**ROGER TINKER IS AN EVIL GENIUS
WITH A MACHINE THAT CAN WORK A
TERRIBLE MIRACLE**

And, as his sexual instructress par excellence,
Dolly Douglas enjoys total control over
Roger. Together, with the aid of his awesome
weapon, Roger and Dolly are out to cut all
her enemies down to size. They are going to
punish all the people she hates from the
darkest depths of her icy heart. Glamorous
Leyna Shaw will only be the first . . .

SMALL WORLD

"A TERRIFYING NOVEL . . .
AN AUSPICIOUS DEBUT!"
—Erica Jong

"IMAGINATIVE POWER . . .
COMPELLING, EFFECTIVE
AND HORRIFYING . . .
HOOKS THE READER"
—*The Washington Post*

SMALL WORLD

TABITHA KING

A SIGNET BOOK

NEW AMERICAN LIBRARY

A DIVISION OF PENGUIN BOOKS USA INC.

This is entirely a work of fiction. Any resemblance between the characters in this story and real persons, living or dead, is coincidental and unintentional. There have been many scale models of the White House, including the one made for the children of Grover Cleveland that is currently displayed in Washington, D.C. The one in this story is purely imaginary. The Dalton Institute, of course, is real, though it does not now and never did have the staff and director I gave it. Any inaccuracies that occur in this story about its day-to-day functioning are entirely my error.

NAL BOOKS ARE AVAILABLE AT QUANTITY DISCOUNTS
WHEN USED TO PROMOTE PRODUCTS OR SERVICES.
FOR INFORMATION PLEASE WRITE TO PREMIUM MARKETING DIVISION,
NEW AMERICAN LIBRARY, 1633 BROADWAY,
NEW YORK, NEW YORK 10019.

Copyright © 1981 by Tabitha King

This is an authorized reprint of a hardcover edition published by
Macmillan Publishing Co., Inc.

SIGNET TRADEMARK REG. U.S. PAT. OFF. AND FOREIGN COUNTRIES
REGISTERED TRADEMARK—MARCA REGISTRADA
HECHO EN DRESDEN, TN, U.S.A.

SIGNET, SIGNET CLASSIC, MENTOR, ONYX, PLUME, MERIDIAN
and NAL BOOKS are published by New American Library, a division of
Penguin Books USA Inc., 1633 Broadway, New York, New York 10019

First Signet Printing, March, 1982

10   11   12   13   14   15   16   17   18

PRINTED IN THE UNITED STATES OF AMERICA

for the Bogeyman,
with love

ACKNOWLEDGMENTS

I would like to acknowledge the invaluable assistance of my sister Catherine Graves and her husband, David; of Chris Lavin, of the offices of then-Senator Edmund Muskie; of my sister Stephanie Leonard; of Kirby McCauley and his sister Kay McCauley; and of my husband, Stephen King.

The Dalton Institute also has my eternal gratitude for the kind offices of its staff.

The only way to discover the limits of the possible is to go beyond them into the impossible.
—*Clarke's Second Law*

Any sufficiently advanced technology is indistinguishable from magic.
—*Clarke's Third Law*

In all his years working in the White House, all his years of brothering, fathering, stepfathering, uncle-ing, and grandfathering, she was, Leonard Jakobs thought, the unhappiest child he'd ever encountered. Like so many of the rich and white, the child didn't seem to know how to be happy. True, the mama drank, secretlike, and the daddy didn't have no time for her, but so what? It wasn't only rich and white didn't love their children enough. But some children got along, and some didn't.

This one tugged at him. She was a little thing, cutelike, but never going to be no true-heart beauty. No, she looked like her daddy, and sooner or later, probably when she was an old woman, the daddy in her would come out. Still, she was tough and willful, like him, and that wasn't all bad. A little tough went a long way in this world.

It was the hopelessness that caught him. The sense that this poor thing was already lost, almost before she began, like some skinny, stupid puppy that never gets enough milk from mama, but too many kicks, and likely gets runned over by a big truck first time it ventures out.

There was little enough he could do for her: kid with her, make her smile when he met her, in the course of his work. And he could do for her what he'd done for a dozen little girls over the years: use the Lord's gifts to him to make her a remembrance of her time here in this great house.

He never had built anything just like this before, so he read up on it in one of the Historical Association guidebooks that even had old plans in it. One passage he read over and over:

It is a serene eighteenth-century vision, founded in the then-visible-and-divine order of the universe. The square of the building is broken symmetrically by the porticoes: the sensual bow of the south, a classically severe pedimented porch on the north, both composed with smooth, authoritarian columns. The detail that disturbs the severe lines is, in turn, purified by the color white that age softens into cream. It is a materialized dream of the republic.

The fancy words tried hard to catch, he thought, his own feeling that it was special, unique, almost living. It was a sad place; no one's home, for all the folks that lived there for their time. The men who had died under its symbolic roof numbered eight; he was not the only long-time staffer who felt their chill presence in its rooms.

Through all the months of patient labor before the child's birthday, he considered these matters and leaned upon the Lord. This house, this image of the Greater Mansion, would always bring joy, pleasure, and delight to the hearts of the children who played with it, for it is those things that the Lord meant the children to learn from their play.

In the end, the Lord humbled him for his pride in the work and made the child turn her face away from the dollhouse he had built for her. Leonard Jakobs beat away his disappointment, resolving that if the child, in her miserableness, rejected his gift, he would not reject the Lord's. Perhaps, in time, the Lord would bless His daughter Dorothy, as He had blessed him.

1

WHATEVER HAPPENED TO PRINCESS DOLLY?

. . . disappeared last Tuesday. Sartoris's once-notorious nude portrait of a presidential daughter at age fifteen had become a nostalgic snapshot from the family album. . . .

3.28.80   —*VIPerpetrations, VIP*

Bells chimed a soft release. Roger Tinker was alone in a three-sided cell, one element in a honeycomb maze of partitions that displayed the museum's collection. The light falling from the skylights had the honeyed richness of late afternoon. Dust motes swam through diffuse golden streams and vanished into the angled shadows of the walls. The whisperings of departing visitors and the "good-days" of the staff intruded on the ecclesiastical silence like muffled prayers.

Roger, clutching his pocketbook in both sweaty hands, breathed his own mildly blasphemous prayer of thanks. He had stared at the painting of the girl so long that her image had dissolved before him into many acid blotches. Moisture trickled in his armpits, and they itched unmercifully.

He stepped back a few paces, pretending to look at other pictures. In high heels that were still a little stiff and pinched at the instep, he felt he was walking in space. He wobbled to rest in front of an enormous gilt frame that ludicrously surrounded about four square inches of a rudimentary portrait of a dog. Roger was certain that he could do a better dog

3

himself, with a cotton swab between his piggies.

The air snuck up his unshaven legs like the mouse that ran up the clock. He shivered. Nylon whispered between his legs as he shifted his weight from one foot to the other. He bit his lips, tasted lipstick, and fretted about how it was wearing. *Shit.* He gave himself a mental shake.

The bells chimed again. A quick glance around the ceiling confirmed that no cameras had sprouted there since last he checked five minutes ago. A handful of guards, white-haired, with big bellies encased in scarlet uniforms, and looking like a troop of off-season Santa Clauses, drifted through the maze one last time. Their attentions settled on the main exit and their wristwatches.

Roger moved casually back to his place of vigil in front of *Princess Dolly.* He stared into the heavy-lidded eyes again. The mouth was wide but ungenerous. Thin-lipped. Suddenly, Roger saw the painting with the painter's eyes. The bottom dropped out of his stomach. He closed his eyes in a spasm of instinctive self-defense. Too late. He felt himself stiffening.

The bells broke the trance. Third time, closing time. And Roger's time. He sucked in a deep, shaky breath. Raising his handbag to his waist, he groped inside, as if for a tissue.

"Cheese," he whispered.

It had been a shock the first time he stood before his mother's full-length mirror. He didn't look like Roger Tinker in drag. He was something else, *someone* else. A woman. Not beautiful, just an ordinary, rather masculine, dowdy matron. But still, a woman. It was embarrassing, even after several times, to glimpse his own reflection. And yet he had to look, he had to see this other Roger.

An hour after stealing the painting, he stood before the mirror again. He was still excited. But his mother would be home soon and he had to be himself again. He stripped off the jacket and long skirt, the blouse and slip. He folded them carefully into the box from the department store where he'd purchased them.

The saleslady in the dress department had been thin, elderly, and very eager to make a sale. There had been no pretense in Roger's awkwardness. He had let her cluck and soothe and admire him for being so thoughtful of his lucky mum. And wouldn't she just love this three-piece suit, so flat-

4

tering to an older woman's figure, and so chic, too. Roger had gone away grinning, with his dress box under his damp armpit, having been maneuvered by the old doll into buying just what he wanted.

Briefly, he admired his artificial bosom in the glass. His own foam creation. Trying on his mother's brassiere, he had discovered that getting in and out of the back-opening sort was impossible. Either there was some trick to it, some secret of the sisterhood, or women had an extra joint in their arms. Finding a front-opener had been a huge relief.

He kicked off the high heels and skinned out of the pantyhose. At last he was down to the blue nylon panties with *Monday* written on the left hip in pink thread. It wasn't actually Monday; it was Tuesday. But Roger liked the blue ones better than the *Tuesday* panties (which were yellow with orange script), and somehow Roger's mother had never thought to tell him it was bad luck to wear the wrong day's panties.

After wearing them, he was sure women must think about their crotches all the time. No wonder none of them could add and subtract without a calculator. The first time, he'd gotten a terrific boner. He'd gotten used to the sensation after a while, but the slide of nylon over his sensitive parts was always there—a secret skin of excitement.

The young and very poised woman in the lingerie department had been used to embarrassed men out of their element. She had batted heavily made-up eyes at Roger, and her long slim fingers with their garishly painted nails had slipped across all the silky things with a sound that had made him shiver. She had smiled knowingly at him, and he had worried, with guilty excitement a knot in his belly, that she *knew*.

He never should have bought the whole week's worth. It was a nervous impulse, a crazy idea that it was more plausible he was buying for a mythical wife or girl friend if he purchased the package instead of just one pair. So now he had white ones, with *Sunday* in pink; and pink ones, with *Wednesday* in yellow; he had *Thursday* panties in green, with white lettering; and *Friday*, black with red script; and the reverse, black letters on red, for *Saturday*. The whole idea of changing drawers every day was so female and sort of cute, like writing the days of the week daintily on each pair. Perhaps it helped them make up their minds.

5

The pepper-and-salt wig went into its own box. It gave him a headache to wear it and, he had to giggle, it wasn't *him* anyway. Hadn't the saleswoman at the wig salon said just that, very sarcastically? Roger had seen right away she didn't believe word one of his costume-party cover story. She had taken one look at him and apparently put him down as someone of questionable sexual tendencies who probably stir-fried small boys for lunch. Roger had suffered her fuming disapproval until he'd gotten what he wanted.

His mother liked to say, in reference to the romantic tangles on the afternoon soap operas, that "faint heart never won fair maid." Roger had told himself that "faint heart never made one fair, either," and had minced wickedly out, winking broadly at the old bitch, as she turned a very satisfactory geranium shade.

The make-up took a lot of scrubbing off. It smudged around the eyes and stained his lips a ghostly red. He couldn't afford to have his mother notice something like that. She'd pee herself. He grinned at the thought of his mother discovering his rubber titties and his panty collection.

At last his face was clean, if a little raw around the eyes and lips. It was disconcertingly bare-looking. He threw the old make-up and the soiled cotton balls he'd used for clean-up into a paper bag, and tucked them into the wig box, along with the high heels and pantyhose.

His own clothes were heaped untidily on his mother's bed. Fishing out his skivvies, he was halfway into them when he realized he was still wearing the blue *Monday* panties. Suddenly hot all over, he kicked off his shorts angrily. He hauled too vigorously at the panties, caught them around one foot, and danced briefly like a one-legged bird to keep his balance. It was infuriating, being tripped up in a shred of nylon. Once out of them, he crumpled them up and stuffed them into the dress box.

With an almost physical sense of relief, he put on his own worn cords and Superman T-shirt. He spirited the illicit clothing to a locked cupboard in his cellar study. There was just time for a quick check of his mother's bedroom and the bathroom, to make sure he'd left nothing incriminating, when he heard her car in the drive. He turned on the television in the living room and shuffled into the kitchen to greet her when she opened the back door.

6

"Hey, Mom," he said, and took the bag of groceries from her.

She presented one soft, peachy, sweet-smelling cheek to him. "Well," she said gaily, "aren't we bright-eyed and bushy-tailed?"

Roger kissed her and dumped the groceries on the dinette table.

"Sure," he agreed, opening the refrigerator, "sure we are."

After supper, Roger settled in front of the television. His mother swapped her girdle for a comfortable housecoat and joined him. They sat in easy silence, fixed in the blue light of the television that was like some unearthly analogue of amber.

Roger paid the minimum necessary attention to the nightly news. The world was going to hell in a handbasket. It had been all his life. No real wonder, so far as he could see. It was a matter of majority vote, wasn't it? The greater part of the population might as well be dead as not.

The girl who had waited on him in the discount drugstore had been one of the zombies. He needn't have bothered with his neat list, ending in Tampax for the sake of verisimilitude. She'd taken back all her marbles and quit the game before Roger ever got there. She had looked at him, at everybody who came in, as if they were already ghosts. If his little list was a lie by omission, so was her life. No matter to her if he were a child-molesting pervert, or the president, or Jesus Christ on roller skates; she had taken the fun out of it.

The last item on the local news broke into his sour recollection. It seemed there had been, that very afternoon, another in a series of art thefts. The newscaster was enormously cheerful about it, as if he personally had pulled off what he called "another shocking heist." A famous painting by Leighton Sartoris, considered by many to be the greatest of the world's living artists, had been discovered missing from the Appt Collection, housed at the Feero Museum of Modern Art. No one had witnessed the heist or had seen the perpetrators. The police described the museum security as "lax," and said the curator of the museum valued the work at three-quarters of a million dollars. It was, of course, Sartoris's 1950 portrait of Dorothy Hardesty Douglas, the daughter of then-President Michael Hardesty.

Roger's mother tut-tutted at the valuation. She tut-tutted quite a lot during the news. Roger didn' pay any attention

7

anymore. When somebody tuts the same for a famine as they do for an act of larceny, Roger refused to take their tutting seriously. He sat back, savoring the word "heist."

Up to that point, he had thought of it as a caper. The truth of it was that the hardest part had been the shopping. It had taken two days to find the right shoes and handbag. A long-haired young shoe-store clerk had been amused with his costume-party story and rummaged happily in the storeroom to find a pair of black patent-leather pumps that would fit Roger's short, wide feet. The pocketbook had been a piece of luck, a treasure hidden underneath a heap of on-sale, long-out-of-fashion handbags in a discount store.

His feet had hurt so much he couldn't face trying the entire costume on all at once. While he had soaked his dogs and watched game shows, Roger had reflected on what he'd learned. Women were tougher than he ever imagined; they went out into the incredible chaos of the retail universe, got what they wanted, and made it back alive. Apparently they even *liked* it.

And then he had tried on his new wardrobe. Suddenly, seeing himself in the mirror, he had known there was more to it, more than just clothes and make-up. There was a stance, a way of holding the body, the expression on the face, a way of moving. The whole idea of disguising himself as a woman was revealed as dangerously complex.

He had felt hopelessly ignorant. Clothing had always been merely clothing, something to cover up the place where God's taste had fallen down. And women, well, there was his mother, and that was the extent of his relations with the other half. Still, he had been pit-deep in the project, his *caper*, and onward he must go, driven by curiosity and perverse excitement.

When the news was over, Roger fled to his cellar hideaway. His mother had given over the cellar to him when he was fifteen. She hadn't been downstairs but twice in the entire thirty years she'd lived in the house. The last time she peeked into the cellar it was a dank cement dungeon festooned with cobwebs and smelling of mildew and mouse poop. When Roger had asked for a place of his own, she took it to mean something in the nature of a clubhouse, crude and masculine and littered with comic books and overflowing ashtrays. She had been rather proud of her tolerant motherhood when she consented.

It had become much more than a rec room. The stairs were lit, as they always had been, by a single low-wattage bulb suspended by its own wiring from the ceiling. From the landing at the top of the stairs, the cellar looked much as it had fifteen years ago. Beyond the dim circle of light thrown by the dusty old fixture was a plywood partition. Roger had painted it a dingy brown to encourage the general impression of gloom and decay. He had hung a sturdy door at the darkest end and installed a good lock, to which he alone possessed the key. On the door, he had long ago hand-stenciled the legend *Fortress of Solitude.*

Beyond that first partition, he had put up a second. One side was lined with unfinished floor-to-ceiling bookshelves. They held Roger's collection of science fiction pulps, and his models of the *Enterprise,* a shuttlecraft, and a Klingon raider. Between the two partitions was the room that Roger thought of as his study.

He had furnished the room with ratty garage-sale furniture: a monstrous chair that leaked stuffing from the wounds in its tobacco-scented horsehair upholstery; a thickly painted and chipped end table; a standing lamp ugly enough to paralyze anyone foolish enough to look directly at it. His mother had contributed an orange hassock that she had once stored her confession magazines in. A melted patch of its vinyl skin had been scabbed over in adhesive tape after she absently rested a hot sheet of brownies on it while changing the television channel one day. Roger had put it to work storing the kind of books she didn't know he read.

Roger had constructed his workshop on the other side of the second partition. It was remarkably and curiously furnished, mostly at the unwitting expense of the taxpayer. There were a number of locked cupboards containing interesting items, including Roger's contraband wardrobe.

Behind one door was Roger's home-made computer, powered by a free and illegal tap into a neighborhood transformer, and connected by an equally illicit telephone patch to the bulk of the government's computer network and to half the bank computers in California. It would have been easy to tap the banks' computers, but it was Roger's conviction that it was also an easy way to get caught. It wasn't conscience, but the odds, that made him prefer alternative financing for his researches.

He was not by profession a thief. It had been a surprise to discover that by nature, at least, he was not unequipped to be one. It made life interesting, and fun, as it had not been for a long time.

He settled down to work, suppressing the impulse to take out the painting and admire his own genius. A good beginning was only that: a point of departure. He was not about to slack off now. Now when he was just getting to the fun part.

Fun and work were much the same coin to Roger. He had earned his coin, all his adult life, working for the government. He had been employed in a series of projects of a classified nature. They were, in fact, but one project, several times sacrificed on the altars of minor democratic idols, only to rise again under new initials, with a deft shuffle of personnel and plant, as soon as it was politic.

As a consequence of these periodic shut-downs, Roger had experienced corresponding periods of unemployment. He suffered chiefly from the deprivation of the work that was his whole life. Unmarried and unencumbered, he was not as damaged as the family men and women, tossed into the ever-deepening storm of the private-sector economy. Still, he had more reason to be frightened, for he had no credentials and a record that would scare off any private employers.

Some anonymous higher-up in the government had looked past Roger's sudden exit from graduate school, examined his rejected Ph.D. thesis, and seen him, not for the crazy heretic his professors took him for, but as a man of practical talents. The government had taken him in from the cold and let him get down to work. He hadn't ever asked them to make him respectable. It was enough to be allowed to work.

His last assignment had been on the sixth floor of a project building known as "the kitchen." It was only metaphorically so. Real food was strictly forbidden there, a regulation Roger Tinker regularly violated. What Roger did there was a very exotic and inedible sort of "cooking," like the varnished food photographed for gourmet cooking magazines. It wasn't exactly experimenting, because seven times out of ten, Roger got the results he predicted. It was more of an orderly progression of random combinations, akin the naming all the names of God.

Roger had been working on one particular *name* for several weeks. He had done a lot of interesting things with it, and had, at last, achieved a degree of intimacy with its attributes. He was beginning to grasp certain basic information about it.

His belly had spoken to him, and he had answered, as was his custom. He had leaned over the computer console, watching a pattern on a graph. With a penknife in his left hand, he had peeled an apple in his right. He had become, inevitably, more interested in the graph than in the peeling of the apple. The tip of the knife had slipped into his thumb.

"Goddamn shit piss fuck!" exclaimed Roger, less in anger than in astonishment, as his blood had dripped onto the keys of the console. Dropping the knife and the apple, he had stuck his thumb into his mouth. For a moment, he had resumed his babyhood, some thirty-two years and two-hundred pounds in his past. He had shut his eyes tightly, for he not only hated the sight of blood but retained a childish certainty that not looking at it contributed to its quick coagulation.

Moaning around his throbbing thumb, he'd opened his eyes. It had been several seconds before the change on the graph registered. The moan had become a gag as he had involuntarily sucked his thumb down his throat. He'd pulled it out, the hurt utterly forgotten. The gouge had continued to bleed for several more seconds at an ever-decreasing rate. Small drops had been scattered by Roger's movements—all over the computer console and in delicate polka dots on his white lab overalls.

It had been two days later that the cut again claimed his attention. He had been sitting in his car in the parking lot after work, his pay envelope and its contents on his lap: a green check and a delicate blue tissue dismissal slip mated to it—the government's sweet regrets. The thumb had begun to throb in counterpoint to the beat of his temples. Roger had stared at the red welt, swollen and clearly infected, and the numbness in his brain had changed into anger.

He had thought if he spoke out now they would take over his discovery. If they believed him. It was possible they would

11

not; he would be perceived as a fantasist, forever beyond the pale. It might be months before he had his proof.

Roger had worked another six weeks on the project before the blue slip turned pink. During that period, most of his thought and effort had gone into stealing an assortment of equipment. Every bit could have been purchased commercially from the same sources the government bought from (probably cheaper), but there would be records of purchase. He told himself it didn't matter; he had stolen from the government before to build gadgets in his cellar and this time it was halfway legitimate. His work was an underground extension of the project; in due time, the government would get the good of it. In fact, he was looking forward to presenting the completed project to his former superiors.

The first device had been the size of a wardrobe. The second one, four months later, had been the size of a color television set. The third, completed in a six-week frenzy, had been a little smaller than a hand-held instant camera.

It was exhaustively tested. Over three weeks, Roger had used up two dozen mice, bought in pairs in a dozen shopping-center pet stores. The neighborhood experienced a puzzling series of petnappings. The Lutzes missed their two tomcats; after a couple of weeks, it appeared they had moved on to softer suckers. The Treats' miniature poodle disappeared from his sunporch basket. Eunice Gold's bob-tailed kitten, last seen wearing Baby Wet 'n Dry's T-shirt and the bracelet Eunice's grandmother had given her that spelled out E-U-N-I-C-E (for the tea party Eunice was planning that afternoon), was among the missing. Andy Stevens's beagle Gilligan, fat and wobbly at six years, failed to turn up for supper three nights running. His mom tried not to hear Andy crying in his closet.

It has been a busy, satisfying time for Roger. The organic residue was rather amusing. Roger played with it for hours before, reluctantly, flushing it down the toilet.

The exhilaration had passed soon enough. *What next* time was at hand. With sudden certainty, Roger knew the project was over, not just his part of it, or his secret project in the cellar, but the project, period. The government wasn't going to call again. And if they weren't going to rehire him, he was finished as a working scientist. He knew what it was like in the private sector for guys *with* papers. With his background, he would be invisible.

If he didn't turn over the device, what was he going to do with it? It had never been his job to decide to what ends a specific piece of work might be turned. Could he use it for himself, and if so, how? It was a relief to go back to the device. It had been his past for so long, it was inconceivable it should not be his future. It was his, by all that's just.

Coming to that conclusion hadn't solved the *what's next* problem. He couldn't go on making the device smaller. Sooner or later he would have to do something with it.

His mother had brought home the answer in a box of out-dated magazines, the old ones from the gynecologist's office in which she worked as a receptionist. She did this every month, when all the new copies had come in. It was mildly embarrassing to Roger, but his mother was frequently mildly embarrassing to him.

It was embarrassing to drop her off or pick her up, as it meant going into an office full of women on the most intimate of errands, and the staff all cheerfully unembarrassed about their work. He might encounter the gynecologist himself, a small, gray-haired man with a twinkle in his eye, seemingly always taking off or putting on a pair of rubber gloves. Then Roger would have to decide whether to offer to shake hands with the good doctor. He couldn't help wondering if the doctor liked his work, and then if the doctor suspected Roger of so wondering.

Since he had been out of work, Roger was sure his mother's co-workers, those relentlessly clean-scrubbed, smiling women, thought he was a lazy good-for-nothing, content to live off his mother and read their old secondhand magazines. It was true enough, but they spent little time discussing Roger and his sins. His mother's endless repetitions of the platitudes and the dullest details of her own life fell on their ears, as they did on Roger's, as background noise, rain on a tin roof. Roger's mom was liked for her good humor and kindliness, but nobody took her seriously.

Still, he'd been delighted when he'd turned up a back issue of *VIP* in the box. It was not that old, the end of the month. He'd recognized the woman on the cover right away, Leyna Shaw, his favorite lady newscaster. She was very tall in heels that looked lethal, and she was bending over to interview a man in a car. Roger didn't give the man in the car more than a once-over, long enough to identify him as the government's energy chief, a pompous pipe-smoking asshole of the first magnitude who had been, not so long ago, Roger's unknowing boss. What Roger was much more interested in was the way the lady's blouse gaped open as she bent into the limo, thrusting a microphone at Secretary Potato Brains. The blouse was white against her dark suit jacket and threatened to slide off her shell-pink body at the next second.

The secretary was having a good look, a view Roger envied mightily. Roger's thumb drifted over the glossy image of her petallike pretty and settled there. He closed his eyes. His thumb rolled ever so gently in a circle. He had never touched a real one.

"Roger?" his mother had asked.

He'd opened his eyes and sat up straight. The couch protested his shifting weight.

"Yes?" he'd answered, trying to sound bright and asexual.

"Would you like a brownie?"

"Sure."

She'd gone away, her head full of brownies. Roger smiled after her genially, drawing his stomach down into its proper place, thinking how truly wonderful it was that mothers couldn't read minds.

He'd turned back to the magazine. The photography was top-notch, practically 3D. She was such a big girl, too big to be a model or a dancer, and hard as a rock. There was a picture of her jogging around the mall in Washington. Roger had been there a long time ago on a high school class trip. He didn't remember much beyond bombing water-filled balloons out the hotel windows (because of being drunk the whole time), but he had a soft spot for the place and could recognize some of the buildings. The public buildings rose behind Leyna Shaw's lithe figure and for once she seemed in scale, reduced to something he could hold in his hand.

He'd read the article avidly. Like all the articles in *VIP*, it was a peek and a promise. Only the photographs were meaty.

He'd meandered through the magazine. There'd been an article on a homosexual fashion show that unaccountably disturbed him. Another piece concerned an old crock painter who lived on an island off the coast of Maine. The name

14

caught on Roger's mind like a burr on linen. There was nothing to interest him in articles on a rock singer, a famous seal, or the case of the comatose teenager whose divorcing parents were engaged in a custody battle over who would get the kid and the respirator. Then, the last-page gossip column to skim, and the teaser in the box at the bottom. Roger came to a dead halt.

YOU CAN TAKE DOLLY AWAY FROM
THE WHITE HOUSE

BUT

YOU CAN'T TAKE THE WHITE HOUSE
AWAY FROM DOLLY

The nation fell in love with Mike Hardesty's little princess when she was a sprite of a tomboy blossoming into a rosebud of a girl. We watched her grow up, break some hearts, and marry Harrison Douglas, the son of her father's oldest ally, in a storybook wedding.

Twenty-five years later, Dolly's been everywhere, has everything. But it hasn't all been good times. Her mother died shortly after Mike Hardesty's ouster from office. Dolly was widowed by Harrison Douglas's suicide twelve years ago. Their one son, Harrison III, was killed in a tragic flying accident four years ago. The loss of his grandson bore heavily on the embittered ex-president, and Dolly lost her beloved daddy within the year.

So what does a still-beautiful, wealthy woman do with the prospect of long life, unlimited options, and no one to share them with? Unpredictable Dolly, and her son's widow, Lucy Douglas, involved themselves in a new hobby that became not only therapy for their shattered lives, but a business and a way of life.

Next week, *VIP* invites you to peek into *DOLLY'S WORLD*, and explore the burgeoning miniatures craze.
2.22.80   *—VIPreviews, VIP*

The smell of fresh, hot brownies had invaded Roger's trancelike state. He'd looked up at his mother, standing over him with a plate of brownies, her forehead wrinkled with worry.

15

"Is everything all right?" she'd asked.

Roger had suspected she was getting ready to feel his forehead for a fever. He *was* hot. He had snatched a brownie off the plate and stuffed it into his mouth.

"Yeah. Fine," he had mumbled around the brownie. "Hunky-dory."

Roger's mother had put the plate down next to him. She had crossed her arms over her formidable bosom. At least Roger was eating. He couldn't be very sick, could he? She had smiled her blessings on her boy.

The next issue had been in the stores. The cover was Dolly Hardesty Douglas's prize dollhouse. Roger could hardly read the article, his hands had shaken so with excitement.

Apparently Mike Hardesty's daughter never completely left the White House behind her. For the past several years, Dolly has given substantial time, energy, and money to the restoration of the scale model of the White House that was a gift to her when her father was still president.

"I was thirteen," she laughs. "I thought I was too old for dollhouses."

So the well-intentioned gift of Leonard Jakobs, a black janitor who worked thirty years in the executive mansion, went unappreciated and forgotten for some twenty years.

It was after the deaths of her son and father that Dolly stumbled over the age-worn dollhouse among her father's effects. It was natural to take it immediately to her son's widow (Lucy), who was already acquiring a reputation as a miniaturist.

"At first I thought I'd have Lucy fix it up for Laurie, my granddaughter," Dolly confesses, "and then I fell in love with it. Laurie's too little for it, anyway."

The dollhouse is a spooky look-a-like for the real executive mansion, and it's been almost as expensive to furnish as the real, one-hundred-times-larger original.

Lucy Douglas estimates shyly that her mother-in-law has spent one hundred thousand dollars on the restoration of her dollhouse. That kind of money would buy little Laurie a lot of slightly less spectacular dollhouses.

Mrs. Douglas, raising Laurie, seven, and Zachary, four, her children by Dolly's son Harrison, says her relationship with her mother-in-law is on a firm and fair business footing. She charges Dolly exactly what she charges other customers for similar work, while admitting that she took on little other work during the period she worked on Dolly's White House. Experts in the field regard her as one of the two or three best miniaturists in the United States; one knowledgeable collector who prefers to remain annonymous states that, if anything, Lucy Douglas undercharged for her services.

"Dolly Hardesty got a hell of a bargain. That dollhouse is worth a quarter of a million today because of Lucy Douglas's signature," the collector maintains.

Still, Lucy Douglas has apparently acquired an unexpected profit on the deal; when Dolly's restored White House came to the attention of Nicholas Weiler, the director of the Dalton Institute, as he was assembling an exhibition of dollhouses, Dolly brought her daughter-in-law and Weiler together. The rumor in Washington is that Lucy may soon retire Weiler from his long-running position as D.C.'s second-most-eligible bachelor, after the president.

2.29.80   —*VIPersonalities, VIP*

The spread had been lavishly illustrated with pictures of the dollhouse, which was full of the choice doodads that Lucy Douglas made. The close-ups had made the items look very real and very plush—much nicer than the trading-stamp furniture in Roger's mother's living room. The photos of Dolly Hardesty Douglas and the talented Lucy had not been hard to take. Dolly was older than Roger had remembered but was still a wickedly good-looking woman. And Lucy—well, that Weiler guy was getting a nice handful. He had turned out to be, in the part of the story that mentioned the exhibition at the Dalton Insitute, a predictably pretty aristocrat who probably had a superlong tongue from licking the cream off his whiskers. His sweat glands had probably atrophied from disuse.

It had been more fun looking at the women. Roger had relaxed, letting the magazine spread over his belly like a small roof. He'd begun to see possibilities.

17

. . . Sartoris has attained the stature of a legend among the locals, people not easy to impress. Isolated on his one hundred and ten acres of island, eleven miles from Margarite (pronounced Mar-gar-right) Port, he survives essentially unaffected by the squeeze between the rising cost of fuel and heating oil and the marginal incomes available from the traditional local economy, based on lobstering, fishing, and farming. The crunch is gradually emptying the coastal islands of their residents who simply cannot afford to live on their ancestral land anymore.

The locals credit the sheer hard work of Sartoris's back-to-the-land existence, the sixties' chimera of self-sufficiency that he has lived since he moved onto the island in the forties, for the painter's good health and advanced age.

"Blame Ethelyn," Sartoris jokes, referring to his housekeeper-companion of many years, Ethelyn Blood.

Mrs. Blood, a Margarite Port woman and the widow of a local lobsterman, comes back quickly: "Blame the devil," she says, "who figures he's got his share of old cusses, and the good Lord, who wants to make a saint out of me."

2.22.80   *—VIPersonalities, VIP*

The old man saw possibilities. He nudged the bit of broken glass with his toe. The sun caught it. It flared green. The old man sipped noisily at a glass of cold tea.

The telephone jangled. He swore at it and stared at the sand under his bare feet, and at the bit of broken glass. The telephone, deaf to his curse, rang again.

"Ethelyn!" he roared. "Ethelyn!"

There was silence from the house. The telephone gave him another Bronx cheer.

"What's she doing?" he muttered. He shuffled through the open French doors into his bedroom, grabbing the telephone just after the fifth ring.

"Hello-oh?" he asked.

The caller asked if he were Leighton Sartoris. The old man couldn't tell if he was speaking to a man or a woman; the voice was blurred by static on the line. How did they get the number?

"Yes, I am. What do you want?" he answered angrily.

The caller stated he was Somebody-or-Other calling from *VIP* magazine, and did Mr. Sartoris have any comment on the theft of his painting, *Princess Dolly*, from a California museum.

Sartoris cackled with delight. "First I heard of it," he said. "Good riddance."

He dropped the receiver into its cradle. Bundling the telephone into the pillowcase, he kicked it under the bed. He knew now where the fellow had gotten the number. Bastards probably had it on file. It had been a great mistake allowing that nosy woman from that miserable gossip sheet onto the island. He wished he didn't know why he had allowed it; it might be easier to think he was getting senile rather than that he was doing foolish things for sentimental reasons.

Picking up his glass of tea, he shuffled outside again. There was a comfortable tussock of grass nearby and he sat down to stare at the green glass. An ancient gray tomcat emerged through the bedroom door and curled up next to him. Idly, he began to knead the back of the beast's neck.

It was amusing to think of that particular picture being spirited away from some bloody museum by an enterprising Yank thief. It took him, a little unwillingly, back to painting it, the way everything wanted to take him backward now.

It had been his eleventh year on the island. He had seemed more of a guest then, still on sufferance in a strange country. When the presidential party, summering south of Margarite Port in the more fashionable Hurd's Reach, invited him to dinner, he went, telling himself it would be rude not to.

But it wasn't that at all. He had just turned sixty and knew he had lost something. During the winter, he had begun to drink more—out of boredom and, he told himself, to ward off the chill. By summer, he had seemed to himself to be a balloon at the end of an insecure tether, floating in an alcoholic ether. There was a terrible urge to escape, and a terrible panic that he might just do that, at long last. So he had asked to paint that silly wicked girl (who agreed out of depthless vanity), knowing that the habit of years would reassert itself; he would stay sober for as long as it took to do it right.

And he had. But the summer, relentlessly hot, had turned hotter in the light of the humid young flesh he had masochistically displayed before him. He worked madly, with the scent of gin, like ice, in his nostrils.

Young Dorothy had reclined half in and half out of a patch of shade in a hollow of sand, just out of sight of her bodyguards, lurking in a grove of pine trees where the sea breeze occasionally stirred. Stripped to a pair of baggy shorts, Sartoris had stood in full sun, the broad brim of his old hat shading his face, and the easel protected from the glare by a strange rigging of umbrellas. She had chitter-chattered like a monkey all the six weeks, and it was all clever and nasty, but at least she had kept her body still. He had never spoken to her; there was nothing they could not say to each other with their eyes.

The afternoon it was finished she had held her tongue for once. Her eyes were busy, as always, speculative, and somehow furtive, and her tongue was forever peeking out between her lips, exposing itself. Her body was glossy, beaded with sweat, and her small greedy hands made a slicking sound as they passed over her breasts. He had watched, in a glaze of sweat, as she made love to herself. At the end, her body had arched, seeking its self-release, and she had laughed. It had been a child's pleased hoot, and so much more sweet and rotten than the low-throated murmur of a woman's pleasure.

Suddenly the old man came to himself again, startled to find he was mildly tumescent. He laughed crudely, as if at some dirty joke, but he knew it was on himself. And he wished deeply he had someone to share it with. Not Ethelyn Blood, who had come to live with him on the island the winter after he had painted the little bitch, nor Nick, who was so often in his thoughts these days. It was Maggie he wanted to share it with, just this moment, and she *would* laugh. Nobody laughed like Maggie.

He would find out if she were still alive and call her up. He must have her married name written down somewhere, the one he had never—probably for much too obvious reasons—been able to remember, and the telephone number.

But no, he wouldn't call Maggie Jeffries. That was history and he was done with that; he hadn't any more time for history, for sitting around, mucking about in the long dead and gone. Nostalgia, a contemptible emotion; memory, so much dead skin, vestigial emotion. It wasn't something he had the energy for anymore.

20

There were too many possibilities to be realized in the way the sun struck that glass bit. The light on the sand. The light.

. . . The only heir to Sartoris's considerable pile is Nicholas Weiler, the director of the Dalton Institute in Washington, D.C., who, though he uses the last name he was legally born under, is Sartoris's natural son by English socialite Maggie Jeffries Weiler.

Lady Eugenie Walters, known as Pinkie to her pals, reports in her memoirs of the period that her dear friend Maggie Jeffries never really loved anyone else but Sartoris. She continued her affair with him after her marriage to Lord Weiler, apparently with her husband's consent. Still, it was a surprise when she had the baby that Sartoris promptly acknowledged as his own. She was forty-two at the time, and the affair had settled into a comfortable and occasional convenience. "Pinkie" says the irrepressible Maggie never could resist a chance to shock; it was not her having Sortoris's baby, or her husband's bemused acceptance of the fact, but Maggie's calm statement that Sartoris was a bloody liar; the child was her husband's that scandalized. It was only after Lord Weiler's death in 1964 that she dropped the pretense. "Pinkie" suggests the farce was Maggie's curious way of apologizing to her much put-upon husband. . . .

2.22.80   —*VIPersonalities, VIP*

Maggie Weiler, who hadn't used the name Jeffries in half a century, laughed so hard she lost her grip on the *News of the World*, and dropped it into the marmalade. Her nurse, Connie, wiped it off with a napkin and gave it back to her when she'd caught her breath.

"Oh, I am sorry, my dear," she wheezed, seeing the mild reproach behind Connie's thick lenses. "The things that go on."

Connie could never really be angry with Lady Maggie. She laughed over the newspaper nearly every day. It had shocked Connie once upon a time before she knew how really good Lady Maggie was, so good it made her think those old scandals must just be wicked lies, but now she defended the old lady to herself, reflecting that one might as well laugh as cry.

21

"The things that go on," Lady Maggie repeated emphatically.

"Please God, none of your friends has died?" Connie asked. It did seem Lady Maggie laughed harder over her friends' obituaries than anything else.

Lady Maggie threw up her hands to screech with delight. The newspaper flew into the coddled egg. Connie, vaguely discomfitted at having said something unintentionally witty, summoned up an uncertain smile. She hoped, may the Blessed Virgin intercede for her, that Lady Maggie wasn't off to a difficult day.

Captain Morrisey wasn't supposed to have the car out. He'd promised his wife to use it only for car shows, parades, and on the ranch, at low speeds. She didn't understand, being a woman, that a machine like this one needed a run now and then. So when she went to Ventura to see her sister in the hospital, he slipped the Villerosi out of its bay in the garage and headed for the freeway, in the opposite direction from Ventura.

He went a good hundred miles, a satisfying run, with just one stop by a cop, who had really only wanted to admire the car. He let the Captain off with a warning and a grin. And kept his grin when the Captain gunned the Villerosi up to ninety right in front of him. The cop probably realized that a man who could own and drive the likes of a 1949 Villerosi wasn't one of those punk kids in their souped-up Camaros, looking for an accident to happen.

The Villerosi was thirsty after a while, and so was Captain Morrisey. He left the freeway to gas up at a big trucking terminal. There was a small bar on the far side from the pumps, evidently catering to the truckers. The Captain parked the sportscar next to a blue van outside the little bar. Considering the time of day the place was fairly lively; the parking lot was nearly full of pickup trucks, vans, and jeeps, but perhaps some were spillovers from the busy shopping center next door.

He settled gratefully onto the cool vinyl cushion of a bar stool and sucked up a pair of Guinnesses. The bartender was obviously unhappy about serving warm beer, let alone warm *foreign* beer, and looked suspiciously at the Captain's canary-yellow trousers and Bally boots. Captain Morrisey had not arrived at his station in life by attending to the stares of the unwashed and unsuccessful. He enjoyed his beer, and also the smoke and noise, the masculine ambiance of the place, subtly enriched by the silence that signified the absence of his wife, bless her. When he came out into the sunshine twenty minutes later and stretched all over, he felt positively sybaritic. He strode confidently to the blue van on the far side of which he had parked the Villerosi.

He stood puzzled for a few seconds. *It wasn't there.* A vague panic formed like a knot in his stomach. Guardedly, trying to appear casual, he glanced over the parking lot. It *was* the same blue van. He remembered very clearly the lettering on the side: *Jim Owen/Caretaker.* No, he was sure he'd left it here. There was a fleeting half-second of relief; his memory wasn't slipping. And then it came to him that if he hadn't forgotten exactly where he'd parked it, there was only one explanation.

Captain Morrisey, the color drained from his face, stood staring at the place where it should be—where a long, low, bullet-shaped pink projectile, a winner of the Targa Miglia and the Targa Firenze, the car driven by the holder of a world speed record for seven months, should be—and saw only the fading white lines on the black hottop, oil stains, dirt, a wad of dirty, deformed bubble gum, a crumpled cigarette pack.

Cold sweat began to bead his forehead, stain the armpits of his shirt. The Guinness in his stomach roiled and surged. For twenty-five-years, he had flown planes, seventeen years in wide-bodied jets. This was how it felt when one of the goddamn wheels wouldn't come down, or when a tire blew on the runway and scared the shit out of everybody. This was how it felt when you hit a monster air pocket and had passengers screaming and pissing themselves as tons of metal plunged to the next floor. He told himself it wasn't as bad as losing the battle for the runway, going into a hundred and fifty mile an hour skid and not coming out of it. Or not finding that next solid floor of good air. Those things had never happened to him, but he thought about them sometimes, in the hotel rooms that were like a chain of paper dolls, and sometimes when he was in the middle of the physicals the company liked to spring on him at what seemed like weekly intervals. No, it wasn't *that* bad.

23

But someone *had* stolen his Villerosi. His beautiful classic racing car. Maureen would kill him. Just kill him. He reeled against the van.

"It could be worse," he muttered, unaware he was speaking out loud.

Something inside him snapped like a rubber band. *O my suffering jesus* he thought, and puked warm Guinness down the length of his yellow trousers, over the glossy shine of his Bally boots.

2

"Lucy!" Pop shouted, "Lucy!"

Then he was in the doorway. The sun behind him turned him into a big black scarecrow, brandishing a chunk of wood at her. Lucy pushed up her protective goggles into her hair and turned off her drill.

The workshop was suddenly quiet, the loudest sound her father's panting breath. The air that Lucy breathed in was hot and dusty, perfumed with wood and oil. Despite the overhead lights and the open skylight above her workbench, it was darker here than outside, where the spring sun fiercely washed out everything. Stepping inside, beyond the backlight of the sun, her father became himself again. He was grinning, excited, thrusting the stick he carried at her. It flopped open in his hands and became a magazine. Her hands were suddenly sweaty. She wiped them on her overalls.

"Finally come," he said, a weight of satisfaction in his voice.

She looked from the magazine in his hands to his face. His unnaturally white teeth gleamed at her. Reluctantly, she accepted the magazine. Her father waited expectantly as she studied the cover.

It was the north side of the White House, a view as familiar to most Americans as their own mother's face. It had been photographed very cleverly, from the same plane as the model of the grounds in which it stood. The crudity of the artificial shrubbery and lawns, the plastic limo in the drive, shouted illusion. Yet it looked the real thing, almost as if someone had pasted a photograph of the real White House onto a false background. But where the sky should be, a band of red-backed black letters declared *VIP*. And about where the Washington Monument should be, another block of letters, smaller and in script, announced *Dolly's White House.*

Lucy's stomach felt as if she were in an elevator, going down. It wanted to stay right where it was, but it had to follow the rest of her, however unwillingly.

She handed the magazine back to her father. "I ought to be going after Zach."

"Oh, it's early yet." He stood twisting the magazine into a roll, puzzled at her apparent lack of excitement.

"I want to wash my hands and take off these overalls. Why don't you put on the soup while I'm gone?"

He nodded. "Don't you want to read the story?"

"You read it first. I'll look at it after lunch."

"Well," he smiled, "I guess that's okay."

"Anything else in the mail?" Lucy shifted tools and fragile items to a high shelf beyond Zach's reach.

"An order from Mrs. Ashkenazy. Accessories for her parlor suite. I'll put it on the order board this afternoon and confirm it. Rest was all bills and junk."

She smiled wearily. "Thanks, Pop. See you in twenty minutes."

Lucy left the workshop before her father. She knew he would look over her work; he wouldn't do it while she was there. And then he would put the soup on and sit down to read the story in the magazine. He had his father's pride. He was patently more eager to look it over than she was. She felt a small thin tide of resentment. It wasn't his ass on the line, not his work, only his daughter's. It wasn't his risk.

She closed her eyes as she leaned against the basin. *Go away, bitchiness* she wished, washing her hands. It was the goddamn magazine, throwing her off balance. Picking at her poor father was just a symptom, the ghost of her adolescent anger at him leaking out of its lead casket just when she thought it was finally rotted away.

It was Lucy's job to clear the dishes and refrigerate the leftover soup. Her father, hunched over the kitchen table with his coffee and the magazine, would do the dirty dishes later in the afternoon.

"Don't you want to sit down and look at this now?"

Lucy dried her hands and sat down, cocking her head to listen for Zach and hearing nothing. Sleep had evidently claimed him.

"All done with it?"

"Nothing else in it worth looking at." He pushed the magazine across the table to her and looked at his wristwatch. "Anyway, it's time for that goddamn stupid show. I need all the chuckles I can get. Excuse me."

Standing up, he scooped up his coffee cup in one thick-fingered, misshapen hand.

Lucy pulled the magazine before her and stared down at it, grinning. She heard the click of the on button and the static as the picture emerged on the screen. The springs of the sofa gave way noisily as her father sat down.

She studied the magazine's cover again briefly and then turned to the feature story. It was like looking at her high school yearbook. She wanted to turn the pages quickly and pretend that she wasn't there.

The largest photograph showed the model White House with the north wall removed, to expose the furnishings and decoration of the rooms. From one side, Lucy bent toward the dollhouse, pointing out a mantelpiece in the Green Room. She didn't need the caption to tell her it was a model of the original Monroe Empire mantel. She knew it in her hands, the hands that had made that tiny reproduction.

The photograph clearly showed her broken nails and calluses. She suppressed a blush; it was a minor price to pay for doing the work she enjoyed. Her mother-in-law would have something cutting to say about it. *Her* nails were perfect, always; her small hands unblemished, soft, and sweet-smelling.

Dolly Hardesty Douglas stood on the other side of the dollhouse. She looked like a little queen, crowned with her own silver hair. She was delicate, but ramrod straight, in white linen with lines sharp enough to cut, like the edge of good paper. Lucy was mildly amused; Dolly would be furious at the front-cover pun on her hated nickname. Her mother-in-law demanded that she be called Dorothy; Lucy did, to her face, but like nearly everyone else who knew Dolly Hardesty, slipped back into the usage of the nickname as soon as she was out of hearing. No doubt, Dolly was ripping the editors of *VIP* up one side and down the other right this second. Better them than me, Lucy thought.

27

Lucy, in the photograph, flattened out and subtly miscolored by the garish inks used in the printing, seemed to herself everything that Dolly wasn't, and most of it was negative. Her father had called her *gawmy* once; it was one of his Yankee words and meant outsized and clumsy. She felt it herself; she was *gawmy,* next to Dolly. Barefaced, big-bosomed, big-butted, a hick in jeans and a blazer, she stared up at herself from the page, as if from some funhouse mirror.

She felt a momentary surge of irritation with Nick. It was his doing. Lucy had never expected to be included in the photographic session. She and the kids were present at Nick's invitation, to preview the exhibition on the day before the opening, a day when the Dalton Institute was normally closed to visitors. Nick had cozened her into it, exactly as he had cozened Dolly into lending her dollhouse to the Dalton's dollhouse show. Nick was a professional cozener; Lucy couldn't be expected to stand against him when Dolly herself had not.

Lucy passed to the next photograph, on the facing page. In it, her children admired the model White House. She knew the photograph to be an illusion. Zach and Laurie had seen the dollhouse many times, in many stages of undress, and had seen each and every element that Lucy created for it. It was not something that impressed them anymore. Yet their faces, in the picture, were animated, their eyes alight, their cheeks highly colored with excitement.

It came of their sudden and total possession of the Dalton itself: its vast spaces, the collections it housed, the staff, many of whom were friends and acquaintances, were all, this day, all theirs. They had whooped through the halls and had been initiated into the mysteries of the radio lecture system by friendly technicians. No wonder when Nick had asked them to have their picture taken with Grandmother's dollhouse, that they had obliged with such aplomb.

Their other grandmother, Lucy's mother, was going to love the photograph. She would buy half a dozen copies of the magazine to send to friends and relatives. "Look on page eleven for a surprise!" or something like that, on an index card paperclipped to the cover. It made Lucy feel a little better about the whole thing. It would bring pleasure to her mother, to whom Lucy had given so little.

Lucy turned the page and encountered a full-page photograph of the Main Hall of the Dalton, taken from the third-floor balcony. It was from an angle that took in the clustered dollhouses of the exhibition in one marble-floored landscape, a scenic view from a turn-off over an alien valley. And Nick was in the middle of it, marking the scale of the houses against the scale of the Hall.

The photographer had apparently been as taken with the Dalton as Lucy always was. She instinctively looked up whenever she entered the Main Hall, where the Dalton climbed uninterrupted for five stories, like an inside-out wedding cake. The successive stories shrank inward as they rose, like a ziggurat, and were topped with a small glass doughnut of a room, an Edwardian version of a skywalk. From it one could look out over the Mall and see the great public buildings made a little smaller. Or one could look down into the Main Hall, a view that was somehow more threatening to the stomach.

Once, while a little high, Nick had told her that he wanted someday to assemble a collection of prisms to refract the light that entered through the skywalk. Now, Lucy could never look up without envisioning the geysered colors splashing over the ornate balconies and columns.

The day of the opening, the day after the *VIP* photographer had taken their pictures, it had been intermittently rainy. The overcast had blotted up the light and the upper stories of the hall had been gloomy and obscure. The chandeliers made little headway against the dank all-day dawn.

Lucy had tramped with Laurie and Zach across the soaking Mall, telling herself that three more would add to the attendance, a comfort to Nick, and admitted secretly that she had to see some public reaction. The buildings around the Mall had been made distant and not quite solid by the blowing rain. They had been as romantic as ruined temples or castles. The wet grass and mud had been slick underfoot. Now and again, the intrepid party had had their slow progress enlivened by a sudden slip forward, and a frantic, momentary jig to regain their balances.

They had encountered the dinosaur in a drift of fog. Its body had been slick and reptilian, the condensed water dripping from its face in huge, mock tears. Zach's hand had tightened in Lucy's a second before Laurie cried out, "Look!"

His steps had dragged as they passed it, and he had stared back at it in wonder as the mist reclaimed it.

The weather had not discouraged hundreds of other children and adults. The marble floors of the Dalton had been slippery and gritty with tracked-in mud. The very air had been moist. Yellow slickers had made the crowd as colorful as a field of daffodils. The excited voices of children, the authoritative voices of adults herding them, the crackling of radio wands, the insectile clicking of umbrellas closing, had made for Lucy a bright tapestry of noise.

The first voice that had spoken from the radio wands that Lucy and the children had obtained on entering was a familiar one.

"Welcome," it had said—Zach shouted, "Nick!"—"to the Dalton Institute's Small Worlds"—people around them had turned to smile at the small boy bouncing up and down in his galoshes—"an exhibition of dollhouses and their furnishings from Colonial times to the present," Nick's taped voice had concluded. Laurie had rolled her eyes in free-floating embarrassment.

Holding hands, the Douglases had moved from cluster to cluster, looking at the dollhouses they had seen set up the previous day. They had not had the radio wands then, the little telephonelike receivers that magically revealed all the secrets, though they had witnessed the testing of them by the technicians. Yesterday the illustrated folder had been their guide, and Nick, as well as Lucy, whose knowledge of the field was considerable. Her own work had been contained in half a dozen of the exhibits, but nowhere had it been as extensive as in Grandmother's White House. Because of the distraction of the photographer and the intimidating presence of Dolly herself, they had none of them examined it in detail. This day they had, walking around it to see it from all sides.

Lucy had been relieved that Laurie and Zach had held their tongues; she had half-expected one of them to announce, "My mother did that!" Perhaps it had been their grandmother's voice, emanating from the radio wand, that awed them a little and invested the familiar bulk of the dollhouse with a little glamor.

They had crept away through the rain after a couple of hours. Laurie and Zach had both fallen asleep in the car. The rest of the day had been washed away by the rain, as dream-like as the dinosaur, or the buildings around the Mall.

The telephone rang, and Lucy jumped. The clock on the wall accused her. She should have been in the workshop fifteen minutes ago.

From the living room, her father declared, "Horseshit!"

It made Lucy smile. One of his chief pastimes was playing critic to his favorite soap.

She picked up the receiver on the second ring. She knew who it was.

"Are you the Lucy Douglas in *VIP?* The yummy one?" Nick asked.

Lucy blew an emphatic raspberry into the phone, and listened to Nick laughing.

"Some of us have to work for a living," she interrupted, "so excuse me."

"Wait," he pleaded.

"I'm waiting, but only out of an overly trained respect for my elders."

"The pictures were great," he rushed, "and you were beautiful. Are you really twenty-nine?"

"Thanks. No, I'm fourteen, I just look old for my age. You're in really hot water because of it too, but you deserve it. You might have warned me so I could wear something more flattering than a pair of jeans that makes my butt look as big as the FBI building."

"I dunno," he mused, "I think your butt looked fine. Besides, if I'd warned you, you wouldn't have come."

"You are horrifyingly devious."

He chortled evilly. "Don't forget, me proud beauty, I have your daddy's mortgage."

Lucy laughed. "Se ya tonight, Snidely."

"You must free yourself, my dear, from this Puritanical, middle-class obsession with work."

"I *am* middle class and Puritanical. And I have these middle-class, Puritanical kids who have wicked appetites. You wanna feed 'em?"

There was a brief, satisfying pause from Nick.

"Well?" she demanded, enjoying the unexpected sensation of having backed him into a corner.

"I'm thinking about it," he said. "They're neat kids. I just don't know if I could take their mother's backchat."

31

"I learned everything I know from you."

"Whew. For a minute there I thought you were going to spit all over the phone again and electrocute yourself."

"You'd better go play with your museum," Lucy insisted, "and let me go back to work."

"Too bad, I was just going to ask you to have dinner with me tonight."

"So ask." Lucy studied the clock. If Nick would ever let her get some work done, she would treat herself to a night off.

"Eight o'clock?"

"Uh-huh."

"Have you heard from Dolly yet?"

"No."

"That's why you're so anxious to go back to work," he accused.

"You're too clever. You forgot Pop. He answers phones, along with his many other fine attributes."

"But Zach's sleeping now. You'll take the phone off the hook. I was surprised I got through, but I surmised you might be entranced with your own image in this glorious rag."

Lucy laughed. "See ya tonight, Snidely."

She hung up and immediately took the phone off the hook, hanging the receiver over the edge of the corkboard next to the phone.

"Pop," she asked, sticking her head into the living room, "will you babysit tonight, after eight?"

"Course." He flicked one big hand in her direction. His eyes never left the screen. "Pure horseshit, this show, know that, Lu?"

She nodded. "I'll be in the workshop, Pop."

Nick Weiler stroked his head and listened to the buzz of the open line for a few seconds. Unwilling to let Lucy go, he listened to her absence.

At last he hung up and stared at the magazine, open on his desk. Lucy had been unnerved during the picture-taking with Dolly. The whole business of the publicity had surprised her, and then too, she was almost always thrown onto the defensive around Dolly. In the picture with her kids, she came into her own.

The photographer had caught the curious upward slant of

her eyes over her cheekbones, which were not the hollow, starved bones of the fashion model, but were fully fleshed and modeled, as if sculpted in some fine-grained bleached wood. The Tartar in her, she explained away her eyes and facial structure, joking away both her ancestry and her temperament.

And then he thought of her hands, with their calluses that were like thin bark, as if she were still caught somewhere in some mythic metamorphosis, still barely Galatea, or just becoming Daphne. But the very center of her palms and between her fingers, at the bases, the skin was smooth and silky.

When the phone buzzed once and one of the numbers lit up, he reluctantly put his thoughts of Lucy away and picked it up.

"Yes?"

"It's Mrs. Douglas, Dr. Weiler."

Not Lucy, he told himself, suddenly irritated with himself for wanting her to call him back, for being disappointed because he knew it wasn't Lucy, it was Dolly, or he would shave his beard.

"Thank you, Roseann." He heard the click of the button being released by Roseann. "Hello, Dorothy."

"Have you seen that goddamn magazine?"

"Ummm." She was going to rant. He would shut up and wait out the storm.

"I'll never have anything to do with those bastards again."

"You shouldn't take it to heart," he ventured, without any hope that she was listening.

A purple curse was loosed on his left ear, followed by "Would you like to be called Nickie, or whatever obnoxious nickname your family tagged you with when you were too young to defend yourself?"

"Nickles," he said absently. "Mother always called me Nickles."

Dolly's low-throated explosive laugh rolled over the line.

"Nickles?" she demanded.

"Until I went away to school."

Dolly paused. "Well, your mother always was a bubble-head."

Nick struggled momentarily between the son's instinctive defense of his mother and the grown man's knowledge that his mother was, at the most difficult times, a bubblehead. Mother love won out.

"She loved me," he protested.

Dolly fell silent. Her father had given her her nickname; *her* mother had always called her Dorothy, or Dorothy Ann. And Nick Weiler knew all that, knew that she hated people calling her Dolly because it was her father's name for her, a love name. Hers. And old Mike's.

"Anyway," she said petulantly, "I'm sorry I lent you my dollhouse. I can't wait to get it back. I miss it."

"You're welcome to visit it anytime."

"Maybe I will."

Nick felt suddenly cheerful, off the treacherous territory of Dolly's name. "It's drawing a lot of attention. We've never had such a successful show."

"Really?" Dolly was pleased.

"Really," he assured her.

"You are taking good care of it, aren't you? The papers are full of art thefts. It's very upsetting."

"Dolly," Nick told her solemnly, "you're the only person I know who'd steal a dollhouse."

She laughed.

"Better than stealing the dollhouse maker," she said.

"Can't steal what isn't owned," Nick came back lightly. He would like to tell her off. She ought to know better than to pick at him about Lucy. But nothing would be gained by letting his anger show.

"I may not own her, but apparently I'm the way to making her, in more than one sense," Dolly said tartly.

"My, aren't we funny?"

"Very funny," Dolly agreed. "What sort of fool do you think I am? You arranged that picture-taking session. I'm perfectly aware that you used me to promote not only your Christly museum, but Lucy as well. Thanks to me, and you, of course, she's got a bundle of free advertising and an instant reputation as the best dollhouse decorator in the country."

"Are you suggesting she isn't?"

"Don't be silly," Dolly dismissed the question. "She's working for me, isn't she?"

"Oh, I thought maybe you were doing it to help support your grandchildren," he barbed.

"That too." She ignored or never sensed his sarcastic attack. "Anyway you owe me for the dollhouse, darling. You be nice to Lucy. I know she's nice to you. She can be a perfect bitch, but you can handle a little bitchiness, and she *does* need a man. I've never expected her to live her life as some kind of virginal memorial to Harrison."

"I'm so pleased to be of service."

"Lovely of you, darling. I'll be talking to you soon. Take care of my precious."

Meaning the dollhouse, of course, not Lucy, not Laurie or Zach. Nick found he was grinding his teeth. Condescending, miserable . . . it was Lucy who had drawn her mother-in-law into miniatures when Dolly was bereft, it was Lucy's work, at whatever price Dolly had paid for it, that was bringing in the crowds in the Small Worlds exhibition. It made him a little sick to his stomach, remembering that once he had known Dolly Hardesty's hard little body, even as he knew Lucy now.

There was the matter of his Christly museum, as she had called it, which needed running, and her goddamn dollhouse to look after. There was a meeting on security later in the afternoon. He had no time to be angry with Dolly or to muse on Lucy. He tossed the magazine to one side and opened the thick file on museum security.

At midafternoon he was walking through the exhibition in the Main Hall. He was one of a dozen or so people in the place who had attained a height of more than four feet, and in the presence of two hundred plus schoolchildren and all the miniature houses, he felt like Gulliver in Lilliput.

He visited the exhibitions frequently. He liked to pick up random responses from the visiting public, but it was as much because he enjoyed the looking as anything else. The commentary of the children and their escorts came to him as the pieces of a jigsaw puzzle, or more correctly, the pieces of two jigsaw puzzles, as the lectures spilled from the radio wands as well.

The lilting voice of Connie Winslow, his assistant for special events, caught his ear. ". . . built in 1876, it features drawers in its base for storage. . . ."

"Brian, don't touch." The strident voice of a harried schoolteacher.

A boy with an eye for a scale. ". . . the doll's too big for the furniture."

"No, it was made that way." His adult escort.

He doesn't give up. "It's still too big . . ."

". . . the Aubusson rug in the drawing room was worked by Elizabeth . . ." a staffer's voice, from a radio wand, one of the girls in the restoring office, he thought.

". . . wish I had that dollhouse . . ." a wistful child.

". . . the extremely narrow hallways. Severely damaged in a fire . . ." Eddie Bouton, his public information officer.

". . . oooh, look at the little chamberpot. I couldn't get my smallest fingertip into it!" A tall young girl, with the gawky look of preadolescence.

". . . typical Victorian cabinet dollhouse divided into two floors of two rooms each . . ." Connie again. Nick had persuaded Connie and several other staffers with good public-speaking voices to tape the scripted information. It involved them more deeply in this specific exhibition, exposed them to other areas of the museum's work, outside their narrow specialties, and saved the cost of professional readers, a satisfying arrangement all around.

". . . made a lamp like that once from a coffee creamer from Sambo's," one middle-aged lady related to another. They would have dollhouses of their own, beloved hobbyists.

"Really?" a squeal of delight.

". . . the first tin dollhouses . . ." Eddie Bouton, in concert with his own voice, from two radio wands at once, ". . . created by cabinetmaker Joseph Pinkham in Philadelphia in 1830 . . ."

". . . it's just like my aunt Theresa's dollhouse, the one with the elevator that really works, you know, when you pull the string . . ." a pair of little girls, twittering.

He could not escape himself today. ". . . the bow windows in the doors are a unique and unusual feature . . ." he heard himself saying.

". . . want to do curtains like that if I can get the fabric . . ." another hobbyist, a collector.

"Brian, don't touch." Boy at work, being supervised.

". . . needlework is exquisite, isn't it? It's all the same woman's work. L. Douglas, it says here. I'm sure Harriet Mushrow's bedroom set was done by her, the one with the log cabin quilt . . ." The subject of the collectors' conversation drew him back.

"Miss Porteous, does the White House really look like this?

36

I went there last month and I don't remember it this way," asked an observant child, near Dolly's White House.

"Not exactly. What does the folder say?" The teacher.

". . . geez, I wish I was the president's daughter and somebody gave me a dollhouse . . ." A chubby girl with a pouting lip.

". . . the 1948 to 1952 restoration was marked with a gift from King George VI, presented by then Princess Elizabeth. It was an early eighteenth-century mirror, here copied . . ."

You tell 'em, Dolly, Nick thought as he passed within hearing of her recorded lecture.

He bent to tap a small boy on the shoulder. "Brian," he said, "touch that," pointing to a large Victorian cabinet dollhouse with oversize windows, the better to peep through, and furnished with relentlessly sturdy pieces. Brian grinned and bee-lined for the dollhouse. Nick caught Brian's teacher's relieved eye, nodded, and made for his security conference.

Lucy's father opened the door to Nick's knock.

"Hello, Mr. Novick," Nick said, shaking the older man's hand.

"Come on in," he was greeted. "She's still getting rigged out. Be right down."

He followed him into the living room where Laurie and Zach were watching television.

"Set down," Mr. Novick invited him.

"Okay." He sat down on the arm of the sofa. "Laurie needs a good tickling, doesn't she?"

Lucy's father snorted amiably and said, "I guess."

Nick reached casually for the seven-year-old, who wriggled away from him, giggling, while trying to keep her eyes on the TV screen. Zach spared a glance long enough to grin at them, and then turned back to his study of Snoopy's ongoing angst.

During the next commercial break, Zach climbed wordlessly into Nick's lap, and sat there, poised as nervelessly as the top man on the circus pyramid, with one thumb in his mouth, and the other hand working the gap in his pajama bottoms. Nick moved his left arm to support the boy. Laurie glanced up and tickled Nick's leg to get his attention. He followed her gaze to Zach's hand and they grinned at each other.

37

Lucy found them arranged in comfortable wordlessness before the TV. She removed Zach from Nick's lap and deposited him next to Laurie on the sofa. Laurie's arm slipped under the little boy's head in a motherly gesture. Lucy kissed the tops of their heads.

"After Snoopy, it's bedtime," she said to her father. "'Night, Pop."

"Did you write down the number for Pop?" she asked Nick, and he paused to jot the telephone number of the restaurant on a piece of paper.

Mr. Novick followed them to the door. "Have a good time," he boomed.

"How is your father?" Nick asked Lucy, when the door had closed behind them and they were walking to the car.

"Well enough, I guess. He had words with my mother tonight, right after supper. She'd seen the magazine; she called about that."

"I didn't know they were on speaking terms."

"There's not much to talk about anymore. The kids." Lucy laughed. "Most of their conversation tonight ran to my father hinting that Mother is missing her grandchildren, to whom he happens to be very close, heh, heh, and her suggesting that he's imposing on me at the very least, and probably drinking my cooking sherry behind my back, too."

"She liked the *VIP* piece?"

"More or less. The kids' picture, anyway. She said she thought you—"

"Oh, oh."

"—you looked distinguished but older than she'd expected. Then she sniffled a bit and allowed I wasn't her baby anymore."

"Oh." Nick couldn't see her expression. She had found something to stare at out the window. "No," he said thoughtfully, "I guess you're not, are you?"

Lucy didn't answer. She apparently didn't want to pursue the subject. Nick wished she would open up to him but she held her past to herself tightly. He knew that her parents had divorced when she was in her early teens and that she had never quite recovered from feeling that she was an embarrassing leftover, the one real barrier to a permanent erasure of the disastrous marriage for both of them. Her mother had remarried and had younger children; she led a busy suburban life around her teaching career and her second family. There seemed to be little energy left over for more than a superficial relationship with her grown-up, widowed daughter.

Nick stole a glance at Lucy as they paused for a stop light. She had her hair up, in the elaborate quasi-Oriental style just coming into fashion. It brought out the barbaric structure of her bones, inviting touch the way a smooth-polished curve of wood did.

"You're beautiful tonight."

She looked at him gravely. "Thank you. You're very . . ."

"Distinguished?"

She laughed with him.

"Did Dolly call?" she asked him.

"Oh, yes. Between your electric raspberry and the endless meeting on security."

"She called me, too."

"And what did she say and what did you say?"

"I said as little as I could. I made sympathetic noises about the sacrilege the magazine committed. Apparently the editors were quite cruel about it when she upbraided them."

Nick snorted.

"She wanted to know how her little darlings were. Weren't they just adorable in that photograph, peeking at Grandmother's dollhouse?" Lucy mocked. "I almost threw up."

"Don't you worry about them taking after her?"

Lucy smiled thinly. "I examined them closely in the cradle. If I'd seen the slightest resemblance, I'd have strangled them, right then, with my bare hands. Which, by the way, she told me were obscene, very distracting in the photographs."

"She must have been a wonderful mother-in-law?"

"Yes. I've earned my heavenly crown. We always lived on military bases. We didn't have the money to visit her, and she wouldn't visit us. The housing was tacky; it offended her. Anyway, I told her Zach was putting gesso on his toothbrush and hung up, before she could lecture me on leaving the stuff where he could reach it."

"I didn't know you ever lied."

"I don't. He was."

"Yuck. It isn't poisonous, is it?"

"I don't think so. Not really nutritious, you know?"

"My little talk with Dolly was fun, too."

"Really?" Lucy smothered a giggle. "Tell all."

"The dear sweet thing accused me of using her name and fame, *and* her dollhouse, to promote you, me, and the Dalton."

"Did she?"

"Oh, yes. And got in one particularly cheap shot about—"

"I can guess. Shit." Lucy's voice faded. "How long have you known Dolly, Nick?"

"Since we were kids. My father painted her picture once."

"I remember. That's the painting that was stolen a little while ago."

"The next summer, I think it was, after her father was ejected from office, Dolly and her mother spent some time in England. Her mother used the connection with Sartoris to introduce herself to my mother. Mother's the original marshmallow, you know. There's no meanness in her; she doesn't see it in other people. I suppose that goes a long way to explaining not only how she could love Sartoris, who's a right old bastard in a lot of ways, and why my stepfather loved her.

"Be that as it may. She put them up for several months. I came home from school one holiday and there they were, ensconced like exiled royalty in the house. I was severely instructed by my mother to ignore Mrs. Hardesty's heavy hand on the brandy bottle, and to suffer what Mother termed 'Dolly's high spirits.' "

"Be a good Boy Scout?" Lucy put in.

Nick smiled at her. He would have been happy to abandon this particular reminiscence, but Lucy pursued it.

"Don't keep me in suspense. Tell me what Dolly got up to. Give me a weapon, for Christ's sake, for the next time she tells me I'm letting her grandchildren grow up like savages."

There was a silence, and then Nick confessed in a funereal tone. "Besides being a miserable spoiled brat, she cock-teased every male in the place, including my poor stepfather, who was by then a doddering seventy-year-old."

Lucy whistled. "That's the kind of weapon that might backfire on me. I guess I won't use it. You, too?"

"What? Oh, yes. I was barely pubescent though."

"Hardly got a rise out of you?" Lucy poked wickedly.

"You're cute tonight." Nick paused. "Funny thing. She stopped it all of a sudden, just like that. Went all demure schoolgirl. I suppose Mother must have stepped on her."

"But I thought you said your mother wouldn't have noticed."

"Oh, she always notices. She just doesn't recognize the idea of sin, or a person who's deliberately bad. No, it's all a matter of manners to her. I don't doubt she thought Dolly had been badly raised and that it was only good manners on her part to straighten the little beast out. She tried anyway."

Lucy shuddered. "Dolly has gorgeous manners. When I first met, I thought, how marvelous. A real lady, in this day and age. Then I found out she uses her manners to suit herself." Then she jumped to another subject. "Did you know Harrison?"

"Your Harrison?"

Lucy nodded, almost shyly, as if she had never claimed possession of her dead husband before.

Nick shook his head. "I remember him, barely, as a small boy. I was not an age to be interested in other people's offspring. I'm sorry. I can't say I ever knew him as a grown-up."

"He didn't ever grow up." Lucy's tone was flippant but bitter. "Lived and died a boy. He really wasn't much like Dolly, except he wanted his own way no matter what the cost. We're all that way, a little, aren't we?"

She was obviously pained. As much as Nick wanted her to talk about the things that were important to her, it was obviously too much for her at this instant. He didn't answer her, pretending to concentrate on changing lanes, leaving the interstate highway.

"How much work do you have to do for Dolly now?" he asked at last.

"The end is in sight." There was a calm satisfaction in her voice. She had recovered herself. "There's some accessories to do, china and whatnot, and I'm trying to locate some French scenic wallpaper so that I can do over the Diplomatic Reception room the way she wants it. And she told me today she thought the model of the grounds that your people at the Dalton worked up was wretched-looking." Lucy cast an apologetic glance his way.

"I admit it was a slap-up job."

"She wants me to do that, the grounds."

"Do you really want to? It sounds like a hell of a lot of work."

"No. I'd like to do something else with my life besides work for Dolly. It's bad enough being tied to her through the kids. I've got other customers if I want them, that I've put off to do her dollhouse. I'll probably never have another project this big, that's all."

It was soothing to talk about the work itself, Nick thought. And foolish to venture away from that narrow path. He was going to do it anyway.

"Has Dolly expressed her anxiety that you're going to run off and marry me and then retire before she has what she wants from you?" he asked genially.

"No. But she shouldn't worry." Lucy looked straight at him, her face expressionless.

"I can't imagine you not working," Nick plunged ahead, willfully ignoring the sense of Lucy's answer.

They were in city streets now, where the light and dark fanned over Lucy's features.

"She thinks I'm going to steal you away, or that someone is going to steal her dollhouse. Little does she know," Nick continued distantly, "the Dalton is tighter than a tick right now. Besides, I've never heard of anyone ever stealing a dollhouse."

He didn't have to add: *And you're locked up tight too.* An uncomfortable silence fell between them that was only eased by the wine at dinner. They left the restaurant in a mildly tiddly state.

He stopped the car on the corner of a quiet tree-lined Georgetown street. Lucy, curled up on the seat beside him and loose from the wine, reacted slowly.

He seized her right wrist, wrapped in the gold chains of her evening bag. "Let's see what's in your purse," he demanded.

Color flared in her cheeks. She struggled a little, laughing, and protested, "No."

He released her and sat back. "Come on." He held out his hands. She thrust the purse at him.

"Fine thing," he scolded mildly, "when I can't take you to a nice restaurant without you stealing the ruffles off the lamb chops and the doily off the candy tray."

"I might be able to use them. They just throw them out," she insisted.

"You don't even know what you're going to do with them?"

"Make something."

"You don't know. And they weren't even our lamb chops."

He gave her back the handbag and started the car again.

"You're a goddamn magpie, Lucy. Would you like to go to my house for a while?"

She had curled up against him again and closed her eyes.

"I'll let you have the egg cartons I've saved," he offered.

She smothered an attack of giggles.

"My old tea bag tags?"

Lucy laughed out loud. Nick bent to plant a quick kiss on the top of her head.

"Let's go," she whispered.

3

Dolly Hardesty Douglas paced her living room. She felt like an exile. There was no comfort tonight in the familiar objects. Her mother watched from the portrait above the fireplace, the focus of the room. The blaze of her mother's hair was the only strong color in the cream, silver, and blue room. Dolly stared at it, for once seeing not the dreaming beauty that she loved but the ghost, locked into her own fantasies, that Leighton Sartoris had painted twenty-five years ago.

She turned her back on it to look out over the city again. Manhattan was its ordinarily spectacular light sculpture. It had rarely failed to delight her. It usually made her feel like the queen of it all, sitting on her steel and glass mountaintop. But tonight she was dispossessed, unable to feel any connection with it.

She emptied a full ashtray in a small silver-reed basket, just for something to do. She tried to think of someone in the city that she knew. It was very painful to acknowledge, abruptly, that there wasn't anybody anymore. Not that she'd want to see. She lit a new cigarette. Very likely there was no one down there in Sin City who knew her either, or cared to.

At the discreet little bar, she poured herself a glass of ginger ale. She had never cared for drink stronger than wine, a taste or lack of it that may very well have preserved her from the alcoholism that destroyed her mother. Her only real vice, she thought, was the cigarettes. She looked at the one between her fingers with distaste. Her father had always held that smoking was unladylike and had warred thirty-five years with her mother on the subject.

Her earliest memories were of her mother, furtively smoking in the nursery, as she read Dolly a nighttime fairy tale. Dolly, old enough to talk at two and a half, also had been old enough to keep a secret when her mother made it a game. Daddy had never come into the baby's room; he was always in his office downstairs, of an evening.

Since then she had done a lot of things in her life, of which her father would not have approved. Not that she was a frigging saint now. She had had lovers for three years. Except herself. She didn't count masturbation as a sin, or even a bad habit. It was wonderful for the complexion and gave the day a good start, and screw her old man, anyway. A typical male, when all was said and done.

If she loved anything it was the dollhouse. It had filled all the little blanks in her life very nicely, thank you. Three years of satisfaction. Not many love affairs yielded that, or for that long. Never mind marriage. The very thought of Harry Douglas, may the bastard burn in hell, gave her the shudders.

She'd look a pretty sight, at her age, anyway, putting herself on the market against the young women with their fresh bodies. Look at Nick Weiler, not that much younger than herself, chasing after her daughter-in-law, a woman with two children, and silly Lucy young enough to be Nick's daughter. Almost. Not that she was jealous of him; Lucy was welcome to him. And he to Lucy. He was, finally, too cold a fish for her. She always had the sensation that he was thinking ahead of her, and that what he was thinking wasn't very complimentary. Just like his father, that old reptile Sartoris.

To be fair, Nick had his attractions. Dorothy sat down with her ginger ale and cigarette and blew smoke thoughtfully at her mother's portrait. It was perfectly predictable, Nick going all soft in the head and hard in the pants for a woman like Lucy. Middle-aged folly, and naturally a girl who was the exact antithesis of Nick's other women. Wouldn't she like to know what Lucy knew about *them*. Not much, if she knew her Nick. He was a past master of discretion when it served his interest, and it invariably did.

She drained her glass and stubbed out the cigarette. Time

45

for a visit to the dollhouse room. She dreaded it, but it would be good for her lazy soul.

It seemed horribly empty, even if it wasn't. There were the boxrooms and the other dollhouses she owned, beautifully displayed. And the great empty space in the middle of it where her Doll's White House belonged.

Goddamn Nick Weiler for talking her out of it. Reluctant to enter into the emptiness of the room, she leaned against the doorpost. It was ludicrous, her twitching around the apartment, working on a case of lung cancer, and speculating on other people's sex lives, like some filthy old woman. All because Nick had convinced her she should share her dollhouse with the world. Snared her in her own pride. She ought to call Lucy and have a little girltalk with her about Nick. Puncture his balloon.

She dialed the nearest phone with almost steady fingers. A wasted effort, for old Novick answered. In his shaky old man's voice, he told her that Lucy was out. He didn't need to tell her with whom.

Her throat closed with sudden rage. The two of them, sucking off her, trying to take her dollhouse away from her. Screwing their little brains out. Her fingers itched to take out their eyes. She threw herself onto her big empty bed and pounded the pillows until she was out of breath. In the lee of her rage, listening to herself pant, she began to giggle. Be generous, she told herself. How did that song go? *What the world needs now . . .*

So nice someone was having fun. She groped for her cigarettes. Sooner or later, it would be her turn to have fun again.

Leyna looked terrific. She knew it. The make-up girl looked at her critically and nodded in approval, but it was just ritual. Leyna waved flawless fingertips at the director and stepped confidently to the mark on the floor. She and Roddie huddled briefly over the script. Roddie loved directing Leyna. She never used notes or the teleprompter and never missed a beat.

Leyna straightened herself to her full height of six feet and three inches, plus four inches of stiletto heel. She relaxed her shoulders and moved her head fractionally, so that her long hair splayed around over her collar. A survey had revealed that male viewers fantasized about her hair. She never forgot it.

Time, signaled by the red light; she gazed directly into the camera.

"It may look like cake-eating in the middle of a revolution, but Washington has never been gayer, more socially giddy, never more glittery and gossipy," she began. "Perhaps people, even in the highest government circles, need such outlets in some kind of direct proportion to the press of world and national concerns.

"One of the ways that official Washington has been exorcising its daily crises is here," and the camera closed its eye on her, opening another one outside, "in the nineteenth-century Dalton Institute, once known as the Penny Museum." She knew the audience, hearing her voice, was seeing the exterior of the Dalton, lit up like a birthday cake in the night, its entrance portico aswarm with elegantly clad officialdom. The camera blinked and returned to her.

"What's here that's so amusing?" Leyna addressed her audience as if eye to eye with it over plump pillows on her bed. "An exhibition of dollhouses," she confided.

A new eye, another camera, high in the upper stories of the hall, scanned the hall, taking the coiffed, gowned, tuxedoed, and tailored embodiment of democracy, making merry among villages of dollhouses. Leyna's voice, light and a little throaty, continued. The camera found her again, as if by accident, a beautiful woman in a slim floor-length dress of faintly shimmering navy blue, separated from the glittering assemblage only by the fact of a microphone, instead of a champagne glass, in her hand.

"Dollhouses," she repeated. "The miniature houses range from goose eggs lined with foil and furnished with paperclip dolls and bead furniture to Victorian cabinet dollhouses to mass-produced plastic and tin cottages to extravagant adult toys worth thousands of dollars." The minicam's eye flitted from one to another of the dollhouses as she spoke and managed as it roved to illustrate her speech, and catch, casually, here a senator or a senator's lady, there the briefest glimpse of the president, his mother on his arm, here a high court justice, a cabinet officer, a grizzled congresswoman, there a trio of prepubescent girls, turned out in crystal pleats and ivory combs, giggling behind fans.

"But the star of the show is this dollhouse." Leyna paused to let the minicam frame the Doll's White House. "Naturally enough. This *is* Washington, D.C., after all. This is Dorothy Hardesty Douglas's Doll's White House, a remarkable replica of the Executive Mansion."

Now, in the camera's vision, there was another person, a small, delicate platinum-haired woman wrapped in gauzy silver.

"Is it true that when you were first given this dollhouse, you didn't like it?" Leyna asked.

"Not exactly, 'didn't like.' I thought I was too old for it. Now I suspect I was too young." Dolly mocked herself lightly.

"You feel differently now?"

"Oh, yes. When I rediscovered it among my father's effects, after his death, I fell in love with it. I determined to make it an ideal White House."

"An ideal White House?" Leyna probed. "It isn't an exact replica of the White House?"

"Not as it is now or as it ever existed. The real White House always seems to be in a state of flux. The obvious anomalies," here Dolly's small square hands flew in delicate gestures over the surprising bulk of the dollhouse, "the lack of wings, which contain executive offices and aren't very interesting, really, and the absence of the underground stories where the present household offices are housed. Essentially this little White House contains the historic public rooms and the private quarters, much as they existed in the nineteenth century."

"And you've decorated it?"

"The prevailing decoration is after Jacqueline Kennedy, modified by my own personal tastes, particularly in the private quarters. She grasped the historic function of the White House very nicely and had excellent taste. Really, though, this White House is the White House I would have, if I lived there."

Leyna looked straight into the camera again. "Leyna Shaw from the Dalton Institute in Washington, D.C.," she cast a brief, amused look at the Doll's White House, "taking a look at Dolly's White House."

The red light on the camera went black and stayed that way. Leyna smiled coolly at Dolly, who stood unmoving, her face a sudden mask. Dolly's head moved stiffly up and back, like a snake bearing its fangs. Her eyes were wide and shocked. She turned on her heel and walked away.

Leyna nodded a dismissal to her crew and handed in her mike, saying *thank yous* as she passed by. She was free to join the party. As she searched the crowd, deciding where to move first, someone handed her a glass of champagne. She found herself hand in hand with Nick Weiler.

"Thanks, love," Nick said. "Dorothy's pissed at *VIP* for that trick, and now she's pissed at you for it, and she's royally pissed at me."

"Good. Maybe she'll drown in it," Leyna said pleasantly.

"You miss the point. She might have endowed the Dalton, she might have given us the bloody dollhouse, the rest of her collection. She owns several Sartorises, you know!"

Leyna shrugged elegantly. "I had no idea old Mike had stolen so much. Sorry, I didn't know. Thought it was all wrapped up. And I think you're being greedy about the Sartorises. Isn't your father going to dump the lot on the Dalton when he kicks it?"

"Who knows what my father's going to do?"

"Well, can't you fuck her out of them?"

"Why don't you talk like that on the air?" Nick couldn't help grinning. "Millions of perverts would be ecstatic."

"I was saving it for you." Leyna swayed closer to him. "I remember hearing you and Dolly aren't that close anymore. Picked up with sweet little Lucy, the hero's brave widow, haven't you?"

"I thought you were looking after the interests of the Republic, keeping an eye on the politicians, and here I find out you spend your time listening to low gossip," he twitted back.

"Same thing, and I do have time for other things. Your ears should be getting red, darling. I just saw your friend Lucy with Dolly. I bet they're comparing notes. Not that you have any shame."

"I was saving it for you," Nick said.

Leyna laughed, low in her throat.

Nick Weiler clasped his hands behind his back. He looked like a cat near a swinging door.

"Will you do the *Sunday* segment on the Dalton?" he asked.

"Roddie's doing enough film tonight to paste something together," she answered him. "We'll need some talkee-talkee with you, of course. Let's plan it out tonight."

Leyna wasn't kind enough to look the other way while Nick fought with himself. He damned her internally for her boldness. But why should she be shy with him?

"I'll be here late, shutting up the store," he said at last. "I'll try."

Leyna nodded. "Good." She waved at someone she knew.

"Excuse me," Nick said, but it was Leyna who moved off, with a vague pat on his arm, and a cool social brush of her lips on his.

The Dalton was empty of all but staff when Nick found Lucy again, curled up in a tangle of wraps on the sofa in his office. She was not so much asleep, as he discovered when he bent to kiss her, as passed out. So much for the prince's magic kiss tonight.

He managed to bundle her into the car. She huddled as far from him as she could, slipping from half-consciousness to sleep and back again many times on the ride home. He was wretchedly aware of the distance separating them. It was as if the sea had ebbed unexpectedly and left him with the endless flats and a distant curl of water catching light.

Mr. Novick was asleep too, in front of the rolling patterns of the television screen. Nick paused to turn off the set, while Lucy kicked off her shoes. She presented a blind cheekbone for a glassy kiss and, picking up her shoes, slipped up the stairs to her bedroom without a word.

Nick let himself out, relieved to escape her silence. It had been bad enough that she wouldn't talk to him, worse that she seemed to prefer unconsciousness to his company. He felt distinctly like a blind date that hadn't passed approval.

He turned back to the lights of the city, aware of not being the least bit sleepy. It seemed as if he might be the only person among millions who was not asleep. A rare and sudden surge of anger tore through him. He wanted to go back into the house and make love to Lucy. Except that he didn't want to make love to her. He wanted her to lie still and unresponsive, like a mannequin, or a rag doll; he wanted to punish her with his sex.

He drove fast, sweating out the fear of his own anger. He might be able to talk to his father about this new experience of rage in love; the old gambler must understand what it was. But his father was far away on his island, sleeping the sleep of the old and justified. Leyna's address was not far out of his way. She would at least return him to himself.

She had removed her silly high heels and they stood eye to eye. A long time later, he was able to sleep.

Lucy was glad when the *Sunday* segment finished interviewing Nick and let him narrate clips from the dollhouse exhibition. She could watch the dollhouses and their contents, and divorce the even, still faintly British-public-school-accented voice from him.

Little girls, and sometimes not-so-little girls, have played with dollhouses for as long as human memory can recall. Generation after generation of children have played at house, with their own child-size or smaller versions of their parents' tools and utensils, furniture, and the rooms to put them in, turning learning into play as children do, practicing at living.

The camera illustrated: tiny blue enamel spatterware pots and pans, a brass sewing machine, a cradle, fairy-size toys for the dolls' babies.

Adults too made miniature forms of their possessions and buildings for purposes other than childrens' play. From the time of the pharaohs, in whose tombs tiny jewellike models of every kind of thing that the people used have been found, people have made what we call now miniatures, not only for religious purposes, but for merchandising. There were miniature objects that were samples of goods too heavy or bulky to be casually transported, or which were models of future full-scale things (many dollhouses, even today, are in fact architectural models of real buildings) . . .

An enameled and gilded altar, one-seventh of the size of the original, was displayed against dark velvet. A toy train, with a tiny, shabby engineer in it; a gleaming, polished piano; an iron oven, showed to less splendor before an elegant Ed-

51

wardian dollhouse; the architect's model of a long-vanished Manhattan townhouse.

. . . or that were samples in the sense of today's commercial samples, enticements to buy. Dollhouses and miniatures have been used as teaching aids, so that little girls of bygone eras might learn the complicated arts of housewifery . . .

A clumsy-looking iron; folded and yellowed linen; rusty knives and spoons of wildly varying sizes; a set of crystal glasses and a decanter; a drying rack; a moth-eaten bellows; all shown in a disproportionately huge kitchen, so crowded with utensils and tools that no self-respecting doll could hope to get a minute's work done in the clutter.

. . . Other dollhouses preserve past ways of life, domestic arts of other times, or sometimes famous rooms or famous houses. It is the grown-up collector or miniatures-maker who is interested in historical illustration, of course. And sometimes, we find a dollhouse that someone's passion and skill has made a work of art, in response to that instinct of human beings to transmute the most mundane objects into something more.

The final vision of the camera was of the Stettheimer dollhouse, the 1920s creation of a trio of sisters that is at once a work of art, a historic illustration of a period life-style, and a never-neverland toy, a dollhouse for not-so-little girls.

What draws us to dollhouses and their tiny furnishings? Perhaps it is a simple, obvious, and appropriately childish reason—littleness: the reproduction of our world on a reduced scale, in which we are in charge, just as we were when we played at being Mom and Dad, parents to our dollies, which become ourselves.

Lucy's father snorted as the segment ended. "Piled that a little high, didn't you, Nick?" he addressed a shiny new luxury automobile being huckstered by a Swedish tennis star. He cast a worried glance at Lucy, silent in her rocking chair. He didn't have the slightest idea what had gone wrong, only that

52

Lucy was unhappy and it seemed to be Nick Weiler's fault. He liked Nick, but Lucy's stolid misery provoked a strong displeasure with the fellow.

"Turn it off, will you, Pop?" Lucy asked abruptly. She stood up and stretched. "That's all over."

The older man watched her walk upstairs, seemingly only tired. He wished he knew what was wrong. Vexed, mildly infected with her depression, he turned the volume down and settled in to watch the late night news.

A few days later, he draped himself into a chaise and read a newspaper in the shade of his straw hat. Laurie and Zach played with a handful of neighborhood kids within sight and hearing. A transistor radio reported a ball game in progress from its perch on a nearby picnic table.

It was all pleasantly somnolent, the sort of spring day he had come to savor. A small cloud hove into view in the shape of Nick Weiler's tapping little Mercedes.

Mr. Novick waved at Nick and took off his hat long enough to tip at the workshop. His speckled pate gleamed in the sun and then the straw hat came down firmly over it. He grinned a broad, dentured smile, and shook Nick's hand in passing. There wasn't anything much to say besides how-dos. He hoped, for the sake of a fine day, that they would make it up.

Nick, walking around to the workshop, was struck with the thought that Mr. Novick was less than ten years his senior. Disability, alcoholism, and bitterness had aged Lucy's father so that he looked and acted twenty years older. He had put even his failures behind him and lived in resigned contentment with what he had salvaged, a backwater life with his daughter. Nick supposed he was grateful for any kind of family at all.

Lucy rarely talked about her father, or the disintegration of her parents' marriage, which she was old enough to remember, or her own marriage to Harrison Douglas, Jr. How long had they been seeing each other before she would talk without apology about her kids? She was so tightly furled; he was only beginning to understand that what she held back, in reticence or discretion or her own need for privacy, weighed against him. He had not gained her complete trust. And he knew it was only partly her fault.

He leaned against the doorpost silently a moment, watching her work. She looked up briefly, to see who cast a shadow over her, and acknowledged his uninvited presence with a sudden bloom of color over her cheekbones.

"What do you want?" she said abruptly. Her fingers pushed sandpaper over wood with a vicious grating sound.

"A fair hearing."

"I'm busy," she responded. Fumbling among tools on the worktable, she seized an X-acto blade and began shaving the thin piece of wood before her.

"I never would have expected this attitude from you, Lucy," he said quietly.

"Really." Lucy didn't look at him. The clutter on her worktable might have been the contents of a treasure chest, so riveted was she by it. "Evidently we don't know each other as well as we thought we did."

"I thought you might be a little more mature—" he was cut off by another savage attack on the wood with the sandpaper. It was almost a relief; he felt like he was saying all the wrong things, and couldn't help it.

"I don't care about Leyna Shaw. Or Dolly. Any of those women," Lucy said suddenly, her voice high with anger.

"Lucy," he said, hating the pleading in his own voice, "nobody was cheated or ill-used. I slept with some lonely women. Not even that many. They weren't lonely for a while. Is that so bad?"

"And you got money for the Dalton, or wherever you were working. Or something, a painting or a piece of sculpture or an invitation to the right party." The tools on the table clinked and clattered as she shoved them around savagely.

"Goddamn it, Lucy, there's lot more to my job than sucking up to donors. I'm good at my job, all of it," he exploded. "It's my job."

"I'm so happy for you. I'd say screw your job but that's what you're doing, isn't it? Is there a woman in this country who hasn't had to listen to that song, 'It's my job.' It ought to be grounds for divorce. Between adultery and mental cruelty, 'my job.'" Her hands moved ceaselessly, frantically, over the wood. She caught her breath and plunged on. "It's sickening enough you'd screw Dolly. And then me. Do you keep a scorecard or was it just for fun, or were you keeping the help happy? It makes me want to puke."

"For Christ's sake, Lucy. Dolly and I were finished years ago. I'm forty-three. Was I supposed to save myself for true love?"

"I told you, Nick. I don't care who you slept with or that you slept with them at all. I care about why. The point is, we don't seem to share the same standards about that. It's important to me, a lot more important, apparently, than it is to you."

"It was never unimportant. I liked them. I never went to bed with a woman I didn't like. Oh, shit," he said helplessly. Why didn't she understand? How could he explain to her how it had been all his life, the women who came to him, the sad rich women with their terrible emptiness? How it had always seemed like the courteous thing to do, the kind thing.

"Rah, rah." Lucy's voice was like breaking glass.

Desperate, he tried to recover lost ground. "You've been listening to Dolly, the fucking witch of the North, and Leyna Shaw. Two of the biggest bitches on the surface of Mother Earth."

"Are you sure you never slept with a woman you didn't like?" Lucy pecked with bloody glee.

"I didn't sleep with either one of them. It was more like horizontal war games. I was lucky to get away with my balls."

"Charming. I can't wait to hear your assessment of me."

"Lucy, you're too harsh," he insisted. "I'm standing here trying to justify myself to you. Isn't that some kind of proof of sincerity?" He passed a weary hand over his face. "I'm telling you the world just isn't always black and white." It seemed to Nick that it was something he had perceived almost literally on his mother's knee. Why was it so hard for her to understand?

"How would you feel about me if you found out the same kind of thing?" Lucy asked in a low voice.

"That's an unfair question. I've taken you at face value from the first. I never asked for proof of anything from you." It was all true but self-serving. He had known from the first she would not come to him, that he would have to seek her out. Was that his real mistake? Falling in love with a good, sweet, fastidious middle-class American girl, who believed that love was always pure and fortuitous, if only you were virtuous enough, as if it were some kind of natural law?

She was slipping away from him. He sensed the slack in the line. Her face, stony and pale, was still turned away from him.

Nick leaned back against the doorpost, looking out into the bright sunlight. He could hear Zach and Laurie and the voices of children he didn't know outside. It sounded like a tag game. He wondered how long it would take before he didn't know their voices anymore. He sucked in breath and turned back to her.

Her hands shoved the sandpaper like a washerwoman. Wisps of hair had escaped her braids and floated around her face.

"I'm trying," he said slowly, carefully, "to tell you that I'm sorry. That's all over. With Dolly, with Leyna, everyone else. I only want you."

"You've got one thing right." She looked at him full in the face for the first time since he'd come to the door. "It's all over." She looked down again quickly. "I have work to do. I know you understand. Good-bye."

He stood silently for a moment, thinking *That's the last marble* as the children's voices faded and died away. He turned and walked quickly away.

Lucy's hands came at last to rest, but she didn't look up. She felt stupid, and somehow, in some shapeless indeterminate way, in the wrong. After a long time, she reached slowly, like a blind person moving through memorized spaces, for an X-acto blade. Carefully, precisely, she drew it this way and that, and then repeated the pattern.

Suddenly, she threw it down and grabbed one hand in the other. A thin red line welled across the palm of her hand. "Shit," she muttered and blotted it on her overalls. She pushed the tools beyond child's reach and tossed the splintered wood in the cardboard box that was doing duty as a waste receptacle. Head down, she abandoned the workshop.

The minivac hummed mechanically along with Dolly as she moved it over and around the tiny settee. The Gingerbread House was having what Dolly thought of as a *nice clean*. It had had dozens of *nice cleans* in the absence of its neighbor, her pride and joy, the Doll's White House. The task felt vaguely like potting around a graveyard, enjoying the hovering spirit of the late departed.

Dolly considered her morning conversation with Nick Weiler on the phone.

". . . record-setting attendance," he said, the way people say *at least he went quick*. "I wish you'd let us keep it longer."

He could have been a little sweeter, a little more enthusiastic. Dolly had to scold.

"Yes, and if I did, you'd pretty please later on to let you lend it around with the rest of the show."

Nick caved in like Wonderbread. "Well, we've got Missy Updegraff's Fondtland Manor to replace it."

"There's nothing tacky about that, now," she told him. "What are you complaining about?" she asked, though really she thought Fondtland Manor was a thoroughly unworthy successor to her Doll's White House, and of course Nick hadn't really complained at all.

"I appreciate your lending it to us, Dorothy. I'd like to point out that it hasn't been stolen."

A feeble, unfunny joke, Dolly thought. How could the silly man believe that there was no threat to the Doll's White House with all the Christless thieving going on?

No, he hadn't been himself. Polite, as always; that old bitch Maggie Weiler would probably crawl out of her antique bed and beat him with her chamberpot if he wasn't. Old Maggie would disapprove of his being so dishwater dull, though, too. All because he and dear Lucy were on the outs. The thought made Dolly hum a little louder.

The idiocy of the man, hopping into the sack with Leyna Shaw, for a rerun, and her living in that complex where half of official Washington lives, to witness Nick's car parked next to hers in the parking garage, a nice symbol, Dolly giggled to herself, of what else he was parking and where. And then the *Sunday* segment, with Leyna purring at him like a cat hearing a can opener, in case anybody had any doubts left. It was more than amusing, the two of them taking care of each other like that, the same way they'd always gotten everything: Leyna, screwing anybody who knew anything plus the necessary network executives to get her promotions, and darling Nick, cheerfully, politely making rich women happy, and his museum nicely endowed. Which brought up the interesting speculation of whether either of them or both had ever screwed the president. Leyna liked to hint around she had, and Matt Johnson wasn't about to deny it. Still, Dolly had never heard of him lusting after any but his own sex, and the best part of that official secret was that Nick Weiler was exactly the type of dear friend that Matt always chose.

Ah, well, Lucy was too quick to miss the signals and there had been some convenient gossip-column talk, and Dolly herself had had a nice chat with Connie Winslow, who Lucy thought was a friend of hers. Connie, with her beautiful voice trapped in a scarred ugly body, knew very well that Nick Weiler would never love her and so kept her yen for him well buried, even to the extent of cultivating his girl friends. Connie had been happy to tell Lucy, by mistake, of course, that darling Nick was a being a bastard, oops, and that was appropriate wasn't it?

Only now, he was a dull bastard, but then, weren't they all, after a while? And it was pleasant to think that snotty Lucy had discovered her true love was just a male whore.

The door bell rang against the hum of the minivac. Dolly ignored it. It was followed shortly by her maid's characteristic knock at the door of the dollhouse where she was working.

"Come in," she sang.

Ruta slouched in and thrust a small manila envelope at her. Dolly examined it quizzically and then shut off the minivac. She ripped the top clean off the envelope.

Peeking inside, she could discern no paper, only a shadowy square like a small flat matchbox. She turned the envelope upside down and shook the contents into her hand. It *was* a matchbox, from a fashionable restaurant. Dolly opened it half an inch and quickly closed it. She waved her hand dismissively at Ruta, whose face was hanging out avidly. The maid rambled out unwillingly.

Locking the door behind Ruta, Dolly opened the box again. With trembling fingers, she plucked the contents from the matchbox. A half dozen inch-long roses, from stems to blossom, the buds less than a quarter of an inch. The stems clung to the skin of her hand without quite piercing it. It was as if they were pricking her. She shook the roses gently into the cupped palm of her hand. They glowed like fresh droplets of blood, set off against a field of green leaves and stems. Dolly raised them to her nose. Her stomach fluttered. The unmistakable scent of roses, real roses, faint as a promise of love, reached her.

She fished out a jeweler's loupe that she always carried in the watchpocket of her apron. Studying the roses, she could see the thorns that had plucked at her skin like small caresses. She examined the matchbox, discovering a small square of paper, printed with minute letters, on the bottom. Using the jeweler's loupe, she was able to decipher the message on it. A name and a phone number.

Dropping the loupe thoughtfully into its proper pocket, Dolly went to the nearest telephone. Her finger shook so, she had to dial three times to get it right.

4

Roger was trying to relax. He had a hamburger and a beer. Between munching and slurping, he rolled the little pink-bullet-car across the round glass top to the coffee table. When he looked up, he could see the digital traveling clock blinking patiently an arm's length away on the nightstand. It was almost time for the appointment, and he finished off the burger with two cheek-ballooning bites. He rolled the little car, one-handed, around the circumference of the table, making squealing noises and revving engine noises and tipping it as if he were two-wheeling it on a real racetrack. He ran it back and forth between the beer can and the manila envelope.

Roger drained the beer can and crushed it with one hand. Sadly, he dropped it into the wastebasket, wishing he'd bought more or that there was time to go out for another bagful. But there wasn't. The digital clock went on blinking its calm alarm at him. He flipped the car casually with his famous fingertip flick, perfected on a series of turtles he had owned as a kid. It was one of those skills, once learned, for which a person never really lost the knack.

Ready or not, he jumped when the knock came at the door. He licked his teeth hastily, in case of onion bits or other flotsam. Grabbing the little car, he dropped it in his pocket. It would make the pocket bulge a little, but Roger didn't care. His car would be on the table soon enough.

He wore his interview suit, an iridescent blue-green, a mark of respect for his visitor. It was profoundly uncomfortable, and he longed for the soft bagginess of his cords and

T-shirt, with their convenient holes for scratching. Roger didn't dress like this for anyone less than a potential employer. It was part of the small collection of self-made rules that he thought of as his code.

His hand was almost too wet with sweat to get a grip on the doorknob, but somehow, he opened the door. He was looking right at the famous lady. It was startling how much she looked like herself. Three dimensions, and nice ones, he thought, and natural coloring. She smiled at him, and the beer and hamburger gurgled in greeting.

"Mr. Tinker?" she asked. Her voice was so *polished*, Roger thought, so high class.

He nodded vigorously and flopped a hand to welcome her hand. After that he felt lost, and could only think to stick his hands back into his pants pockets. She stood there, expectation all over her face. Then she looked significantly at a chair.

What next came to him abruptly. He asked her to sit down, which she promptly did, in the graceful way he thought only ladies in automobile ads did, and then he offered to call room service for a drink or coffee. She said no thanks and Roger was on his own again.

Then she spoke quickly. "I'm Dorothy Hardesty Douglas," she said. It was puzzling for a moment, since Roger knew that, and then he realized she was trying to help again, to keep the old manners rolling, making him comfortable. Her eyes were, he fumbled for the right way to put it to himself, *kind*, but there was something more. Amusement?

"The flowers were," she paused and looked straight at him, "extraordinary. How do you do it?"

Roger flushed with pride. He chuckled. "I can tell you," he told her, with what he hoped was a suitable degree of mystery, "I *don't* grow 'em."

The lady's calm smile turned to bewilderment. She fumbled in her handbag, and Roger, recognizing the gesture, knew immediately what for. He whipped out his Winstons and offered her one. She took it with a grateful little puckering of her lips that made Roger feel weak, and stuck in in her mouth. Roger remembered he was supposed to light it, too. There was another box of matches from the famous restaurant in his suit pocket and he had them out in a jiff, scraping one down the side of the box so hard that it broke.

"Flimsy," he muttered, and she nodded. "I didn't really eat there," he confessed.

"Intelligent of you," she assured him warmly, "the food's overpriced and wretched."

Roger was inspired by her confidence to try another match. This was the magic one that hit the lady's cigarette. Roger was thrilled. Here he was, lighting a cigarette, the other end of which was between the glossy lips of a famous, rich and still wickedly good-looking woman.

"You don't grow them?" she repeated thoughtfully, coming back to the point. A fine blue puff of smoke shredded before her face. For a moment, hers was the cruelly beautiful face of the stepmother queen in *Snow White*. Roger remembered the Disney cartoon very well; it had scared him silly when he was old enough to have to pretend it hadn't. But he had never forgotten the villainess, the best, he thought, of the whole long Disney line of witches and bitches, much more appealing and sexy than the simpering little-girl heroines.

"Well," she continued, "they're not manufactured. They're real, goddamn it."

The swear fell from her lips as easily as how-dee-do. Roger was almost too startled to enjoy this moment, so long imagined, come round at last. He breathed deeply.

"I shrink 'em," he said calmly.

The lady's rainwater-gray eyes widened for a fraction of a second and then narrowed, and she puffed her cigarette as if she were a stoker in hell.

Roger slipped a hand casually into his jacket pocket and curled it around the cool metal comfort of the bullet-shape car. He giggled just a little. Slowly, he brought it out, hidden in the fleshy rack of his hand, and held it out to her. She raised her eyebrows. Very slowly, one finger at a time, he uncurled his hand. Silence settled like a hundred years all around them.

She stared thoughtfully at the little pink car on his palm. After a moment, she dropped her cigarette into one of the hotel's tinfoil ashtrays and produced, from the depths of her handbag, a jeweler's loupe. Taking the car calmly from Roger, she slipped the loupe to one eye and studied the tiny vehicle for several long moments. Then she dropped the loupe into her free hand, placed the car on the table top, and sat back.

"Anything else?" she asked conversationally.

Roger admired her cool. Anybody else would be hysterical by now. Like his mother. He slid the small manila envelope over the table top.

Opening it quickly, with a barely perceptible tremble, she slid out a tiny rectangle. This time she gasped. It was a distinctly satisfying reaction.

The jeweler's loupe went back to her eye. She had to steady the hand holding the miniature painting with her other hand. This time the examination did not take long. When the loupe dropped from her eye again, and she sat very still, the painting in her hand, she stared at Roger as intensively as she had at his wares. Roger felt vaguely uncomfortable, like a much-handled grapefruit in a market. She might as well have kept that bit of glass in her eye.

At length, she whispered, "How?"

"I minimize them," Roger explained. "I have this device I call the minimizer."

It was in the closet, in a neat leather camera case. But he wasn't going to tell her that. He might be crazy but he was no fool.

"Minimizer?" she asked. Her mouth twitched with some joke to which Roger was not privy. But then her gray eyes clouded.

Roger could see she was having trouble with the whole concept. He whipped out the Winstons again. This time he helped himself, too.

"I used to work for the government," he told her, offering her the butts, "on a project."

She took one, nodded.

"Well, the numb bastards, excuse me, shut down the project. Fired me." He lit her cigarette again, feeling like Humphrey Bogart.

She held up a hand peremptorily. "Let me get this right. There was a government project to shrink things?"

Roger shrugged. Close enough, and she was quick, too. "A little more complicated. That was one of the things they were looking for. It was pure research, but of course, they wanted something out of it. You know what I mean?"

She dragged on the cigarette. It must have tasted good. "The things that go on," she said around the butt, amused, again.

"Yeah," Roger agreed. "The project actually started in your father's administration. I was drafted for it about fifteen years ago."

She no longer seemed very amused. One elegant eyebrow arched dangerously.

"So, I finished it. Zap! I guess they don't want it, anymore. I guess it's mine."

The lady puffed on. It was apparent to Roger that she followed his logic. To the user go the spoils. Hadn't it made America great?

"So how does it work?" she asked.

"Great," Roger said. "See?" He pointed to the painting in her hand.

She looked at it again, and then back at Roger.

"I see. I meant could you explain the mechanism to me?"

"No," he replied flatly. He was pleased to note from her stunned expression that he'd thrown her a loop. Apparently the lady didn't hear no too often.

"Why not?" she persisted. Her cigarette was getting the shit ground out of it in the ashtray.

"Because I can't."

"Oh. You're sure?"

"It's much too complicated. There's probably only two or three people in the whole world capable of understanding how it works, assuming they had the proper theoretical information. And me, of course, and I'm not too sure myself sometimes that I've got it right."

Roger felt the pack of Winstons carefully. She was going through them fast. He hesitated, then offered it to her again.

"I think I understand what you're saying," she said slowly. She lit up again, taking the match from his hand. "Can't you tell me a little of the theory. I'll try hard not to be stupid." She smiled dazzlingly.

It didn't matter if he did tell her, he knew. She couldn't do anything with it.

He sat down in the chair opposite her.

"You sure?"

"Oh, yes." Her eyes all bright and eager.

He thought for a minute and then plunged.

"Well, when I was a little kid, I used to think the world was run by buttons. I suppose I heard people talking about pushing The Button and just figured if there was a button that could destroy the world, then there must be other buttons. Maybe even buttons that ran people. It's crazy, but I really thought everything that happened, happened because someone, somewhere, pushed a button. Some adult. I used to go around feeling under chair arms and things, looking for the buttons.

"It really worried me. I didn't know how you were supposed to know which button did what. I was afraid I might accidentally hit one, maybe *the* button, and, whoosh, there goes the world, down the hopper. Or the one that would kill my mother.

"Probably it seems like a silly story to you."

She looked puzzled but was still listening.

"Anyway," he continued, "in the course of the research I was doing for the project, I found out that my crazy kid idea was right. I found one of the buttons. Yeah, there really are buttons."

He was wet with sweat but somehow relieved, as if he had confessed some childhood transgression to his mother. Someone else knew, now.

"Someday," he mused, "when I get enough money, I'm going to look for the other buttons."

The lady's cigarette had gone dead between her fingers. Her mouth was a little open, the tip of her tongue slipping nervously along the inside margin of her upper lip. She cleared her throat.

"But you can control it effectively?"

Roger nodded. He leaned forward, his hands clasped on his knees. "You mean, can I shrink what I want as much as I want?"

"Exactly."

"Sure," Roger said casually. He gestured to the painting and the car, sitting on the table between them. "You want either of these things? I have to make back my investment."

She started, apparently thinking about something else. She sat a little straighter, and sucked in a long, shaky breath.

"I have no use for the car. My dollhouses are period pieces, you know. It wouldn't do to have anachronisms in them. None of them even has a garage."

That was fine with Roger. He had a soft spot for the little car. It was a good-luck charm. It had been luck that he wandered into that shopping center just as the old cock walked away from his gorgeous racer. It had been luck to have the minimizer with him. He couldn't question, whenever he held it in his hand, that in some fundamental, mysterious way, his luck had changed.

"The painting," she paused delicately, "well, I can't hang it in one of the dollhouses, now, can I?"

Not good news, but Roger understood. He was prepared to write it off. How was he supposed to know stuff like that? It seemed this business was a little more complicated than he had figured. But at least he had proved to the lady that he could produce a better miniature anything than her daughter-in-law.

"Still," she continued, startling him, "I'll take the painting. It has associations for me. And I suppose I could hang it privately."

Roger clapped his hands. "Great."

She fondled her cigarette and smiled at him. Then she socked him again. "I don't suppose you'd let me buy the device from you?" she asked lightly.

Roger was stunned to silence. He glanced nervously at the closet and then reddened when he realized she'd seen him look. Now her smile said she shared his secret. He felt panicky.

"No," he blurted. "No."

"Just thought I'd ask," she said soothingly. "But we'll have to work out financial arrangements and what exactly I will be buying." She relaxed into her chair.

"Sure." He was willing and eager to get down to brass tacks. And change the subject.

She looked at her wristwatch and frowned. "It's getting on. Perhaps the best course of action would be for you to come to my apartment and see the dollhouses I have there. Unfortunately, my best one isn't there right now." She smiled apologetically. "We can talk more comfortably there. Have dinner. I can teach you a lot about miniatures."

Roger's heartbeat bounded. She was right. And he'd never had dinner with a beautiful woman in a fancy apartment before. It was not an experience he was going to pass up. She was still beaming at him, as if she wanted to pat him on the head.

Almost without being aware of it, he went to the closet and retrieved the minimizer from the chest.

66

"Might want to take some pictures, for reference," he mumbled.

She stood up and slipped her hand around his left arm. Roger breathed heavenly air. He allowed himself to be led away.

Dorothy Hardesty Douglas lived in one of those glass towers. Roger wondered, staring up at it as they passed it on the street below, how much window washers were paid for a job like that.

They entered through an underground garage packed like a box of Christmas ornaments with Mercedes-Benzes, Rolls-Royces, and a sprinkling of yet more expensive and exotic vehicles. Roger could imagine the lot of them shrunk to matchbox size and tucked neatly into a shoebox. The place smelled like a garage and looked like a garage, but it summoned for Roger memories of celebrity funerals at Forest Lawn, when there were lines of dinosaur cars like these, rolling slowly by, as if to some nearby tar pit.

A pair of security guards watched a short, glossy lobby that led to elevators. The guards were courteous but not what Roger would call warm. They looked about eight feet tall. Their eyes passed over Roger, seeing him and not seeing him, like the klieg lights in prison movies. Or perhaps more like X rays, looking for malignancies, but not much interested in recording the presence of healthy tissue.

The elevator was empty but for Roger and the lady. It carried a perpetual passenger, a rubber plant in a glass booth. The plant looked healthy enough, but Roger thought it must be boring, riding up and down in that glass booth day in and day out. Better the rubber plant than Roger.

The lady did not seem to be in a communicative mood. In fact, she was about as stiff as the rubber plant. Roger examined the control panel, the only other thing to look at besides the plant and his withdrawn companion. One button indicated the building had its own swimming pool and some kind of health club.

Rich people lived differently from regular people, that was something Roger knew. They owned apartments instead of renting them, and had these little private clubs together. They must feel safer in gangs.

The lady's apartment was impressive. It wasn't what his

mother would call cozy. It was . . . glamorous. About what he'd expect his fairy godmother to live in. The colors were all shimmery.

A doughy-looking woman in a charcoal-gray uniform appeared and Mrs. Douglas instructed her to fetch Roger a beer. Then she excused herself and disappeared on the heels of the maid. Nobody told Roger to go sit in the kitchen, so he sat down. He presumed the lady wanted to fix her face, not that it didn't look fine to him, or visit the can, or something private like that. He savored the luxury around him. A maid, for Christ's sake.

Wallowing in the pale blue sofa, he studied the picture over the fireplace. He recognized the woman, Elizabeth Payne Hardesty, the lady's mother, may she rest in peace, and probably a saint by now, considering who she married. Roger struggled to summon up a faint, ghostly memory of a ceaselessly, painfully, smiling woman trailing around after the old toad, Mike Hardesty. He didn't recall her as being as beautiful as the picture painted her, but then he'd been just a kid. It was a funny painting; just the woman's head and shoulders, life size, with hardly a brushstroke visible. The colors were translucent, filmed over the canvas. It gave Roger the spooks.

He hauled himself out of the sweet embrace of the sofa and looked out a big window at the city, spread out like a carnival midway, far below him.

The maid came back with his beer, poured into a glass and presented on a silver tray. She looked down her nose at him. He ignored her and took the beer. It didn't taste American, but it was beer okay. He sipped it happily, reflecting happily that the maid could sneer all she wanted. *She* was serving the beer; *he* was drinking it.

The lady returned, dressed in different clothes. She had swapped her tailored suit for some funny material that Roger could only fumble to name, a shimmery loose thing that sort of went with the room. She asked if the beer was acceptable and offered him a cigarette, out of a little silver box shaped like a vampire's coffin. Roger was amused; someone's little joke about coffin nails. He was also relieved. He was running low, supplying her with his butts. Politely, he accepted one but he didn't figure he would ever catch up with her.

They didn't talk much for a while. He finished his beer and she did in another cigarette and there they were.

"Would you like to see the dollhouses?" she asked.

He jumped up, relieved. "That's what I'm here for, ma'am."

"I wish the Doll's White House was here," she fussed, leading the way.

It wasn't as big a room as the living room. There was a whole wall of glass and no conventional furniture at all. Two large dollhouses on what appeared to be specially constructed tables filled two corners. A half dozen boxes containing single suites of furnishings hung on the walls. The middle of the room was dominated by a great empty plain of a table.

Dorothy Hardesty Douglas skirted the empty table, avoiding even looking at it.

"This is the Gingerbread Dollhouse." She touched the roof on her left gently, and then gestured, like a stewardess pointing out the exits, across the room. "That is the Glass Dollhouse."

The Gingerbread House was a re-creation of one of Roger's favorite fairy tales. Each Christmas, he ordered a gingerbread house, usually faked from plastic or cardboard with a little edible trim, from one of the catalogs that peddled cheese and smoked sausages. It was supposed to be his contribution to the Christmas decorations, but he often left it sitting on the table until Easter.

This was the best he'd ever seen. Even the ones blueprinted in his mother's women's magazines didn't come near it. It was about four feet high and constructed of wood that had been painted to resemble gingerbread, frosting, and candy. The trim seemed to have been molded or carved into the most pleasing and whimsical arrangement of candy canes, gum drops, and assorted other goodies.

There was a cage suspended near the hearth. Roger was delighted to see the little wooden boy inside, a fair-haired kid in shorts and a hand-knitted sweater, a little ragged at the elbows. His little cheeks were flushed with the mock fire in the fireplace nearby and his eyes glittered, with the reflected fire, or with terror. A girl was chained to a table leg and sat cross-legged and morose on the stone-flagged floor.

The witch was not at home, in any of the four rooms, up or down. Not in the low attic of the cottage, hung with arcane herbs and lined with colored glass bottles of unidentified substances, or in the bedroom where black robes and pointed hats hung on pegs, and the four-poster's canopy was woven with the night sky. Nor in the kitchen, where the children waited, with plates of cookies near at hand, fresh from the brick oven alongside the open hearth. Nor in the smaller room, for which Roger had no name, where the floor was drawn with mystic patterns, and there were no furnishings, except a cheval mirror.

Roger loved it. He loved the bundle of faggots on the hearth, within reach of little Gretel, and the cauldron hanging on the spit, and the table set for one, with the wicked-looking knife plunged into the carving board.

"Wow," he said simply. Dorothy Hardesty Douglas accepted the compliment gravely.

The Glass Dollhouse was more like a sculpture than any house Roger had ever known or imagined. It was like origami, all angles, facets, and sides, and shadows of itself, only transparent. Roger was bemused to see that it was empty, unfurnished, undecorated. Just itself, playing abstract games with light.

The woman laughed at his transparent puzzlement.

"Who could live here?" he blurted.

She nodded. This man had a knack for the central question, the bottom line, in the current cliché. No doubt it was one of the characteristics that made him such an extraordinary scientist or inventor or whatever he was. She shook her head as if to clear away a sudden puff of smoke. It was all unbelievable. But she had *seen* the painting. She had no doubt of what it was.

"Well," she said in a teasing drawl, "I can think of two sorts of individuals who might live in this house."

Roger studied the house. He couldn't imagine living in it himself. No Fortress of Solitude, no solid-walled bathroom.

"Ghosts or flashers." Mrs. Douglas grinned. They laughed, united in a larger joke.

The Glass Dollhouse was like modern art to Roger, mostly incomprehensible. He preferred the Gingerbread House, the sticky seductive trap for children, a house where devilment dwelled. It whetted his desire to examine his other dollhouse, the miniature White House.

She led him away again, this time to dinner. It was a

scanty feast by Roger's standards: too many raw vegetables, thin little pancakes of no substance filled with seafood in a sauce, and not a plate of bread or rolls to be seen. There was at least beer for Roger, and a bottle of French wine for the lady.

Roger did most of the eating, and Mrs. Douglas, beginning with "Call me Dolly, darling," did most of the talking, and a lot of wine-drinking. Roger himelf had no taste for wine at all. He associated it with the sourest of vomit and the foulest of hangovers in his college days, and, at the other end of the spectrum, with food snobs.

He was happy to listen, while sponging up the available food and knocking down beer from a glass that seemed to have no bottom. She talked well, this fine-boned, porcelain-skinned lady he was now free to call Dolly. It wasn't at all like listening to his mother. She knew a lot about dollhouses and miniatures and she was making that information available to him. He recognized a seminar when he heard one, even if this one had fancy restaurant-style grub, Dutch beer, and French wine laid on. When the meal was over, he knew what Dorothy Hardesty Douglas wanted for her Doll's White House.

They left the table, when he allowed he didn't want any coffee, tea, or dessert, and he would be very happy if he had just a few more beers within reach. He felt comfortable asking for them, buoyed on what he had already consumed, and since she took the remnants of the wine with her. He heard her tell the maid to clear up and out as he shambled back to the living room. There was a pleasant buzz in his ears. He felt so good, he just glowed.

"I've got to see this Doll's White House," he told her, when she joined him.

"You will," she promised.

Roger liked that cozy future tense. It would be nice to see something more of this warm, elegant woman. A pleasure for his eyes and nose. It was incredible to think she was old enough to have had a son who if he'd lived would have been less than five years younger than himself; that she had grandchildren. Bluntly, she was old enough to be his mom, had she gotten a precocious start. He wondered foggily if he should bring up money again, and then it went right out of his mind.

Dolly was suddenly sitting a lot closer to him than he'd re-

71

alized. Had he moved or had she? She sighed in a contented, cat-by-the-fire way, and leaned against him, batting her silvery eyelashes at him.

At once, Roger's hands and armpits were nearly as wet as the rock that Moses smote. He slipped one arm around her gingerly, and waited for her to crack him one across the face, or jam her wine glass up his nose, or possibly drive a fist into his crotch. She just cuddled closer and giggled, to his complete astonishment. He closed his eyes. It couldn't possibly be this easy. He and/or she must be drunker than he thought. Surely now the phone would peal obscenely, like the stroke of midnight, and his mother would turn him back into a pumpkin with one searing scold. But she couldn't; she didn't know he was here, did she?

He moved his hands through the shimmery stuff of Dolly's gown and shivered all over. His throat went dry and he wanted, desperately, another beer. He couldn't figure out how to extricate himself to grab one of the enticing bottles on the tray. She was positively mewing now, rubbing along his thigh and torso.

Black panic descended on him like a hangman's hood. He told himself to open his eyes; if she were still there and he wasn't stiffening embarrassingly against the sofa pillow or her fat maid, he would believe what was happening to him.

Since she had knocked at his door, he had had the sensation of walking the rim of a maelstrom. He was out of his native element, walking a razor's edge, risking everything from one moment to the next. Now the silken rush of her dress caught at him, caught him, it seemed, feet first, and he felt himself slipping, letting her catch him up in her own churning, centrifugal power. Into the whirlpool, he slipped, into the eye of the hurricane, into the tornado, with a woman named Dorothy.

Sex was not as he had ever imagined it. It was less and it was more, like a whole cheesecake eaten in a frenzy. How long had he persuaded himself that there could be only marginal differences between what a person got out of making love to another person, and what they got out of making love to their own good fist? Another theory disproved. But he discovered something much more important. Another button.

Roger came to the next morning with a poisonous hangover. He felt like a rotten bucket in a well of stagnant and distinctly physical misery. The silky sheets entwined him much as she had, mocking his tortured flesh. He was only too aware that he was not actually dying. He needed a cigarette, a quart or two of clear, cold water, and a ten minute pee, as close to simultaneously as could be managed. If only he could find a way out of the goddamn bedsheets.

Once out, and relieved, by means of a violent and courageous effort, he buried his head in the pillows. All he wanted now was a small measure of oblivion, just until he felt right again.

Instead, the night's exertions came back to him, not nearly as vaguely as he wished. In living color and 3D, all his failures played on the video screen in his brain, within the secret room of his skull. His mother's voice, nasal and certain, warning him for his own good about beer, bars, and bad women, was the sound track.

Deviled by roiling innards and a gigantic black bird that was pecking savagely inside his skull, he drifted into a fitful semiconsciousness. She was with him, he noticed after some time, sitting in a chair with her feet propped on the bed. She coughed politely, and he saw her watching him, with narrowed eyes through an aura of cigarette smoke.

Reddening all over, he yanked the sheets a little higher. She was so delicate, from her daintily painted toenails to the gossamer disarray of her platinum hair. She made him feel gross and clumsy, and now he approached a distinctly madder red, remembering exactly how clumsy he had been with her. And what she had said to him at one delicately-fraught moment. His mother would have fainted to hear it.

"How ya feeling?" she asked, around a cigarette.

Roger tried to smile bravely and could only grimace.

She blew more smoke at him and then tossed a box of butts and her lighter to him. He scrabbled for them gratefully, careful to clutch the sheets with one hand, for the sake of modesty, and moving gingerly, so as not to have a stroke.

"Stupid thing to do," she told him. He looked up, startled, from trying to make the lighter flame with fingers made of Play-doh. "All that boozing. Spoils things, every time, doesn't it?"

He sucked on the cigarette, relieved. She was offering him

73

a screen for his injured pride. He'd take it as quickly as he took her cigarettes.

Dolly moved easily to scoop up something by her chair. He glanced up from the solace of his cigarette, his eye caught by the rising shadow as she lifted it. The black bird in his head cracked his skull and exploded outward. For a second, Roger could see nothing at all, nothing but the bolt of black lightning just behind his eyes. Then his vision cleared.

She sat there calmly with the minimizer, in its leather case, in her lap, the shoulder strap twisted in one hand. Her eyes met his. It was like looking at a big endless snake as thick as your thigh that was going to eat you, no matter how fast you moved. Then she smiled, like the angel she looked like, and tossed it ever so gently onto the bed at his feet. He couldn't move to claim it. He was all light and empty as a bird's nest. The slightest movement would knock him out of the tree.

It was she who moved first. Dolly dropped her cigarette into an ashtray. It struck him that she must carry them in her pockets. There was always an ashtray there when she needed one. She stood up and stretched, as elegantly as a pedigreed cat. Her silky pajamas, the color of champagne, shook and rippled like leaves in moonlight.

She crawled onto the bed from the foot. The pajamas gaped in front. Roger could see her small breasts trembling in the silky shadows. The first wave of excitement rose in his belly, washing away the residual ill feeling, as if it were debris on a beach.

She sat cross-legged next to him. He could smell her fragrance and was, somehow and absurdly, touched. A woman smell. She drew fingertips over his mouth. At once he tasted the sourness of his saliva, the nasty nicotine flavor of his teeth and tongue. She began to hum very softly.

Roger couldn't move. She moved for him, arranging them as it pleased her. He looked up at her, her throat arched, her chin high, as if she were flying and he was her broom. He felt her gathering him, taking him with her. He forgot, again, the device that had brought them together into this new world, tangled in the sheets at his feet.

"I want to minimize something," she said.

"Ummm?"

She blew cigarette smoke into his face. He waved it away, refusing to open his eyes.

"I want to," she repeated.

"Yeah," he mumbled.

She poked him in the armpit. It really hurt. He flinched and opened one eye in protest.

"Come on." Dolly was out of bed, dropping the pajama top on top of the bottoms she had flung to the floor earlier, when she wanted something else.

He closed his eyes again.

"No," she cried, and slapped his bottom flat-handed. It made a sloppy sound that demoralized him immediately.

It was evident she wanted his attention. He rolled over, trying not to grunt with the effort.

"What time is it?" he asked.

"Just before noon."

He thought a moment. "Can't," he decided, and flopped back onto the pillows. From that vantage he could watch Dolly hauling on a pair of jeans. Roger admired them. They were cut like a second skin, and probably cost more than his mother's best coat.

She planted her bare feet on the floor and her hands on her jeaned hips. If she was unaware that she was blouseless, Roger was not.

"Why not?" she demanded.

"Too many people around," he informed her. "Unless you want to shrink something you own, or want to buy. If you're going to steal it, the first thing is to do it when there's next to nobody around. Unless you want to get caught."

She sat down unhappily and crossed her arms. "You could be right."

"I'm not in any kind of shape for it, anyway," he complained, feeling righteous.

"You're not in any kind of shape for anything," Dolly snorted.

Roger was effectively deflated. She was right, but still, it was unkind. He heaved over onto his belly, the better to hide it, and remembered that he'd left his rear exposed. In a back-handed scramble to cover all his faults at once, he missed Dolly putting on a brassiere and shirt.

Still, she wasn't hard to take with her clothes on, either. He couldn't complain about the shape she was in. Her body was spare, not an ounce of extra flesh, and what there was, was tight and smooth. It didn't seem quite normal for a woman her age to look that good naked. Roger felt his ignorance of women. He suspected that she cheated. There were operations if you were rich enough, he knew. And then he felt guilty and rather slimy. She probably just worked like hell at it.

She didn't look like a nearly fifty-year-old woman who had been drinking and carousing the previous night. Well, maybe a little. Delicate blue veins on her eyelids, faint lines around her eyes and mouth, suggested a touch of age and dissipation. Roger liked them fine. There was something piquant about them, a suggestion of experience.

"I still want to shrink something," she announced. She was plying a silver-backed hairbrush vigorously through her hair. The spray of silver hair, the rise and fall of her shirted breasts with the swing of her arm, stirred pleasant sensations in Roger's groin.

"Well," Roger decided to keep her talking and brushing if he could, "tell me about it."

So she did.

5

The Statue of Liberty stands in the harbor, afflicted with what appears to be a bad case of psoriasis. Every other city landmark (the Empire State Building, the Chrysler Building, the World Trade Towers, and numerous others) has been mauled by the strongly acid rains of recent weeks. Business for dermatologists, the sale of acne medicines, raincoats, umbrellas, hats, car refinishers, and hair stylists is up. Jogging and dog-walking is down, and the cabbies have a new and violent complaint. Con Ed's new coal-fired generators in New Jersey are blamed for what has so far been a mostly localized pollution, but neighboring states are waiting nervously for the wind to shift.

With no hope held out for its recovery, the bizarre disappearance of the Central Park Carousel was one more embarrassment to an already red-faced city administration. Small face was recovered when a fund established to accept donations from the public to replace the eighty-five-year-old landmark amusement was quickly exposed as the enterprising if fraudulent venture of a Queens garbage man and his brother-in-law, a city bus driver. It seemed, at week's end, unlikely that the facts in the mystery would ever be discovered, but the city-dwellers joked that the Carousel was just one more victim of the acid rain. . . .

5.11.80   —*VIPerpetrations, VIP*

It was drizzling nicely. Roger relaxed in his seat and reached out to squeeze Dolly's hand.

"What do you think?" he asked, craning his neck to peek out the top of the windshield at a low ceiling of dirty clouds above them.

"That nobody in their right mind is in the Park," she answered triumphantly. "Or out of doors." She withdrew her hand quickly to return it to the steering wheel.

"Even the muggers," Roger grinned.

Dolly's silver Mercedes-Benz crawled down Central Park South. It shared the road with a few cruising taxis. Another few cabs were parked and idling—despite the new emergency air-pollution regulations—near hotel awnings. It was too early for the street vendors or the horse-drawn carriages, which would not come out today anyway if it did not clear, for there was no really effective protection for the horses and their harnesses. The only pedestrians were much too interested in getting where they were going to get out of the rain to notice passing vehicles.

The target was not very far into the Park from this end. That was just as well, given the drizzle. And Roger was not as convinced as he had tried to sound that the Park wildlife was in fact seeking shelter from the evil elements.

Dolly parked around the corner on Central Park West, moaning when she glanced at the hood of the car, which had developed an unhealthy looking sheen of bubbles and smelled faintly of dead rats. She and Roger had covered all of their vulnerable flesh that they could, and shared an umbrella, walking quickly as if they too would rather be inside, into the Park. Roger carried the minimizer, in its case, slung over his chest, as well as an empty duffel bag.

At the top of a rise they came to a halt, looking down on an unglamorous, oddly shaped building.

"Shit," Dolly muttered. "I forgot about the doors."

Roger shrugged. "No problem."

He unlimbered the camera case. Dolly watched him carefully. Now and again she glanced around, looking for unexpected company. A large black dog bounded by them, trailing a frayed leash. No baying owner pursued him. The dog squatted in the patchy grass and then was off again, his spirits as undaunted by the foul weather as his unkempt rusty fur was.

The minimizer looked like no camera that Dolly had ever seen, but it did sport something that looked like a lens. It occurred to her that for all she knew cameras, without their skins of plastic, chrome, and leather, might look exactly like the device in Roger's busy fingers. She had watched Lucy use a Polaroid often enough, taking pictures of dollhouses and dollhouse furniture at shows, taking pictures at home of Laurie and Zach, and it might as well have been magic to her, the way it spit out squares of paper that mysteriously showed images within seconds. Dolly was watching Roger when he brought the device to his right eye, blinking into an aperture that looked like a piece of a L'eggs container. He depressed an obscure button. She whirled around to see the target building.

Where it had been, the ground was a crude naked octagon bordered by the pavement. *It* was still there, at the center of the octagon, about the size of the duffel bag. Roger had deposited on the path. She bolted down the path, but came to a sudden stop at the edge of the octagon Roger, the duffel bumping against one thigh, the minimizer in its leather disguise thumping on his chest, scampered down the rise after her. He went without hesitation to the center point.

He bent to pick it up but she broke her freeze, lunged toward it, and snatched it up. It took both hands for it was a couple of feet in diameter and still heavy. Her breathing was shaky and excited. She looked straight at Roger for a brief triumphant second. His heartbeat jigged and jogged. She was so beautiful, with her fair hair capturing the feeble light, her cheeks ablaze with excitement and exertion. He couldn't mind her snatching it up like a greedy kid.

Between the two of them, they crammed it into the duffel bag, which was severely strained. Dolly carried the umbrella while Roger toted the duffel bag back to the car. Once in the car, on the way back to Dolly's apartment, Roger found himself idly patting the minimizer, as if it were an old pet.

The city was coming awake. There was more traffic in the streets, more early pedestrians. A couple of joggers, a few dogwalkers, were clearly headed for the Park. Dolly and Roger passed them by, oblivious. Roger was thinking of breakfast, Dolly of getting home.

The Park kept its silence. The black dog drank sour water

from a dead pond. Bits of paper rolled fitfully and aimlessly at the urging of an occasional gust of wind. The drizzle glossed the rocky outcroppings, the pavement, the serpentine drive.

A sign near the Central Park South entrance pointed forlornly into the Park. *Carousel* it said. A few yards further on, another signpost stood high above the heads of potential passersby. It pointed down on the forking of the path to *Carousel*. Up the gentle rise of the roadway and the roof would be visible, an eight-sided roof, damp with light rain. *Carousel* the signs directed hopefully. *Carousel*.

The black dog, doubling back, trotted cheerfully over the exposed ground to the middle of the octagon. He paused to sniff the very center. Then he whined, as if spoken to harshly, and trotted away. No Carousel there, for sure.

It wasn't precisely tiny, sitting there on the glass coffee table. Twenty inches high, twenty-five or so in diameter. Roger tapped the doors, bays really, light in turn. He studied the cupolaed roof. Dolly paced around him, making him nervous as an ungrounded wire. He decided to take off the roof. It was a simple matter with a chisel dug in between the roof and walls, used as a lever to rip the sucker off. It came unevenly, in chunks, but it came.

Now it was possible for Roger to look down into the Carousel. A central drumlike structure that housed the machinery was revealed to him like the contents of a can of tuna fish. The dark forms of the Carousel were frozen in motion on the round green table that formed their endless pathway.

He set about removing the side walls, and then, with utmost care, the concrete floor. It was nearly noon before the carousel stood free of its housing, and Roger's stomach was in a state of violent revolt. Dolly at least had stopped twitching and, with a cigarette clenched between her teeth, cleared away the debris into shopping bags. And she was mercifully quiet, except for a propensity to hum. Roger could imagine his mother, in the course of an operation like this one, chipping away at his brain with her chisel of a tongue, while he tried to work.

At last he laid aside the tools he'd borrowed from Dolly's

cupboards, and looked pridefully at Dolly. She was much more interested in the Carousel.

"Look at it," she breathed.

He had been looking at it all morning, he thought, and from some damned strange angles. He looked at it again anyway and grunted.

"How does it go?" she asked.

"With a motor. Like just about everything else," Roger said shortly. "It won't work like this. It has to be modified."

Dolly became very cross. "Shit. How long will that take?"

Roger shrugged. "I'll have to take the mechanism apart, to start. I need to think about it. Let's have lunch."

Dolly ground out her current cigarette mercilessly. Roger winced to see what she was doing to the pathetic little cancer stick.

"This isn't any fun." She plumped herself down onto the sofa, pouting.

"I'm sorry," Roger explained patiently. "It's electrical. You can't just plug it somewhere. The wire couldn't take the charge. It needs a different set of works."

Dolly looked doubtful. "Oh, hell." She examined her nails. "What do you want for lunch? I'll tell Ruta."

Roger nodded happily. A quick lunch and he would get right down to it. She would be amazed how fast he could whip the Carousel into working order. He watched her leaving. Her bottom sure was nice to watch. It didn't move like his mother's at all. Actually, with her girdle on, his mother's didn't move. It sort of waddled. He settled back on the sofa, remembering the nice things he knew about Dolly's behind.

The music began at last. The horses plunged and reared in undulating ranks of four. The chariots glittered as they rushed by, drawn by glossy steeds. Roger decided he liked the white ones best. The outer white reached with his head for something, something that wasn't there. A brass ring, freedom from his elegant colorful trappings, for joy? His tail was cropped and gold; the mane on the arch of his neck also gold.

"It's *Blue Skirts*," Dolly said suddenly, and hummed with the music to which the Carousel revolved. Roger recognized it too; it was what she hummed earlier, when he was freeing the Carousel from its building, and what she hummed during lovemaking.

A blue-wheeled chariot, emblazoned with colorful dragons and silvered moldings, went by. Above the sculptured beasts, a frieze crowned the Carousel. On it cupids shot arrows and captured doves and danced about in red diapers. Roger liked them, too, especially the little rabbits the arrow-bearing cupids seemed to be chasing. He'd always thought cupids shot love into peoples' hearts. Perhaps the rabbits were symbolic hearts. Whatever, he wasn't up on that stuff. It wasn't his field.

On the walls of the drum, which now housed an electric train transformer, among other things, clowns and monkeys dressed as clowns cavorted. Roger twitched his nose and sighed with pleasure.

Dolly studied the rise and fall of the merry-go-round as it circled. She was entranced. Her face was sunny and gentle. She patted Roger's head absently, and leaned against him.

"Oh, Roger," she breathed, "let's do it again."

Nick Weiler tossed the newspaper to one side of his cluttered desk and tipped his chair back. Muck, all muck. One could always hope that sense would come bubbling up out of the muck. The unfortunate thing about muck was that bubbles from it usually stank like a month-old string mop. He closed his eyes. His head ached from thinking about the bizarre article in the newspaper.

The only verifiable fact was that during the previous night the Central Park Carousel had been removed. By whom, to where, for what purpose, was a mystery. So was how. In the night, and in Central Park, which meant overtime for union workers, and while the unbarred zoo of humanity was restless. The most curious, the most oddly shaped piece of the puzzle was that the building housing the Carousel had also been removed, the sort of debris that workmen usually leave behind had been meticulously cleared away. Curiouser and curiouser. As if it had been moved all of a piece.

Nick shook his head to clear the cobwebs. It was only too likely that the whole business was some colossal piece of idiocy on the part of the parks workers and their masters. Very likely the whole thing would be discovered, someday, in some storage area, or at the city dump, or in New Jersey or

Nevada in the hands of some wide-eyed, hard-working, and crooked-as-old-Mike-Hardesty entrepreneur.

He sat up straight, thumping the chair's front feet to the floor. Had anybody considered the possibility that the Carousel had been broken up for separate dispersal into the murk of the antiques industry? Nick rang Roseann, his secretary, and asked her to call a man he knew at the FBI.

He drew the newspaper back out of the general chaos. There were two small photographs with the article: the Carousel itself, reduced to a dark unidentifiable puzzle, and the Parks Commissioner, looking as if someone had just goosed him as his picture was taken. Nick felt a tiny surge of sympathy with the poor guy. Some job.

"Mr. Tucci, returning your call." Roseann, over the intercom, interrupted his thoughts.

"Roscoe," Nick said genially, "how are you?"

He listened to Roscoe Tucci admit he was still among the living and suffering.

"Listen, Roscoe, I was thinking about Mark Hardesty and how he got started."

Roscoe laughed. "He was a supply sergeant in Southeast Asia, wasn't he? Dealt everything there was going and never got caught."

"Right. And he got to be president and was out of office and pardoned for every sin he ever committed, back to his First Communion, before one of his partners went public. Anyway, this crazy business of the Central Park Carousel stirred it up in my mind. I remember he used to fence stolen Chinese and Tibetan antiquities. I thought the Central Park business smelled of his work, you know."

"Nick," Roscoe protested, "you're slipping. Hardesty's roasting his ass in hell."

"I know that," Nick paused. "I'm sorry I sound flaky. The whole thing is as flaky as anything I've ever run into. I just thought maybe somebody had taken a leaf out of his book. Maybe somebody doesn't want the Carousel. Maybe they want the parts."

Roscoe was silent for a count of ten. "Jesus, that's beautiful."

"You bet, Roz. Private collectors who aren't too fussy about who really owns what would eventually pick them up. Pieces of a merry-go-round, who knows how they fit together, how to identify. Whoever has it may even sit on it for a while to let it cool off."

"And the pieces will fetch a better price than the whole will."

Nick agreed. "Priced by the glass instead of the bottle, the pop instead of the gram, classic Mike Hardesty thinking."

"God bless you," Roscoe said fervently. "I see a promotion in this for me. You're invited to the party. I'll call you back when we get something tangible on this."

"Yeah," said Nick.

It was nice to think Roscoe would be commended for Nick Weiler's clever ideas. Roscoe would return the favor someday. Thought of the old Harry himself, Dolly's darling daddy. Loathsome old bastard. Slimy as a snail. Poor Dolly.

Screw Dolly. Poor Nick. He missed Lucy. He hadn't heard from her in weeks. She used to bring the kids to the museum once a week. It made him a little sick, thinking that she didn't miss him, avoided him, even to the point of avoiding the Dalton.

His desk was as messy as the inside of his head, his heart, and the rest of the world. Roseann and Connie fussed over him until he thought he would scream. The museum itself, his beloved Dalton, that he had rescued from the swamps of penury and bordeom, was closing in on him like some medieval torturer's device. It was time for a vacation. Perhaps he would see his mother, who would soothe him, or his father, who might goad him, and either way it was a way of getting off dead center. But first, and he grinned, finding the other end of the logical circle, he had to put things in order.

. . . The thefts—which included several fine gold and silver heirloom pieces, occurred, coincidentally, with a visit to the Borough Museum by dollhouse hobbyist Dorothy "Dolly" Hardesty Douglas—puzzled both police and museum officials with their random nature. The thieves are believed to have made away with the Stillman dollhouse and the other booty while visitors and staff were distracted by Mrs. Douglas's visit. She is well known there, and has donated several items from her father's estate to its presidential collection. . . .

6.2.80   *VIPerpetrations, VIP*

The day that Roger Tinker checked out of his hotel room, between his first encounter with Dolly and their adventure in the Park, he had changed his life as well as his surroundings. At times, he thought he might have actually changed skins with someone.

Dolly had come back from her dancing class that day and there he was, sitting awkwardly in her living room. She was still wearing her dancing costume, one of those leotard things that looked like a second skin. This one was white. She wore a skirt over it, the kind that wrapped on, and it was tied with a lot of thin ties circling her waist over and over. Her perfume was tinged with a faintly athletic scent, fresh, light, woman sweat.

She had looked him over as if he were a particularly virulent specimen of plague germ. His excitement at her entrance had dissolved into a violent wash of embarrassment. His fly was zippered; it was just his instinctive reaction. Some people believe they were born with original sin. Roger was born with original embarrassment.

The peach-colored leisure suit hadn't helped. He couldn't explain to Dolly that his mother made him buy it for his cousin's wedding two years ago. He had tried to make it a little classier with a black shirt, but that had shrunk, along with the suit, and he was afraid he looked like a very low-ranking underworld hit man in it. Still, it was all he'd brought with him, besides his interview suit, and his socks, shorts, and pajamas. He hadn't planned on staying more than a couple of days. Or on this sudden lady in his life.

She sat down and lit a cigarette.

"Dear Jesus, Roger," she had murmured. She jumped up and punched him, none too gently, in the gut.

He had been too surprised to react.

"You're impossible," she had said.

He had known exactly what she meant. Impossible that he should be with her. He had hung his head at the disgust in her voice.

"Well, it can be helped," she had gone on.

He had looked up in surprise and, seeing the set of her mouth, felt the same dreadful excitement that he knew when she had first touched him.

"We're going to buy you some decent clothes. Get rid of

85

these," she had fingered the collar of the black shirt distastefully, "*California* rags."

Roger had smiled gratefully. She was telling him it wasn't his own terrible taste, just where he had hailed from. Another small door from one world into another. Thank you, Dolly.

"Not too many," she had continued, "because you're going to be too small for them, very soon."

Life became more physical than it ever had been for Roger. There were painful hours at the Health Club in Dolly's building. Sparrow meals. A constant gnawing hunger. He cheated every chance he got, but he spent so much time with her, and she watched him. And Ruta, the maid, couldn't be tickled out of so much as a goddamn soda cracker.

The hours of physical misery alternated with delicious, lubricious hours with Dolly. She conducted him through another seminar, not miniatures, not dollhouses, but a more basic course. Introduction to Skin, his own and hers.

In his cellar Fortress of Solitude, he had wondered if real people did the things that he read about in books hidden in the hassock, or if it were all a huge slobbering practical joke on the innocent and lonely. Some of the goings-on sounded very far-fetched to him. He had never ventured into the grimy, obscure, grind houses where pornographic films could be seen, fearing, perhaps rightly, some terrible blow to his fantasies from the lewd light shows.

The real thing was the more satisfying for being unexpected. She tutored him; he was happy to play the student. At the beginning she would sit on him and ride him like the white horse in the Carousel. It was easier for him, and perhaps for her, considering his weight. He would have been pleased to do that forever. She wouldn't let him stop there. Soon enough, there were variations.

It was all either so pleasant or so excruciating that he had a hard time remembering to think about anything at all except what was happening to the small imploding universe of his body.

He did remember to call his mother, who thought he was interviewing for a job with a mythical scientific supply company. He told her he had to stay on a few more days and that he might take a consulting position with them. She was doubtful. Roger knew she was afraid that he might ask her to move somewhere with him, or even leave her for good. They had managed to avoid long separations or his moving in the past. She would move if he wanted her to, of course, because she couldn't deal at all with the possibility of losing him entirely, but it wouldn't be easy to leave her home of thirty years, or likely that she would find a new job at her age. Having been reminded of all that, Roger hung up with relief. He couldn't say how long he might stay, he didn't know. It all depended on Dolly.

The rewiring of the Carousel was a welcome diversion from the carnival of flesh. His brain was still a refuge, it still worked. He carried the minimizer with him everywhere, locking it in a public locker when he had to, and sleeping with it in reach of his hand. He made some modifications so that it was a little harder to use, a little less automatic. Dolly gave him a small bedroom in the apartment; it became instantly cluttered with his tools, accumulated like a little boy's toys in no time at all.

Other than those minor matters, Roger had little to think about except Dolly, what she was doing to him, and his absorption into her life. She continued to teach him about dollhouses and miniatures and to educate him about the other people in her life. There were the people who did her hair, her clothes, her apartment, who taught her dance and tennis. There were the people who were the closest thing she had to friends, like Nick Weiler, and these she avoided, saying she was bored with the precious little mandarins.

And then there was her daughter-in-law, and the two grandchildren. Dolly talked with her grandchildren several times a week by phone. A pair of silverframed photographs of them hung on her bedroom wall, along with a picture of her dead son. Outside of the five minutes occasionally spent on the phone, and the family photographs, Dolly never mentioned her raggle-taggle family. Roger figured she didn't want to and that was fine with him.

Having no friends himself, he didn't find the isolation of Dolly's life unusual. He presumed he was in love. If it was possible to love one's fairy godmother. He did not allow himself to consider whether she was in love with him. She might care for him the way she did for a shabby old dollhouse that wanted restoring. It was enough for him that she allowed him into her bed.

She was so excited about the Carousel that he determined

to do something else for her, soon. Perhaps in Washington, where she would have to go in the near future, to retrieve the Doll's White House from that museum. He found himself included in her plans for that trip. It was necessary that he hang around long enough to see what he could do about that dollhouse, for Dolly.

In the meantime, in the odd hours that were his own, he wandered through the shops of Manhattan and the city's art galleries and museums. The museums were laughably undersecured. The shops varied. Some of them exhibited rampant paranoia. Some of them should have displayed signs reading *Help Yourself*. Roger practiced a little basic thievery from time to time, lifting a scarf here, a pair of socks there. But most of the shops fell in the middle, resorting to enough mirrors to make a funhouse. This gave him the opportunity to admire himself frequently in duplicate. The way the new regimen had trimmed noticeably in such a short time. The cut of his new duds. The roses in his cheeks. He patted the camera case that hid the minimizer. He looked, he thought, prosperous. Well laid. Lucky.

The day they were supposed to drive a rented truck to Washington to pick up the dollhouse, Roger invited Dolly to visit a downtown museum with him. It was one she knew well, and where she was known, as it housed a small and precious collection of dollhouses and their furnishings.

A quick look at him, and she started to dig in her handbag for cigarettes.

"Really?" Excitement shook her voice.

"We'll have some fun."

Her eyes sparkled and she drew hard on the butt. She offered him one, which he took. She smoked nervously. He smoked because he liked it. He enjoyed it to the last drag.

"I want you to stir up a stink when you go in."

"Be the famous lady, you mean?"

"Sure. I want to poke around across the hall while you look at the dollhouses. Give me fifteen or twenty minutes, in case there are people there."

"Then what?"

"You'll leave as soon as I come into the room. People will be paying attention to you, I hope."

"I'll see to that," she promised.

He went in before her and drifted into the gift shop on the left of the lobby. A trio of elderly women preceded her; she waited graciously for them to negotiate the steps, push through the wheezing, old-fashioned doors, and traverse the length of the lobby. The woman at the lobby information desk took one look at her and reached for an in-house phone. Half a minute later, a balding gentleman with official written on all his wrinkled features in triplicate appeared, and the fuss Dolly had promised began in earnest. Roger slipped away up the central staircase to the reedy trumpeting of the official.

"Mrs. Douglas! How good to see you again!"

Heads turned. Roger grinned. Dolly was a class act; she could handle the show.

He moved casually to a Y-shaped room at the same end of the second floor as the room where the dollhouses were displayed. This room, across the corridor from the dollhouses, was lined with glass cabinets. More glass cases filled the floor space, leaving only narrow aisles to walk through. It was rather badly lit, but within the glass cases, a collection of silver, gold, and vermeil objects glinted righteously.

Roger had been there once before. He knew what he wanted. First, though, he wanted to be the only person in the room. Normal traffic here was never very heavy. With any luck at all, he should have, sooner or later, five, maybe ten minutes to himself.

He waited for a middle-aged man clutching a cold pipe to peer at some of the specimens. The man was driven out by a noisy gang of schoolchildren, under the unsteady hand of a young teacher. The children, too, passed almost immediately out of the room, with announcements that they were bored. Roger breathed a sigh of gratitude to Loki, the god of thieves, and picked at the camera case strapped to his chest.

He was disappointed when a woman with a stroller full of sleeping baby entered. He stared unseeing at his own reflection in the glass over a batch of coffee and teapots. The woman left quickly, looking as if she'd gotten the wrong room.

Outside, Roger heard the museum official burbling, Dolly laughing politely, and the whispering and shuffling of a goodly number of people. She was playing Pied Piper. Her entourage should be entering the room across the way. He slipped the minimizer from the case.

The glass cases were locked, by the kind of locks that look like small cylinders and are fitted into the frames. Roger focused the minimizer on one of the locks. A tinking sound recorded the impact of the lock with the floorboards. Where the lock had been, there was now simply a cylindrical hole in the wood. Roger stooped down and scooped the tiny lock from the floor. He dumped it into his pocket.

Looking up to check the doorway, he saw no one. The noise from the dollhouse room was steady. A considerable hullabaloo, as his mother would say. He pushed gently upward on the glass. It slid away a few inches. Plucking a card of four rings, he dropped it into his pocket and closed the case.

He moved quickly to the next case, a wall display. After zapping the lock, he minimized and removed a silver-backed hand mirror, handled brush, handleless brush, button hook, shoe horn, and a small round dish suitable for the holding of hairpins, faded rosebuds, and lovenotes. Roger was sweating heavily. He wiped his forehead with his handkerchief and stepped to the back of the room.

There he unlocked another case. His prizes this time were an early Victorian coffeepot, creamer and sugar bowl. He popped that lot into his pocket, the minimizer back into his camera case, and strolled out.

Slowly, he worked his way through the crowd into the dollhouse room. Dolly saw him and looked straight through him. It was faintly disquieting. He had to admire her acting. It was just nerves that made his stomach flutter and his head hurt.

In another two minutes she was leading baldy out at the head of a parade of children, elderly ladies, and young mothers trailing after her, whispering. She caught the anxious eye of a child autograph-seeker and summoned the kid with a quick melting smile and an outstretched hand. The kid pressed a sheet of notepaper and a sweaty pen into her hand. The dam broke, and the crowd flooded around her, begging for signatures. A jam developed just outside the doorway, where she had stopped, so that no one could get into the room of the dollhouses and no one still in could get out. The few left inside were much more interested in the goings-on in the corridor than in the displays. For all practical purposes, Roger had the room to himself.

It took very little time. He pushed his way rather rudely through the now-thinning crowd around Dolly and left the museum. It was extremely hot for so early in the spring and Roger thought he might melt. He bought an orange drink from a street vendor and it tasted like sugared piss. He drank it anyway. It was wet.

Dolly found him slumped wearily in her car.

"Too much," he said, smiling weakly.

She slipped in next to him. "Show me."

He shook his head. "Let's get the hell out of here."

She pouted but drove off anyway. At least the air conditioning was on.

When she saw the dresser set and the coffeepot and its mates, she whooped and jigged. For no reason he could articulate to himself, he held back the card of rings, the only part of the loot he had not yet minimized. He was startled, though, when her first delight quickly clouded over.

"Jesus, Roger, I didn't know you were going to do that." She had the little house in the palm of her hand. She put it down as if she thought it was one of Great-aunt Helen's favorite knickknacks. He wondered, without daring to say it, what the hell she thought he had been proposing.

"Don't you see?" she went on. "I was there. There's bound to be suspicions that I had something to do with the disappearance of the dollhouse and this other stuff. Just because they're all gone together."

Roger shrugged. "What are you sweating? The point is everybody in that whole creepy old tomb was looking at you. You obviously didn't have it under your arm."

Dolly turned the silver pieces over and over.

"You may be right. But no more risks like that, please. I don't want to be publicly near anything like this again."

Roger patted her hand. "Let me get you a drink."

A small grateful nod from Dolly. She was weary, he could see, from her Great Performance, but was going, valiantly, on. And on.

She allowed them each one glass of wine a day, taken at odd moments to fill the silences, or to mark small events. Roger hummed to himself as he poured. Her song. The little merry-go-round piece. He wasn't ever going to care for the aftertaste of wine, a taste of rot, he thought, but he could at least tolerate it now. She called it her little glass of civilization. He called it relief.

It wasn't a bad thing for Dolly to get the wind up. She was uncomfortably interested in the minimizer. It would be better if she put some distance between herself and its use. Better if he kept control of the thing. It was *his*, after all. It was fine with him if she wanted to play innocent.

"We have to start for Washington," she told him, when he gave her her glass. "We'll need a good night behind us to get through the packing tomorrow."

"Here's to a good night," Roger said.

"I can't wait to see my babies." Dolly leaned against him comfortably.

Roger could wait to see her babies. Her grandchildren. The wine washed down his throat in a cool oily rush. They'd managed very nicely to avoid each other's families. Tomorrow he was going to have met not only the little darlings, but their mom, and much more appallingly, another Dolly, their grandmother. What might happen to them he could only fear. He braced himself.

It would be better to be out of town for a few days, especially on a trip planned for weeks in advance. The police could search the apartment all they pleased. They would not find Dolly's safe, into which Roger had shoe-horned the Carousel. They would not find the other things, because they would be looking for the wrong size. And perhaps today's take would come along to Washington with Dolly and Roger, to be lost in the numerous furnishings of the Doll's White House.

Well, whatever happened, the trip would be interesting. Meeting some new people, seeing some new things and places. That was one of the great virtues of his entanglement with Dolly. Life was almost always interesting.

6

"Mrs. Douglas is here," Roseann told Nick via the intercom.

He abandoned the work on his desk and rose to greet her. If he was surprised to see that she was not alone, he didn't show it.

She had changed subtly. It was as if she had stripped away ten years since the Founders' Day Gala, when he had last seen her. She had been brittle; now she was soft, and pliant, blooming. He was reminded of the young woman she had been. It was suddenly only last night's nightmare, that piquant interlude of theirs, after her husband's suicide.

He kissed her cheek formally, and breathed in her familiar perfume. It too was a little clearer, a little more essential. Wounds he had thought were merely scar tissue opened inside him. He was grief-stricken but for Dolly, or Lucy, or himself, he could not say.

"Nick, this is Roger Tinker," she introduced the man who had entered with her.

Nick met Roger's uncomfortable eyes. "Roger," Dolly said, "this is Nick Weiler, the director of the Dalton."

The two men shook hands politely and looked each other over. It was immediately clear to each that there was no hope of a civil relationship.

Roger saw a tall, bearded blond man, who wore his expensive clothes too well. A man who, all his life, had had all the money, women, and power that he had ever wanted. The sort of man, exactly, that Dorothy Hardesty Douglas might have,

93

so much more logically than the likes of Roger Tinker, as a lover.

The man who put up Nick Weiler's well-mannered hackles was painfully out of place. He wore his new suit and his new haircut as if they itched. He didn't know, and his body spoke it, what to make of this well-appointed office, in this over-blown statement of Victorian sensibilities that Nick Weiler thought of as his museum. He most certainly didn't belong with Dolly. Not casting possessive glances at her.

"Mr. Tinker is writing a book about miniatures," Dolly elaborated.

"If we can assist you in any way . . ." Nick offered. Roger didn't seem enthused at the thought of professional assistance, if the sour grimace on his face meant anything.

Nick, reflecting that Dolly had some odd pals, turned his attention to her. "Are you sure you don't want my people to do the packing for you?"

She took him by the arm. "Oh, no, darling. We want to get right at it. Lead on."

Nick didn't stay with them any longer than it took to turn them over to the collections manager, and a pair of packers. Wednesday was the day the Dalton closed its doors to the public and did its housekeeping. He had legitimate excuses of work to be supervised. Dolly, like some high school tease, clung to him and smothered him with *dears* and *darlings*. Roger Tinker's fierce foo dog glare was childishly irritating. It was a relief to leave them to their own devices.

After examining the packing materials, Dolly sent the museum packers on their way, saying she would call them if she needed help. The packers were happy to go. It wasn't as if Dolly were known to be fun to work for. She wanted her dollhouse to herself, and now she had it.

The disassembling and packing consumed hours. Dolly didn't seem to notice either the passage of time or Roger. She went on wrapping all the tiny objects from the Doll's White House and placing them, patiently and lovingly, into frames of foam. Roger did the heavy looking on.

It was Roger's first examination of the dollhouse. He told himself it wasn't the creeps whispering on his shoulder like a big nasty black bird, that it was not just an overgrown doll-house. The perfection of detail was uncanny; it called out for tiny people to populate its precious rooms.

After a while it was too much, and he wandered away to stare at the remainder of the exhibit. But the spooks wouldn't go away. Something kept pecking at his brain, a kind of mental itch that *would* be scratched.

Sisterless, and raised in a firm straightjacket concept of masculinity, he had not been exposed to dollhouses as a boy. His childhood was past before the craze for little boys' dolls, disguised as "action figures," and all the attendant paraphernalia of appropriately scaled space ships, motorcycles, automobiles, and secret headquarters, arrived. He had read about it, but here, in the Dalton, he saw the physical evidence: the toys of generations children had been metamorphosed into an adult hobby, and for some adults, more than a hobby, into an obsession.

The why was just beyond his grasp, solid and tangible, but smooth, hard, and inaccessible, like a polished stone, a piece of fused glass. Why was the reduction of every aspect of human life so fascinating?

Working the subject over in his mind, he drifted to the second-story gallery where a new exhibit was being assembled. The place was ass-deep in technical staff and electrical equipment. The staffers, mostly electricians were a swarm of buttercup-gold uniformed bees, fitted out with belts of tools.

Roger figured out that they were setting up a whole series of projection screens, each of which required sound systems and a video disc unit. It was interesting to watch, so he stayed for quite a long time, trying to stay out of the way, and itching to give a hand.

He was able to see bits and pieces of the video recordings as the equipment was tested and discovered the whole zoo had to do with showing processes, preindustrial processes. One three-minute slice was of an old man making barrel staves. Another detailed the making of maple syrup and sugar. The tapes were as interesting as the equipment.

With each screen, antique tools were being arranged in realistic settings. A girl from the graphics department told Roger that visitors would be encouraged to handle the old tools. Roger privately thought someone would kite the whole display, piece by piece, and that Nick Weiler must be as pussy-wrecked over Dolly's daughter-in-law as Dolly said he was, to approve that idea.

Once the idea of thievery was in his head, Roger remembered he'd wanted to find a little something for Dolly and started to look around in a casual fashion. His survey was interrupted by the sound of a voice he'd heard once before and he looked up just in time to see Nick Weiler's unwelcome face across the gallery. He made his way out and found himself, after a few minutes on a back staircase, in the third-story gallery.

It was proportionately smaller than the second story gallery, and in atmosphere, totally different. Quieter, darker, given over to portraits. Roger drifted around it, studying the faces of ancestral Americans, painted in the early primitive way. He was bemused by the kaleidoscopic quality of the Dalton. It was more like Disneyland than the museums of his school field days, or the ones he had poked around in New York. All those fucking wires! He'd always thought of a museums as being like a big old Roman Catholic church during a funeral. Only the museums had glass coffins instead of wood, and dozens of them, full of dusty, arcane, dull objects instead of bones. Nobody of any active scientific intelligence would be interested in the contents of his mother's head. But apparently museums had changed since Roger quit the hot-lunch line. This one, for sure, was fun like a rich kid's toy-box.

Roger found his way back to Dolly by means of an elevator.

"Nick came back to ask if we would have lunch with him," she told Roger briskly, barely looking up from her task.

"Whatever you want." Roger had no trouble restraining his enthusiasm for Nick Weiler's company.

Dolly sat back on her heels and regarded her handiwork with satisfaction.

"Never mind then. Give me a hand with this and then go find one of Nick's munchkins, preferably well muscled, to help us with the crating."

She was so cheerful and energetic that Roger shrugged off the shadows of the Dalton and fell to. The Doll's White House and its furnishings were deposited in the rental van by midafternoon. Roger's stomach rumbled noisily. He was looking forward to a well-earned late lunch.

"What do you think of him?" Dolly asked Roger as they drove away.

Roger looked back at the portico of the Dalton, where

Nick Weiler, good host that he was, stood seeing them off. The late afternoon sun glinted in his blond hair, making spun gold from straw.

"Pretty," Roger grunted.

Dolly reached over to pat his hand in mock consolation.

"You should have seen him when he was a little boy, living with his mother. Rattling around in a rotten, damp old mansion, like two buttons in a drier, with the old man, his stepfather, squatting in his library, half gaga, and a dozen antique servants trying to keep the place up."

Roger watched the city as she threaded the van through the crowded streets. He was looking for the FBI building, which hadn't been built when he was last in the capital. She broke the silence as they approached their hotel.

"Poor Nick's always been pretty. It's a curse," she said thoughtfully. She glanced at Roger and smiled. It was a pleased, satisfied smile.

"You," she declared.

Roger straightened up to await her verdict.

"You," she said, "are smarter than you look."

Roger grinned. "I'm hungry," he confided.

Dolly looked severely at his barely noticeable gut. "You can afford to skip a meal," she scolded.

Roger's heart sank. It looked like a long haul to dinner.

It was. Dolly refused to lock the goddamn crates in the trunk and leave them in the parking garage. They had to be trucked through the garage, onto the freight elevator, and up to her suite. She supervised the whole operation too so that Roger and the pair of bellmen who had been pressed into service had no opportunity to be slack.

Roger had to go out for a disposable razor. He told Dolly he would be a few minutes, that he might do a little sightseeing around the hotel. It was convenient to the tourist attractions; Roger was able to buy a hot dog from a street vendor and consume it while staring righteously at the Capitol. He wandered by the Library of Congress and bought a T-shirt that said *Wet Paint* in multicolored dripping letters from another vendor. Dolly would be revolted by it, but it made him feel better. A man had to have something he could feel comfortable in, once in awhile.

He was in the shower, struggling to strip the paper off the

hotel soap, when the FBI came. If he'd heard the knock on the door, he would have hurried to finish, assuming it was room service, but he didn't. So he wandered into the middle of things, damp around the ears, with his hair curling wildly from the humidity. He found Dolly sitting on one of the crates and smoking while a pair of FBI agents looked up foolishly from where they squatted over an open crate.

She introduced him. He sat down on the couch to pull on his socks and shoes and comb his hair while the agents efficiently tossed the crates. Dolly came to sit beside him. Then she discovered she was out of cigarettes.

"Oh, shit," she said appealingly.

"I'll get some," he volunteered, after patting his pockets and turning up none. He picked up his camera case and made for the door.

He missed her silvery laugh behind him. He would have recognized it. Dolly had used it on him often enough. Put him at ease. Like ice on the sidewalk, oops.

In the hotel room, one of the agents fumbled for his notebook and pen.

"Would you mind answering some questions, ma'am?"

Dolly was amused. Gold star for politeness from Uncle Saint J. Edgar. If they wanted to play out old scripts from the televised mythology of the FBI, she would milk what fun she could out of it.

"No, of course not."

"About Mr. Tinker?"

"What do you want to know?"

"Well, what does he do for a living? Where does he come from?"

"Oh." Dolly shifted around and picked up an ashtray. She twirled it slowly on the tips of her fingers. "Mr. Tinker is writing a book about miniatures. I'm helping him. I believe he's from California, but I know very little about his background."

The agent nodded helpfully. "Do you know his permanent address?"

Dolly smiled. "The same as mine."

Duly noted. "Is he in your employ?"

"Not exactly."

The agents pursued the question. "What is your relationship with Mr. Tinker."

"We're friends. He's a little helpless. I look after him." Make them work a little. Challenge is good for the soul.

The agent exchanged a nervous glance with his colleague. He didn't want to have to ask the question again, more bluntly. It was worse because he couldn't see any reason why the FBI had to know the answer but he knew his supervisor would ask, and he'd better have the right answer.

"Oh, no," Dolly exclaimed. "I didn't mean that. Roger is just as gay as Mardi Gras, darling."

"How did you meet Mr. Tinker?" Relief. Move on to the next one.

"Oh, somewhere. Some party. I don't remember, really."

The agent closed his notebook. "Thank you, ma'am. Sorry to bother you."

Roger passed them in the corridor. He smiled at them genially, and was disappointed to receive nothing for his effort but neatly paired sneers.

"Good fucking riddance," Dolly said, as he came through the door. "One more 'ma'am' and I'd have screamed."

Roger presented her with the pack of cigarettes. He slipped the camera case from around his neck and dropped it into the nearest drawer.

"At least that's over. What did you tell them?"

She looked uneasy. "You won't like it. I had to fib a lot."

"Sure. So what did you tell them? I ought to know in case they try to catch us up with different stories."

Dolly looked at him from half-closed eyes. She put out the stub of her current cigarette.

"I had to tell them I picked you up, the way people do. And that you are gay."

"What?" Roger was flummoxed. "For Christ's sake, why?"

"I didn't want them to suspect the true nature of our relationship."

"Shit." She sounded like she was quoting some frigging soap opera. "What does that have to do with what they were looking for?"

"Don't talk to me like that." She turned her back on him.

Roger could think of only one reason why she should tell such a lie. She was ashamed of him. Abruptly, the true nature of their relationship, as she called it, stared up at him, like his own reflection unexpectedly encountered. He had something she wanted, the minimizer, and what the minimizer could do. And she had the money and she had her body.

He saw the set of her spine and knew she could grind him down. What hadn't he already done for her? Tortured himself with her goddamn diet and fitness program, jumped to her every whim. So that she could deny him to a couple of FBI agents whose opinions were of no significance to either of them, or shouldn't be. He had only himself to blame. His mother would have told him so.

Except for his acute awareness of the state of his wallet, he would walk. After paying for her carton of cigarettes, he had exactly fifty-seven cents in his pocket. Then he decided that was okay, too. He would get along, if he had to wash dishes. He opened the drawer where he'd dumped the device.

When he looked up, she had turned back to him. There was barely controlled panic in her eyes. Moving to him quickly, she pushed her small iron body into him. He clutched the minimizer a little tighter and pulled away from her.

"Roger," she pleaded, "please."

He shook his head. "I'm broke," he blurted. "I can't stay anymore. I'm going home. Cutting my losses."

"No," she said. Then she laughed lightly. "Silly boy, why didn't you say so? I'm so absent-minded about money, you know. I never thought of it." She reached for her handbag jerkily.

Roger stopped. He knew better. She thought about money all the time. He hadn't lived with her as long as he had and not noticed that. He had an ugly suspicion that she was as slim as she was because she didn't like paying for a decent menu. He'd leave as soon as he had the satisfaction of her begging him to stay. The minimizer hung heavy on his chest. He felt his heart beating against it.

She was coming to him now with a wad of cash in each manicured hand. Stuffing the money in his pockets.

"There, darling," she murmured, "I'll see that you have what you need. Everything."

Her hair tickled Roger's face with its silky tendrils. Her hands, emptied of the money, slipped around him, hugging him. Roger closed his eyes, breathing in her perfume.

"Oh, Ma," he muttered.

"What?" Dorothy looked up at him.

"Oh, nothing."

She ran a hand through his kinky hair. "Listen, darling. I have been a *bitch*. I haven't thought about you at all. I want to make it up to you."

Roger nodded, numbly. He understood, just then, exactly how flies felt as they dropped into the spider's web. He wanted the bait, could almost taste it, and his appetite was not diminished, no, it was excited by the vision of the spider at the center of the web. Even the sticky stuff had its own electric feel.

"What do you want?" she whispered.

He heard it *Do what you want.*

Clearing his throat, he said, "I saw this statue today."

She was unbuttoning his shirt. "Yes."

"It was this god, or something. The sea god."

"Neptune," Dolly supplied the name.

"Yeah. With mermaids sort of all wrapped around him."

She had stopped her caressing and rubbing and unbuttoning. She just looked at him.

"Would you mind," he stammered, "ah, pretending to be a mermaid?"

Dolly thought about it, decided quickly. "Of course not, darling. It's sort of cute. Tell me, just what do mermaids do?"

"Well," explained Roger, putting the minimizer back in the drawer and hoping she wouldn't notice how much he was sweating. "I imagine . . ."

"What?" she encouraged him.

"I think we'd better fill a bathtub first," he decided. "Then I can show you."

Roger thought she was asleep. Since he wasn't the least bit sleepy himself, he slipped out of bed and into the living room of the suite. Flicking on the television, he watched the tail end of a movie. He waited patiently through what seemed like an hour of commercials and then the machine music of the late-night news came on. He slid out of the chair he was sitting in to a belly-down position on the pile carpeting. Settling his face in his hands, supported by his elbows, he prepared to worship.

She looked wonderful, as great as in the *VIP* feature. Her make-up was fairly heavy, her hair done a little more elaborately. She was wearing a V-neck sweater, reminiscent of the fifties. Those incredible boobs did amazing things under the fine soft weave of the wool. The color on the hotel TV wasn't just right, and Roger didn't have the energy to fix it, but he could tell the sweater was supposed to be a deep rich red, the same as the gloss on her full lips.

He wondered idly if Dolly would ever consent to pretend she was Leyna Shaw. She might be offended if he asked her to be a real person.

Dolly must not have been sleeping as heavily as he thought for Leyna had barely gotten through the economic news, all bad, when she appeared, shrouded in her white satin robe, and took his chair. She said nothing, only watched and listened.

Roger was surprised when after a few minutes he felt her cold foot jabbing his naked bottom.

"Turn that crotch off and come back to bed. I want to sleep."

"Sorry," he mumbled. He scrambled up and punched the on/off button on the TV. "I couldn't sleep."

"So jerk off," Dolly said rudely.

Roger grinned. "I could, if I could watch Leyna Shaw while I was doing it."

She didn't seem to think that was very funny. She slammed into the bedroom.

"Hey," Roger said, following her, "I was just joking."

"I'd appreciate it," she informed him coldly, "if you didn't mention that bitch is my presence again."

"Is she your enemy, or something?" Roger was genuinely curious. How could anyone really hate a woman that beautiful?

"Yes, that's exactly what she is. She'd like to make a joke out of me, that's what."

"Well, I'm sorry."

There was a long silence in which they both tossed and turned.

"Roger." Dolly probed with her fingers into his armpit, to see if he was still awake. "You'd better know this, now."

"What?" he asked, finally sleepy.

"I have a lot of enemies. There are always people who hate anyone who has something they haven't got. Money, power, physical prowess, good looks, the right family. You know?"

"Sure." Roger understood that rap. His mother hadn't raised any fools. It was a rough old world.

"So there are people who hate me, even though I haven't done anything to them."

Roger made sympathetic murmurings.

"She's one of them."

"Who?"

"Leyna Goddamn Shaw!" she exclaimed.

"Oh."

"You're a darling, Roger," Dolly went on, "but you have to start paying attention. You're like a kid. You only think about what you want to think about. You have to start using that wonderful brain for day-to-day living."

"Ummm," Roger agreed. He was slipping away.

Dolly sighed, sat up, and reached for her cigarettes.

What a fuck of a day. At least she had the Doll's White House back. Her hand shook, holding her lighter, and she had to steady it with the other. She must be experiencing something like the post-Christmas let-down. Wanting a thing so badly and then, once having it, it wasn't quite enough.

Or maybe it was just postcoital blues. She studied the dark bulk of Roger rolled up in the sheets. She'd had to be drunk to do it the first time. He was such a nebbish, utterly classless. She'd heard of women who liked to screw their chauffeurs and gardeners, but it had never had any charm for her. They must, she thought, have been bloody bored with the alternatives, their husbands and their friends' husbands.

Still and all, she must have intuited something about him because there was something special there. Inexperience, which was a little startling in this day and age, and a natural wild talent. Aided and abetted by the same plunging desire for knowledge that made him a crackerjack, if slightly mad, scientist.

Nick cast Roger in a shadow today. But she could testify, couldn't she, that when it came time to turn down the sheets, she'd take Roger. Nick was a few years back, but she hadn't forgotten. He had his basic carnal acts down cold but there was no real feeling, except for the chilling sensation that he was holding back because he didn't really care. He might have been feeding his cats. Roger, now, didn't know the meaning of holding back.

An ash drifted onto the bare skin of her torso. She brushed

it away languidly, not minding the secondary prick of fire. Goddamn, life was complicated. And always changing. Roger had reminded her what men were good for after she had given up on them; he had brought a dead part of her back to life again. All she really wanted now was the dollhouse and the minimizer. And Roger. Like all men, he would become boring quickly enough. She never doubted that. But she knew she would get along just fine when that happened. The certainty of it added the spice of perversity. She would have her fun, however long it lasted.

The city fell away behind them rather quickly. It was always a surprise to Dolly to realize how small Washington really was. They drove the interstate highway through the suburbs and patches of undeveloped countryside. For the most part, the traffic was bound the other way and they made excellent time.

Roger showed Dolly the model of the Washington Monument with the pencil sharpener in the base that he had purchased for his mother. She spared a distasteful glance from the road.

"I could have shrunk the real thing," Roger boasted like a small boy.

"Why didn't you?" Dolly asked. She thought to herself that his mother might as well have the original ugly as a copy.

"Too many tourists."

"Excuses, excuses. So shrink them."

"Jesus," Roger said, "I think we'd get stomped on good. It's a little obvious, you know."

"No, darling," Dolly retorted, "we could stomp on the tourists, then." She laughed.

"Be messy," Roger observed, to stay in the spirit of the conversation. The idea wasn't really very appealing to him.

Dolly negotiated an intersection. "Really, we ought to zap a little souvenir while we're in town."

"What did you have in mind?" Roger was prepared to be reasonable, although another adventure might be a little close on the heels of the last one. "How about the real White House?" he joked.

"Uck. Wouldn't have it."

"Too many people anyway," he said. "Would you really

104

want a houseful of little tiny press secretaries and secret service men?"

He noticed a passing truck. It was full of frozen dinners. It said so on the side. He could use a frozen dinner. He had managed a hot dog again this morning while sightseeing, but Dolly showed no signs of noticing that the lunch hour was passing even now, as surely as that truck full of chicken pot pies.

"Actually," she was saying, "what the Doll's White House needs is some dolls to live in it. And," she poked him, to get his attention, and then punched the cigarette lighter, a familiar cue to Roger, "the one thing that nobody makes in miniature that's any good is dolls."

Roger gave her a cigarette. "Lucy can't?"

"She said no. Won't touch it."

Roger had to admire a person who said no to Dolly. He was beginning to look forward to meeting this Lucy.

"Why?"

"Not her area. She said she'd ask around, try to locate someone for me. But outside of the Disney operation, I suspect there's nobody that could do it for me. Except you."

"I could zap one of those big animated robots they use at Disneyland," Roger offered.

Dolly hissed smoke through her teeth. "Sounds perfectly hideous to me."

"Oh." Roger turned it over in his mind.

Dolly tossed her cigarette butt out the window.

"Listen, Roger. Have you ever minimized an animal?"

"Of course. Laboratory-size animals."

"Did it work okay?"

"Sure. Great. I had a terrific beagle, an inch and a half long."

"Can't you do that to people?"

She stole quick glances from her driving at him.

He fingered the camera case in his lap.

"Jesus."

"Well?" she demanded.

"Well," he took a deep breath, "so far as I know, and I know more than anybody about this, the process isn't reversible. You can't unminimize something."

"Oh." This time she did the thinking. "I wish you'd consider it as an option. Really think it over. Maybe we could work it out."

"Yeah."

They were within sight of the white picket fence that enclosed a generous patch of lawn and trees, fronting on Lucy's house. Roger could see a small shallow plastic swimming pool sitting in muddied splendor in the very green grass. Dolly tooted the horn on the truck.

Zachary Douglas, sitting on the edge of the pool, in a pair of faded swim trunks, was trying to stick his toes, one by one, into the nozzle of a garden hose. His feet were very muddy, up to the ankles, almost to his knees; and the grass immediately around the swimming pool looked satisfyingly wet.

Laurie, serving tiny plastic cups of tap-water tea to her mother and grandfather, shouted when she saw the truck turn into the driveway, where it stopped behind Lucy's battered old compact wagon.

"Gee!" she shouted.

Zachary looked up for a second and then returned to the serious experimental work in which he was engaged. It was much more interesting than the grandmother he called Gee. He knew from past experience she wasn't into mud.

Mr. Novick was listening to another ball game, broadcast over the transistor radio in his shirt pocket via a plastic plug in his ear. He was half-asleep as a consequence of lolling a good part of the day in the sun and heat and having consumed two ham sandwiches for lunch. Only the incipient demands of his bladder, overloaded with cups of Laurie's "tea," kept him awake. He straightened up to present a more dignified front to his daughter's mother-in-law.

Lucy, lazing on a chaise in the midday sun, sat up quickly and checked the metal snap on the top of her cut-off denim shorts to make sure it was closed. The zipper was zipped, too. She stood up and stretched.

"Hello, hello," her mother-in-law was shouting, as she came around the picket fence. "Lucy, darling, you look marvelous."

Lucy did, indeed, look very good. She nodded.

"Thanks."

"Oh, this is Roger Tinker, Lucy. He's writing a book on miniatures."

106

Lucy shook Roger's slightly damp paw in polite puzzlement. Miniature-making and collecting was a relatively small world that she knew well and she had never heard of Roger Tinker.

"Pleased to meet ya," he mumbled. He stared down the front of her halter and stuck his hands back in his pockets, nodding his way through an introduction to Lucy's father. The camera case dangled from his neck like an outsize pendant.

"And this," Dolly was saying proudly, "is my cutie-pie, Laurie." She was clutching the little girl fiercely. Laurie Douglas squealed, making the most of the attention.

Dolly looked expectantly at Zachary. The little boy ignored them all.

"Zach!" his grandfather scolded, "say hello to your grandmother."

Two little spots of color appeared on Dolly's cheekbones. Zach looked up from his business and stared at them solemnly.

Dolly laughed. "Come on, you silly. Come see Gee."

Slowly, with a sense of ritual, Zach stuck one finger delicately into one nostril. This was too much for Lucy.

"Zachary," she said.

The finger came out, and disappeared into his pocket guiltily. He shuffled to within reaching distance of his grandmother.

" 'Lo."

Dolly considered him. Mud covered his legs to the knees like dirty stockings and he was gloved to the elbow as well in the stuff. She found a patch of reasonably clean skin over one eyebrow, ducked in for a hasty kiss, and withdrew to a safe distance.

"Don't let me keep you," she told him archly.

He looked to his mother hopefully, received a nod of dismissal, and trudged back to the pool, where there were still worlds to explore.

Lucy smiled apologetically at Dolly; he was only four.

Dolly raised her eyebrows.

"You might have cleaned him up. You knew I was coming."

Lucy's mouth set stubbornly and she ignored the reproof.

Laurie broke the tension by offering them all a cup of tea. Roger looked eagerly into the cup in her hand. Hope rumbled away as he realized it was plain water. Dolly laughed, and refused the offer. Rudely, Roger thought, since she didn't bother to ask him if he wanted any.

"Thank you, darling," Dolly was hugging the kid again, "but I have to talk with your mother first."

"I'll keep an eye on the little ones," Lucy's father offered. He touched his cap lightly in Dolly's direction, and settled back in his chair.

Laurie shrugged and went back to her tea party. Grown-ups were always busy with themselves and their work. It must be boring.

Lucy led Dolly and Roger away to her workshop, giving Roger a chance to walk behind the two women, from which vantage he could admire Lucy's behind in her denim shorts, and Dolly's, in linen trousers. A good view, he decided. Worth the trip.

Lucy stepped to one side and let Dolly look over the set-up on the worktable. It was bare except for a tiny wardrobe. One of its two doors stood open just enough to permit the light to glint off the mirror inside. A pool of red glowed in the mirror, a reflection of a garment hung within.

"Very nice," Dolly murmured. She opened the door a little more with a light push of one long fingernail. The red within developed a white shadow. She drew out two tiny gowns. She stroked them in an unspoken compliment.

"Perfect." She put them back.

"I have something else, a surprise." Lucy produced, magically, from some dark corner, a tiny silver bowl perched on a silver tray. The bowl was piled with fruit.

Dolly took them in the palm of one hand. She popped a loupe into one eye and stared at them. Then she sniffed. She looked up in amazement.

"Lucy!" Plucking a tiny orange from the bowl, she sniffed at it curiously. Roger drew closer to see what she was so excited about. She held it out to him and he sniffed too.

"Marvelous!" Dolly exclaimed. "Smells like a real orange."

"And the apples smell like apples, the bananas like bananas, the grapes like grapes," Lucy chimed.

Roger grinned at Dolly. "Not bad," he grunted.

She caught his eye. An unspoken thought passed between them: *but we can do it better.*

"It's a gift. For you." Lucy blushed.

"Why thank you, dear." Dolly was a little startled. Lucy would do something like this and make things even more awkward. She stalled.

"How did you do it?" Roger jumped in helpfully.

"I've been fooling around for weeks now with artificial scents. For the grounds. I wanted to get the roses right and the flowering shrubs and perhaps the grass. It would be awfully complicated. But I see possibilities now I didn't know existed three months ago. Been writing to chemical companies and perfume manufacturers, giving myself a crash course. I know I can do better than plastic grass on a mat and wired plastic roses."

Lucy noticed her enthusiasm didn't seem to be catching. Dolly didn't seem particularly interested. And her friend seemed peculiarly amused, as if he'd caught her picking her pants out of her crack. Confused, she plunged on.

"The stickler's going to be the grass. Real grass has so many properties, like moving in a breeze and feeling silky and smelling good, that it will be hard to do it right."

Abruptly she stopped and faced down Dolly. Roger looked away from the two women. He didn't really want to listen to what was coming next. Lucy seemed like a hard-working woman. Cute, too. He studied the workbenches and the tools on the pegboards, the materials neatly arranged on industrial shelving.

"Lucy, dear," he heard Dolly say in a low voice, "I don't want you to do the grounds."

In the silence that fell like a shadow over them, Roger fiddled with a neat little jigsaw. Lucy didn't seem to notice. She was so still she seemed not to breathe. Her face was white and faraway.

Roger looked around some more. He noticed the sun coming in through an old storm window that had been stuck in the roof as a skylight. There was a sliding glass door at the rear of the shop, behind Lucy, that looked out onto a big kitchen garden. The place had a homemade air that made Roger think of his own cellar hide-out, back home in California. He found himself feeling terrible for Lucy.

"Is there something you wanted me to do first?" Lucy asked in a puzzled tone.

"Well, no." Dolly turned back to the dresses in the little

wardrobe. "Actually I'd like to leave the Doll's White House as it is, for now."

Lucy straightened. "Do you want the wardrobe?"

"Oh, yes. Very much. It's delightful."

"I'll pack it for you, then."

Lucy scooped up the piece and began wrapping quickly and carefully in a fibrous brown paper. She didn't spare a glance for either Roger or her mother-in-law. The way she moved made Roger think of the spare violent motions of a butcher. He began to sweat heavily.

Dolly drifted to the sliding glass door and stared out into the garden. Roger studied the tools. Tiny sawblades, gouges, a jeweler's frame saw, a small power drill, a disc sander, a pin vice. Fine tools. Anyone who worked with these as well as Lucy Douglas did, Roger could respect.

She opened a drawer to take out a thick elastic band. Roger glimpsed small clamps, pliers, the nose of a jeweler's snip, tweezers, the debris of anybody's tool box. Lucy slipped the elastic around the small cardboard box and set it carefully on the table before her. Then she slipped the fruit bowl into a penny-candy paper bag.

Dolly was watching the operation now, smiling as if the air were not charged with Lucy's unspoken anger.

"Do you want the files?" Lucy asked quietly, her voice carefully purged of emotion.

Dolly nodded.

The younger woman began rummaging in a small filing cabinet that stood in one corner of the shop. Odd pieces of carpeting were piled unsteadily against it. They looked as if they had been used as a slide by some small child.

Idly, Roger picked up a sweet little X-acto number two handle and slipped it into his pocket. A number eleven blade followed it. Dolly was busy, groping for cigarettes in her handbag. The files, once found, went from Lucy to Dolly to Roger. Roger held them the same way he would hold a baby if anyone were fool enough to hand one to him.

"The correspondence with Dud Merchent about the wall-paper you wanted is in there. I was going to ask if you wanted the sample he sent, but I guess you want to handle that yourself now."

Dolly flicked her lighter. She was bored. Roger recognized the signals.

"And the photographs of the vermeil from Linda Bloch are in there. And of course everything I've done to date about the grounds. I'll bill you for the wardrobe and the exploratory work on the grounds model. I hope you understand I consider myself free to use what I've developed."

Dolly picked up the boxed wardrobe and the little bag of fruit. "Good afternoon, Lucy," she said, not bothering to keep the amusement from her voice. She strode out of the workshop. Roger trotted after her, bearing the files.

She departed smiling and waving like royalty at Lucy's father and the children. The old man tipped his baseball cap again. Laurie waved back. Zach, stuffing mud by the fingerful into the nozzle of the hose, ignored the whole business.

When Lucy failed to reappear after a long time, her father went looking for her. The workshop was empty, the door to the garden open. He found her picking bugs off the tomatoes.

Her cheeks were wet with tears she had already failed to stifle and her nose was red. She looked up at him, managing a stiff, brave little smile. She held up a slug in the palm of one hand.

"This slug's name is Dorothy Hardesty Douglas, Pop." She dropped it into the tin can of salt water at her feet. "Goodbye, you miserable bitch."

"Oh, Lu," her father said. He squatted down next to her.

"It's the best thing, really," she continued. "She just uses people. She doesn't care. When she's done with you, she flushes you down the nearest toilet. I'm glad to be done working with her. I wish I could be rid of her entirely."

Mr. Novick nodded. "Right you are. But you don't like being fired, do you, baby?"

Lucy grinned. She examined the underside of a leaf. She liked the musky smell of tomato plants. They always made her feel better.

"No. You know what, Pop?"

"What, Lu?"

"I hate the thought of that rotten cu—bitch having all those things I put so many hours of my life into. I feel like I sold myself on a street corner somewhere."

"Ah, Lu," he drew closer, hugged her. "Lu, now you can do some of the things you've been talking about. It's for the good. You're right."

"Sure, Pop. That's what's next." She stood up and

111

stretched, so that he could see she was over the weeps. "Did you ever think when I brought Harrison around to meet you that it would be so important?"

Her words evoked a vivid picture in her father's memory: the shy, whipcord of a boy in a summer uniform, holding hands with his nineteen-year-old daughter on the rickety old porch swing, the pair of them so young and beautiful. His daughter had grown up; the boy had not, but it was his children who played in the swimming pool out front and his mother who had savaged a perfectly good summer day. He shook his head. Life was a complicated curious business, and he didn't need to watch the soap operas to know that just because it was a cliché, that didn't mean it wasn't true. Magical and painful, the way time doubled back on itself, and nothing ever really seemed to end.

"No," he answered, unable to put his emotions into words.

"Let's barbecue tonight. I'll make the lemonade if you'll do the hot dogs."

"Better get the coals going. Where's those kids? I'll put them to work setting up."

Lucy wiped her hands on her shorts and set off for the kitchen. Her father watched her go. He wished she hadn't broken up with that Nick Weiler. She was almost happy with that fellow. But she'd get along. She always had. Tough little creature, though not so little anymore. Who would have thought Louisa and he would produce a child like Lucy? Not he. It made him smile.

In the kitchen, Lucy dialed the telephone.

"Is Nick there, Roseann? This is Lucy Douglas. I'd like a quick word with him, if I may."

"I'm sure he's in, Lucy." Unmistakeable surprise in Roseann's voice. And curiosity.

"Thanks," Lucy said.

"It's nice to hear you again," Roseann said unexpectedly and cut out.

"Lucy?" Nick sounded anxious.

"Nick," she began and had to stop and think what she was going to say. "Nick, I'm sorry to bother you. But something funny just happened. Would you come and see me tonight?"

7

In her hotel suite, Dolly tucked the small package of the wardrobe into one of the crates of dollhouse furnishings. Opening the bag of scented fruit, she rolled the pieces into her palm and sniffed at them ecstatically.

"Dear, dear Lucy," she purred. "She's so sweet."

She shot a quizzical glance at Roger.

"Doesn't she just make you want to gag?"

Roger, loosening his tie, and trying to ignore seismic hunger pangs, sensed he was on shaky ground.

"She's . . . cute," he said, covering himself with a word with notoriously broad shadings.

"Fat ass," Dolly pronounced. "Peasant."

It was unclear to Roger whether she meant her daughter-in-law or himself. Either way, he decided it was safer not to dignify it.

"Isn't it typical, though. Men. My son, marrying a woman so completely opposite to his mother."

He didn't know Lucy Douglas well enough to be sure, but thought that the set of her spine was not very different from Dolly's. And the two women had shared Nick Weiler, which indicated at least a taste in common. The thought of Weiler irritated him. Dolly, telling him about that old fling, had called the museum director The Widow's Comfort. *Don't be jealous, darling, it makes your face red. Besides, that was practically before you were born.*

Roger took off his jacket and hung it on a chair, humming noncommittally. The less said, the safer.

"Bitch lets the old man raise the children. No wonder their manners are wretched. She's out having a good time. On my money and Harrison's death bounty. And everyone thinks she's a saint. Too good to screw other people's leavings, and all that."

Dolly was working up a good head of steam.

"She's really pissed at you," Roger ventured. "Aren't you afraid she'll cut you off from the kids?"

Dolly, lighting a cigarette, laughed.

"No, silly. She's so *fair*. Totting up points for a halo. And she feels guilty because she killed Harrison."

Roger, just putting his feet up on the couch, almost fell off. This was a whole new version of events that had been so much historical newsprint to him.

"I thought he was killed when his plane crashed."

Dolly sank onto the couch at his feet and grew quiet. Roger sat up, drawing close to her, preparing to receive a confidence with the proper attention.

"They were so young," she said at last, "when they got married. I didn't like it, of course, but they were of age. Well, before you could say hi ho Silver, they had one child and another one on the way. I mean, I *love* my grandchildren. There are days I go on living just for them. But I knew what the responsibility would do to Harrison. He did take after his father. He felt trapped. And he had to prove he was one of the men. That's why he insisted on being a test pilot. And she wouldn't say a word to him. Said he had to work it out for himself. Worked out fine for her. She's got a nice fat pension from the government."

Her left hand, passing wearily over her brow, trembled slightly. Roger could see she wasn't putting it all on, she was upset. He didn't really know what to do with a weeping woman and hoped just quietly holding her would be enough.

Nor did he know what to do with this embarrassment of family history. Lucy Douglas had struck him as a nice enough woman. It must have something to do with the age-old enmity between mothers and their sons' wives. Weiler going from Dolly's bed to Lucy's, however indirectly, was a kind of re-enactment of the loss of the son to the daughter-in-law, a nasty little fillip to a stereotypical family tension. Probably both women deserved some points for staying on

114

civil terms, until today. But Dolly was too tender to take any kind uncle advice on the subject from him.

He fumbled for words. "Hey. You've got the dollhouse back and you're quits with Lucy about it. You can do what you want to now. You ought to treat yourself to a good time."

Dolly sat up, blew her nose, and sighed eloquently.

"Have a nice dinner," he suggested. "A little champagne."

"I guess I deserve that," she conceded.

With visions of dinner dancing in his head, Roger hugged her close and kissed her chummily on the forehead. Maybe he was learning something from her. Getting smoother, as well as thinner. Wasn't life grand?

Nick Weiler found them on the screened porch at the back of the house, sitting around an oil-cloth-covered picnic table. Lucy's father rose to shake Nick's hand eagerly. Laurie, in wispy summer pajamas, jumped up to kiss him. On Lucy's lap, Zach grinned and held out one hand, palm up, to reveal a muddy-looking ball of dough. Nick bent to kiss him and was surprised by a sudden very strong smell of fruit. It was as strong as the rush of belonging that overcame him coming into their presence and for a moment he was disoriented by his own confused emotions. Lucy always smelled of wood and varnish and paint and never wore scent that he knew. But of course it was too strong for any perfume. He wrinkled his nose and Lucy laughed at him.

"It's the dough," she explained.

He accepted the lopsided ball that Zach still held out to him and sniffed. Lemon, for sure, and strong enough to dry his mouth.

"Smell this," Laurie ordered, and thrust an inch-long bruised worm of dough at him.

"Banana!" he exclaimed.

"And cherries, and coconut, and a bunch more." Laurie showed him a paper plate on which half a dozen mounds of the same grayish dough were lumped. It was like sniffing a fruit salad.

"Amazing. Is it edible?"

Lucy shook her head. "It's not toxic, but it's not very nutritious either. I don't think it would cause any more than a case of the trots."

115

"Is this going to make your fortune, competing against the commercial play doughs?"

Lucy started. "Good heavens, I never thought of it. It's just for making miniature foods. I guess I wouldn't trust little ones to keep it out of their mouths."

"I made a grapefruit," Zach announced. "Want a bite?"

"Gobble, gobble," Lucy said, picking it up. She palmed the minute ball of dough. "It was great."

"It's bedtime," her father put in.

Laurie groaned theatrically. After a second's intent study, Zach produced a fine imitation.

"It is," Lucy agreed, ignoring their objections. "In to brush your teeth and wash your mugs. I'll be up in five minutes to tuck you in."

"I'll ride herd." Mr. Novick picked up Zach and slung him over his shoulder in a fireman's carry. The boy squealed delightedly.

"Careful, Pop," Lucy warned. She looked at Nick. "I'm afraid he'll hurt his back again, heaving that kid around. But I can't stop him."

Her father grinned, showing his perfect false teeth. "No, you can't. Come on, Laurie."

For a brief, awkward moment, Nick and Lucy found themselves alone together on the porch. Lucy suddenly found a great interest in the dough. She fell to, packing it into small plastic containers. Nick examined his hands nervously, deciding not to offer any help. If he got in the way, it would only irritate her.

"I'll show you finished pieces of fruit later. There's some in the workshop." She lined up the containers on the table. "I have to say goodnight to the kids. I'll be right back." She was gone through the door into the kitchen.

Nick was suddenly more depressed than he'd been in weeks. Coming here was like falling off a wall. He'd been comfortably perched for days and now he was going to crash again. And she could hardly stand being in his presence.

He dropped into the old porch swing with its musty-smelling pillows and stared at the sky. It was clear, if the heat had not much lessened from its strength in day. He didn't mind. In the city, the heat drove up the gate, as the tourists galloped into the big cool marble tombs of the public buildings.

She came back with a tray, bearing lemonade in an old-

116

fashioned glass pitcher and tall glasses clinking with ice cubes. She didn't sit down immediately but stood leaning against the porch screen, studying him by the low, buzzing lights.

"How are you Nick?"

He shrugged. "Getting along."

There was an edge in her polite laugh. "Aren't we all?"

He cleared his throat. "You look wonderful."

"Thank you." Her voice was very low, and to his surprise, pleased.

He hesitated and then plunged. "Are you seeing anyone?"

She cocked her head. "Yes."

His stomach turned like a dry leaf in autumn. "Don't be so goddamned smug about it," he blurted.

"Oh, Nick." She turned her back and considered the night sky.

"Nevermind," he said finally. "What did you want to see me for?"

She turned back to him, presenting a face that was suddenly tired and strained.

"Dolly was here today."

"She picked up the Doll's White House yesterday. Then she came here today?"

"Ummm." Lucy fidgeted. "Well, she fired me."

Nick sat bolt upright. "What?"

"She took delivery of a piece I'd finished. The last big one, really. And then she canceled the work on the grounds and the accessories. The things we hadn't finished."

"Hoo. Cool bitch, isn't she?"

Lucy nodded. "I thought she'd be so excited about the stinky dough."

"Stinky dough? Is that what you call it?" Nick laughed in spite of himself. "I'm sorry. You have my sympathy."

"That's what Zach calls it," Lucy explained the name. She sat down abruptly, next to him, and leaned back against the nearly shapeless cushions. She went back to the subject of her dismissal by Dolly. "It's a little like getting divorced must be. Relief, and frustration at not making it come out right, all mixed together. We've never been close, but we've gotten along. Now it's going to be painful every time she comes to see the children."

Nick settled back to look at her. He wondered if that's as

much as how she felt about him, too. Wisps of her hair fell against his shoulder as she leaned into him.

"It makes me angry to have her treat you badly, Lucy, but you're better off without her. It's a bloody shame you can't be rid of her entirely. If I were you, I wouldn't knock myself out to give her access to Laurie and Zach. She'll just make trouble."

"That's true enough. Everything you've said. She's very bold when it comes to my kids. Likes to tell me what a lousy job I'm doing, in front of them if she can. But she's not the only miserable mother-in-law in the world, I'm sure."

"Still, you can carry patience and goodwill too far. She'll take advantage of you. Be careful."

Lucy smiled. "I think I can handle her."

"Now you can get on with something else. I know you want to do other things. What about the museum shop ideas we talked over, a hundred years ago?"

Lucy leaned forward intently. "I want you to see something I've been working on in odd moments. In the workshop. I think it's something that Pop and I may be able to produce in enough quantity to keep up with the shop. At a reasonable price, of course."

"I knew you could do it, if you put your mind to it."

"Well, I'm tired of making expensive playthings for rich women, Nick. I'd like to make children's toys. Pop's got a project of his own. He wants to build a simple sturdy dollhouse he's designed that can be added to with increasing sophistication. He's really hot to go but he doesn't like to get in my way. And he feels he has to take care of Zach for me."

"Zach will be doing half-days at kindergarten this fall, won't he?" Nick asked.

She nodded. "That's five mornings or afternoons, depending on which set he's assigned."

"And the year after that, he'll go full days, right? It sounds ideal to me. Your father could start gradually."

"So it's possibly a good time. He's scared, you know."

"Afraid of failing?"

"Partly. More, I think, of succeeding, and of the changes it means. He's got a comfortable little rut; his life is settled. It's hard to take chances."

She looked away from him. Nick sensed then she was talking about herself as well.

"Whatever he does, Zach is going to start school. He's going to keep on growing and so is Laurie. They're not going to need your father the way they have."

"Or me, either," Lucy added ruefully.

"Has he ever thought, do you think, that you might marry again?"

This time she looked him straight in the eye. "He hasn't seemed concerned one way or the other. He's always pleased when I'm going out with someone."

"Perhaps he knows you better than I do. Knows something I don't know."

Lucy grinned. "Maybe he's just generous."

Nick glanced upward, to the upper stories of the house. "He hasn't gone to bed, too?"

"No, just watching television and trying to stay out of our way. He was really pleased when I told him you were coming over tonight. I think he likes you, or something."

Nick laughed. "Has anybody ever told you you're something of a tease?"

She ignored him. "I want to ask you if Dolly said anything to you that would indicate why."

"That's changing the subject but, if you mean why she fired you, no. She never mentioned you at all. I just assumed she would see you, since she was in the neighborhood."

"Umm." Lucy bit her lip. "What did you make of the fellow she was dragging around after her?"

"Strange. Dolly may be getting peculiar, change of life or whatever. Collecting odd hangers-on."

Lucy giggled. "He certainly was odd. She said he was writing a book about miniatures, but he didn't seem very interested in them. Poked around my tools mostly, and acted bored."

"They put up at Dolly's favorite hotel together. I don't think he's writing anything either."

"Really." Lucy seemed genuinely startled. "I was joking. I didn't think he was the sort of man she would be interested in."

This was delicate ground, the subject of Dolly's taste in men. Nick thought carefully before he spoke.

"He isn't, so far as I know. Although there's no accounting for taste in sex."

This drew another rueful glance from Lucy.

He continued. "But he may toady or something. Supply her with wicked cocaine. It's impossible to guess, Dolly being Dolly."

"How do you happen to know all this?"

"A friend at the FBI. A funny thing happened in New York."

"What?"

"You remember the collection of dollhouses at the Borough Museum?"

"Sure."

"One of the dollhouses was stolen, apparently at about the same time that Dolly was in the museum."

"Jesus. I missed that one."

"She was surrounded by people, she couldn't have done it. In fact, it's a bit of a mystery, how anything that large could be removed from the premises with no witnesses. In the middle of the day, yet. And of course, there were other things taken from the Borough's collection of gold and silver."

"So it looks like some kind of extraordinary coincidence?"

"Indeed. Except she's Mike Hardesty's daughter, and he never stopped when he wanted something. It's in her blood."

Lucy leaned forward on her hands, thinking. "I'm flummoxed, Nick. All of a sudden there's a big black cloud of confusing activity from Dolly. I mean, this guy, what's his name?"

"Tinker."

"Tinker. And stopping the projects she had going with me, and now this crazy theft from the Borough Museum, just when she's there."

"Dolly's always been unpredictable. Just how much work did she have contracted to you?"

"The grounds project, the newest and most extensive. The scenic wallpaper in one of the reception rooms, odds and ends and doodads. A lot of what was left was going to be subcontracted to other people, anyway. China and paintings. And we talked very casually about some dolls someday."

"To whom would she be taking the work?"

"She could deal with the subcontractors directly, of course. Save my fee. I don't know, really, about the other things. The grounds."

"You do know."

"Well, I can guess. But I don't want to know who's doing it."

Nick slipped one arm around her and drew her close.

"Got attached to it, didn't you?"

"Ummm."

"I'm sorry for that."

"Me too."

Lucy pushed him away and stood up. She gathered up the small containers of dough and went into the house, returning almost immediately.

"I told Pop I'd be in the workshop. Do you want to see those things?"

"Of course."

He followed her around the edge of the garden. The view from a few paces behind her was disturbing but too exciting to abandon. He reflected, not for the first time, that Lucy brought out the seventeen-year-old in him. He had had so many years of careful discreet sex that this outburst of passion was as uncomfortable as it had been in his teens, when the sex drive had been so great as to be painful.

The fluorescent lights in the workshop flickered on. Insects seemed to spontaneously generate around the long bluish bars of light. Lucy left the glass doors from the garden open, and the smells of the vegetation followed them in, to mingle with the workshop's own peculiar woodsy perfume.

She showed him a tiny fruit crate filled with bunches of bananas, a silver fruit bowl piled with assorted delectables, a minuscule cherry pie. He was delighted with them. The small perfections, the sensual smells, fed their pleasure in being together again.

Next he received a small box, about the size a pound of butter might be packaged in. He opened it to find a curious puzzle composed of pieces of wood. Reduced to its components, it was revealed as a miniature dining room suite. From another, identical box, he turned out a puzzle that reduced to a bedroom suite: bed, dressing table, nightstand, and a tiny wooden thunderjug and lid, which formed the core.

"How fast can you turn these out, Lucy?" he asked, examining them closely.

"Myself and Pop? Two or three dozen a week, if we didn't do anything else."

"They're just what I want for the museum shop. Something identified totally with the Dalton."

"We can do another that's all designed. It's a kitchen. I have an idea for the bathroom. Eventually I should have an even half dozen choices, six small roomsful."

"Marvelous. I knew you could do it. How long have you been at this?"

"Off and on, since you first asked for something."

Her face glowed with pleasure at his approval. He put down the toys and seized her happily by the shoulders.

"You deserve kissing for this."

"Oh, oh," she began to protest, but with such a teasing note that he drew her tighter. Good intentions vanished like the moths around the lights. He found himself eye to eye with her, willing her desperately not to turn away or close her eyes. She leaned into him slowly, with a small sigh, like a deflating balloon.

"I missed you," she admitted.

He stroked her hair. Abruptly she broke their embrace. Nick caught his breath and leaned back against the worktable. Lucy began pawing at the pile of carpeting remnants that were heaped a few paces away. She flung them onto the tiled floor near the garden doors. For a second, Nick wondered if she had gone berserk. Then he realized what she was doing and, with a sudden bark of laughter, joined her in the task.

There were more than enough pieces to make an acceptable bed. They closed the doors halfway, but the smell of tomatoes on the vine, onions, the musk of squash leaves, invaded still. A night bird chirped nearby and dogs barked in the neighborhood. Lucy put out the lights, so that only the moon gave them a gentle light. They knelt down together. She reached out, hesitantly, to touch his face.

"Good enough," she said. "Good enough."

Nick reached for her. She had said all that needed saying.

In a king-size bed in Washington, Captain Kirk, a.k.a. Roger Tinker, romped with an alien adventuress from Alpha Centauri whose name was unpronounceable by human lips but who answered, in other dimensions of time and space, to the name of Dorothy Hardesty Douglas. The fantasy was disturbed at a crucial moment by the clanking thunking descent of several almost empty bottles of Dom Perignon from the foot of the bed to the carpet, where they dribbled fragrant foamy dregs.

Just after dawn, the view from the hotel was of the Potomac and a stretch of sidewalk along the embankment of the river. There were concrete planters filled with red and yellow flowers dividing the slick silver surface of the water from the gray concrete of the walkway. The night had not broken the heat; the atmosphere was muggy and a little misty so close to the water. Roger sat on the balcony in his shorts and studied the small patch of the world below him. He heard a dog yapping happily in the distance. Joggers passed, singly or paired or in small flocks. A straggler from one group huffed by, damp, and red in the face. The barking dog shot by, an Irish setter, a pretty patch of color, pursued by an old man with white hair who moved as easily as the dog. Then a woman. The woman's hair was loose, floating as she ran. Roger stirred in his webbed chair. She was a big girl, and there was something familiar about her.

He leaped to his feet, possessed by an irresistible urge to go running.

She had gotten her stride, moving effortlessly and almost thoughtlessly. If she thought anything at all, it wasn't about politics or her career or what she was going to do about the husband she saw once a month. She thought, if it was a real thought defined from the delicious flow of sensation, that she was almost flying.

Her route was elaborate and changed each day. This day she ran by the river and then turned through the city to the Mall. Once around the Mall only, instead of two or three times as she sometimes did, and back to her apartment, a precisely clocked ten-mile run.

She waved to a jogging senior congressman headed in the other direction from her, toward the Capitol. She didn't really look at anything, so often had she run the route that it was as familiar and uninteresting to her as another woman's kitchen might be to the lady working in it. Leyna's kitchen was a bar and a miniature fridge, stocked with fruit juice, yogurt, and eggs. If she couldn't make a meal out of that, she went out.

It was early yet, but the sun was beating back the haze. Early commuters were out, and a scattering of tourists. She didn't pay any attention to the sweaty-looking tourist with the

123

camera slung across his chest. People took pictures of her nearly every time she ran around the Mall. She made her living having her picture taken. Why notice the little man unstrapping his camera as she drew up to him?

"Miss!" he shouted and she had time to think that that wasn't the usual greeting. "Leyna!" they shouted, as if they had her in to cocktails regularly. But this man shouted a cheerful "Miss!" at her and she looked his way. Just a smile, and she'd have another fan for life. Little grains of sand, but that's how beaches got built.

She turned her elegant neck and flashed her expensive, almost perfect, teeth at him. A red light popped. A flashbulb in this sun, she thought, the picture would be overexposed. And then it hit her, a wave that knocked her backward, breaking her seven-mile-an-hour momentum. *I've run into something. Something's hit me* flashed through her mind and she was angry at herself for not looking where she was going and angry at the tourist for distracting her. She thought *Now he'll sell me ass over teakettle*. She didn't have a chance to imagine what it would be like in *Newsweek*, or *Time* or *VIP*. A joke if she were mildly injured. A scoop if she were killed. The pain hit her, and an awful cold penetrated all through, and then *thank God* she didn't feel anything at all.

Roger was there with two quick strides and had scooped her up in a handkerchief and turned away, stalking as fast as his short legs could carry him across the Mall. He passed a few people who ignored him in their own haste to get to work or to breakfast or just because he wasn't very interesting. In two minutes he was headed down a side street. The Mall was swallowed up by the big buildings all around until it was just a wedge of screen behind him.

He had dumped the minimizer hastily into the camera case and slowed down to shift it around so it fit properly. Roger didn't like even as many people around as had been there, but it was a hell of a big Mall, it was, and it shrank the early visitors down to a riskable size. He hoped she was okay. She was so beautiful, with her hair flying out in great glossy wings. It was like snatching a rare and beautiful butterfly in flight.

When he entered the hotel suite, Dolly was having her morning shower. Making a bed of tissues in one of Dorothy's fancy soapboxes, he placed the tiny form of Leyna Shaw in it. It was a relief that she was still breathing, but her color was a little off. He wondered about the possibility of shock. And then he had to chuckle, thinking how this would set Dolly on her can.

The water thrummed on the floor of the shower and flowed over Dolly's shoulders and down, to make two little waterfalls off the tips of her breasts. It sheeted down her back and over her bottom. She lathered soap, her own, not the insulting little paper-wrapped squares the hotel deposited, like nasty candy, in likely places. It reminded her of how much she loved individually wrapped pieces of candy. The wrapping added a measure of hesitation, delay, and then a small surprise, to the sweetness of the treat. But there should be candy inside the wrapper, not soap, especially not the kind of soap the godly preferred for washing out the mouths of naughty children.

She lathered patiently, shoulder to toe, according to a routine of some years standing. Then she rinsed, and stood squeaky clean in the spray. When she took up her soap again, after a second's pause to set her mood, she only lathered between her legs, and while she lathered, slipped from a standing position to a crouch. It took only a minute or two to bring herself off. And she would admire herself in the mirrors when the steam had begun to dissipate. It did so much for her color.

Roger, poking needle holes in the soapbox with great care, heard the water stop its seemingly everlasting drumming. Dolly took the longest damned showers. His mother's Sunday soaks took at least an hour, but it was only once a week and perhaps just before special occasions, like Mother's Day. She seemed so pink and happy afterward that he couldn't resent being locked out of the bathroom for so long. But Dolly spent literally hours in the bathroom, most of it, to judge by the sound of running water, in the shower. He didn't mind her smelling of the fancy soap she carted around with her in its own handy box. That was okay. Mostly he wondered if she wasn't washing healthy germs off her skin, but just looking at her, she looked so good that that couldn't be. Just after the showers, she glowed. He suspected that women were supposed to smell like something besides soap and had heard rumors that their natural smell was either wretched or wonderful, depending on who was mongering the rumor, or which sex book he consulted. It was the kind of thing he couldn't ask his mother about. Or Dolly.

She emerged, in a loose wrapper, her skin still moist from the steam. Her hair curled all over her skull, outlining it in silvery cupid ringlets. She glanced at him without much interest and went to look out the window.

"Looks hot out, and it's not even eight-thirty," she observed.

"Yeah," Roger agreed. "It's a bitch out."

Dolly raised an eyebrow at him. "You've been out."

"Good deduction." He held out his right hand, palm up. The box balanced there precariously.

Dolly stopped still, staring at the box. The uneasiness she had felt almost automatically hearing him say *it's a bitch out* burst into black fear, like the ink out of an octopus. Roger grinned at her as if he were trying out for village idiot.

"You're going to love this." He advanced on her, pressing the box on her.

She drew back. "You haven't done anything stupid. Have you?"

His face creased with rejection but she didn't notice. She answered the question herself.

"There's nothing open this early. You couldn't have."

Relaxing visibly, she extended her hand to accept the box. It would be flowers, or a bagel, or some other little curiosity.

He presented it to her and withdrew a little ways, clasping his hands behind him and watching her. She opened the box with the air of a woman receiving a corsage, aware of an honor, but prepared to find something to which she was allergic. Then her eyes widened, the color drained from her face, her nostrils fluttered. She closed the box carefully and put it down quickly, on the nearest table.

Roger watched her fighting for control, uncertain if she was angry or so ecstatic that she had no means to express herself or was just too surprised to speak. She opened her mouth a couple of times, as if to say something, or as if to take in air before the water closed over her head, and her hands shook so that she thrust them hastily into the pockets of the gray silk wrapper. She turned away from him, slunk away to the window, and muttered at the glass.

Uneasy, Roger approached her.

"What?" he said.

She turned to him, her back straight and her eyes flashing. "You goddamn idiot," she hissed.

Roger blinked. He backed away and sat down on the sofa, clasping his own hands for comfort between his knees. He was too stunned to think.

"You goddamn fucking *genius* idiot," she said.

He looked up blindly at the sound of her voice and caught his breath in a sob of relief.

She had taken command of herself and him. Her face was serene and smiling.

"Got a butt on you, kid?" she asked.

Roger wanted to jump up and shout. But he was a man of the world now. So he found her cigarettes and matches and presented them to her with a glowing smile.

"We've got to get the hell out of here," she continued. "Let's go home."

"Whatever you want," he agreed.

She took one of his hands in hers. "You're a madman, I think. And I'm crazier than you are. But I'd rather be crazy than not, right?"

"Right." And he felt like a butterfly that had escaped some predatory enemy. He still had his wings, and the sun still shone.

8

It was Lucy who informed Nick Weiler of Leyna Shaw's disappearance. She called him at the Dalton after hearing it on the noontime radio news. It was a brief conversation, a hasty exchange of facts and plans to see one another, and then Lucy had gone off to make lunch for her family. Nick had bulled through the work on his desk before leaving at a run for lunch with an important donor and an influential senator.

Late in the afternoon, on the way home, Nick heard a repeated radio news item that brought the incident to the forefront of his thoughts. In the wake of his reconciliation with Lucy, the press of work at the Dalton, and planning a trip to England to visit his mother, it was like finding a missing lucky coin in a bank vault. It grabbed at him, puzzled him, troubled him, made him feel aimlessly guilty, and was more than he wanted to think about. He wanted to think about Lucy and very little else, and there was too goddamn much going on.

Entering the cool silence of his co-op apartment, he was greeted by the pair of ancient and oversize tomcats who had been his closest companions for an inordinate number of years. First of all, he fed them, and was dismissed from their attention immediately, as always. He stayed to watch them chow down. What came unsummoned to his mind, idling in the kitchen, was the way Dolly had looked the night of the Founders' Day Gala at the museum when Leyna had used her private childhood nickname in a way calculated to dismiss the passion of Dolly's middle age, her dollhouse, as childish. And Dolly was in town. But it was ridiculous.

Very likely Leyna Shaw had been kidnapped for money or political reasons. If her enemies had played any part in her vanishing, and it wasn't just a terrorist spasm, there were dozens of others who had more compelling reasons for hating her and harming her than did Dolly. It was just that Dolly was as good at hating as her old man had been and had no softness in her that he knew. Still, he had no personal fear, so why should he think of her continually as potentially dangerous? Because she had tried to hurt him through Lucy?

He shook himself free of the whole sticky web of speculation. It was a dead end. He was going to shower off the sweat of the day and trim his beard carefully and take Lucy out to a quiet restaurant to hold hands. It was rotten to have the shadow of whatever tragedy had befallen Leyna hanging over them. But he was just selfish enough to want to cherish what he had almost lost entirely.

The following day he heard from his FBI contact that Dolly had returned to Manhattan with the Doll's White House and her odd friend in tow. The FBI had searched the crated furnishings and dollhouse before the disappearance of Leyna Shaw. They were satisfied that Leyna had not been spirited out of the city disguised as a box of dollhouse furniture. There were many other possibilities to follow up, including suicide and French leave. For the FBI, it was destined to become an open file.

For Nick Weiler, it remained for a long time a nagging doubt, an unsettled question, buried under more engaging, urgent explorations.

A week later, he went to England. He tried to go a least once every three months, for at least a week. Sometimes, museum business took him there irregularly, and he was able to look in on his mother. This time, he could spare only three days. He went feeling guilty.

At ten in the morning, Lady Maggie was at the high point of her day, well rested, breakfasted, bathed, dressed, made up, and bejeweled, and entertaining her only kitten in the splendor of her morning room. Nick, feeling and looking more like a raffish tomcat after a night out than somebody's kitten, lazed on an old-fashioned chaise.

His mother had her nurse pour a restorative cup of tea for him while she sat enthroned in her favorite William and Mary chair. Her expression was calm and serene but her hands trembled occasionally, showing him clearly that she was pleased and excited by his presence. Her happiness weighed on him, making the physical hangover of the long flight from one time zone to another more miserable. His mother might be queenly, in her Lalique necklace and earrings, but she was just another lonely old woman and *that* was his fault.

When she had imparted the news of her own ever-shrinking circle, the bits and pieces of gossip she had hoarded over the past weeks to tell him in person, and they were at ease with each other again, she let him sip his tea in peace awhile and let the sun from the high old windows warm her.

"So how are things with you, dear?" she asked, at last.

He smiled a secret smile. "Good enough, Mother."

She looked at him critically. "Despite your best efforts, that last letter seemed very depressed. You aren't conning me, are you?"

"I'm seeing Lucy again," he admitted.

She clapped her hands together. "Oh, good."

"Would you like to come to Washington? I'd be pleased to have you, if you'd fancy it. You'd meet her then. If not, I'll persuade her to come here."

"I'm afraid not," she laughed. "It's too much for me now. I have had to accept some limitations, you know."

Nick knew. She looked very fragile, much frailer than the last time he had seen her, three months ago. The heavy necklace seemed to bite into her scant flesh; he thought it must be painful to wear. But she always did, on important occasions, had for years. It glinted and flashed in the light, paled by the sun but still elegant, barbaric, cruel.

"Well, I'm relieved," she said. "I had great hopes for that connection. It was very distressing to think you'd flubbed it."

Nick laughed. "I really think the lady was more scared than angry."

"Of you?" His mother's eyebrows arched. "My Nickles, the ladies' terror?"

"Not anymore."

"I'm glad of that, too. I don't know where you got the idea that making love to anyone that asked you was the only polite thing to do. Not from your father, I'm quite certain, and not," Lady Maggie insisted, "from me."

Was that what it was, he wondered, an excess of manners? He could no longer remember any one woman, only their several parts: this woman's shoulder, that one's breast, another's neck, a small greedy hand weighted with rings, including a wedding band.

"Perhaps it was Weiler?" his mother speculated.

Perhaps it was, but he kept that thought to himself as well. Perhaps it was old Blaise Weiler's sweet inoffensiveness that had been his chief inheritance from his stepfather, and not the fortune Blaise had gone so far as to leave to Nick, a rogue's bastard borne by the old man's wife. Appropriately, Nick had accepted the inheritance only because he didn't have it in him to offend the man's memory. He had placed it in trust, to pass on to his children, if he ever had any, along with his stepfather's name, not that of his natural father. Lucy's children, he thought, I'd like that.

He reclined in the thin summer warmth of England and savored the moment. I'll remember this, he told himself, and marked the pale, cream, silk-skinned walls, the portrait of his mother and himself as a child, painted by his father, the only picture on the walls, the delicate antique furnishings, the silver Georgian teapot, the sun-warmed air, fragrant with the smell of tea and his mother's perfume, the clear sweetness of roses.

"Now tell me, darling, whatever did you do to offend that lovely young woman?"

She was perhaps the only person he could tell who would not judge him, not because she was his mother, but because she was Maggie.

"Do you remember the journalist I introduced you to a year or so ago, when I was here for the settlement of the Wilkins estate?"

His mother nodded. "Striking woman, if rather hard. It's very sad, the kidnapping or whatever it is, isn't it?"

"Yes. Well, I . . . embarrassed Lucy over her."

The old woman was silent, letting him condemn himself. He struggled on, just as if he were confessing to some mischief at school.

"I was in the wrong. I nearly lost Lucy. But it brought me to my senses. I realized what I did want."

"However did she find out?" The criticism was unspoken but he heard it nonetheless. *The least I would expect of my son is discretion.*

Why? He might have asked bitterly but he didn't have to, because he was her son.

"Dolly."

"Dorothy Hardesty?"

"And Leyna herself, I think. Apparently Dolly was feeling meddlesome."

"You have been rather naughty too often," his mother chided amiably. "I don't suppose you had the sense to avoid *her* clutches."

"No, I didn't have the sense, and no, I didn't miss her clutches, as you so colorfully put it. She knew everything because she knows everybody, has an uncannily filthy mind, and I was stupid enough to fall under her spell, though not for long, small blessing."

"Silly. And your Lucy didn't understand, did she?"

"No. She's rather vulnerable. Tries to be tough on herself and it spills over onto other people."

"Just what you need."

"Someone to keep me in line."

They laughed together happily.

"Ah, well, you worked it out. She came round."

"Yes."

"That's good. You know, I'd be very happy if you married before I die." She held up one hand to still any protest, though Nick had none to make.

"I know I shouldn't say that but I've done it, haven't I? I love you and I've let you make your own mistakes. Perhaps I shouldn't have.

"You're not a bad boy. Too pretty for your own good, for sure, and rather careless for fear of being thought cowardly. That's what happened to your painting. You couldn't let yourself care about it for fear it might become too important. You might start putting your daubs before people. And then, you couldn't help seeing most people aren't worth a daub, are they?"

He couldn't dismiss it. She had him, as always.

"My fault. Your father's. I wish we'd been better people." Suddenly she was tired, her eyes glittering with tears.

He was too. He rang for her nurse and packed her off to

bed for a rest, admonishing her to save her strength for a riotous dinner out. Then he trundled off to curl up under the puff on his narrow boy's bed, beaten emotionally as well as physically. He loved her dearly but it was hard to visit her, just because of that; there was so much grief and regret, guilt and sadness between them. He drifted off, determined not to let the past, his own and his parents', dictate his future, and knowing just how impossible that was going to be.

. . . When no authentic ransom demands were received by midweek, the focus of the investigation shifted to a closer examination of the journalist's private life. Architect Jeff Fairbourne was genuinely distraught by his estranged wife's disappearance, authorities believed. Friends of the couple agreed that while the marriage was clearly over, Jeff and Leyna remained on good terms. Shaw dated a wide spectrum of politicos, bureaucrats, and media stars, but there were not, apparently, any deep or passionate attachments. The case remains a painful puzzle. . . .

5.9.80   *—VIPerpetrations, VIP*

. . . Dorothy "Dolly" Hardesty Douglas, in Washington last week to retrieve her Doll's White House from the Dalton Institute dollhouse show, had a mystery man in tow. He was clearly younger than she, underlining what's been suspected all along: that Dolly's young at heart. . . .

5.16.80   *—VIPairs, VIP*

The dark, soft and yielding, promised walls, corners, edges. Even without light, it was not hard to know what was herself and what was her environment. Herself. Every part of what she called herself felt crushed. Every breath was paid in teeth-clenching pain. She willed her body to an unnatural stillness.

After a time, there was a lightening of the pain, so that she could think, in starts and stops. This was bad. Whatever had happened to her. Scary. She could still, and did, reject the creeping insistent thought that this was more than bad, this was dead.

The darkness overtook her frequently, blotting out the pain

and speculation. She dreamt, eventually, of earthquakes, volcanoes, meteors, shooting stars. She was a small spaceship. Or a stray bundle of gases hurtled loose from some far sun. Space was great, black, cold, and curiously scratchy.

She woke in bed, a satisfaction. Naked but not cold. Very warm, in fact. The sheets were pleasantly heavy and textured. She was in shadow, the bed draped to veil the light. An oxygen tent, she thought, relieved to be able to identify it. Carefully, she let herself down into the gentle cradle of the dark. She was safe.

Dolly was setting up the dollhouse, a task, she told Roger, that would take two or three days. She gave him the bed for Leyna, a dismissal he recognized.

He found a shelf in a closet for it and installed her. He had other tasks to attend but he came back, compulsively, to check her. It was almost more than he could do to tear himself away from the wonder of her. She was still in shock; it worried him but he was helpless. Once, while he watched, Dolly came up behind him.

"Is she okay?" she asked anxiously.

"Fine," said Roger, telling himself, too. "She's fine."

They stood staring at her.

"Did you ever read the story of the teeny tiny woman? Or maybe your mother or someone told it to you when you were a kid?" Roger blurted at last.

Dolly shook her head. "No."

"I look at her and that's all I can think. The teeny tiny woman."

"Oh." Dolly twitched impatiently at the obvious. "She's that. So what's the story?"

"It's a kid's story. It goes something like: There was a teeny tiny woman who lived in a teeny tiny house. You can go on forever describing all the teeny tiny things she lives with, her teeny tiny cat, and her teeny tiny canary, whatever. Anyway, the teeny tiny woman starts feeling a teeny tiny bit hungry. She goes out and for some reason, goes to the graveyard. She finds a teeny tiny bone on a grave and takes it home. She's so tired when she gets home, that she puts the teeny tiny bone away in her cupboard—"

"—her teeny tiny cupboard?" Dolly interrupted, caught up in the tale.

"Yeah," Roger agreed. "Anyway, she goes to sleep. In the night, she's wakened by this teeny tiny noise. She hides under the covers and it gets a teeny tiny bit louder until finally she understands it's the teeny tiny bone, saying, 'Give me my bone.' I always thought that was silly, the bone asking for itself, but I guess you're supposed to understand that there's a ghost that owns the bone and it's as much in the teeny tiny bone as any of its other bones. And it's not going to be happy in a teeny tiny soup or that cupboard. It wants back to the graveyard. So the teeny tiny woman ignores the cries of the teeny tiny bone and tries to sleep, but every time she dozes off, the damn thing starts crying again. And each time it cries, it gets a little louder. So finally she screams back at it; she screams 'Keep your old bone.' "

Dolly, her face flushed with delight, was puzzled. "It doesn't seem to be a very logical story, though."

"No. There's all kinds of questions to ask. Was the teeny tiny woman a cannibal, making soup out of bones from the graveyard? Why was the bone lying around to begin with? And why, at the end, is it sufficient that she say 'Keep your old bone'? Anyway, I like it."

"It's cute," Dolly said. "I like the part about the teeny tiny house."

"You would," Roger teased, but she had dallied enough.

"Don't you have things to do?" she chided.

Sighing, he put the little bed back out of harm's way.

There was the little matter of the grounds. She handed him that one like it was going out for a bag of fries and burgers. It was going to be legal, though. She handed him a whopping wad of cash and told him to buy the turf.

Done almost as soon as said. A trip to Connecticut in a rented pickup netted a satisfyingly discounted deal with a big landscaper. Zip zap at the nearest rest stop and the enormous rolled strips of turf were in two shoeboxes. Another landscaper in another county was the source of a quantity of shrubbery, a truckload that fitted nicely, after alterations, into another shoebox. One more stop, just like the others. Rosebushes, perennials, a list of vegetation in Dolly's precise upright hand. It took two days to assemble everything necessary but the trees, and most of that was spent driving, or visiting McDonald's. It was hard work, all that driving.

"Nobody sells mature trees," he explained to Dolly, who hardly even looked up from the drifts of packing materials that threatened to inundate her.

"Steal them, darling," she advised. He replayed that throaty rasp dozens of times, driving around Westchester, looking for the right trees. It gave him shivers that started somewhere in his testicles. How many women, he marveled, understood that a man needed a challenge?

He did his best, as always, and substituted a mere four trees on her list. Central Park turned out to be a surprisingly rich source. Then there was a long, endless day putting it all together, over a rambling discussion about zapping fertilizer and laying on the water and artificial light for the plants.

At last Dolly staggered away from the Doll's White House, cramped up and hungry in the wake of her frenzied reconstruction. Roger put aside the work on the grounds until the next day. They wallowed together in the Health Club pool at the peculiar hour of 3:00 A.M., and then wallowed a few more minutes in Dolly's bed. Roger was inspired to get up again, and returned to serve corned-beef hash with fried eggs on the top and beer on the side. Dolly ate as much as he did, rolled over, and dropped into the sleep of utter fatigue. Piling the dirty dishes on a tray, Roger left them in the kitchen, a little treat for Ruta in the morning. He felt too excited, too nerved up to sleep and decided to check on his teeny tiny woman before he gave in to the tug of satiety.

She was a bundle in the shadows of the canopy, curled like an unborn baby. Her hair was splayed across the pillows in dark wings, her eyelashes melted in the dark smudges under her eyes. She was alarmingly insubstantial. Roger's stomach gurgled happily, full of corned-beef and eggs and beer, and he felt guilty. He touched her gingerly, and she winced away in her dark sleep. At least she was still alive.

A tiny foot slipped from beneath the covers. He moved it, between thumb and forfinger, back under the quilt, and tucked it in. He was awash with strange and alien emotions. Rubbing his chest idly, he wondered if the eggs and corned-beef had not been a mistake. The teeny tiny woman in the dollhouse bed evoked feelings in him that he had never had for anyone. She was his. Even Dolly wasn't really his. Roger Tinker created this small person. It made him feel godlike.

He wanted to take good care of her. Make her happy. With that vow, he made his way back to bed.

For a moment, waking up, she thought that she was in her old room. It was delicious to be back in her white four-poster with the rose petit-point canopy. Her mother would call her soon, and have breakfast waiting for her, so she wouldn't miss the bus. No, that wasn't right. No bus, it was summertime. She could stay in bed as late as ever she pleased.

Except she couldn't. Lying perfectly still on the pillow, she held her breath. The shadowy room around her faded. She did hurt still, all over. And she was horribly hungry and thirsty. There was no way she could be in her old room because it was someone else's room now, had been for years and years, and the house was someone else's, too. Since Mummy married David, and Daddy married Ruthann.

She lifted her head carefully, ignoring the pain. Now she could see that the posters were some dark wood, not white. The canopy was rose, though, but a solid rose silk, not rose-on-white, as hers had been. She laid back, staring into the curve of the tester over her. Not an oxygen tent.

Then she wasn't badly hurt, only in ferocious pain from bruises, from healable things. Not in a respirator or a kidney machine or a body cast. Nothing heroic. She could stretch her limbs a little and the pain was even reassuring. Everything seemed to work, on the surface.

The desire to pee came on without warning. She struggled upright. No bell for a nurse with a plastic bedpan, not one that she could find. With more effort, she got her legs over the side of the bed. The pressure in her bladder was enough to make her feel panicky. She could see the rest of the room, beyond the gap in the bed hangings. Some of it anyway. A dresser. A fireplace. A door. Maybe a bathroom door.

She stood up and fell back, nearly fainting. On the edge of the bed, she gathered her strength and concentrated, suppressing the outrage of her body. A hospital room this wasn't. Not with a canopied four-poster and a fireplace with a marble mantel. Not any hospital she knew. But she did know something about four-posters in rooms with fireplaces and the kind of wallpaper whose patterns were shadows on the wall from where she sat. Groping her way along the side of the bed, she pushed the hangings out of her way. Just to the right of the bed, hidden before by the folds of rose silk, was a commode. She slipped to the floor beside it, and opened the cupboard door.

A tear of relief seeped from her left eye. She pulled the chamberpot out and weakly shoved at the lid, until it clanked to the floor. She drew the pot painfully between her legs. It hurt to sit on it but not nearly as much as it hurt not to. Her urine hissed into the pot endlessly, its fumes rising hotly to her nose. Her stomach roiled in revolt and another tear escaped. At last it was over. She managed to replace the lid but was afraid she would spill the heavy pot putting it back into its cupboard, so she left it by the bed.

Now she sought the covers like a refuge. The tears streamed, her nose was running, and she was almost too weak to wipe it. Using a corner of the sheet, she rolled it carefully away from her. The effort had tired her so much that hunger and thirst faded in urgency. She slid almost immediately into a fitful doze.

"Is she all right?"

Roger looked up from the chaos on the floor. It was necessary to modify the base that supported the Doll's White House so that the new green stuff would keep on growing. It was more of a problem in gardening than anything Roger had a strong interest in, but it was something to do.

He couldn't, however, ignore Dolly's genuine concern. Taking care of her possessions, he knew. There was no sudden love of Leyna Shaw springing in Dolly's small bony bosom, just because Leyna was now tiny and vulnerable. The thought of Dolly's bosom naturally kindled memories of Leyna's, once a full seductive pair of moons peeping rosily from her blouse on a magazine cover.

"Well?" Dolly demanded.

"She's just compensating. She'll come out of it."

No point in adding *I hope.* Roger could only project her response to minimization from the small amount of data he had accumulated testing smaller mammals. It was one of those risks that had to be taken, like when the first A-bomb was exploded and some of the scientists on the Manhattan Project thought there was a chance that it might ignite the universe, but hoped mightily that it wouldn't. And it hadn't. That was the operative point.

Roger glanced at his wristwatch. "Time for exercise class," he told Dolly cheerfully.

After that, it was lunchtime. Amazing how sanguine he had become at the prospect of a cup of plain yogurt and a quarter of a cantaloupe. Nasty stuff, cantaloupe. Sherbert of boogers. With the yogurt and fruit clotting in the pit of his stomach, and a nice touch of heartburn, not from the yogurt, which he didn't mind anymore, but from not eating enough, he would cease to be cheerful. In the afternoon, he would finish the grounds model and become cheerful again, as dinner approached. He was taking it as it came.

Dolly put out a cigarette in the ashtray she was carrying. She peeked at Leyna once more, now sweetly ensconced in her replica of the Queen's bedroom.

"I'm going up, too, for a swim," she announced, and stalked away.

Roger nodded his approval but she was gone, leaving cigarette smoke behind her like a trail of vapor from a train. She seemed jittery; a swim would be good for her. He'd have to speak to her about smoking though. It wasn't good for the plants, or for the dollhouses with their fine furniture, or for teeny tiny Leyna.

Hunger and thirst, those ever popular apocalyptic twins, woke her. She felt so weak. Even the ache all over her body was weak. She could barely open her eyes.

The light in the room had changed, but she could not judge what time of day it might be, except that it was not nighttime. A small lamp shed a little over the bed.

She had lost weight; she didn't need to look. She could tell just by moving that she was down twenty pounds, at least. This was the way she'd felt after a bout of flu three years ago. It had been weeks before she was herself again. The only compensation had been not having to diet for a while. Coffee milkshakes and sticky buns. And real cream in her coffee.

She was salivating. It relieves the thirst a little, she thought dully. She rolled over and sat up. Her chest immediately protested the effort. Her heart was thudding like an old water pump. She closed her eyes and waited.

This was what a person got for trying to stay in shape. Flat on your ass. She would like to know what had happened to her. And where she was.

Opening her eyes again, she looked at the room. The same room she had seen before through a veil of pain. An old-fashioned room, with antique furniture. Large windows covered with expensive looking draperies. A fireplace with a fire laid and unlit in it. A mirror over the mantel that was disturbingly familiar. The commode by the bed, thank God for that.

Reminded of it, she slithered out of bed and unlidded the pot. The stale force of her own urine assaulted her nose. She wrinkled her nose and held her breath long enough to do her business. This time she was recovered enough to wish for a tissue, but there was no roll of paper hidden discreetly in the back of the little commode.

Back on the bed, she rested from the effort. Someone would come soon and tell her what had happened and where she was. Probably someone had been in and out while she slept. She ignored the evidence of the pot that surely would have been taken away and emptied if anyone had been about. She would find a real bathroom, she decided, and empty it herself. A real bathroom would have water in it, and another of her needs would be answered.

Two doors in the bedroom, and one of them logically had to be a bathroom. Once out of the bed again, she was chilled into consciousness of her own nakedness. Her breasts were cold lumps on her chest. It was as if she had not flesh left on her, only her cold hard bones. There was something embarrassing about standing mother-naked in the middle of a strange place, but she chided herself. The president wasn't going to come walking in. And that was a strange thought to intrude itself but then, she knew she wasn't herself. She fumbled, nevertheless, with the bed linen, wrestling the top sheet off the bed and draping it to cover her shoulders. She was slightly warmer.

She limped across the floor, supporting herself on furniture as she went. Once she stopped to rest against a beautiful old wardrobe. It smelled of its finish, polish, sachet, and sawdust, all mixed together. It was necessary, though, to abandon its silken support and make for the nearest door.

The door opened onto a hallway that was one with the room, carpeted with an old Oriental rug and dotted with antiques. Furniture that was by definition old and well made and nearly useless, except to fill appropriate spaces, on the excuse of holding up a pot of flowers or a tatty bust. There were more doors along the way. It was not what she needed just then. She closed the door.

Groping her way along the wall on the other door in the room, she had to pass the fireplace. In the mirror on the mantel, a glimpse of herself as her own ghost, shockingly white, bony, jumped out at her. Her eyes were sunken and dull in great smudgy pits. She couldn't look at herself.

The knob of the second door gave way to a feeble push. She staggered in, taking in the room at once. Another old-fashioned room but a bathroom. A chain-pull toilet, a claw-footed tub, a basin of the kind that had always reminded her of a heron, asleep on one foot. Her first trembling touch on the basin told her it was cold, sleek porcelain, not plastic or fiberglass. Ignoring the small glass in the filigreed holder on the wall, she reached convulsively for the faucet. The small *c* written on the ceramic button inlaid in its handle filled her vision. She jerked the faucet. The water would not come. Again she jerked it, cursing her own weakness. Still, no water. The hot water faucet turned as easily but it, too, gave nothing.

Stumbling to the bathtub, she turned both faucets on, to no result. Groping from bath to toilet, she seized the seat with both hands and lifted it. The bowl was dry. When she dropped the lid, defeated, it sounded like a shutter being dashed against a wall by the wind.

She sank to the floor and buried her head in her hands. The fantasies of soaking baths, cool drinks, and a proper bowel movement dissipated like an oasis in a mirage. What sort of bathroom had no water?

"Goddamn, goddamn, goddamn," she mumbled.

The tears came suddenly, the taps of emotions opened violently. Why was she here, and where was she and why was she all alone? Who had turned off the water and why? There were so many unanswered questions and she couldn't think, not without food and water. Shivering, she gathered her sheet around her. She was growing colder.

Leaning against the cold surface of the toilet bowl, she whispered, "Mummy, I want Mummy."

In a moment or two she stopped crying. The cold, thirst, and hunger had become more demanding than mere grief and terror. She would grope her way back to the bed and at least be warm. As she rose to her feet, she noticed there was a roll of paper next to the john. Fumbling it from its holder, she clutched it with one hand and her sheet with the other. A very small profit on so painful a journey, but it was something. Later she would empty the chamberpot into the toilet. At least then she would not have to smell her own waste, even if she couldn't flush it.

The pillows, the velvety quilt, were gifts for which to be grateful. She drew them around her, and closed her eyes again. She was so tired, so tired. Perhaps someone (*Mummy*) would come soon and take care of her.

Roger peeked in at the window. She'd moved. Excitement burbled in his stomach, driving away his heartburn. The bedclothes looked like a war had happened in them. And the little pot was out of its cupboard. She slept now and he didn't want to wake her, so he held his breath. She needed all the sleepy-bye time she could get. It was part of the compensation process. He wished she didn't look quite so terrible, diminished, the way his dad had the last six months of his life.

He would bring food and water for her. She would be wanting that when she woke again, especially if she had been awake long enough to use the potty. But first he had to tell someone.

He trotted off to look for Dolly and found her in her bedroom, changing her clothes.

"Guess what?"

Dolly looked up from doing her shoes. They were all straps, about a million buckles. Roger loved them. Suddenly, though, she fumbled and bit her lip. "She's been awake," he announced before she could ask what.

Dolly sucked in a long, shaky breath. "At last." She bent over her shoes, hurrying now to finish up. "I can tell you now I was beginning to get worried."

"I'm going to cook up something for her." Roger stopped to hug Dolly. "I'll be right back."

So transported with his little plans was Roger, that he didn't see she looked after him with the edge of jealousy in her eyes. Seizing a tube of hand cream, she rubbed lotion in her hands, to stop their sudden trembling.

Roger found her peeking through the dollhouse windows when he returned. He bore a plate of scrambled eggs, with a slice of wheat toast carefully quartered, and a glass of orange juice.

"She won't be able to eat all that," Dolly objected. "It'll go to waste."

"I'll eat what she doesn't want," he volunteered bravely.

Dolly glared at him. He ignored her, happy to have, once at least, put her in the corner. Either she tossed away the small change represented by the grub or she let Roger off his diet. Hee Hee.

She struck back. "You can't put that Christawful huge plate in there."

Then she proceeded to pull up one of the walls of the dollhouse. It made a hideous noise, and Roger peered at Leyna anxiously. She didn't move.

Rummaging in a china cabinet, Dolly came up with a couple of display pieces, samples of one of the many presidential dinner services. She examined the pieces critically before giving them to Roger. Unsure of what he was to do with them, he stared at them.

"Lenox," she informed him. "Harry Truman picked them out. I like the lilies, don't you?"

Desperately trying to hold up his end of what seemed to him to be a perfectly insane conversation, Roger mumbled, "I like the ones with the eagles."

Harry Truman, he thought, had nothing to do with these tiny dolls' dishes; they were copies of dishes the former president had selected. Dolly talked about the furnishings of her Doll's White House the way his mother talked about her soap operas, like it (or life as lived in the television romances) was more real than real. It must have something to do with women's monthlies, one more evidence of their cyclical craziness.

"Eagles!" Dolly fairly spat. "Every goddamn thing in the White House had an eagle on it. I hate them."

Roger shrugged. His mother would have said what can't be changed, must be endured. Dolly could stand a dose of that philosophy. He set about apportioning a tiny quantity of the eggs to the small plate.

"Put the wall back," she ordered.

Roger didn't want to but he tried to do it as gently as possible, for Leyna's sake.

"Now take that one out."

He hesitated.

"She's sleeping," he objected in a whisper.

"Well, shit, she's slept for days. Why did you make this food if you weren't going to feed it to her while it was hot?"

The logic was unassailable. He moved the wall.

She heard the voices in the distance. They were like the soundtrack of a movie, heard from the theater lobby. Opening her eyes, she sat up. Someone had said something and then "eat," she was certain of it. There was a rumbling noise, like an old elevator struggling up or down and then the voices again. "Eagles," she heard. And an emphatic, "Well, shit" and then the rumbling came again, like a small earthquake all around her, and the wall with the windows in it was gone. She stared at it, going, rising upward, and the light poured in, making her blink rapidly. She thought she made out enormous shapes like nothing she had ever seen in her life.

She sat bolt upright in the bed and opened her mouth. Her throat was paralyzed; she could only make a kind of piteous mewing. And then the Hand, a hand as big as she was, bigger than her bed, reaching in.

The scream she had been trying to scream tore from her throat. She covered her eyes.

Roger cast a reproachful glance at Dolly. It was fruitless; *she* was staring at the teeny tiny woman, who was crouched in the farthest available point of the bed from the intruders. Dolly reached into the house again. Roger grabbed her elbow. Surely she could see the extent of Leyna's terror. But Dolly stopped of her own accord, as the thin agonized whine reached their ears. The teeny tiny woman was moaning. It was terrible to hear.

"What's wrong?" Dolly asked Roger in a low, faint voice. There was genuine alarm in her expression.

"She's scared."

Roger placed the little silver tray with its china dishes at the very edge of the room. He began to move the wall back into place, as carefully as he had removed it. Dolly drew back and watched. Leyna watched, too, wide eyed and wary, from a cocoon of bed linen. When the wall hid her from their view, Roger took Dolly by the hand and gently tugged her away.

"I want to see," she hissed.

With both hands on her shoulders, he pushed her out.

"Sure."

Roger closed the door between Dolly's bedroom and the dollhouse room. He sat on the edge of the bed.

"Have a butt," he said, tossing a pack of cigarettes at her.

She caught them reflexively, stared at them as if she had forgotten what they were. Sighing, she ripped the pack open.

"Let her get used to it a minute. It won't take long. The human mind can accept anything."

Roger flopped back onto the bed. His own thoughts fixed on the rest of the scrambled eggs, cooling beside the Doll's White House.

"Gimme one of those," he requested. Any port in a storm, his mother might say.

The wall descended. She did not breathe until it completed the room once more. She stayed frozen a few seconds, watching to see that it stayed where it was supposed to and then scooted weakly across the floor to claim the tray, simply unable to resist the siren scents.

The smell of eggs and orange juice and warm bread rolled over her, fragrant as the first smells of spring, and her stomach gurgled in anticipation. For one uneasy second, she thought she might vomit, and then it was all right. The tray was heavy, made of silver and chased with a delicate design, but she didn't really look at it. It was to be expected; it went with the room. It was enough of a struggle to get it to the bed, and then to heave herself up next to it. Blackness swam behind her eyes; she had to lay back until it passed.

At last, she could lift the fork to her mouth. It was the best food, she thought, she had ever eaten. Five stars. She giggled. She ate it too fast.

Her stomach rolled again and the orange juice sent up an acid aftertaste. She pushed the tray to one side of the bed and pulled the sheets and blankets tight around her. For the moment she was all right again. Warm. Not hungry. Not thirsty. The pain had become merely aches and bruises.

The wall and the Hand came back to her. She pushed away the thought of them. They could not have happened. They had not happened. She had been delirious with hunger, and perhaps a continuing shock. She still did not know what had happened to her. She had had an accident, that was apparent. She could have sustained head injuries, concussion, something, that was not serious enough to require hospitalization, but still might cause her to see things, nightmare things. She closed her eyes tightly, shutting it out.

Someone had fed her, at last. All would be explained and understood, in time. She was sick. It was enough to do, to try to heal herself. Her body demanded her attention again. She *was* sick, sick to her stomach. She felt all greenish and low. The too-quickly consumed food gathered in a nasty, greasy lump in the pit of her stomach. She groaned.

She had not the strength to fight it. Over the side of the bed, aiming for the floor, she opened her mouth, and it all came up and out, still quite distinctly eggs, and toast, and orange juice. She felt rather distant from it, could look at it as if it were someone else's mess, and note the sourness.

"Oh goddamn and shit," an enormous rasping voice boomed, "she's being sick all over the bedclothes."

She closed her eyes instantly. It was enough that the sour food was in her nostrils and mouth, right back to the back of the throat. It was enough that her ears heard voices from outside, voices larger than human. She couldn't bear to see, again, the wall disappearing, or that Hand, God's or Whoever's, probing the room, reaching for her.

The rasping voice went on, berating her and someone else, she was sure someone else was being dressed down. The someone else responded, a deep, hesitant protest. Someone Else was protecting her, defending her from the rasping voice that was angry with her for being sick.

It was a dream of being seven again, the evening of her birthday party. She had gorged all day, at Grammie's and Aunt Reenie's and at home, at the big party, on the sweets she loved. Her mother objected repeatedly, warning she would be sick, and the others kept saying *It's her birthday, Leona.* Before that incantation of privilege, her mother fell silent. And Leyna had gone to bed and been terribly sick in the night. Her mother, summoned by the choking cough of her vomiting, flew into a rage.

"How do you like your birthday now, you little pig?"

And her father, following her mother, trying to calm her. "For God's sake, Leona."

"Where's your mother now, and your sister Reenie?" she screamed at him, "now there's puke all over my coverlets and on my rug?"

"Lee, the child is sick."

"I see that! I see that!"

And she pushed Leyna from the bed, cursing the whole while and calling her a pig. She swept the bedclothes and the rug into a heap and snatched the soiled nightdress from Leyna's shivering, feverish body.

"I'll bathe her," her father had offered, and started to lead Leyna out of range of her mother's wrath.

But she wouldn't let go. "Don't be silly, go back to bed. You have to work in the morning. I'll do it."

And do it she did, as roughly as possible, and muttering between buckets of cold water poured over Leyna's head, "How do you like your birthday now?"

"What a goddamn mess," Dolly said in disgust.

"I'll clean up," Roger volunteered.

"Of course you will. It's your fault."

Dolly was looking for a new cigarette. She stuck one in her mouth and rummaged for her lighter.

"Are you sure she's all right?" she continued.

"Sure." Roger drew the wall gently out of its slots. "Probably ate too much on an empty stomach. Or too fast."

Dolly inhaled the cigarette smoke gratefully. It covered up the faint smell of sickness nicely. She loathed sickness.

"Why don't you get something to bathe her in?" Roger suggested.

It was something to do and would take her out of the room a minute, away from the stench. She came back from her bathroom with a small basin full of water, a bar of soap floating in it, and with a hand towel on her arm.

"This do?"

"Sure."

Roger barely glanced at it. He was engaged in the delicate operation of unwrapping the teeny tiny woman from the soiled linen without getting too much of the sick around the bedroom.

"She all right?" Dolly asked again.

Roger nodded. The small body, wrapped in a sheet, was in his palm. She was curled up like a sleeping child, her hair in damp dirty tangles that made a dark pillow under her head.

"She looks ghastly," Dolly observed.

He smiled. "She's been through a lot. Shocks. The physical shock and then the mental one, that's only just starting. It'll take some adjustment. But she'll be okay."

" 'The human mind can adjust to anything,' " Dolly quoted. She rolled the cigarette between her thumb and forefinger gently.

"Yeah. Exactly."

Roger unwrapped the sheet. She was entirely naked. The bruises were dark patches on her skin. Some of them were as dark as the patch of her pubic hair. The aureolae of her breasts were the faintest of all the shadows on her skin. He dipped her into the water with one hand and used the other to move a little of the tepid fluid over her, as gently as he could.

"Will you wash her hair?" he asked Dolly.

Dolly put aside her cigarette. She touched the small skull tentatively. It was creepy, like touching a mouse or a squirrel.

"Just a second," she said and left the room again. She came back with a teaspoon.

"Like that," she told Roger, rearranging Leyna so that Roger's hand supported her body up to the base of the skull. The head was free so that her hair hung down between Roger's thumb and index finger.

Dolly used the teaspoon to wet the hair thoroughly, and then lathered it with the bar soap. It wasn't the best thing for hair but it would do for the moment. It was surprisingly pleasant to rinse out the soap, to feel the silky strands of hair slipping squeakily between her fingers.

"There," she announced, with some satisfaction. She looked at Roger over the basin and smiled proudly.

"Good job," he murmured, and carefully lowered the little body into the hand towel.

"I don't know how she can sleep through that," Dolly said. "The water should have brought her to."

Roger grinned. "She's not asleep. She doesn't want to look at us. I'm going to wrap her in a dry handkerchief and put her on your bed, okay?"

"Ummm."

"You ought to get some clothes for her."

"That's all taken care of, darling." Dolly's voice came to him through the dollhouse. She had her face right in it.

"Now for this mess. Oh, ugh."

Roger wandered back to find out what she was fussing over. She held out the little chamberpot.

"Good," Roger said. "Everything normal."

Dolly pushed it at him. "You like it, it's yours."

"I'm going to test it. See if she's all right."

"Better you than me. I thought you said she was."

"Well, she is. But there's nothing like a spot of pee to really tell the whole story, is there?" Roger giggled.

"Blecch. Don't make any messes, please. There's been enough of those made today."

She turned back to the dollhouse. "Listen, you'd better hook up the water system. I don't want to spend the rest of my life emptying a thunderjug and giving baths and shampoos. It's too much like being somebody's mommy."

"Do it right away," Roger promised, "after I have a peek at the pee. I'm all set for it."

It was a chance to sneak a burger or a hero or maybe even a pizza and a beer, while ostensibly at the drugstore collecting the urine-testing equipment. It wouldn't take any time at all. He really did want to test the sample. Then he could be sure his teeny tiny woman was really all right.

She awoke tucked between sheets so crisp and clean-smelling that they were glassy to the touch. Astonishingly, she herself smelt of soap. Felt clean. She lay still for an instant, enjoying the sensation of being cared for. It was the sound of running water that made her sit up. It was insistent, no mere drip, a definite gushing. In the bathroom. She slipped from the bed, this time not bothering to pull a sheet off to wrap herself. The bed was freshly made. She couldn't disturb it. It was time she acted like a proper guest in someone else's house. With the aid of the furniture, she reached the bathroom door.

Her laughter, weak as it was, spontaneously joined the splashing of the water into tub and basin. She flipped the lid on the toilet gleefully and looked down into her own reflection in the small pool at the bottom of the bowl. She closed it

149

and sat on the lid to catch her breath. After taking a glass of water to soothe her dry throat (but not too fast, she warned herself), and another one to put by her bedside, she turned off the taps she had left on. She crawled back into bed, marginally stronger, and with a feeling of delicious well-being.

The nightmare was over. She had closed her eyes and feigned sleep until it really was sleep, and the horrors had passed. She looked around at the solidity of walls and furniture. This was sanity (cleanliness, running water) by any measure.

Now she was not much troubled by hunger. She knew why. It was like fasting; she'd fasted before. Not for a diet, but in a seige she'd gotten caught in, the one that had made her name in television journalism. Five days the crew had gone, cooped up in a shell-shattered Hilton in the no-man's land of a Middle Eastern city's center. Four days before the Canadian soldiers who were the United Nations peace-keeping force had escorted them out, the beseiged had consumed the last stale candybars in the vending machines and drunk the last warm Cokes. The hotel kitchens had been looted by the employees on the way out, and what little remained had been fouled by vermin. One of their number was wounded, with a bullet-shattered knee, and nearly died from shock and blood loss. The hotel had been strewn with bodies, and bodies piled up by the entrances and by certain windows with useful views. The vermin had become very active in the five days of the film crew's imprisonment. After a while, appetite hadn't been a problem.

During her recuperation, a military doctor had told her that stress would kill appetite, as the body concentrated on survival. The genetic inheritance of a foraging species, he told her. And after a certain time without food, the body's chemistry changed, and the stomach ceased to clamor. The body settled down to consuming itself. It was at this point that sustenance had better be resumed or real damage would occur.

But euphoria was a common side-effect of starving, and so were mystical visions. She was close to euphoria, so strong was her sense of well-being. The mystical visions, she reflected, she could wait for. She had her nightmares, that was enough.

And the wall rumbled and complained and rose again. She

sat up straight and screamed as if in agony. She shook her fists at the rising wall.

"It's not my birthday!" she screamed. "It's not my birthday."

This time the Hand did not stop at the outer wall. It entered and she fell silent, paralyzed with fear. It moved closer and she saw the chamberpot, grasped between thumb and forefinger like a china acorn. It passed her and descended. The enormous loglike fingers poked and prodded at the commode. She stared at them, the knuckles that were all leathery wrinkles like an elephant's knees, and at a scar, shaped like a blunt arrowhead, that pointed across the back of the Hand. It withdrew at last, with a flash of scarlet, a great pool of shiny scarlet, and she knew it was a Woman's Hand.

"There now," the voice like a fingernail drawn over chalkboard said, and it was very close and loud, so that she winced away and covered her ears. "Roger?" it said questioningly, and faded away, taking with it a cloudy mass of lilac and gray. She dared not look up, to see if it had a face. Hadn't she learned in Sunday school that the sight of God's face was reserved for Judgment Day? And even the strong possibility that the joke was on the human race, that God was a painted female, did not erase the certainty that on Judgment Day, we would all be dead.

She curled up tightly under the covers. She prepared to die.

"Roger," Dolly said softly, "did you know this was going to be a problem?" Her tone of voice suggested he should have.

"Should have," he confessed, using a ploy that worked well with his mother. He thought of it as Beating Her to the Stick. "I'll set up a sound system. Something to magnify her voice and damp down ours."

"What about the test? Is she all right?"

"Basically, yes." He drew out a notebook and a pen, opened the notebook and stood very still, thinking. "She's got to start eating. But," he smiled slyly, "I've got that licked."

"Oh?"

"I'm going to minimize the food for her. I think it'll be easier for her to digest."

"What about water?"

151

"She's drinking it and keeping it down and it's coming out the other end okay. I don't know why. Maybe it's just psychological."

"Well, as long as it works."

"Right. One of us should try to calm her. We don't want her going into shock from fear or distress."

"I'll do it," Dolly said.

Resigned, Roger let it go. Dolly showed signs of being really ham-fisted in dealing with Leyna. But there was a lot of work that needed doing, and he would have to let her handle this part, at least for now.

The wall stayed up. Minutes passed and there was silence. Leyna's heartbeat slowed, adrenaline ebbed. Her head began to ache fiercely. She remembered her mother's old nostrum for childhood headaches—water. That was something she had. Warily, she watched the place where the wall had been, and sipped water from the glass she had carried from the bathroom. It was tepid, but still sweet and soothing. The muscles of her throat, dry and cramped from screaming, and wanting to scream, from sheer terror, relaxed a little.

She put the glass down and lay back, shutting her eyes. *Headache commercial: celebrity journalist, in the middle of a stressful, exciting day in the course of her meteoric career, is wiped out by a migraine, just before the cameras go red. She flops on a handy chaise, has some water and the product patent medicine, puts her lovely legs up while the camera lingers on them and on the gap in her blouse. Minutes later, she opens the six-thirty news with a stunning display of teeth and shining, healthy, untroubled eyes. Take Blecch. Or whatever.*

A rustling crackling sound intruded into her daydream. She saw the Hand once more disappearing. She began to tremble all over. The urge to crawl under the covers nearly seized control of her. It was the sheet of paper that stopped her. The Hand had left a piece of paper, mysterious as an antique treasure map, on the floor near the wardrobe.

She crept up on it, wrapped in the coverlet from the bed. Nevermind wrestling the sheets. She wasn't going to expose her nakedness to God, or Whomever, out there. Snatching up the paper, she scurried back to the safety of the bed. In the shadow of the bed hangings she spread the paper, as if she were opening the *Times* on Sunday morning. It was as wide as her arm span. The printing scrawled across it, inches high.

But eminently readable. Leyna giggled. She'd never before received a note from God.

Don't be afraid. We mean you no harm.

The clichés of a kidnapper's note, or a bankrobber's threat: *Nobody will get hurt. Do what we say. We won't hurt the kid if you pay up.*

Shit.

She stared at it, unseeing. She was in a room, a definite place. It was furnished in the best of taste, beautifully wallpapered and carpeted and curtained. Beyond the door was a hall and the hall had its own doors to other rooms. What she had seen was familiar, but not anyplace she had ever lived in. How many rooms like this in how many old houses were there in this country? Very likely it was familiar to her simply because it was a type, a cliché itself.

Then there was the mad part of it. Walls that moved and were gone. When the walls went away there was no out of doors, no street, no other buildings, no garden, no trees, only those enormous, amorphous nightmare creatures. Who wrote notes.

Her best, most cynical, explanation was that she was in a private loony bin. The aberrations in this room, perhaps the room itself, were all in her head, as a consequence of the accident, of which she still had no certain knowledge. It could have jarred loose her sanity. She was not, before this accident, either neurotic or unstable. She had known who she was and what she was doing with her life. Professional hand-holding, the crutches other people commonly used, had never been necessary. Nor booze, nor drugs. No, she had been sane enough. And there was still some essential balance that could tell her quietly that some of what she perceived was fantastic, impossible, and mad-as-a-hatter. And go on to reassure her that it was most likely the consequences of some organic damage, and not any mental defect on her part.

It was that certainty, arrived at in her usual painstaking way, as if crossing a line of stepping stones over running water, that stilled the terror. She did not scream when the Hand returned.

It came directly to her and she winced away instinctively, dread rising in her like water around a drowner. The Hand stopped and waited and at last came on and touched her. It had great heat. The skin touching hers was stiff, leathery, and unyielding, like a battered but once superior suitcase. It scooped her up gently, rolled in the quilt she had pulled around herself.

She closed her eyes. She always did, during take-offs and landings, and during the rare instances when she had been lured into riding rollercoasters. There was nothing to do but close her eyes, take a deep breath, clench her teeth and fists, and ward off death by sheer willpower.

The quilt, like a winding sheet around her, was too warm. The Hand generated its own enormous heat, and she was quickly awash in sweat and grimly fighting off nausea and faintness. Release was quick and gentle, down into a feathery softness. Opening her eyes in a strong natural light, she saw that she had come to rest on something that looked like a cloud cover from a plane window, an enormous undulant field of white. It was formed of stalks, like a field of grain, but she knew by touch and sight that the substance that rose to midthigh, white and slender and very smooth, was not any kind of plant. There was no soil under her bare feet but something woven, like the backing of an Oriental rug. It smelled dusty, but there was no vegetative scent, no plant smell, no *green* reaching her nostrils.

Surveying the field of white, she could name no other features. It ended, but what was beyond it was all mass and color. There were no dimensions, no perspectives. The stalks around her rippled mildly and she turned, instinctively, to the source of their agitation. She found a wall of stiff, shimmering drapery. It was very coarsely woven and had no perceivable frame, no solid wall around it. It just rose upward to the farthest point she could manage to see by painfully crooking her neck.

And it moved, at last. She realized it was moving not horizontally, but vertically, and downward. Holding her breath, she drew back, as it descended without any break.

Abruptly it changed and was not a wall at all but a Face, clearly a face, very close and as large, no larger, many times larger, than she was herself. A moon face, a mask on a stick, unreal in its enormity. She remembered, suddenly, the face of the Wizard that had so awed and frightened Dorothy and her companions. And of course it was a trick, a projection, created by the charming old rogue who was and wasn't the Wizard of Oz. A giggle of relief died in her throat. She knew this Face and why it brought to mind the Wizard of Oz. Moaning, she buried her face in her hands.

"Don't be afraid."

The Face had a Voice, the same rasping one she had heard before in her mysterious bedroom. The Voice of God, except now she recognized it as Dolly Hardesty's voice. The tone was soothing, the volume vast, as if it came from a loudspeaker. Despite its message, she could not help retching dryly.

"You're safe. Nothing can harm you."

Willfully, she forced her hands downward and raised her eyes. She summoned her voice, putting all her remaining force behind it.

"Dorothy?"

A soft chuckle rolled over the field at her and whispered in her hair.

"Dorothy?" she cried out again, fearfully.

"You may call me that, if you wish. And I will call you Dolly."

Leyna drew the quilt tightly around herself. A terrible stillness welled up in her. She breathed deep and calm.

"Dorothy?" she asked, a third time, though her throat hurt to shout the name again.

"Yes?"

"Am I crazy?"

The silence spread around her almost palpably, for as the stalks trembled as the Voice of Dorothy spoke, they remained motionless when she did not.

"Oh, yes."

She was assured, with sorrow in the Voice, and condescension like half-cooked egg. There was nothing more to ask and nothing more to say. Leyna sank slowly to her knees; the stalks rose up around her and made a low wall. Closing her eyes again, she waited. She would open her eyes again on reality, on sanity, or not at all.

Roger, behind Dolly, heard the last part of their exchange. He seized her by the wrist and drew her away, to the farthest corner of the room.

"What the Christ are you doing?" he demanded of her in a hiss like boiling water.

Dolly met his eyes coldly and wrenched her wrist free of

his grasp. Turning on her heels, she stalked out. He followed her into the kitchen, where she opened the refrigerator.

"What were you doing?" he persisted.

She looked up at him and smiled.

"Really, darling," she said, "I don't think you've thought this business through."

That's what he'd been thinking of her.

"Well, tell me what I haven't thought of."

Turning back to the refrigerator she produced two bottles of imported beer. She held one out to him. He had to come close to her to take it. He could feel its wonderful coolness even before he touched it and his mouth watered for it. He looked around hastily, for the can opener he'd left on the chopping block at lunchtime.

When he looked back, she had a drawer open and a church key in her hand. He had to smile at her prescience. She was not only permitting him a beer but was going to have one herself. It was a large gesture for Dolly. He regretted the force with which he had seized her wrist.

"It'll be a lot easier to deal with her if she thinks she's non compos," Dolly explained over the beer.

Roger thought it over. It made a crazy kind of sense. She might be more compliant. On the other hand, they had the advantage of her, didn't they? He was uneasy. The human mind was so unpredictable to begin with, and this one had experienced a unique trauma already, at their hands. At his, he corrected himself, but it didn't make the uneasiness die down. He didn't say anything to Dolly. There was enough else to discuss.

"She'd better be fed soon, very soon. Do up a new tray and I'll zap it. She's weak. She needs clothes. A good chill would be risky."

"Of course. What if she won't dress herself?"

Roger considered. "I wouldn't touch her if she were hysterical. If she lets you, just be careful, very careful."

"Cheers," Dolly said, raising her bottle to him.

She was drinking straight from the bottle, the way he did. Noblesse oblige. But the work waited. Roger finished his beer quickly.

Leyna was genuinely faint when the Hand came back. She lay limp and unresponsive in its embrace. The smell of food again assaulted her when she dared open her eyes again. She was back on her bed. The commode next to it supported the silver tray. This time the smells were of broth and buttered toast. When she lifted the covers from the dishes, she cooed with delight. She didn't notice the wall being replaced. The broth was astonishingly good and she couldn't help slurping a little as she consumed it.

Afterward she could lie back and feel almost whole again. Amazing what food does for a person, she thought, and wondered if it had something to do with the question of her sanity or not. It was true that hunger could make a person crazy, create chemical imbalances that distorted one's perceptions of reality. That wasn't what the Voice of Dorothy had meant though, she was sure of it.

The Voice was her madness and the Face that went with it and its terrible Hands. This room, the bed, the food she had just eaten, that was all as real and sane as could be. The fullness of her belly told her that. She had to be a little bit sane just to be able to consider the question.

Then the Voice spoke again. Leyna flattened herself into the pillows, thinking *no, no, no.* If It heard her thoughts, It ignored them.

"Look in the wardrobe. There are clothes for you there."

She waited for It to speak again. For one, two, five minutes, It was silent. She decided It had delivered its message and gone away again.

There was no reason not to see if It spoke the truth. She felt as if she were trying to put together a jigsaw puzzle, though she had no idea what It pictured, and that this might be one small piece. And she was cold and self-conscious when she was out of bed.

When she left the bed, she was certain that Someone watched her. A quick survey of the room revealed no visible cameras in the corners of the ceilings. Sometime soon, she promised herself, she would search for hidden ones.

The wardrobe was one of those relentlessly well-made pieces of furniture that testified to some ancestor's personal solidity. She admired the smooth, deep finish and the brasswork, the japanning on the doors. It was the sort of thing that fetched tens of thousands of dollars at auction. The appraisal made her reassess the room. It was very well furnished, indeed. A rich person's room, in a rich person's old house. Another piece of the puzzle.

Musing on that, she opened the right-hand door of the wardrobe and peeked into the empty darkness. She hesitated, then threw open the left-hand door. Red and white gleamed at her, throwing the light back to her in brilliant clarity. She reached out instinctively to caress the material, silk the color of blood, a satin that was as blindingly white as a snowfield at high noon.

She chose red. Examining the dress, she reveled in its elegance, its complete simplicity. There was a line of hooks hidden under a discreet seam in the back. It took some time to unhook them all. How she was going to hook them again was a problem she would defer to the future.

The dress settled over her shoulders and slipped down the length of her body, caressing her now with its texture. She shifted from one foot to the other in an ages-old female motion, the first dance step, and it shook out, falling in the flawless lines of its design.

The mirror in the door of the wardrobe reflected her, the dress blazing against her bleached skin. It was sleeveless and the neckline formed a gently squared U. The perfect frame, she thought, to show off her sickly face and prominent collar bone. A step back confirmed what she had sensed. The dress was too short. It was without ornament or trim, depending on its cut, color, and texture for effect. Falling without a break in its clean lines to the hip, the material was there gathered on the left hip, from which it flowed in a spray of folds to the hemline. The hemline itself had been softly gathered.

Obviously post-World War I, she thought, and meant to fall to the ankles, which would be clad in real silk stockings in satin slippers. On her it stopped six inches too soon, a ludicrous effect. The dress wouldn't do; she'd have to try the other and hope it was a better fit.

At least she didn't have to try to hook herself into and out of the silly rag. It came to her suddenly that ladies of the era of this dress had had maids and button hooks to do the job, anachronisms, or perhaps the tools and skills of a more civilized way of life, now forever lost. She shook it off her shoulders and it slipped right to the floor. Skinny broad, she reflected wryly, and that dress had been made for a slim woman. She stepped out of the pool of red silk and reached for the white.

In the light, it was transparently obvious that the white dress wouldn't do either. It was a very small woman's dress, almost childish in its proportions, and a real piece of period costuming. She had to grin over the ruffles on the short sleeves, the extravagant off-the-shoulder collar that plunged in a vee, repeated in the waistline, from which yards of material fell to form the bell of the skirt. It wanted petticoats and long gloves and some sort of headdress, perhaps with feathers, to look right. On whomever it had belonged to, not her. It would never look right on her, thank God for little favors. She put it back in the wardrobe, for a moment very grateful to have been born in this particular period of history, when women wore comfortable clothing, by and large. Bar the occasional spike heel or crotch-cutting jean. Good-bye Queen Victoria.

That was it, the connection. The dress looked like something that antique monarch might have worn, and most probably when she was young. Pre-war, only pre-Civil War, maybe pre-Mexican War. A nice little museum piece.

She hung up the red dress thoughtfully. Odd things to turn out of anybody's closet. She was troubled with a sense of the familiar, and dismissed it. It was a syndrome with her. Too much information to be absorbed and after a while nothing much *was* absorbed. Sensory overload. She knew others in her profession who were plagued with that constant sense of déjà vu. It was the basis, she thought, of paranoia of the grandest kind.

Thinking about that she ignored one of the details that was obvious about the pair of dresses. The styles were unquestionably antique. But the dresses weren't. The material was crisp, clean smelling, and taut; the seams were tight and clean. The dresses were newly made.

She gathered up her quilt and crawled back into bed, suddenly tired out. Nakedness was her lot, she decided. Unless the drawers of the serpentine front dresser contained something, and that would have to wait. She needed a nap. Something would present itself when she woke again. It was very comforting to know she would wake again.

"She's asleep," Dolly informed Roger.

159

"Good," he grunted.

Roger was sitting on the floor, watching the Carousel go round and round. He had provided a passenger, the little Gretel from the Gingerbread Dollhouse, who rode in one of the chariots. She could not be imagined to be enjoying the ride, for her face was forever fixed in the expression of cornered terror appropriate to the witch's hearth. She still wore the dog collar, glinting like a wedding ring, around her neck; Roger had slipped the chain but found the collar glued to her bisque skin.

But Roger was enjoying the ride, if she wasn't. He listened to the turn-of-the-century music that tinkled from the tiny speakers and the counterpoint of the mechanical grinding and rubbing of the merry-go-round itself. It was a nice bit of work.

"The dresses didn't fit," Dolly said, bringing him back to the real world.

"What about her own things, the jogging clothes?"

"I washed them and put them away."

"Leave them out for her. It's better than nothing."

"She would be difficult," Dolly sniffed.

"She kept down her broth?"

"Ummm." Dolly was searching for a cigarette.

He interpreted that as affirmatory. "I figured she had. I didn't hear you pissing and screaming."

Dolly laughed. "I never liked sick kids. Harrison was always sick. Just pigging, mostly. One of those children that refused to eat anything but junk, you know? And then, after marrying Lucy, he converted to health foods and was obnoxiously virtuous about it."

Roger did know about that kind of kid. He had been one himself, though blessed with a digestive system apparently superior to Dolly's dead son. And he hadn't given it up, not until he met Dolly.

He sat back on his heels. Dolly rarely talked about her family. He couldn't help knowing things about her in a vague way, absorbed as if by osmosis from the media. It was like meeting a neighbor everyone talked about but that one didn't, well, neighbor with.

Of the few family pictures in the apartment only the Sartoris portrait of Dolly's mother was accorded any prominence. It had given Roger the creeps until he figured out why; it was perfectly life-size, just like looking at someone else's face, at least as far as the scale was concerned. Hinting around about it, he realized, too, that Dolly was not aware of it.

Beyond that, the near-total absence of family portraits didn't require a degree in psychology to understand. Dolly didn't want to be reminded that the late husband, or late Dad, had ever existed. Just Mom, the late son, and the grandkiddies, and the last three in discreet silver frames in equally discreet corners.

"Hey," he said, trying to be light about a potentially dangerous subject, "I thought rich people had maids clean up after their brats."

Dolly grimaced from within a halo of smoke. "The little darling always managed to do it on nanny's night off."

"Rough," Roger observed insincerely, turning back to the Carousel.

"What do we do next?"

"What?"

"What do we do next? About *her?*"

"Feed her up. Try to get her healthy. That means keeping her warm and giving her something to do."

"Like what?"

"She's used to strenuous exercise. She ought to be getting it again, as soon as she can. She should make her own meals, read books, listen to music, walk in the garden. Take up knitting. Shit, I don't know. Anything to stimulate her. So she won't deteriorate and go crazy."

"Basket-weaving?"

"Call it what you want. She's people, not a pet or a prisoner. She needs to be occupied."

The word *occupied* had unpleasant connotations to Roger. It was what the Germans did to the French and the Poles and half of Europe, what the Americans did to the Japanese, the Russians to the East Germans. What the victors did to the losers. But that wasn't what he meant. It just felt like something walking on his grave. He didn't like it; it had just slipped out.

"This is more complicated than I thought it would be, Roger. It really is," Dolly complained.

"That's what makes it interesting," he grinned, though he didn't feel it. "Hey, maybe she could make her own clothes."

"She may have to. I can't very well go out and buy clothes

for someone a foot taller than myself for you to minimize, not when the FBI and half the world is looking for her. Maybe later. But not in the immediate future."

The thought of the world looking for Leyna Shaw made Roger feel funny. He and Dolly, they were outlaws.

"When the heat dies down," he said.

He wished he had a white fedora and a pinstripe suit. Dolly would make a great moll. *Dot* he would call her, and she'd wear a red dress with white polka dots on it and a scalloped collar, and those strappy heels that were so sexy. He realized that she was smiling at him.

"What were you thinking about? You had such a funny look on your face," she said. The tip of her tongue crept out and touched her upper lip.

"My mug," he told her. "Mug's the word."

She leaned back against the closet door. Her eyes were alive with speculation.

"Mug," she repeated, and Roger knew she knew all about mugs.

9

The room was dark when she woke. Feigning sleep in case the Giants were watching, she lay quiet, listening. The depth of silence convinced her at length that she was truly alone.

Ignoring ravenous hunger, she took a long bath, drawing it out until the water became tepid. The one light in the bathroom, an old-fashioned lotus-shape fixture, spread a feeble, rather romantic cocoon of light over the tub. She was surprised to feel some faint heat from it.

Quickly chilled, probably because she was down to skin and bones, she abandoned the bathtub. She could see the fading glory of her bruises, at least down the front of her. Despite the fact she was ready to kill for food, she appeared to be healing.

She examined herself in the mirror of the wardrobe door. Her backside was decidedly dappled with the ghostly motley of healing bruises. Her hipbones stuck out like the edge of a child's sandpail half buried in the beachsand. She dismissed the examination with an internal *ugh* and proceeded to pull the bed apart so that she could drape a sheet around herself.

This time she devised a tied-on, draped costume. She looked, in the mirror, quite a lot like a walking pillow slip, after knotting the sheet at the shoulders, wrists, and ankles. It made her giggle. Rolling a real pillow slip, she tied it around her waist as a belt.

"Good-bye best-dressed list," she muttered.

The draping at least covered those awful bones.

Opening the door to the hall, she stepped out of her bedroom for the first time. She stood in the doorway at the end of the hallway, a curious scarecrow backlit by the light from her room. The light glinted off the fixtures on the walls of the passageway, on the glass of framed pictures, and in her eyes, curious and feral as some predator. Turning on lights as she went, she padded slowly down the hall. At the end, she turned and looked back. Now the hall was smaller, shorter than it had seemed in the half-dark. It was simply furnished with a marble-topped pier table and a pair of delicate armchairs with white brocade seats. Automatically, she typed them: Duncan Phyfe.

She arrived at a choice of two doors. One of them, at the very end of the corridor, promised to lead to another hall or stairway. The door on her left was either a bedroom, bathroom, or closet door. Opening, she peeked into complete darkness. The door itself blunted the light from the hall. Moving sideways into the room, she tried to guess where the light switch might be. After a panicky moment of blundering and groping, she located a lamp. She saw immediately if she had moved left instead of right, she would have found the wall switch immediately.

Once illuminated, the room turned out to be another tastefully decorated bedroom that she recognized, to her amusement, as a close but not exact copy of the Lincoln Bedroom in the White House. Whoever had done it had at least had the good sense to chuck the cabbage rose carpet that had always produced nausea in Leyna. It must have cost a mint to assemble the right pieces, but there was plenty of money spent on odder things, and it was beautifully done. Finding the right furniture would be sticky but not impossible. The Lincolns had been very much people of their time and class; the taste that had furnished their original bedroom was probably duplicated in the tens of thousands, if not millions.

She sat down familiarly on the white crocheted bedspread. Mrs. Coolidge's? She couldn't remember. She would much rather have stumbled into the kitchen than this mid-Victorian museum bedroom, but it would do for a rest before pushing on. The springs creaked abominably and she was glad, feeling the lumpy mattress, that she was in the other bedroom. The windows, in this room and her own, showed her only the dark of night.

She thought about the rooms she had seen and lived in the

164

last few days. They were all the information she had about where she was, her real location. She could say to herself, *I am here* in this bedroom, this hall, this bathroom, wherever. Beyond that, they ought to tell where they were.

She had stayed in houses like this, in Virginia, New York State, New England. Eighteenth-century manor homes, signified by the dimensions of the rooms, the moldings, the decoration, tributes to the Enlightenment. Big houses, they were carefully preserved or restored by hefty chunks of cash. Real, awesomely expensive, and well-made antiques furnished them. Washington alone was full of houses like this, the residences of every type of top-level politico, legislator, bureaucrat, high-court justice, lawyer, special pleader, diplomat—the list went on forever. And she knew, personally and professionally, so many of them.

Why would she be in one of their houses, and which one might it be? It had that familiar quality to it that might mean she had been in it in the past, at least once, but it might also mean that it was just another example of a type of house she had been in too frequently. So tasteful, so Colonial, so boringly careful. She was stuck with the thought that it was possible she knew this house better than she could remember. If she had injured her head, she might have knocked loose pieces of memory that might or might not come back. It was only too likely that the mystery was in her silly head.

She closed her eyes, resting them. A slight headache, not worth working up an advertising fantasy for, brought on by hunger as much as too much thinking about her situation. Onward and probably downward. If this trek was going to be worth the energy expended on it, there had better be food at the end of it. Leaving the lights on, she left the room. A vague defiance stayed her hand from the light switch. *Let mine absent host turn the goddamn things off*, she thought, *or send His monstrous butler, the Hand. If I leave them on, perhaps He will notice that I'm here.*

The next door gave onto a broader hall and an elevator in a brass cage. After turning on all the wall sconces, she summoned the elevator, which creaked ominously downward from somewhere above her. Waiting for it, she noted nervously, as if to distract herself, that the hall was furnished with a pair of pier tables, lovely Federalist pieces, supporting expensive bric-a-brac. A single Aubusson runner covered most of the dark wood floor. A chased brass umbrella stand with a walking stick in it occupied one corner; a rubber plant half as tall as herself squatted in another.

The elevator arrived and its doors opened with a rattle. Suddenly her mouth was dry—*it was too much like an open mouth*—and sweat trickled in her armpits. She gave herself a mental shake and stepped firmly into the cage. It settled abruptly and she grabbed the handrail inside convulsively.

The panel inside read *1-2-3-4,* but there was no indication of which floor she presently was on. Concentrating, she guessed the second floor because that was a place where bedrooms were likely to be located. She pushed *2,* thinking if her guess was right, nothing would happen and she would make another choice. But she had guessed wrongly; the doors rattled shut, and the elevator lurched downward. Above her, machinery ground painfully. She remembered then, the horror story she had read on her honeymoon. About a haunted hotel, with an elevator that ran itself at night. Empty. It was like this one, an antique curiosity.

She told herself she was being silly, giving into the jim-jams, on the strength of a fiction. It wasn't as if the elevator in the Overlook Hotel had really existed, really been haunted. Gritting her teeth, she forced herself to touch the cool satiny brass of the doors. They smelled like brass; she didn't have to rub her nose on them to know that. They were real. This was just an elevator, a box on a pulley.

It was a very short trip. The elevator lurched to a stop almost as soon as it started. Apparently she had traveled one floor down. She looked through the brass grill into darkness. Her fingers lingered near the plate, wanting to push *3* and return to known territory. But the hollow in her interior, and a growing uneasiness about the elevator persuaded her to continue. She would brave the secrets of this floor because she had no choice. Stepping out carefully, she waited for her vision to adjust to the lack of light.

Waiting, she thought affectionately of her apartment. Furnished monastically with a narrow bed, carpeted in low-pile navy blue that climbed the walls to the blank white ceiling with its transparent plastic squares covering chaste fluorescent tubes, it had few secrets. The self-indulgence of an enormous closet, invisible when its doors were closed, was one. She told herself she had to keep her duds somewhere.

There was minimal furniture: the bar, a modular sofa, a hidden stereo system, a single shelf of hardcover books, all weighty tomes of great literature, with one each in Chinese and Russian, signaling that she was not a jumped up actress but a serious person. There were no plants for she found few houseplants worth their keep and was allergic to cut flowers. She didn't like cats and thought it cruel to keep a dog in a city apartment. That left small and necessarily caged animals for companionship and a touch of the vulnerable.

After ruling out birds as too messy and fish as hard work and temperamental, she settled on a pair of female gerbils. They turned out to be pesky little beasts, given to midnight noises, nearly constant pooping, and squirming attempts at escape, whenever she cleaned their cage. Once they achieved sexual maturity, they took to fighting with each other, bloody battles that left their cage smeared with gore and littered with bits of tails. At last, sickened by one such tiny night-war, she gave them to the daughter of the building supervisor.

The one really striking piece of furniture in her apartment was an Irish hunt table that had been a wedding present from her husband. It seated ten around its glossy mahogany oval and was invaluable for entertaining, being not only functional but a clear statement that she had excellent taste and could afford it.

There were no pier tables, no commodes, no end tables, no glass coffee tables. She loathed small tables. Her husband's family possessed houses full of tables, underfoot at every turn, like kids or harems of small dogs. Perhaps they knew something she didn't know about the intrinsic value of small tables. Maybe the damn things were as good as gold in a pinch, but to her, being rich was simply the Curse of Tables.

In the near dark outside the elevator, she sensed that she was in another hall, some kind of foyer. She thought she could discern a railing, as if on the landing of some stairwell. Moving along the wall, she felt for a light switch. It was a long and unrewarding grope, in which she became intimate with a stretch of brocade wallpaper and the moldings. She reached a corner and turned it, flailing desperately. Then made contact with a new surface, solid wood, paneled like a door. Her hand flew instinctively to knob level, swept the width of the door, and found the cool brassy sphere. She let out the breath she had not even been aware she was holding in one sour hiccup. The knob turned easily. At least the door was unlocked. She pushed it slowly open. She licked salty perspiration from her upper lip. The sense of trespassing was very strong now; she felt like a little girl exploring her mother's dresser drawers, or listening in the dark of night outside her parents' bedroom door.

Once through the door, she explored the nearest wall until her fingers encountered a plate, a cold ceramic rectangle, studded with nice, round, ribbed buttons. Rheostats. Grinning in triumph, she pressed them all at once.

The lights came on at their highest settings. Small suns like flashbulbs exploded in her now dark-accustomed eyes. She crouched, flinching away from something she could not name, but feared as much as death. Her heartbeat seemed enormously loud in the cavernous hall illuminated by a series of chandeliers and from standing candelabra as tall as young saplings ranked along the walls like guards. Walls of white marble rose from a white floor. The pillars, also of white marble, and as big around as a big man's chest, reached to the white ceiling. It was blinding. Except for the red carpet that ran the length of the room, it was as cool and chaste as a mausoleum. It made her shiver, curled up in the corner, barefoot in her sheet.

She knew then, looking down this hall, why she was possessed by déjà vu, why the other bedroom copied Lincoln's, and her own, she realized, the Queen's bedroom. The place was a ghost of the White House. She had been in and out of that ark often enough to see immediately what this was meant to be. The fear left her, to be replaced with puzzlement. It made her a little dizzy to think about it. Or perhaps she was dizzy from lack of food. She could not think about this crazy duplication now. She had to locate food, keep her body and soul together, nevermind her free-floating mind.

Walking slowly down the hall, she glanced into the entrance foyer that mocked the North Entrance of the White House. It was bizarre, seeing it empty even of the guards who should be sitting near the private staircase. Except the private staircase wasn't there, either. It just didn't bear thinking about. She pushed through the door at the other end of the hall, wandered through another short hallway where there was a massive staircase in dark wood. Knowing what was on the next floor, at least in part, she felt she could ignore it, for the time being. She was sure there was no kitchen up there, anyway. It didn't make sense, on the basis of what she knew.

The light switches to the next room, on her left, were easy to find in the spill of light from the huge Cross Hall. Pushing them, she turned the knob on one half of a pair of double doors. She walked through into what was obviously a dining room. Leyna didn't notice the handsome draperies in the windows or the mirror gloss of the table. The flowering of the chandelier and the blooming carpet went unnoticed. First, she saw the fruit bowl on the table, part of a rococo surtout-de-table that had been abbreviated into a more elegant centerpiece. The colors of the fruit gleaming in the gold, reflected in the mirrored base of the surtout which was like a filigreed tray, glassed at the bottom, and gold on its base and sides, left her weak in the knees. The warm fruit colors were almost the only colors in the room, with its white walls, gold fixtures, gold and silver flowered carpet, and dark wood furnishings. And the scent of apple, banana, pear, grape, and orange started saliva in her mouth, obliterating any other odors in the room as surely as the fruit colors drew the eye from the cool decoration.

She snatched a Red Delicious apple from the bowl. Touch should have told her, for the weight, the density, the surface were not right, but she was very hungry. Perhaps her senses were unreliable. Food. She bit into it greedily, thinking she would like it very much if the juices ran down over her chin. One bite was enough.

She sprayed the mouthful of scented dough over the glossy wood of the table and hurled the false apple against the wall. It exploded softly, showering the carpet, leaving a smear of lipstick red on the white wall. She spit little bits of dough all over the carpeting, and then the small amount of spittle she could summon. The taste and texture of the stuff was like scum on her teeth, and she couldn't get it out.

The tears came silently, dripping into her mouth with their salt taste. A guttural moan escaped her and then rose in a wail. She seized an orange and a banana in either hand and pitched them at the portraits on the wall. The grapes, more apples, oranges, and pears followed until the bowl was emptied and the room spattered with bits of dough and smears of color on the white and gold surfaces.

She sank into one of the high-backed upholstered chairs

and slumped over her hands. They made a lousy pillow, all knots and bones, and were almost thin enough to see the grain of wood through. They confirmed the trouble she was in. The tears were utterly undammed. She descended into pure misery.

Roger, on his way back from a pee, decided to look in on her. He was trying to tie the strings on his pajamas pants, almost impossible in the dark, half-asleep, when he backed into the dollhouse room. *Pee and a peek,* he mumbled to himself, chuckling at his own wit, and stopped in his barefoot tracks. The half-tied strings of his pajamas were totally forgotten. There were lights on in the Doll's White House, not just in her bedroom, but all over.

"Oh, shit," he murmured.

Instantly, he decided not to wake Dolly. He would see that everything was all right. Tell *her* about it in the morning.

First, he took his promised peek into Leyna's bedroom. He didn't expect to find her there and she wasn't. The bed looked like an army of whores had staged battle games in it. The lights led him, like a path of big fat breadcrumbs in the moonlight, to her.

But it was no relief to find her. Huddled up in a chair in the State Dining Room, her sobbing was distressingly audible, a faint hiccuping sound. It had been a serious mistake not to have gotten speakers and cameras in, he thought. Now he would certainly frighten her if he spoke, adding to her upset.

"Please," he whispered.

She sat up and stared around her, poised to scurry away like a small animal.

"Please." He kept his voice soft and gentle. "What's wrong?"

There was no response. She just sat there, fixated on his eye that peeked at her through the window. He waited. Patience, he told himself. That was how the cat got the mouse.

He studied what he could see of the room. The broken pieces of ersatz fruit puzzled him. Then he understood.

"You're hungry!" he exclaimed, forgetting about frightening her.

She moaned and shrank away from him.

The Eye blinked rapidly and went away. She wanted to run and hide before it came back. But it would find her, she was sure of that, and she was so tired and hungry. Maybe it would feed her. The thought evoked a mad chortle. She was certain that hunger caused these hallucinations of Giants and their Parts. And her delusions of Giants, in turn, fed her. She could make nothing of it. Insanity.

It took Roger fifteen minutes to sneak into the bedroom to retrieve the minimizer from the closet and then to rummage the kitchen for some grub, zap it, and return to the Doll's White House. She was dozing by then, slumped over the table, still hiccuping irregularly in her sleep.

It was necessary to remove a wall, actually less noisy than trying to open one of the windows. He did it as if he were a surgeon cutting something nasty out of someone's brain. Moving slowly and smoothly, he piled an assortment of miniaturized fruits and vegetables, a chunk of cheese, a loaf of bread, and a six-pack of Heineken neatly on the table. He could feel her small heat near his hands. It made him want badly to touch her, comfort her. But he resisted, feeling she would only be frightened. Some other time.

To wake her, he rattled the wall just a little putting it back in place. She jerked convulsively, coming out of her doze, and he saw saliva glistening on her hands where she had drooled as she slept. He was sure from her dazed expression that she had not seen the wall out of place.

She might not have noticed if he'd left it out. Stock still, she stared at the food on the table. Then, with a deep pleased sigh, she reached out for the banana. He suppressed a chuckle when she sniffed it carefully. He wished he'd been around to see her try the fake fruit. Lucy's unknowing revenge, and it made him marvel at how the world went round. Good thing the stuff hadn't been the kind made out of pins, but surely she would have noticed that. She must have been pretty hungry to go for the dough fruit.

A good appetite, he told himself, was a good sign. She crammed the banana into her mouth in a very unladylike way. She looked around at him, with her big wide unblinking eyes, and shoved the last bit of banana into her mouth with her fist. Just like the monkeys at the zoo. She dropped the peel on the table and looked away from him, back to the business at hand.

A tiny hand went directly for the beer. Roger grinned. Best

thing for her, full of good stuff. He watched her upend the green bottle and gulp a nice mouthful. It made him a little thirsty to watch. Not too fast, he wanted to tell her, savor it. She seemed to hear him without his ever saying it. She looked at the tiny twist-off cap in her hand as if she had never seen one before and dropped it on the table. One more good swig and she wiped the back of her hand across her mouth and put down the bottle, in favor of a bit of the cheese.

The Eye watched her and she watched it, out of the corner of her eye. It was not Dolly Hardesty's eye; this one was brown and seemed, perhaps because it *had* fed her, rather kind.

The weakness was passing off. She was starting to feel the food, not just filling the hole in her middle, but in the steadying of her trembling muscles, the diminishing of her headache. It all tasted like manna from heaven. She did savor the tastes, deliberately slowing the rate of her consumption.

She finished off the first bottle of beer with a round, satisfying burp. It brought up the mingled flavors of the Heineken, banana, bread, and a creamy Danish cheese she had always liked. The combination was no less wonderful the second time around. Tipping back her chair, she surveyed the remains of her feast.

After some consideration, she decided that one end of the centerpiece would do for a three-sided tray. With the rimless side held against her body, she could safely transport the rest of the food and drink back to her bedroom. A head of Boston lettuce tried to get away, rolling off the heap. She propped it into place, and moved slowly out of the room, bearing her tray pregnantly before her. It was immensely satisfying to climb back into bed and picnic on more beer, bread, and Havarti cheese. By the time she had upended the second bottle, she found the whole situation amusing. She belched loudly and giggled.

The Eye that wached her followed her passage back to bed. It peeked in at the bedroom window while she wallowed in the sudden, incredible luxury of a full stomach. She ignored it. It was much more fun to slip into a tipsy doze. If she dreamed of a liquid brown sun in a land of bread and cheese and strange, doughy bananas, she had forgotten by morning.

Roger watched until she had fallen asleep. Passed out. He couldn't help grinning. The dollhouse was still lit up as if for some state entertainment. He hit the main switch. It hit him all at once that he was dead on his feet. He had forgotten, watching his teeny tiny woman, that it was very late and Dolly, sleeping while he looked after Leyna, would not allow him to sleep in. She had a busy day all planned for him. With a faint surge of resentment rising in his heart, he crept off to his own bed.

The next day began badly. Ruta bitched to Dolly that she didn't know how she was supposed to cook when her vital supplies were pilfered in the night. Dolly jumped on Roger before he had so much as a sip of his coffee, accusing him of breaking his diet. Wearily, he showed her the state of the State Dining Room, its walls still smeared, the fruit like Ichabod Crane's pumpkin in shatters, and the evidence in Leyna's bedroom that the food had gone into her, not Roger.

"Beer!" exclaimed Dolly. "You gave her beer?"

She had to find something to pick at, if he was innocent of the first sin of which she had accused him.

"It's full of carbohydrates and good stuff," Roger defended himself.

"She looks like she passed out to me."

Roger took a peek in the window. Leyna was sprawled across the bed, snoring gently. There was a distinct aroma of stale beer in the room.

"You have to take better care of her," he muttered.

"Me? I didn't give her the beer."

"No, I mean she's really thin. She's got to be fed up, get some weight back on her. And the clothes. She still needs some clothes."

"I'll give her the jogging outfit. I haven't got anything else just now."

"How about dolls' clothes?"

Dolly's eyes narrowed as she thought rapidly. "I'll check into it."

Roger stared down into his coffee cup. Black and bitter and about as filling as a gust of wind.

173

"Okay," he sighed. "I'm going to the gym."

Maybe he could sneak out and find a jelly doughnut somewhere. He didn't mind the workouts. While his body was occupied, he found he thought better. It was a curious phenomenon to him. He'd like to look up the scientific literature and find out what was going on inside himself. Something to do with the old alpha waves, no doubt, but that would be the obvious, surface development. Something had to trigger those brain waves.

That morning's workout he devoted to thinking about Leyna. He was more and more convinced that she should be left alone to make the best adjustment to her new life. She should do for herself, to give her something to do. And the shocks would be, ah, minimized. But he was too out of breath to laugh at his own witticism. Yeah, the walls should stay in place; their hands should stay out of the Doll's White House. It disturbed her to be watched, therefore their watching must be unobstrusive.

Obvious solution: Zap television cameras and install them. Dolly would wince at the expense because he would have to use the best color cameras, not the cheap black-and-white boxes banks used for security. It was something they should have done right away.

Maybe he was getting soft, but the kicks were mostly gone from the act of stealing. He had Dolly, at least some of her, some of the time. And he had his teeny tiny woman and his minimizer. That ought to be enough for any sane man.

Dolly lit a cigarette impatiently. She couldn't believe Roger's reaction. Take a man's advice seriously and get it blown back in your face every time, like so much cigarette ash.

Roger fingered the dolls' clothes she'd purchased, and giggled. Slipping an index finger and a pinkie into the sleeves of one dress, he bent the two middle digits down below the necklace for décolletage and danced his new puppet across the coffee table. When he picked up a pair of trousers and started to push his fingers into the legs, Dolly snatched them away.

"Jesus Christ," she hissed at him.

"I was just fooling," he apologized.

He looked at his fingers as if they had grabbed a strange tit without asking him first.

174

Dolly folded the little garments and returned them to their box.

"Got a letter from my mother," Roger announced.

"That's nice."

Dolly wasn't very interested in Roger's mother. One glance at the picture Roger carried in his wallet had made it clear she should save her energy.

From his breast pocket, Roger retrieved a much folded sheet of paper and smoothed it nervously on his knee.

"I really think I should go home and see her," he told Dolly earnestly.

"Oh, wonderful." Dolly sat down and crushed out her cigarette. "Is she sick, or something?"

"Well, no. But I think I should make a quick trip back home and set her mind at ease. She worries about me."

Dolly's eyebrows rose skeptically.

"Me too," she muttered.

Roger sighed and passed the sheet of paper to her. Taking it a little reluctantly, she grimaced at the scent of violets and shook it once, as if to bring it to order or shake off an insect.

It was written in a fine, spidery scrawl; she read:

Dear Roger,

How is my baby doing in the Big Bad City? I couldn't help it after you called last night I just cried. You'd think I would be used to being an old lady all by myself now. But when you went away to college, you came home every weekend and I never felt like you were really, really gone. But nevermind me. I am just an old woman all by myself with no husband and no chicks to cluck over.

I am okay, except for slow bowels and I asked Dr. Silverstein about that, and he said I have to expect some change with age. I have a new girl to train in the office and she is so stupid but what do you expect. All she is interested in is her hair and her boyfriend. I guess I can remember what that was like, old fossil that I am, and probably I was foolish to pass up my chances to get married again after your daddy passed to the Other Side but I felt my boy needed me and I had to think of you first. Thanks for the scarf with the Big Apple on it. It goes real good with my pink pantsuit and I feel like a regular world traveler when I wear it. The girls at the office ask me did I get it in New York visiting you and I say, "No, I haven't been there yet but I expect Roger will ask me anytime now, as soon as he's settled."

Well, I won't take up any more of your valuable time, hon. I like the postcards you send but I sure would like a nice long letter or another call, or better yet, to see you at the door when I get home from work some night. Supper's a dull business without my boy cracking jokes to me. I just sit in front of the news and can't get my meal down for the terrible things going on. Then I just sit around watching the shows until bedtime with not a soul to pass the time of day with. Probably you're out on the town with some cute girl, eating in fancy restaurants, and going to shows. I hope you don't overspend your pay. Foolish living always catches up with a person, hon; you may think me an old foggy, but lots of girls are not very nice, especially in a place like New York, full of homosexuals and other wicked people.

Well, I am going to try to get some sleep tonight for a change (a woman just three years older than I am over on Ocean View Drive was murdered in her sleep by a burglar or pervert or someone last Thursday night; she was a retired schoolteacher and a spinster and all by herself). Maybe I will have the beans to tackle some of the chores around here tomorrow. The screen door is awful loose. If I can't fix it, I'll have to hire someone and I'm afraid it's going to be terribly expensive. I don't guess on my income I can afford a Mexican gardener yet.

Spare a thought for your mom, baby. She's thinking of you all the time.

Love,
Mom

Dolly finished the letter with a fine bloom of red in her cheeks. She folded it up and thrust it back at Roger.

"Does she always write like that?"

"That's the longest she's ever written." He put the letter carefully back into his breast pocket. "She's not used to me being away, not for this length of time. She's dependent on me."

176

"Do you think it's wise to give in to this kind of blatant emotional manipulation?"

Roger's chin set stubbornly. "I think I should go home and calm her down a little."

"Do you?" Dolly stood up and stalked to the window to stare angrily at an oblivious Manhattan. "Well, I wouldn't want your mother to get all upset and trembly."

This was genuinely distressing to Roger. He had dared hope for some understanding from Dolly. It had not been an easy choice, torn as he was between his concern for Leyna, his need for Dolly, and guilt over his mother.

He made excuses. "I should close up my workshop there. There's stuff I could use here, and it isn't safe to leave it behind."

The hint of finality in his plans soothed Dolly.

"You're going to work here?"

"If you could find me a corner, that would be tremendous."

"I want you to. You won't stay away long, will you?"

She had only to look at him to make Roger waver.

"A week, no more," he promised.

She smiled and leaned against him, "Just don't go off and forget me like an umbrella or something."

"That's not very likely, is it?"

Roger put his arms around her. He was a spy leaving his little woman to plunge into some mad, foolhardy act of daring-do. He kissed her lightly. Let her remember him at this moment, a thin smile on his lips, acting as if he really thought he might survive to return.

When the door closed behind him, Dolly smashed a Chinese vase that was old when Christ was crucified onto the tiled hearth of the fireplace. It was the only available substitute for shouting at him, dancing on his frigging head. He was taking the minimizer away. What if his goddamn plane crashed and it was destroyed? What would she do then? He had no right to take it. It wasn't fair.

During her dance class, she worked herself into something like calmness. Lunch was deadly quiet. She had gotten used to Roger's foolish face staring at her over the avocadoes and shrimp. The place seemed so still and empty and she knew that only meant she was lonely.

She thought she had given up married-people habits forever. Now she would not be able to sleep on his side of the bed, not for a long time, when the invisible property lines disintegrated. To whom would she talk, to whom tell the silly things that happened every day? She knew the drill; she had been through it before. It was just a habit, she consoled herself, more breakable than the tobacco habit with which she fouled her mouth and lungs every day.

Of course, she would miss bedtime. He had a wonderful sexual pliability. Tabula rasa he had come to her and she had written the stage directions until suddenly, he caught on. It had been amusing; still, when did that kind of thing ever last? Let him piss away his time holding his dreary mother's hand.

She drifted to the dollhouse room, standing in the doorway a long time. It wasn't her room alone anymore. Roger had claimed it, altered her Doll's White House substantially, and in doing so, made it partly his. It was Lucy, all over again, only more so. Lucy was circumspect in her possessiveness. She never forgot who paid the bills.

And now Roger dared to tell her how to take care of their house guest.

"Leave her alone," he said. "She has to learn to live in a new world."

Dolly circled the room restlessly, trying not to look at the big dollhouse. When she decided to allow herself one small peek at the bedroom window, she found the room empty. Listening carefully, she heard nothing. The bathroom door was closed. Was she in the can or not?

Going from window to window, she wished Roger had put in the cameras he had been talking about, seemingly forever. At last, she found her in the China Room, studying portraits. Lucy had discovered some extraordinary teenage boy in Texas to do the reproductions of the paintings in the White House. The Christy portrait of Grace Coolidge that Leyna was looking at just then was one of his nearly flawless efforts. As Dolly looked through the window, Leyna seemed to sense her presence and turned to her. Neither woman so much as blinked.

"The red dress in the wardrobe," Leyna said in her high tiny voice, "it's that one."

Her color was high; she was apparently both excited and frightened by her discovery.

"Yes," Dolly agreed. "I'm sorry it didn't fit."

Leyna shuddered.

"I'll get your clothes," Dolly offered.

Leyna stood silently before Grace Coolidge's portrait. She had seen it before, the day that Matt Johnson had given her the Grand Tour. It was just a publicity stunt, meant to generate speculation in the gossip columns that she and the nation's first bachelor president since Wilson's widowment were romantically interested in each other. You scratch me, I'll scratch you, and only the public is conned.

Nevermind that the whole press corps and his mother knew that Matt Johnson was a single-track homosexual. Women took to him as quickly as men did, because he was a relentlessly charming bastard, but his sexual bent was clearly defined. He had no personal friends of either sex, only allies, enemies, and sex partners from either camp.

It flitted through Leyna's mind when she first began to identify the curious place where she found herself that for some reason, Matt Johnson had elected to tuck her into a state bedroom while she recuperated. It was a wild thought, dismissed immediately. There were too many things out of place for this house to be the White House she had known. It was not quite right, as if it were in a different dimension, another world.

Yet here was Grace Coolidge's portrait, and all the china patterns she had seen the day of that publicity tour. Ugly china she thought it then, and still thought now, and that made her remember some of the more notable examples. She couldn't be mistaken.

Struggling out of bed with a mild hangover, she had eaten everything left from the previous night's meal. It made a screwy sort of breakfast, but it did the trick. The carbohydrates and about a quart of clear water flushed the shakes from her system. She had a nice soak in the tub and rewrapped her sheet. It was getting a bit crumby and smelled distinctly of spilled stale beer, but it was all she had. She brushed her freshly washed hair with a silver backed brush from the set that gleamed on the top of the dresser. Lovely things, sensual in their cool grace.

The wardrobe mirror told her she looked a little more alive. She twitched her sheet at herself and grinned. Now that she had satisfied, for the moment, her hunger, she discovered a new appetite. She had always been a solitary, content with herself. It was not any real desire for friendship, or companionship, that blossomed in her. Just the need to see a person the size of herself, a whole, sane being, to corroborate her own perspective. Not parts of people the size of fairy tale giants. Not Eyes, Mouths, Hands.

She steeled herself to go exploring again. The unnatural silence of the place had to end sometime. Sooner or later, the house must answer back.

Still, Dorothy's gray Eye found her in the China Room. Leyna wondered what part of her mind had thrown up the Other One, the brown-eyed Giant who seemed so much kinder and gentler to her.

When Dolly returned with the clothing, she found Leyna had returned to the safety of her bedroom. Opening a window noisily, she slipped the neatly folded pile of clothing into the room. Then she waited avidly for the little woman inside, watching her from the shadows of the bed hangings, to dress.

When the Fingers had withdrawn a safe distance and time from the window, Leyna retrieved the bundle from the floor. She knew them instantly: her jogging shorts, shirt, and brassiere. Once she touched them, she couldn't help hugging them to her. The first concrete evidence that she had once existed in another world.

The Eye returned to the window. Stricken with irrational guilt, Leyna hid the bundle behind her back. She stared back at the Eye, appalled by its enormous gelatinous sphere mooning at her through the glass. At last she could hold herself no more; she broke and ran for the bathroom, slamming the door behind her. It was a mistake. She was still too weak. The sudden exertion made her vision swim red and black behind her closed lids. She staggered and sank onto the toilet seat. Her stomach rebelled. Just in time, she turned and flipped the lid, losing her breakfast in the bowl.

Huddling by the cold wall of the bowl she wished to slip back into bed, into sleep, to wake up with the new nightmare behind her. With an ear-shattering grinding and shuddering, the bathroom wall was abruptly torn away. She screamed, more in anger than in fear. There was no place to hide in the narrow room; she was trapped.

The Eye, now part of a Face as large as the bathroom wall it displaced, stared in at her. Its Nose was as long as she was. A great, gaping, red-rimmed Mouth breathed foully on her. She could fall into the Mouth like Alice down the rabbithole and never be seen again.

"Don't hide from me!" Dolly roared at her.

Leyna covered her ears. Tears streamed over her cheeks. The bundle of clothing slipped from her grasp to the bathroom floor.

In a softer Voice she was ordered, "Get dressed and I'll put the wall back."

Leyna moaned. Spittle bubbled down her chin. She had to seize the side of the bathtub to pull herself upright. The knots she had tied in the sheet to costume herself were rocky and stiff. Fumbling with them, she broke fingernails and scraped her papery knuckles raw. In a few minutes, the sheet puddled on the floor around her feet. She shivered violently, covering herself unconsciously with her hands.

"Come now, we're all girls here," Dolly said, and hooted. "Get dressed."

Leyna began, trying to remember what she had done with her clothes. She fished them out from under the crumpled sheet. The bra was the hardest part. A sports bra with no hooks to catch, it had to be pulled on and kept from twisting itself. Then the shorts and shirt and she stood clothed again.

"Nasty thing," Dolly reprimanded. "Don't wear panties like a good girl, do you? Always ready, aren't you?"

Leyna shook her head vigorously in denial. She was not a bad girl. There was enough spittle in her mouth to explain her personal idiosyncrasies about running dress.

"You ran away," Dolly went on.

Leyna bowed her head.

"You didn't wait for these."

Leyna looked up. On the tip of an enormous Finger, her jogging sneakers, with socks stuffed neatly under the tongues, pointed their red toes at her.

Dolly began to hum as she slipped the wall back into its slot. The sound broke over Leyna in continuous waves that vibrated like the tires of huge trucks passing in the night. In the silence that followed, Leyna went to her knees. Her mind was a blank screen. No clear thought focussed on the white wall of emotion. She crawled, on hands and knees, back to the bed.

Holding her breath, Dolly watched her. For long moments she stared at the huddled form under the blanket. She smiled, toyed with a pack of cigarettes, but did not light one. She had no desire to smoke. For once, she was having fun.

10

The screen door was off its hinges just enough to throw the whole door out of line. Roger made a mental note to fix it before he left. It was just one of half-a-dozen superficial out-of-order flags around the house. His absence showed in minor ways.

Dropping his duffel bag on the porch, he pushed open the door, carrying only the minimizer in its camera case with him. The house was empty, silent except for the drip of the kitchen faucet. He had planned it this way, wanting a quiet time in which to look things over and gird himself before his mother arrived home from work.

He opened the refrigerator. She had stocked it for her prodigal son. Hesitating for a second between a stick of pepperoni and a jar of pickled eggs, he chose the pepperoni, hooked a beer, and trotted purposefully down the stairs to his Fortress of Solitude.

Among the dusty cobwebs of the cellar, the beer went down like lemonade. Anticipating the soldiers that remained in their neat plastic nooses in the refrigerator made him feel mildly perverse.

His absence showed in the workshop in the film of dust over the grime and trash of his past life: fingerprints, rusty can rings, grease, and oil smears. The place smelled stale and looked tacky.

He ran a hasty inventory, rummaging through cupboards and shelves, mentally marking what he ought to ship East, what he ought to destroy or discard. In the morning, he would go to a market or liquor store for boxes.

Overhead, the screen door opened with a scream, and he heard the clip clap of his mother's sensible heels. Wiping mouse turds from his hands on a handy rag, he picked up his pepperoni. He locked up quickly and trotted up the stairs, shouting gaily, "Mom! That you?"

That night, they went to dinner at a fancy restaurant in a big new shopping mall. She prattled; he slipped easily back into the old habit of hearing without listening. Bending his elbow over steak Diane and getting mildly plastered on an expensive, sour-tasting wine, he allowed the flow of her chatter to pour over him like a caress. Deep in his own alcohol-dimmed thoughts, chewing lustily on a chunk of rare meat, he didn't notice for some time when she stopped talking. He looked up when the silence penetrated to catch her watching him with a gleam of tears in her eyes.

He wiped his mouth, feeling distinctly like a terminal patient whose condition is being kept from him.

"Something wrong, Mom?" he asked, unable to think of anything else to say.

Slowly, sorrowfully, she shook her head. But she reached across the table, grabbed one of his hands and clutched it convulsively. Roger let her hold on, but he shifted uneasily in his seat, hoping no one in the restaurant would notice.

"I'm just so glad you're home again," she snuffled. Burying her face in her hanky, she muffled her sobs.

There was nothing Roger could say to any of it. And it didn't seem quite the right moment to mention he was going back East as soon as he could dispose of his gear and settle her.

A couple of days later, Roger shocked himself by losing his way to the Salvation Army store on Redondo Street. After delivering a box of his old duds, he wandered around the store, having a look-see at the old baby stuff and flaky television sets. A woman pawed over a jumbled heap of second-hand nightwear on a table. Another tried on an assortment of shoes. A clerk grinned hopefully at each of them in turn. Roger was overwhelmed, in a most un-Roger-like way, with sheer anomie. It was giving away his old and comfortable clothing, he told himself, and knowing that soon, strangers would pluck them from the general ruck and hold them up in a critical light. And losing his way, in a town he had lived in most of his life. The sense that something was happening to him, something he couldn't stop and that might never end, that would be forever, oppressed him.

He passed down a rack of coats. Idly he caressed a shabby fur coat. The fine silky hairs passing through his fingers recalled the day Dolly had sent him to bring her coat from its closet. There was an enormous walk-in closet in her bedroom, full of more clothes than she ever wore. She never gave any of them away, so the range in hemlines and style was an education in the whims of fashion for a couple of decades. The closet had a closet, a chilly slice in the very back where she kept her furs. He had stepped in casually, ready to grab the right one and walk out, but the fur had been like water, all around him. Instinctively, he held his head, keeping his nose in the air, which was heavy with the peculiar dusty smell of the coats, and stagnant and cold as well. Simple claustrophobia created the sensation of drowning, but it had been a wonderful drowning, caressed by the furs.

She became impatient and found him there, shook him loose of his trance. She might have guessed, for that evening, she allowed him to jump her while she still wore the coat. He pretended he was a crew member of the Starship Enterprise, establishing good interstellar relations, this time, with a native of the planet Nutria.

It was light years from the Salvation Army store. He diagnosed space fever, only to be expected when an old spacer like himself makes a planet-fall, after years among the stars. He gave the balding raccoon a final pat and left the store, hoping he could find his way home better than he had found his way to this place of the cast-off and abandoned.

His last day home was a work day for his mother, but she took a sick day so that she could see him off. She thought it was the least she could do, seeing that he had worked so hard, putting the house to rights. There was nothing Roger could say that would make her go back to work. He was not going to leave without her farewell.

In the space of a week, he'd made the necessary minor repairs around the house. He'd had her car serviced and arranged to sell his own, which had been garaged while he was away. After cleaning out his study in the cellar, he shipped a number of innocuous-looking boxes to Dolly's Manhattan address and carted several loads of one thing or another to shopping-center dumpsters. He was careful to do his cleaning out while his mother worked, in the hope that she wouldn't notice. What she would feel when she discovered his teenage clubhouse, his home at home, was now empty of all but the mouse-gnawed, scarred furniture, and the dust kitties and spider webs, he preferred not to think about.

He put his duffel bag on the porch. There was nothing else to take besides the minimizer, in its carrycase on his chest like some exotic good luck charm, to deposit in the rental car. His mother waited in the living room, which was dark in the middle of the day, the shades pulled against the sun. Standing near the door, he couldn't help twitching, wanting to run, to be done with her.

She broke the silent tension between them as if it were a sewing thread, with a quick snap of her teeth.

"You aren't coming back, are you, Roger?"

And he had kidded himself that mothers couldn't read minds.

"Don't be silly, Mom. I'll be back," he lied.

"You took all your clothes away," she accused him.

He shrugged. "They were too big for me. I gave them to the Salvation Army."

"Your car. You sold it."

"I told you. It's not worth maintaining one here. I'll rent one when I come home."

She had more evidence to marshal.

"You took your books away, too."

"I gave the kid books away. The other ones I might be able to use, so I sent them to New York. Where my work is."

"And where you're going to live. You'll stay there, and never come back." Her slack chin trembled in emphasis.

"I'm staying as long as the job lasts. For Christ's sake, Mom, a job is a job. It took me months to find this one, and it's a good one."

"Don't swear at me, Roger. I'm still your mother. I expect some respect."

"Sorry, Mom," he mumbled.

"Why can't I go with you?"

There, the big question was out of the bag. The last thing he wanted to hear.

"It's a bad time," he told her. "Maybe later, when I've got a good apartment, and I'm all settled. When we can get a decent price for the house. And I'm making enough so you won't have to worry about working for anyone." He couldn't think of any more conditions but he tried.

She watched him suspiciously. The set of her face told him she was buying his line about as much as she once bought his defense of being kicked out of graduate school. Behind the close imitation of an Incan mask, the only indictment was made: *If they say you're crazy, you must have been acting crazy. What's wrong with you, throwing away an education? Dad and I sacrificed for you. How could you put your opinions first?*

And his answer then: *I was right. They were wrong.* Now she was *they*. The issue wasn't so clear-cut.

He stepped hard on his growing panic. He was an adult man; he didn't have to quail before his mother's disapproval. It was his life, goddamn it. And excruciatingly late beginning, too.

"It's a woman, isn't it?" she said suddenly. Her eyes were bright, searching out the truth in his. "That's why you're so skinny and you got all those fancy new clothes."

Roger blushed. "Mom," he protested.

It was answer enough. Turning her face away into the shadows of the room, she acknowledged she had lost the undeclared war for her son.

He approached cautiously, bent, and kissed the cheek she presented to him. It was cold and slack, with the texture of an aging peach. But it was dry, and that was a relief. She was letting him go easily.

Driving away, he argued with himself. What place could he make for her in his new life? He might as well be living on another planet. What would Dolly make of her? No, he couldn't go back, not for good. He shrank from the implied promises of future visits as if they were something catching. It would be sinking back into the past, into a tar pit of guilt. His choice was made. A man had to live his own life.

He distracted himself finally by worrying about Leyna. Before leaving he had zapped a week's supply of food. No more than that, as a signal to Dolly that he would be back when he promised, drawn by the magnet of both his dollies.

Feeding Leyna had turned out to be more of problem than they'd anticipated. Ruta fussed about invasions of her kitchen. He'd installed a bar refrigerator and a microwave in the dollhouse room so that it was now possible to prepare food for their tiny house guest with a measure of discretion. The neat little appliances rather excited him; he would like to have one of each in his own bedroom. But soon, when Leyna was strong enough to care for herself, he would zap them and install them in the Doll's White House.

Roger thought eagerly that he would be happy to see her again. Very happy. And then, like a pinprick or a bee sting, he realized he meant Leyna.

There was a new meal: steak, potatoes, green stuff, pie, with a rose in a vase. She thought of restaurants she had been in that affected a single flower on a table. And in those pretentious places she had eaten similar meals, pretty and no doubt high-priced, but with the meat and other cooked food not quite hot, and the cold elements of the meal limp with sitting around. Someone goofing off at the microwave and everything done up hours and hours before the actual meal, to save work.

Still, she ate it. Wouldn't send it back if she could. Starvation is a wonderful way to keep the customers in line.

It seemed that the terrible hunger might be at an end. She had a bowl of fruit to snack on, a tin of cookies, a can of nuts. Nourished on a regular basis, thoroughly rested, and in her own clothes again, she felt herself once more. A desire for the physical exercise to which she was so long accustomed formed. Her thigh muscles had thinned and slackened. The bruises were the faintest shadow but her color was too pale, her bones too prominent. If she no longer looked like death warmed over, she still thought she might qualify for a place on a refugee boat. But she had gotten used to it; most of the time, she could look in the mirror and not wince.

She left her bedroom and wandered through the house. The place was uncanny. It gave her the creeps. She was constantly stumbling over objects she recognized. Even more unsettling were the times she expected to find something, a door, a desk, a rug, and it wasn't there.

At last she found the kitchen, in the lowest story of the house, along with a laundry room equipped to handle a huge establishment. It was all strictly pre-World War II. The laundry room took her back to the one in her grandmother's house in Chicago, with its huge sinks and presses and wringer washers, but it lacked the distinctive odor, the perfume of bleach, and soap, and heat. The enormous, old-fashioned kitchen was barren of food; if she had managed to find it before she could have starved to death in the middle of it. Like the laundry, it gave no sign of ever having been used. Bewildered, she wandered back upstairs.

She began to feel cooped up. There had been glimpses of green through various windows, but she had not had strength to venture outside. Knowing the South Portico would open onto the greater garden, she chose it for her exit.

Pressing her face to the glass doors, she could see the green of grass, trees, and shrubbery, encircled by a drive that passed just outside. A blur of colors centered in the green; she thought it was some kind of fantastic structure, like a circus tent, or a brilliantly flowered garden. When she pushed open the door, the greenery scented air rushed in upon her, and the faint sound of music reached her ears. The freshness of the air made her realize how long she had been inside, in rooms where the atmosphere was not precisely stale, but rather preserved, as in a library or museum.

Beyond the distortion of the glass, she saw that the blur of color was a Carousel. It was from there that the music emanated. She was drawn to it as if by a magnet; whoever can resist a merry-go-round? She watched it whirling by, riderless and ghostly. When it slowed and stopped, she hoisted herself onto its platform without thinking.

After circuiting the parade, she selected a black charger as her mount. She intended to sit on it for only a second or two, pretending to ride, trying to recall the sensations of her childhood, but the merry-go-round wheezed and creaked and began to spin again. As it slowly revolved, she had ample time to jump down. But she chose not to; it was simply too much fun to sit astride her magnificent black horse, riding it up and down, while the breeze of their passage lightened her hair. The smells of the vegetation intensified in the air current, as if they were being sucked liquidly along for the ride. It was glorious.

She stepped down when it stopped. Sometime she would ride it again. First there was too much else to be explored, much more that she needed to know, that the merry-go-round could not tell her. It started again as she backed away; apparently it was operated automatically. It was hard to leave it. As she stood and watched, a memory tried to form itself, struggled in her brain, and then faded beyond reach.

Thoroughly distracted, she turned her back on the music and sauntered down the lefthand arm of the drive. Peeking back at the house she came from, she was disconcerted to realize that a thick copse of trees obscured not only the additions to the White House on either side, but the buildings that should have been visible from the site. It struck her then that there were no additions, for she had not found any of the entrances to the wings within. The exterior was indeed that of the White House, but it was smaller, more compact, more the original White House than the one she had entered as Matt Johnson's guest. And of course it was only habit that made her look for the familiar landmarks around the White House. If this was not the White House, but some copy, it was unlikely that it existed within sight of Pennsylvania Avenue.

It made her head reel a little. She began to trot slowly away down the drive, looking back at the house every few seconds. The merry-go-round was not as unlikely an addition to the grounds as it might have seemed; she had witnessed enormous colorful tents erected in that very place for garden parties. Nor was it beyond the reach of Matt Johnson's imagination to plant a whole carousel in the backyard of the White House.

The confusion in her mind cleared suddenly. She remembered the curious disappearance of the Central Park Carousel. Only a few days before her accident. It brought her to a sudden stop, with a pain in her stomach as if she'd been punched. Abruptly, she sat down and covered her eyes, trying to work it out in her head. None of it made sense. A fierce black headache cramped her thinking.

She was carrying a handful of nuts in the pocket of her shorts. When the headache began to ease, she nibbled them. Slowly, her body relaxed and then, as the pebbled surface of the drive began to pinch her, became uncomfortable again. Scrambling to her feet, she shuffled on. Details, she told herself, enough details would paint the picture for her, in time.

Never having been much interested in plants and trees, it was hard for her to recall much about the grounds of the White House. Grass she knew when she saw it, all kinds, and a tree she recognized as a tree. She could tell an evergreen from a deciduous, a red maple from a willow. Shrubberies were bushes, and flowers came in different colors and tended to hug the ground except for climbing vines and sunflowers and hollyhocks. Not hopelessly ignorant, she could grin, but close to it. She knew magnolias by their smell, and a rose is a rose, isn't it? All that foofaraw came down to not being able to say exactly why this garden, like the White House she resided in, was strangely out of focus.

Her leg muscles were cramping. She slowed to a crawl and left the driveway, moving toward the wrought-iron fence, straining to see what might lie beyond it. A mild panic, or possibly the handful of nuts, knotted her stomach when she failed to discern anything beyond the fence itself. The need to know what lay beyond the boundaries of this small world kept her walking, though she told herself she needed to loosen the muscles that were protesting their sudden use. She blinked rapidly, hoping she had something in her eye that would presently, before she reached the fence, clear.

When she reached it, she touched it. Cold, not quite smooth, very distinctly what it appeared to be: iron. Her fingers traced the curleycues and uprights, the spear points, the bars and stylized flowers. They came away almost clean. Cautiously, she moved one hand between the iron tracery and beyond it. The tips of her fingers immediately encountered a hard, smooth, cold surface. Feeling through the gaps in the fence, she followed the wall she couldn't see to the top of the fence and as far beyond it as a tall woman could reach. She leaned hard against it, and felt no give. Staring very hard, not quite against it because of the intervening fence, she tried to see what it was made of and was startled to discern, abruptly, her own, scarily faint image. In anger and fear, she struck it with the flat of her palm. It did not care. She was the one who cried.

Turning from the fence after a moment, she crossed the grass back to the drive, blinking back the tears that now really did obscure her vision. Stumbling once or twice, she kept on going, because there was nothing else to do. At the bottom of the steps, she sat down. There had to be an explanation. If only she could stop screaming inside long enough to think clearly.

"What's wrong?" Dolly rasped.

Leyna cringed. She was still teary-eyed, blinking fast to clear her vision but not really wanting to see the being who spoke.

"You ought to be ashamed of yourself."

Hot breath blew over her as Dolly bent to scold. Instinctively, Leyna warded her off with her hands.

"Lots of people don't have such nice homes, you know. Lots of people don't have lovely meals, like you do."

Her great Hands were in motion overhead, like leather-winged birds of prehistory, with their enormous shadowy wingspreads. There was a grinding, groaning noise that Leyna had learned to recognize, the sound of a wall being moved.

"Look at this!" Dolly exclaimed in disgust. "What a mess! This room is a disgrace. It looks like pigs live here."

A Hand swept down and seized Leyna around the waist with two fingers.

Her scream ended abruptly when she was dumped roughly onto the bed and had the wind knocked out of her.

"I'm not your maid," the rant went on. "You just clean this awful-looking room up, and I mean right now. I worked hard to make this room nice. Special. *You're* not anything special, you know. Not now, you aren't. You just pitch in."

Leyna sat on her knees, seeing the room as if for the first time. It *was* messy, much messier than she had left it. The tray had been overturned, spilling dirty dishes and the dregs of her last meal to the carpet. The bedclothes had been ripped from the bed. The towels she had hung on their bars in the bathroom were now a tangled heap in the bathroom doorway.

"Get out of bed, you lazy cunt." A huge Finger flicked at her impatiently, catching the side of her head and knocking her backward.

She crawled away, crouched like a cornered animal in the farthest shadows of the bed-hangings. Her hair wild around her face, she screamed in a high, thin voice, "It's not my birthday!"

Dolly chuckled. It sounded like a breaker at the ocean, rumbling over the rocks.

An hour later, the room was flawlessly neat. The spread was smooth and tight across the bed. The towels hung in precision ranks in the bathroom. The tray was washed, dried, and stacked with spotless dishes. Leyna had knelt on the carpet and picked up crumbs with her fingers, scrubbed at the stains of coffee dregs and grease and salad dressing with a washcloth, later washed and rinsed in the bathroom. Now she sat by the fireplace in a prissy little Brewster chair, the nearest available dunce seat, with its caned bottom, high turned arms, and rigid back. Her hands were folded in her lap, her face smooth and empty. The wall was raised and removed. Dolly stood there in its place, a new wall that flowed like drapery and breathed.

"I forgot," she said calmly, "to give you clean linen."

A Hand hovered in the room, dropping a pile of folded bed and bath linen in a small heap on the carpet. With one Finger, she hooked up the spread from the bed and tore apart the neat tucks and corners. The towels were ripped from the bars and strewn over the room in a small tornado of damp cloth. Leyna ducked but not fast enough; the wet cloth caught her once, squarely in the face, as it was centrifuged from the Finger. This time Dolly laughed from her belly. It was like a train screaming in a tunnel.

The War had commenced.

Late in the afternoon, she woke. She had slept on the top of the spread, but Dolly had not returned to inspect the bedroom again. Her bladder was full and she was hungry.

She had been without plumbing recently enough so that she had no doubt that happiness was a dry bladder in a working bathroom. Almost cheerfully, she made for the bathroom and sat down. It struck her then she hadn't menstruated in some time. She had been nearly due when the accident happened. She supposed the trauma had caused her to miss one period. Surely now that she was better her cycle would begin again. When she stood up, with this female matter of no small importance on her mind, she pulled up her pants with one hand and pulled the chain with the other. The toilet flushed with the satisfying waterfall of the overhead tank.

What would she do when she did menstruate again? There was none of what her husband mockingly called feminine équipage in this bathroom. She would be compelled to ask for what she needed, a prospect that made her stomach ball with dread. It was bad enough to have those Eyes peeking at her while she slept, dressed, ate, and eliminated.

She stooped to wash her hands, splash water over her face, and fill a glass of water from the tap. Her mouth was dry with sleep; her thinking thick and muddily resentful. Abruptly the water slacked off when the glass was half full, and then, with a discolored dribbling, failed altogether. She turned both faucets to their most open position. Nothing.

Curious, she checked the toilet bowl. There was water, but it was disconcertingly low. She nibbled at the interior of her lip thoughtfully. Absent hosts make awkward landlords. Who to complain to when the water stops? So much for the little business of her menstrual cycle. Not that there was anyone she could complain to about the missing flux of blood, either. But the everyday plumbing of this house was more important than her monthly plumbing.

"Shit," she muttered.

She belly-flopped onto her bed. An orange would assuage her thirst for the moment and boost her energy as well. She selected one idly and made a small hole in it. Sucking it dry, she was as amused by the shriveling of the orange in its skin as she had been by the same trick, taught to her by her father, when she was a kid.

While she sucked, she considered her plumbing problems. Water was not some magical juice of the pipes through which it flowed. It had a source, a domestic source, such as a well, or a reservoir, or else a connection with city mains. Racking her brains, she could recall only one bit of knowledge about the White House water supply. It was not drawn from the city supply but from reservoirs, filled by tanker trucks from Virginia springs. It was a useless piece of information. She wasn't in the real White House. However uncanny a copy this place was, it was all too obviously a reproduction. Certainly Matt Johnson and his cohorts had not suddenly abandoned the Executive Mansion for her exclusive use, nor torn down their precious ugly offices in the wings on the way out.

Leyna was bored. She hadn't done a damned useful thing in days, other than cleaning house for the Great Bitch. Dropping the desiccated orange back into the fruit bowl, she determined she would give herself a quick course in plumbing. She might find a blockage, a leak, some explanation of the mysterious disappearance of the water. Nevermind that it had stopped as suddenly as it had started. It didn't bear thinking about. Action was the thing. She went looking for tools.

Padding down silent corridors and stairways to the domestic offices in the basement story of the house, she felt her skin crawl with the emptiness of the place. Passing the elevator, which she avoided using now that she had strength enough for the stairs, was a special trial. She wondered if it would help to whistle, as for a graveyard.

The institutionally ugly cupboards in the warren of rooms devoted to the baser needs of the mansion yielded one mean wrench and a cutting blade of the type she recalled from college art classes. The blade was strangely out of place, but potentially useful, at the very least as a fruit knife. She turned up a drawer of linen napkins, helped herself to one, and used it to wrap the blade, setting it aside to take with her when she finished. The wrench in her hand evoked a sudden feeling of competency, efficiency, in-chargeness. She began a futile search for access to a water system. There were rooms for ironing, washing, polishing the goddamn silver, but no suitably obscure entrance to a musty cellar full of engines for heating, cooling, and plumbing. No dusty grimy tanks to explore, with one ear listening for strange sounds in the gloom.

Disappointed, she returned to the kitchen. Turning on the faucets in one of the enormous porcelain sinks, she was not surprised when they were as dry as the ones in her bathroom. She dipped to her knees and examined the pipes under the sink. A couple of taps with her trusty wrench established that they were empty. Following them to the wall, she noted that they entered the wall at a slightly upward angle. It was puzzling. The angle would create a sure trap, a certain blockage in a kitchen sink, even to the eyes of an amateur.

Of course, this was a singular kitchen, absolutely spotless, utterly empty, and obviously as virginal as a busload of nuns. Where her daily bread was coming from, she could only guess. Staffing a mausoleum like this would be a problem for anyone less than the government. Her meals were evidently catered.

She shied away from the subject quickly. She knew perfectly well her meals had been delivered on several occasions by Giants. But they were figments of her disordered imagination, the dreams of illness and trauma. She had to presume that perfectly ordinary human beings brought her the grub on silver trays. It was her brain that put them in Dolly-masks and blew them up into monsters.

She carried the wrench and the linen-wrapped blade back to her bedroom. After hiding the blade between her mattresses, she emptied the fruit bowl onto the bed. The bowl might come in handy in the bathroom, to catch the dregs in the pipes.

She banged and wrenched for an hour under the bathroom basin, trying to move the joints of the pipes. At last she threw down the wrench in frustration and sent the bowl spinning against the wall with a quick kick. It clanged hollowly and came to rest with an enormous dent in the side. The pipes under the basin were apparently empty, anyway.

Her fingers were sore and grimy. She looked at them with distaste. Her nails were a mess, a disaster. She would have to find a pair of scissors or try the art blade, ugh, on them later. But first she was going to have a try at the water tank over the toilet. If there was anything in it, she would have it to drink in an emergency.

The connections to the porcelain tank separated easily. It was surprising that they had not sprung a leak. The threads in fact were damp; moisture beaded the joints. She positioned the bowl underneath and was rewarded with a pint or two of rusty looking water, mostly from the pipes above the tank, rather than from the tank itself. The pipes emptied themselves with a gassy gurgle and were silent. She stored the bowl of water in the wardrobe, out of sight.

It had given her an idea about where the water supply might be located. But first she needed a rest; she damped the end of a towel and cleaned her hands and nails as best she could. That left her with nothing immediate to do but with a definite thirst, and a growing desire for something besides fruit to eat. She'd like another steak. Or a nice ham sandwich. Or a coffee yogurt.

The room was growing dark. She switched on lights, made up the bed to a military neatness, and plumped the pillows. Her hands itched. She was conscious of their grimy second skin and tried hard to ignore it. She studied herself in the wardrobe mirror.

Tangled hair, a smudge on her nose. Her jogging shorts

hung loosely on her stringy muscles. Her sole perfume was the stale sour scent of her own sweat.

"Ugh, ugh, ugh."

She would have spit at herself had she any spittle to spare. She stretched out on the bed, beat. Climbing to the top of this crazy house, where the water had to be, would have to wait until the light came again.

In the morning she breakfasted on fruit. She could feel a canker forming in her mouth and her bowels were painfully gassy. She used the toilet; she had to. Then she started upstairs, looking for the water.

Out of breath, dirty, slimed with her own sweat, she came out onto the roof after a long, fumbling search. A white tank stood at the other end of the roof. She trudged to it, becoming gradually aware that it was semitransparent. She could see the waterline; it was three-quarters full. It was a long rectangle, lying on its long side, and its corners were blunted. One end was squarer than the other; when she investigated, this end appeared to be nearly flat, except for a pair of symmetrically placed dimples. The other end was very gradually tapered and ended in a blocky device that clearly controlled the flow. The stopcock was huge; Leyna had to straddle the neck of the tank to obtain leverage, and then tore most of the skin off her palms moving it. The pipe that descended from the stopcock into the roof let out a reassuring burp and the water in the tank began to burble.

She jumped off on the other side from her approach to watch the water level in the tank drop noticeably as the pipes below filled up again. This side was not purely white as was the other but had a faded legend on it. It was unreadable close up, so she stepped back a ways and pieced it together, a letter at a time. O-A-K-H-U-R-S-T and then there was another line, reading top to bottom, D-A-I-R-Y. Smaller letters on the next line stated F-A-T space F-R-E-E space M-I-L-K. She stood reading it over and over for a long time. It was always possible, she supposed, that someone had used an old milk tank to hold the household water supply. But she had never seen one that was semitransparent, clearly made of plastic. There's lots of things she'd never seen, she might scold herself, what does that prove? Not much, but the thing still looked like a goddamn plastic milk carton to her. Another detail for the lady journalist.

"Shit," she sighed out loud. Shit never ended, did it?

Dolly decided to do something nice for poor little Leyna. She had given her something to do, and it had been rather amusing, watching the little beast solve her plumbing problems. Well, Dorothy Hardesty Douglas was not some kind of unfeeling monster. She would give her little dollie a reward.

She started by calling Lucy Douglas, who was, from word one, quite obviously hostile.

"Let me talk to my little darlings," Dolly began.

"Pop's taken them to the swimming pool."

"Oh. What swimming pool is that?"

"The Y pool. In the town park."

"Ummm. I hope they don't catch something there."

Lucy fumed silently.

"Well, actually I'll like to talk to you, dear."

Lucy came back bluntly. "I really don't want to talk to you, Dolly."

"Oh, come now. Mustn't be a baby, now. Let's be grown-up. You've been wanting something to be mad about ever since I wised you up about Nick."

"Dolly, I don't have a grievance list. It's not worth my time or effort. I just don't feel friendly; I don't want to talk. And your interfering between Nick and me hasn't come to anything."

Lucy bit her lip; she hadn't intended to let that out.

It gave Dolly pause. That was satisfying.

"So you're back together." Her voice was cool and amused.

"Yes, we are."

"Well, it's your life."

"Yes, it is."

"Isn't that nice. Really. You know I'd be very happy if you remarried. I'd dance at your wedding. I don't bear you any ill will and I wish I could convince you of that."

"What do you want, Dolly?"

Another pause. Dolly, from the sounds of scratching, and thunking, was looking for a cigarette, nevermind the phone bill. The click and whoosh of her lighter, a sudden sucking breath and immediate exhale confirmed Lucy's supposition.

Finally, "Well, this isn't actually for me. It's for a friend. She saw the little reproductions you did of Grace Coolidge's and Angelica Van Buren's gowns. She wanted me to ask if you might do some dollclothes."

Lucy knew immediately she didn't want to do any more dollclothes and suspected Dolly's friend was in fact Dolly, but she couldn't help asking, "Period reproductions, you mean?"

"No. Simple contemporary children's clothes."

"Oh."

"On a slightly larger scale than the two pieces you did for me."

"Ummm. Sounds interesting. Who is this?"

She waited patiently to see if Dolly would continue her lie.

"No one you know," Dolly said airily.

Lucy's grim smile was intimated in the tone of her voice. "Oh, come on, Dolly. I'm not a complete idiot. You can lie better than that. Why do you want dollclothes? Have you found someone to make dolls for you and they can't do the clothes?"

Dolly's silvery laugh frosted Lucy's ear.

"Aren't you clever? Well, I didn't think you'd work for me again, that's all. You do hold a grudge, don't you? Yes, I've got some dolls. No, the maker can't do the clothing."

"Well, I can't either. I'm too busy right now. And you're right. I hold a grudge. I won't work for you again."

Lucy rolled her eyes at Dolly's long-suffering sigh.

"Of course, if you feel that way . . . Nick must be keeping you very busy." There was a poisonous pause. "Tell me, is he any better in the kip than he used to be?"

Lucy dropped the receiver into its holder with a clunk.

"Fuck you," she said calmly at the phone.

Dolly, listening to the dial tone, laughed again, but without much amusement.

"Fuck you," she said into the open line. Then she hung up.

Sucking fiercely on her cigarette, Dolly stalked into the dollhouse room to peer at Leyna, undressing in the bedroom. The water was running in the bathtub.

But while she watched, her thoughts were on Lucy. For Lucy, she fantasized, she would like a nice hot cauldron. And for every time the bitch had bitched her up, she would add a new and more painful poison. Starting with Harrison, their marriage, and his death. The grandchildren, being raised in the self-righteous bosom of the middle class, by Lucy and her dotty father. And her visits so graciously, so fairly permitted by darling Lucy. Everything they ever argued over while renovating the Doll's White House, because Lucy, the craftswoman, had *her* standards. Nevermind who was paying the freight. Signing everything, while Dolly signed the checks. And the little matter of friend Nicholas. She was welcome to him and he to her, and Dolly hoped that Lucy's younger body wore the bastard out.

Now she would not have new clothes for her dollie unless Roger could be persuaded to buy them and shrink them. He would say it wasn't safe yet. Piss on him, too; holding his mother's hand and probably sucking her watermelon old tits, too.

It was all enough to make her feel quite irritated.

Leyna was soaking in the tub when the wall was taken away. She winced but fought to control her panic. The Giant Dorothy stared in at her.

"This place stinks."

"The water was off," she cried out.

Sitting straight up in the bath, she lifted a soapy fist in unthinking anger. The charge was true. She had flushed the toilet but the stench remained, a lingering, still rotting ghost in the air. The bathtub was foamy with soap, partly to clear away her own grime, but mostly to perfume the air.

Dolly was deaf to her defense. "Smells like a cage full of mice."

A Hand hovered and swooped. Leyna heard the bedclothes being torn apart.

"Where's my fruitbowl?" Dolly demanded.

Without waiting for a response, she poked noisily under the bed, into the commode, and then into the wardrobe.

"What!" she hissed. "It's dented."

Leyna trembled in the breathless stoppage of Dolly's scolding.

"You'll be punished for this," Dolly muttered.

It was like a low roll of thunder to Leyna. The bathwater was suddenly cold and clammy.

A Hand passed the open bathroom door towing bedclothes like flapping ghosts behind it. It returned immediately; there was a cool thump on the floor as it dumped the clean linen.

"Clean this place up, you lazy bitch, and I'll bring your breakfast."

Leyna climbed out of the bath and dried herself quickly with shaking hands. Her shorts and shirt were filthy. She had planned to rinse them out in the bathwater. There was no time to drape a towel into a toga, so she did the bed quickly, still naked.

The Giant Dorothy returned, a mountainous, moving monster with breath that wheezed and rattled. There was a curious smell, like grass, around the tray she carried.

"That's better," she said.

The Hand intruded into the room, depositing the tray on the commode. Leyna sidled forward, watching Dolly. She didn't want to eat in front of her. But hunger overcame her inhibitions; she lifted the cover of the tray. There was an enormous tureen of something that looked like a dry salad of coarsely chopped green and white cabbage. It smelled strongly of chlorophyll. There were no utensils, dishes, or beverages on the tray. No condiments. Leyna dipped her hand into the stuff. It was dry, papery in texture. Pinching a couple of pieces, she lifted it to her mouth. As she tasted the stinging, papery strips, she heard the first violent explosion of the Giant's raucous laughter.

She spit out. Dolly was peeking in.

"Didn't you like the gerbil litter? Best gourmet litter in town? It was a special treat, too, just for you."

And she laughed again. And again.

Leyna was convulsed with anger. Seizing the tureen with both hands, she heaved it upward at the Giant. She watched it flash briefly in its arc and then descend, far short of its mark, into the garden below. The anger disappeared with it as she realized she might now have nothing at all to eat, if Dorothy chose to be offended by her attack.

Dolly's laughter trailed away.

"Temper, temper," she chided.

There was amusement in her tones, to Leyna's relief. Then she went away.

Leyna waited a long time before retrieving a mushy apple and a blackened banana from her hiding spot behind the pot in the commode. With the art blade, she sliced the apple in two and returned one half and the banana to the commode. Bananas, she told herself, may look like shit and be fine inside their decayed peel. But apples, apples that look yukky usually taste yukky. Her half in hand, brown spots and all, wasn't as tasteless as she had anticipated. The sauce of hunger, she thought sourly, nibbling at the half core.

The Giant's shadow fell over her again, long after she had deposited the scant, inedible remains of the half-apple in the toilet bowl. Dorothy came with a wonderful smell of tomato, garlic, and olive oil. Her Hand entered to place a new tray on the floor by the bed. The rich odors of the pasta and sauce made Leyna a little dizzy. She scooted to the tray, her mouth watering, made bold by hunger.

Under the silver dome the delicious smells kept their promise: even the oilshiny leaves of the salad had their own delicate perfume. There was a small bonus, a bottle of Chianti with a note taped to its side. Hungry as she was, Leyna had to investigate. Mail, she thought, and grinned. Unfolded, the note revealed an unpracticed typescript of just five words: *Bon appetit, your friend, Roger.*

"You'll burn yourself if you eat that in your birthday suit," the Giant scolded cheerfully.

Loathing for the huge being rose in Leyna's throat as sour bile.

"You just thank Roger for this feast. He thinks you're cute."

Leyna tried to ignore her, concentrating on forking up pasta. A Finger reached out and touched her left breast before she could move away. She jumped from it but the Finger followed relentlessly.

"Cute little titties. Roger thinks they're cute," the Giant's voice murmured in a curious flat tone.

The Finger traced an invisible line down Leyna's belly and tickled the patch of hair furring her pubis. Abruptly, with all the force she had in her, Leyna drove the fork she still clutched in her hand into the Finger.

The Giant yelped and withdrew the Finger hastily. She comforted herself with a string of curses.

Stunned by her own rashness, Leyna stared at the fork in her hand. The moment in which to seek shelter passed almost before she considered it.

The next time the Hand came swiftly, and pushed her backward roughly. Leyna saw bright red drops welling on the index Finger, red as the polish on the shieldlike nails, as she staggered against the bed. It pinned her there, hard against her chest. When she struggled to raise the fork in her own defense, the other Hand entered like a great dark bird from above and snatched it from her. The struggle came to a standstill.

"Bad girl." Leyna was reproved.

She closed her eyes in resignation. If she counted to ten, the Giantess might go away. It was harder than it should have been. The smell of food rose around her until she was weak and had trouble recalling the numbers. Suddenly, at the count of seven, the pressure lifted and was gone.

Exhaling raggedly, she opened her eyes.

And the Hand returned, in a blur. Her legs were thrust apart, the Finger separating them effortlessly. Leyna screamed and screamed but the Finger probed at will. The Giant Dorothy hummed some Giant's song.

After a time, Leyna was left to herself. She curled on the bed, her thumb in her mouth. The perfume of congealing spaghetti was heavy in the air.

"Why, dollie," the rasping Voice of Dorothy said in mock surprise, "you're upset. Don't you like being five inches tall? I thought it would seem perfectly natural to you. Just like being on television, isn't it?"

Tears leaked from Leyna's closed eyes. She tried to count again. This time the magic worked completely, and the Giant went away.

She woke in utter darkness but to total awareness. She was not afraid. She could hear the emptiness of the Doll's White House in which she now knew she was imprisoned.

11

Sleep had thrown up the ancient, minor incident to which all this terror referred. Dorothy Hardesty Douglas, the Queen of the Monkeys, and her miniature White House, at the Founders' Day Gala of the Dalton Institute. Tiny Dorothy had blown all her circuits because Leyna had dared to use the little princess's darling daddy's name for his baby. It all had been so unimportant at the time, a bit of cattiness, a mere showing of claws.

What she really remembered of that night was the few hours that had bridged it and the next day, the time when Nick Weiler had been with her. She knew he had answered her imperious summons because he had been on the outs with his new girl, partly Leyna's doing, and because he had wanted something from her. It hadn't cost the network anything, but she had seen to it that it had not come exactly free to him. All because she had wanted him to erase, for a few hours, the polite murder-suicide of her own marriage.

She hadn't thought about Jeff much lately. Not for months, really, before she had gone jogging on the Mall on the last day of what she now thought of as her real life. The state of their marriage had been just a fact of life that would, in time, work itself out. There was no rancor, no bitterness, no emotions involved on either side. Just an arrangement that hadn't worked, loosening like a badly made sweater, soon to unravel.

It too was unimportant. She had her work. That was part of the problem, of course. They neved had had much of a marriage. They both had had their work. His and hers. A careful separation of careers, personalities, lives, leading quite logically to a parting of their hearts and bodies.

Now there was no work to take her mind off the accident of themselves that had befallen Jeff and Leyna. She had to look at it, the way she had to look at herself in the wardrobe mirror, a mass of bruises, a rack of bones, skin the color of an evil moon.

Something Bad had happened to Leyna. Somehow, Dorothy Hardesty Douglas had made her crazy. Or made her tiny. She pushed that possibility away. She was crazy, just crazy, that's all, and her particular craziness put her inside Dolly's goddamn dollhouse.

So she would never see Jeff again, not in a lawyer's office to settle their marriage like a real estate deal, not in his mother's table-cursed mansion in Philadelphia, over a mile-long linen-covered dining table bordered with horse-faced relatives, and not in her naked little barracks of an apartment, with its pricy view of the Potomac. Her marriage would end, not discreetly, with the promise of a civilized nostalgic encounter in a luxury hotel, one last bittersweet romp, but here, in the mad birthday party of her own mind. In rooms that mocked the Center of Power she had served.

She pulled herself hastily from the bed and ran to the bathroom. Squatting on the toilet, she ran out of evasions. There was one small fact she was tucking away, like her cache of elderly fruit in the commode. Dolly, the Giant Dorothy, had mocked her. Would her own mind do that? Surely, not even Dorothy had the power to reduce full-grown adults to the size of fairies, to the stature of a doll, a plaything? It wasn't possible. Human beings were not reducible, not shrinkable, like cheap underpants.

Leyna returned to the tray on the floor. There was no longer a fork, so she ate with her hands, and nevermind the mess. The wine was tepid, sour-tasting, but she drank it directly from the bottle, ignoring the glass that had been provided.

It came back to herself, she decided, as she swallowed the gelid mess in great gulps. She was the end of the circle. She had created her own mad prison out of bits and pieces of an antagonistic relationship with a woman who meant, in the total context of Leyna Shaw's life, next to nothing to her. The Giant Dorothy was an insane metaphor, her present existence her own crazy poem. She had hoped, when she first began to suspect that she was living an irrational hallucination, that her mind would heal itself. Now, with her mouth and stomach full of the spice and grease and acid of her meal, she thought she couldn't bear the terrors she was inflicting on herself much longer.

When the light came around again, there was a new tray, laden with aromatic delicacies. She didn't move to claim it. The room was fragrant with the odor of coffee, croissants, eggs benedict, strawberries in cream. Curled in her quilt, she inhaled their perfumes and then became inured to them. The rush of saliva subsided; her stomach growled in protest once or twice, and fell silent when she didn't respond.

Late in the afternoon, she left the bed to empty suddenly liquid bowels on the chilly porcelain throne. She shivered and trembled, shuffling back to the bed, but took no water to ease her throat or cleanse the bile from her mouth. When dark came, she crawled on her belly across the floor, and consumed the cold contents of the breakfast tray, and the lunch tray of cold lobster in avocado, and the tepid supper tray, abandoned with much clucking about sleepyheads by the Giant Dorothy. She ate with her fingers, stuffing the food in slippery fistfuls into her mouth, swallowing it whole. No sooner did the last pasty glop of mashed potatoes follow the last fibrous chunk of roast beef down her gullet than she was stricken with cramps. Scuttling across the floor to the bathroom, she lost most of the day's meals into the bathtub, while suffering spasms of diarrhea on the john.

Grasping the basin for support while she gathered her strength to go back to bed, she glimpsed herself in the dimly lit mirror. There were sores around her mouth. Her hair had become curiously dull and colorless. She touched it gingerly. Threads of it came away with her fingers. She was losing her hair. She moaned softly and began to cry. The oblivion of sleep between the sheets came much later, a careless boon from indifferent gods.

The War ended, or a truce fell. She wasn't sure; she was sick. Her meals came on time, silently, and the intrusions of the Giant Dorothy were brief and unthreatening. Sometimes she heard the Giant humming and she felt dread, but nothing else happened. Dorothy did not speak to her. The days began to assume a new, more normal rhythm.

Leyna ate frequent, small meals and slept long hours of

mostly dreamless sleep. When she felt a little stronger, she walked through the nearest rooms, never venturing as far as the elevator. She listened for it often but it never moved. In the other rooms on the third floor, she found a few books and took them with her to while away the time. The fevers and chills gradually left her. Her bowels returned to something like normal. Her hair seemed slightly more secure on her scalp. She washed it very carefully and one day, feeling especially strong, used the art blade to chop it off close to her scalp.

Another day there was a gift of clothes that fit her. They were ugly clothes and ill-made but a change that kept her warm and covered. It amused her that they were exactly the sort of clothes she had once dressed her Barbie dolls in. Flashy, tarty things, meant to show off a plastic figure that was far, far from her present bag of bones.

Feeling better, she was able to achieve boredom. Her restlessness must have shown in the disarray of the bed and the clutter in the room. One morning the Giant Dorothy appeared, to take away the breakfast tray, and lingered, noticing the mess. Leyna trembled. So far her illness had absolved her of household duties.

But the Giant only clucked mildly and then, surprising her, said, "I have a treat for you, if you feel up to it."

Leyna watched her warily, clutching the bedsheets, white-knuckled.

"It's a little gift from Roger."

This made Leyna twitch visibly. Dolly noticed it with amusement. She was no doubt remembering she had paid dearly for her last treat from Roger.

"Trot outside, dolly-mouse. Your chariot awaits. No treats for *me*. I have to clean this nasty room."

The wall began to move in its slot. Leyna slipped from the bed and vanished into the walled warren of the house as fast as she could move. She had to take her treat, she knew. There was no hiding. But the elevator that had before given her the creeps was safety this time. Within its cage, going downward, she realized that for a moment she was beyond the Giant's reach.

Once it reached the ground floor, she dared not remain in it. Now Dorothy's cleaning activities reverberated through the house. Apparently she had not lied about that. So Leyna padded down the corridors in a pair of gold lamé Barbie pajamas. The seam along one leg was shredded, and the collar, sewn with fine plastic thread that felt like suturing stitches to Leyna, irritated the back of her neck. She peeked back over her shoulder at intervals, but the Dorothy noises remained a safe, same distance away.

She left the house by a side entrance, one that in the real White House was used for discreet diplomatic visits and by the president and his family, when he had one. It meant walking around the side of the house to the drive where, presumably, "the chariot" stood, but she could pass through the Rose Garden which gave at least a feeling of cover to the South Portico.

The tinkling music of the Carousel came to her before she saw it. She had heard it before, from the safety of her bedroom, and it tugged at her, calling her to ride again. She always refused the summons, convinced in her heart that another time the magic would be lost, perhaps forever. Glimpsing its circus colors, she slowed and shrank as much as she could into the cover of the shrubs. But no Giant Dorothy shadow waited to pounce on her, only a small racing car, a garishly colored projectile, sitting quietly in the drive.

Leyna looked up. The sky was the same uniform blue it had been every day. The orb of the sun was never visible yet the light was strong, warm, and diffuse. It came and went at regular intervals. There was never rain or cloud cover; the garden remained lushly green and colorful thanks to a sprinkler system that operated every day. It was all evidence that this world was artificial, and yet, because it was evidence gathered by her suspect senses, she could not believe it.

The little car attracted her. It promised power and speed. The dashboard was not what she was used to, but then she was very out of practice driving anyway. She had never really mastered standard shift and noted the stick shift on the floor nervously. There was something intimidating, sweaty, and masculine about its black leather knob and cowl. She climbed in and sat there, examining the display of dials and buttons she did not comprehend. At last, she began a systematic exploration, trying them out. Wipers swept across the low curve of the windshield; lights came on all over the dashboard. Leaning across the horned half moon of the wheel to twiddle the various knobs, she put her elbow squarely into the horn. It blatted. She sat back hastily.

Nervously, she scanned the roofline of the house. The protest of the horn might draw the Giant Dorothy. After a few tense moments, it appeared that it hadn't.

Leyna settled back, closed her eyes, and concentrated, calming herself. She wanted, very much, to master this odd gift. Opening her eyes, she looked at the stick shift. She moved it idly through its pattern. The little car jerked once and then was still. Suddenly, she was sure that the little automobile had been parked in neutral. That was new to her. Still, she had never had anything to do with this hot a machine before, so for all she knew, they were all parked in neutral. She moved the stick into the most forward position. Then moved it back to its original position. She would have to assume that was the parking gear.

Then, she resumed her study of the dashboard. Magically, her exploration was rewarded; the engine turned over after a couple of tentative twiddles, and after a polite cough, began to chug smoothly. It had a diesel sound to it, reminding her of a Mercedes-Benz that her husband had run while in college and now kept in storage in fond hopes of its attaining classic status.

She d ₋ed nervously on the foot peddles and with much jerking and some minor league cursing on her part, she had the little pink car rolling at a sedate pace down the drive. It was a very pleasant sensation, passing through the sweet fresh garden smells, along the gracious curving drive. Picking up speed after a time, the rush made her feel almost euphoric. She had forgotten how an automobile could free her. Behind the boasting roar of the car's engine, she was no longer a prisoner, not of the Giant Dorothy or of madness, if they were not the same.

Passing through a bridge of shadows, she realized they had not been in that place on her first few circuits of the drive. Looking up, she saw Dorothy. Then her attention was given to regaining control of the little car. She slowed then and stopped it, waiting to be told the treat was over, or that it might continue a little longer. As she waited, it came to her how foolish it had been to stop. It might be fun to see if the Giant could catch her. But the car would run out of gas and

209

then she would be punished. The illusion of freedom vanished as the shadow and its substance hovered over her.

"I see you figured out how to run it. You must remember to thank Roger for being so good to you."

Leyna giggled wearily. Her mother talking. She would write him a thank you note.

"Isn't this little track rather boring? Wouldn't you like to ride somewhere else?"

Leyna listened without hearing. What did she mean?

Dorothy showed her immediately. An enormous Hand descended, and while Leyna cringed, trying to fold herself into the well of the seat, closed round the car and lifted it. Leyna sensed upward movement and peeked over the edge of the car door. Below her, the White House she lived in was shrinking as she was carried away from it. It receded and disappeared, no longer a compass point.

The journey was quick. The car and its passenger felt solidity beneath them almost immediately. The Giant Dorothy crouched beside them, the currents of her hot breath flowing over Leyna, reinforcing the nausea that was already strong under her breastbone. And as quickly as she had come, Dorothy withdrew a considerable distance. Her smell and sounds were still heavy in the air, but the mass of her blurred and became blue like a mountain on a not-quite clear day.

Leyna turned on the car again. As it chugged patiently, waiting to be shifted up, to run as it was meant to, she looked around. The surface she was on was smooth, reflective, and hard, a brick-red in color. The sky overhead was the same one that she had seen so long, except that it did seem farther away. The horizon was completely flat in all directions around her. As she turned in the seat, craning to see as far as she could, Leyna made out indistinct shapes and colors but had no name for anything she saw.

So she sped away, not too fast, slow enough to observe what she could. She moved in the opposite direction from Dorothy, not out of any sense that she might escape her, but in distaste. Escape was the farthest thought from her mind. All this was in her own mind. How could she escape herself?

She passed enormous square pillars that supported a roof, a structure that would have to be measured in acres. There was a familiarity about its dimensions but nothing she understood as yet. After some time, she passed another of the strange, heaven-scraping columns. This one was festooned with thick cables that made her think, wildly, of the bean stalk that Jack climbed. Behind her, she was aware that the Giant Dorothy moved but at a distance.

She stopped the car, suddenly very tired. The red plain around her stretched for hopeless distances. Its nakedness made it seem even larger and more abandoned than it was. It was a vast dead end; there was no place to go. It was suitable only for racing, only at great speeds.

A knot of anger and resentment formed in her chest. The Giants' gifts were always sawdust in the mouth. Just another form of torture, she thought, and brought the heel of her hand down on the horn, driving it into its own well. The blatting rose in an angry crescendo as she pumped up and down and then, when she released it, fell silent.

The mass that was Dorothy was silent, watching. Why should she respond? She was the one in control.

The tiny car jerked and then shot away, turned a perilous wheelie to face Dorothy and came roaring at her, except that to her ears the roar that Leyna heard was the angry hiss of a hornet. She couldn't see the tiny face hunched over the wheel of the car but she understood, instantly, the meaning of the sudden fierce race, with her as its goal.

She laughed and stood up. Deliberately, she placed one foot in the path of the little car, too close for it to be able to swerve away. The projectile slammed into her shoe. She felt it. It was like stubbing up against the furniture, a mild ache that would not even bruise. The car bounced off her shoe and stopped.

She picked it up and regretted it immediately. The hood was hot enough to scald. She held it gingerly in her palm. Its tiny occupant flopped like a rag doll in the seat. The windshield was patterned with an abstract sunburst of cracks. The car's pink metal skin was wrinkled; the bullet end flattened and fissured.

Dolly pulled Leyna's unconscious body from the little car and deposited her in her bedroom on the neatly changed bed. Brushing back Leyna's hair, Dolly could see that her forehead was rosy and swelling. The skin was barely broken, dotted with a few dewdrops of blood.

"Ice," Dolly muttered, and remembered that Roger had neglected, while he was busy shrinking ten days' worth of food for Leyna, to zap a few ice cubes. Even a single cube would be like dropping an old-fashioned cake of ice on her. Besides, the mess from its melting was unthinkable. She would have to crush some herself and use the tiniest pieces.

"Silly little nit," she scolded the still-unhearing Leyna.

While Ruta looked on surreptitiously over the top of her movie magazine, Dolly crushed the ice personally in the food processor. It made her feel wickedly efficient. Roger had charged her with the care of their tiny house guest and no one could say she wasn't doing it, taking care of her. The thought made her laugh out loud. Ruta dared to drop the magazine and stare at her directly.

"I spilled some glue. If I freeze it, I can pick it off," Dolly told her.

Ruta grunted. If she had any real curiosity, it appeared to be satisfied.

In the dollhouse room, Dolly spilled a chip of ice from the bowl she had carried from the kitchen onto one of the miniature washcloths from Leyna's bathroom. When she piled it gently on Leyna's forehead, the tiny woman groaned, almost too faintly to be heard. Dolly had folded the cloth neatly in a band, and it looked as if it were going to stay put.

The silly thing was going to have a rotten headache, if she didn't already, but it was her own fault for being so careless. Too bad Roger hadn't zapped a little aspirin, too. Perhaps she ought to crush some of her own, but then again, it might be dangerous. Poor little Leyna might just have to suffer the consequences of her own bad temper. Might teach the little beast a lesson.

At least Dolly had done her duty. She deserved a cigarette. Before looking for one, she picked up the tiny pink car from the drive where she'd absently set it while looking after the foolish driver. It was rather sad-looking. Perhaps Roger could fix it. He would be very displeased with his teeny tiny woman when he saw what she had done to his treat. She couldn't help smiling just a little at the thought.

Leyna had more than a headache when she came to, in darkness that was relieved only by the light from the bathroom, a faint blue of white that cast fantastic shadows into the room. The pain in her head was intense, radiating from the enormous tender bruise that was her forehead. She was still all over, from the back of her neck to the base of her spine and in all her limbs. Flexing her reluctant muscles as she lay waiting for her vision to adjust to the near-absence of light, she inventoried a hundred small aches and pains. Sitting up at last, she felt her bowels lurch, adding their unease to the general symphony of discomfort. She groped her way very cautiously to the bathroom, becoming thoroughly dizzy along the way. Bending her head into her hands, as the room reeled around her, she emptied her bowels in a spasm of delayed reaction.

The dizziness was so persistent and steady that she feared drowning and did not dare soak the aching muscles in a hot tub. Back in bed, she kept her eyes closed. It seemed to help with the vertigo. She dropped back into a fevered doze, full of chaotic dreams that were less coherent dreams than nightmare collages, underlined in hot sensations of pain. As she thrashed, she found a wet washcloth on her pillow and sucked it for its tepid, soothing moisture. The darkness dispersed at an agonizingly slow pace. Sometime in the predawn, she slipped into real sleep.

She woke to the noise of the wall rising but did not open her eyes. When the wall was replaced and the sound of intrusion ceased, she peeked, pretending to be waking. The morning tray, already announced by its comforting scents of toast and coffee, orange juice, and eggs, assumed a solid form, within reach on the commode. A heap of white chunks in a soup bowl sat next to it.

Leyna sat up, suddenly hungry. The quickness of her movement was quickly regretted; she was promptly dizzy and had to close her eyes again and wait for her body to catch up with her. The smells of breakfast were maddening. There was a faint acid undertone that piqued her curiosity. As soon as she was able to open her eyes, she reached, but slowly and carefully, for the mysterious white chunks. A deep sniff and a quick lick identified them: aspirin. The residual ache in her head, so deep as to be mere background music to the rest of her aches and pains, seemed suddenly stronger, as if it wanted the magic potion. She nibbled the stuff quickly, hating the burning acid taste in her mouth, and washed it down with a slug of orange juice. Breakfast followed, a deeply satisfying, filling experience. At the end of it, with her stomach full and the plates empty of even the smallest crumbs, she realized the aspirin and food together *had* worked magic. The headache and its cohort of lesser pains subsided to mere discomfort.

She felt strong enough to trust herself to the tub for the long soak she wanted, but she moved slowly, like an old person, to minimize the dizziness that was still there, in a lower key. Squeaky clean and dressed, she neatened her bed and reclined on it. The dizziness prevented any other course of action, beyond minimal self-care. There were books at hand, but she could only page them idly, putting them aside in the shadow of headache. Unable to do anything else to distract herself, she was forced to remember and to think about her situation. It was not pleasant; the headache grew stronger.

She was sick of being miserable, of pain, nausea, and hunger. Since the day she had run around the Mall into the sights of that tourist's camera, she felt as if she had been tortured, like a fly captured by a sadistic boy. A pair of Giants (mad visions) made appearances to her, and she saw no other identifiable human beings. She was not only physically discomforted, she was lonely.

Her rational mind insisted that what had happened to her in this strange doppelgänger of the White House was insane, the product of her own disordered brain. And there was nothing illogical about the division in her thoughts; presumably, the insane could and did suspect that they were not sane. Still, her delusions were wonderfully consistent. If they were hallucinations, she had successfully created a tiny world in which she was imprisoned by giants. The details were worthy of a novelist. Perhaps she had missed her calling, and didn't belong posturing before the television cameras but dreaming at a typewriter.

Her fingers trailed over the quilt on her bed. She could feel the stitches in it, the nap of the fabric. With her eyes closed, she used her other sense to inform her of her world. The faint smell of breakfast, yet lingering about the tray, and the soap from her bath, the vague sachet, a potpourri of roses and spices, that perfumed every drawer and pocket of the room. The smell of sunshine itself, a little dusty, reminiscent of a hot iron, and the warmth of it, on her skin. She felt the cloth under her, the smooth wood of a bed post against her toes. What she touched spoke back to her about herself: her toes were warm and a little leathery on their bottoms; a current of air ruffled the downy hairs on them. The nappy cloth of the quilt brushed her smooth skin and she was aware, because of its caress, of the muscle that lay, dense and bloodwarm, under the epidermis. Her jogging shorts were snug around her bottom, and a little loose at the crotch, so that the warm air penetrated there, among the glossy pubic hairs. She tightened her stomach; once upon a time, before she came to live in this house, she had had a husband, and lovers. They had clothed themselves in her flesh, as she was now clad in her velour shorts. She touched her breasts, weighting the sweat shirt with their silky roundness, and suddenly they ached, for what she could not say. A lover's caress, a child's mouth, a letting down of milk, a knife. Tears trickled over her cheeks, lining her face, with its fine bone structure, its velvety, flawless texture. She tasted the tears, salt wetting her soft lips, and good upon the rough tastebuds of her tongue. Her shoulders ached, the back of her neck ached, as if from bearing some insupportable burden, and yet the pain reminded her of the muscles, the good and faithful meat of her own body. All clothed in skin that was more wonderful in its texture and properties than any cloth, breathing and sweating, feeling all there was to feel. She drew air shakily into her lungs, heard the pounding of her heart that pumped the hot blood throughout her body.

"Oh, God," she whimpered and hugged herself, curling slowly in upon herself. "Oh, God."

The agony passed. She lay in the lee of her emotions (like an infant after squalling) in the peace of exhaustion. Lunch was delivered; she didn't notice until after the smells had penetrated beyond her closed eyes. Pulling herself to a sitting position, she ate, slowly and with great savor, the spinach salad, soft cheeses, crackers, and pâté. The wine was a California Riesling, a silky delight. Pacing herself, she felt the first glass almost immediately in the warming of her knees and thighs; the second was also her last. She recorked the bottle firmly and hid it in the commode. With it, she hid the corkscrew which she discovered, after examination and trial, to be sharp enough to pierce the tip of her finger, given a good hard jab.

Curling up under the quilt, she feigned sleep again. Within the hour, her ears informed her of the Giant Dorothy's presence. The Giant seemed pleased about something; she was humming. A puff of cigarette smoke wafted into the room. Leyna turned her face to the pillows and held her breath until the smoke dissipated. Distantly, she heard the Giant chuckle. When the tray was gone, and the room silent again, she remained by force of will as still as she could be. She wanted to be sure that her enemy would not return immediately.

At length, she crept out from the cover, smoothed it automatically, and retrieved the art blade and the corkscrew from the commode. Crouched by the side of the bed, she unplugged the bedside lamp from its floor socket and began patiently to strip the black plastic skin from the wire by scraping it with the art blade. When she had exposed about eight inches of bare wiring, she wrapped the wire around the lamp and hid it under the bed. If she was lucky, Dorothy wouldn't notice its absence.

After tidying up, returning her tools to their hiding place, she drew a bath and had a long soak and a shampoo. The dizzy spells were not quite so insistent, but she was not sure if they were really diminishing or if she was just getting used to being chronically lightheaded. After her bath, she spent some time poking in the wardrobe, which was now filled with her Barbie doll clothes. Finding nothing she wanted to be caught dead in, she pulled on her shorts and sweat shirt once again.

Suppertime came around and found her genuinely napping. She woke to the prodigious clatter of the wall's removal and pushed herself up into a sitting position with exaggerated care.

"Din-din," the Giant Dorothy sang.

Her perfume was very strong. Leyna thought her face seemed elaborately made-up, a garish moon above her shimmering garb. Perhaps she had plans for the evening. It was convenient for Leyna, perhaps too convenient. The Giant left the supper tray, replaced the wall, and went away immediately.

It was a huge, festive supper: breast of turkey, wild-rice pilaf, pureed hubbard squash, new green peas like small sweet pearls of jade, cucumbers in vinegar, rye bulkie rolls, and sweet honey butter, and a banana split for dessert. There was a split of rosé to drink, and a pot of coffee. Leyna set the wine aside, and savored the rich coffee in its fragile porcelain cup.

Afterward, she brushed her teeth and waited patiently for Dorothy's return. The light failed and the room grew dark and still, but the Giant did not come for the tray. It was not unusual; she had left the supper tray all night previously. Any of the trays might sit for hours before she bothered with them. The possibility that she was out for the evening cheered Leyna immeasurably.

With the art blade in one hand and the corkscrew in the other, she began the second phase of the War. She began with the pillows, slashing them until their feathered entrails flew around the room. Next, the needlepoint upholstery on the two chairs in the room. When they had been slashed and stabbed, she went to the draperies at the windows. It was tiring but exhilarating, tearing the heavy cloth from the rods and slashing it in long hopeless rents. Tearing the clothes from the bed, she piled the linen in the middle of the room.

Sweating and panting by the pile, she realized that so far she had made little noise.

"A little night music," she whispered, and a frenzy broke in her.

She spilled the tray with its china and silver to the carpet. It clattered and crackled as it fell but the carpet muffled the sounds disappointingly. She kicked the silver pieces, then stooped to pick up china and pitch it against the wall. There was a satisfying crescendo of smashing crockery. She paused again to listen for the sound of approaching Giants.

The room grew still and darkened. She turned on the overhead lights, the better to see by. It was time to do the real work now. Retrieving the lamp, she plugged it in, carefully avoiding the exposed wiring. She shredded an obnoxiously scratchy blouse from her wardrobe and heaped its nylon and Lurex around the base of the lamp and the naked wires.

Tucking her art blade and corkscrew into her waistband, Leyna picked up the split of rosé and the half-bottle of Riesling that remained from her recent meals. Pausing before the mirror, she inspected herself, seemed satisfied, and closed the wardrobe door. Without looking back, she turned off the overhead lighting, and left the room, leaving only the lamp on the floor for light, and the spill from the hall through the partly opened door to disperse the dark.

She vandalized randomly as she went through the house, slashing wallpaper, upholstery, draperies, paintings, and then carving obscenities into the long, shining table in the State Dining Room. She drove the corkscrew savagely into the wood of furniture doors, moldings, frames, and chipped futilely at the marble surfaces of the Entrance and Cross halls. Tiring of it, she pitched it through a window. The bottle of rosé, drunk as she progressed, oiled her rage and boosted her flagging energy. She grew dizzy and fell against things, knocking over pier tables, potted plants, busts, and chairs. The wine slopped from its open carafe onto the carpets when she staggered.

She giggled once or twice but mostly did her damage in a wordless, panting fury. When the carafe was empty, she used it to smash a mirror. With the end of it, she ran out of hysteria.

Calmly, she dragged an elegant little Boston rocker to the Blue Room from its place in the East Room, and stationed it so that she could look out onto the grounds. The lights that illumined it at night had come on automatically. She could make out the Carousel, standing silent in the middle of its circle of blackgreen grass, and the fantastic shapes of the trees and bushes around it. She wished she knew how to turn it on. It was the Giants who controlled the Carousel. If it were running, by chance or choice, she might have chosen it over this room, and would have liked to hear its music again. Here, though, she could ruin the carpets. In fact, she had a considerable start on most of them already.

A spasm gripped her bowels and she withstood it. Standing up, she walked to the center of the room, slipped down her shorts, and peed on the Aubusson. That done, she ignored the acrid smell of her own urine, and took her seat again. The art blade was a little dulled by its recent use, and her hands trembled, but she found the proper vein in her left wrist with very little effort. Dropping the blade, she snatched up the bottle of white wine, and chugged a good portion of it. It spilled out of her mouth and ran down her chin. Her head was notably unsteady; it was an effort to keep her balance in the chair. Closing her eyes, she leaned back. She took a deep breath, and thought she could smell, somewhere, a tarry smoke.

"Some birthday party," she whispered. "Happy birthday to

me," she sang softly. "Happy birthday, dear Leyna . . ." she paused to collect a shaky breath ". . . Happy birthday to me."

She wanted to clap for herself but her left arm was numb and unresponsive, her right growing very weak. She opened her eyes to stare up at the chandelier that hung like a huge lit birthday cake overhead. She thought it swayed, that the flames of its false candles wavered, and then she realized it was her own vision. From somewhere in her brain, black explosions obtruded into her sight. She heard something that might have been a faucet dripping, but her nose, curiously acute, told her it was warm, salt, coppery. She could feel it spattering her bare feet. With great relief, she remembered it was not her birthday at all.

In the third-floor bedroom that had been hers, the facsimile Queen's bedroom, the scraps of cloth around the stripped wire glowed. The smell of ozone was strong in the room. At last, a faint explosion, as the synthetic cloth, heated to the point of combustion by the electrical wiring, burst into flames. There was a lot to burn; it was a well-furnished house. The fire fed itself on fine cloth and wood, glue and paint, varnishes and wood stains. Like a living thing, it breathed the air that came in through the many tall, well-proportioned windows. It burned twenty minutes before the smoke detectors in the dollhouse room went off, thirty before the sprinkler system automatically flooded the room.

It was an excellent system. The fire was quickly out, and the sensors, detecting no more smoke and heat, turned off the water. If the room was a miasma underfoot, and stank of wet charred wood and cloth, if the Doll's White House was a sodden wreck and the rest of Dorothy Hardesty Douglas's prized collection damaged, at least the apartment and the rest of the building was safe. No one would die as a consequence of this fire, inside or outside the no-longer quite-white dollhouse. Leyna died, as she planned, from blood loss.

No one heard the smoke alarms. Maid and mistress were both absent, on similar errands. The sound-proofing between apartments was more than adequate. The morning would have to come round to expose the business of the night.

Dolly came in at ten the following day. The apartment, always quiet, was preternaturally still. She shivered involuntarily and then shook off the sudden, inexplicable shadow on her good feelings. It was not the shadow of anything real, she decided, merely the ghost of cocaine. It was unlike Ruta not to be up and about her work. She had spoken to Dolly about seeing a new boyfriend the previous night; undoubtedly, she was hungover. Not knowing that Dolly had eaten breakfast out, Ruta would be contrite about not being on hand to serve Dolly her morning coffee.

Dolly, bored with life without Roger, had gone to a dinner party and encountered an old boyfriend, a French record producer. Armand had a pretty boy in tow, and one thing had led to another. It all made her feel like a world-beater, her father's old expression for postcoital self-esteem. How could she have imagined she was getting old? She was just beginning.

Consulting a mirror, she thought she did look a touch dissipated. Roger would be home in the evening but there was nothing much to do today. She could sleep the day away and greet him fresh-faced and innocent. But first she had to feed their dolly-mouse. Roger would notice any signs of neglect. He might punish her by withholding the use of the minimizer, by refusing to supply any more little things to her.

There was no warning. The hermetically sealed dollhouse room had kept its secrets from the rest of the world, from Ruta, never really welcome in the sanctum sanctorum anyway, and from Dolly herself, until she unlocked and opened the door. She looked right at the Doll's White House. For an instant, nothing registered. Then the odor of wet char reached her nose, and after that, the pit of her stomach.

Approaching the house as if a sleepwalker, she slipped in a puddle of water and slid heavily into the dollhouse and its base. The Carousel shuddered; its mechanical music-maker was jarred and issued a distorted, rasping note in protest. Gaining her feet again, Dolly saw both the charred East Wall and the South Portico, where a rusty stain seeped from under the doors and across the floor of the Portico to the steps. In a daze of disbelief, she reached out to the fire-blackened wall. Her fingers came away smudged with soot; she wiped them distastefully on her cocktail dress.

Dipping a finger into the stain on the Portico, she stared at it. The water from the sprinklers had not diluted it because the roof of the Portico had covered it. But it had not dried;

the room was now too humid. It was darker than when it flowed from Leyna's veins, to be sure, and the smell of death was strong in it.

Dolly had only to bend a little and look in. Leyna had chosen the obvious place, center stage. She was slumped in the rocker like a doll, abandoned by a child called away to supper. The chair, squarely under the chandelier and facing the windows, was painfully out of place. Under it, a hideous rug of brick-red puddled around it, and the rockers were spattered with the same substance. There was so much of it, Dolly thought, for such a tiny being.

Her first instinct was to smash the little dolly-mouse, to grind the teeny tiny corpse into the floor, but she could not bear to touch her.

"Good riddance," she whispered, "good riddance. I'm glad I broke you."

Leyna's unseeing eyes stared up at her; she made no reply. The little body, limp and white, seemed to waver, as if it were becoming a ghost that very instant. But it was only the tears in Dolly's eyes, blurring her vision. They were not tears of grief, but tears of rage.

"What happened?" he said, when she showed him the small body in the coffin-shaped cigarette box. His voice was as dead as the teeny tiny woman.

Dolly's hands shook as she put the coffin-box in his hands. She fumbled frantically for the cigarette she had put down a few seconds before.

"I don't know. She seemed all right. She ate her meals."

He didn't seem to hear her. His eyes traveled feverishly over the Doll's White House. He fingered the slashed curtains, the scars on the furniture, the char marks, as if he were a pathologist performing an autopsy. When at last he spared a look for Dolly, his eyes accused her.

She said nothing in her own defense, thinking it was the best defense to simply act shocked and innocent.

His hand found her face in a haze of unreality. She was astonished that it hurt. She fell backward, against the sofa. His voice struck at her with as much violence.

"What the fuck happened?"

"I don't know," she choked out. "She went crazy, I guess."

He turned his back on her, to stare at the corpse.

"I had to put her in the box myself," she told him, aggrieved.

He stared at her and didn't seem to see her.

"When I gave her the car, she tried to kill herself. I couldn't stop her. When someone wants to die, that's it."

Roger sat down abruptly in the nearest chair and covered his eyes.

"It's your fault," Dolly burst out. "You did it to her. You did something wrong!"

The slump of his shoulders and his hidden face voiced his own secret conviction. Now Dolly could be nice to him. She moved close to him, brushed the nape of his neck with her fingertips.

"We'll make a nice funeral for her," she murmured.

He sighed raggedly.

"Listen, darling," Dolly pushed on, "we've learned a lot. Next time will be better."

There would be no next time, Roger promised himself, staring at his late teeny tiny woman in her silver coffin.

Dolly sensed his withdrawal from her. It made her a little sick. She must have new tenants for her White House. Somehow, she would have them, when the house was repaired. Roger had to give them to her. She'd see to it. Only for now it was necessary to smooth things over, ease his evident pain. Just like a kid with a pet mouse, she assured herself, he'll forget it quickly enough. She knew how to make him forget his own name, let alone his teeny tiny woman. She knew how.

Investigators admit privately that they are baffled by the strange disappearance of TV journalist Leyna Shaw. After weeks of intensive cooperative effort by law enforcement agencies, there was no visible progress in the case. With no authenticated ransom demands to support the theory that Shaw was kidnapped, for money or by political terrorists, the focus of the investigation shifted to Shaw's private life. There too, there was a painful scarcity of clues. Childless and separated from her husband, architect Jeffrey Fairbourne, but on verifiably good terms with him, the journalist apparently had few close friends, and no serious relationships in her life, though she dated a wide spectrum of media colleagues, upper-level government bureaucrats, and politicos, including his Elegance the President, Matt Johnson. Inevitably, her disappearance sparked wild rumors, which were dismissed by no less an insider than the president's mom, dowager Harriet Caithness Johnson, as "poppycock. The girl and Matthew were never more than acquaintances." Almost-ex-husband Fairbourne has his own information in the matter: He claims Leyna told him that His Eligibility had paid more than one midnight visit to her plush Potomac co-op. Fairbourne plans on revealing his suspicions in a roman à clef, now being shopped to major publishers.

6.6.80   —*VIPerpetrations, VIP*

12

The station wagon, awash in popcorn and paper cups that trickled sticky red puddles of Kool-Aid onto the carpet, stank of sugary artificial strawberry and salty butter. The kids were limp on the backdeck, in a sea of pillows and old quilts. Laurie snored softly; Zach was lost in the deep unreachable sleep of very small children. The second feature was just half-over.

Nick and Lucy, entwined quietly on the front seat, were not watching it. Lucy, her head against Nick's chest, murmured, "Are they asleep?"

"Ummm."

"Is that a yes or a no?"

"Ummm."

She dug an elbow into his side. "Ha."

Nick laughed softly. "Hey, is this what being married is like?"

"Wall-to-wall popcorn and Kool-Aid orgies? Yes. If you have kids, and live in the U.S.A., anyway. I wouldn't know about the other half of the world, the childless and un-American. This," she enclosed the interior of the car in one quick gesture, as if she were catching a butterfly, "is a closed universe."

"I was really thinking in terms of going to the drive-in with the kids in their summer pajamas, and you and I necking in the front seat while they cork off."

"We don't come very often. Once or twice a summer is enough. You forget, from one summer to the next, about the bugs and the mess in the car. Anyway, I never before brought anybody along to neck with."

He buried his nose in her hair and they tussled briefly. She backed out first.

"Wait," she giggled.

"Aargh," he mock-groaned.

Glancing out at the cars parked in curving ranks before the wall of moving pictures, he grew thoughtful.

"I'm glad I don't own this place."

Lucy was quiet, looking around them.

"It looks run down, but they always do. It's part of the ambience, isn't it? Drive-in tacky?" she observed.

Nick grinned. "Yes. But I meant it's obsolete. Unless somebody invents an automobile that doesn't use gasoline or uses a hell of a lot less of it, the drive-in movies is only a footnote on the long list of American institutions that are going to stall out permanently."

"I never thought of that."

After a time, she slipped a hand into one of his. "Now I feel like a goose walked over my grave, or something. I never think about the Future, with a big F. It seems like there's enough to do, thinking about getting along on our own. Do you think Laurie and Zach will lead lives very different than ours?"

"It's hard to imagine anything else. If the pace of technological development continues, their lives will be as unimaginable to us as ours would have been to our great-grandparents. If technology stalls out, life is very likely to be a lot grimmer and harsher than ours. Different, for sure."

Lucy shivered. "How could we all be so stupid?"

Nick smiled and squeezed her comfortingly. "We're not stupid. We're too clever for our own good. My ancestors—I can't speak for yours—the blue-blooded English landowners on my mother's side, and the good high class butchers who produced my father, would have said that a proper respect for God and one's place in society, plus a heartfelt devotion to hard work, was the best road to survival and prosperity, in this life and the next, for any man."

"Jesus saves, and so do I, at the First National Bank?" Lucy mocked.

"Just right. Our generation, and to be fair, our parents', with the attitude you just displayed for religion, and a certain cynicism as well about hard work and its fruits, puts its faith in technology, or science. Mary Shelley warned us about that some time ago, but we haven't taken her message, or all the others, along the way. Our technology is at once the most dangerous thing in the world, and our most likely salvation."

"I've never heard you talk like this. I would have expected you to say something about art."

Nick shrugged. "My early upbringing has soured me a little on the almighty importance of art. And then, you can't eat art, when the crops fail."

"That sounds bitter."

"I know." Nick sighed and drew her closer. "We should be making love, not talking about the end of the world as we know it."

Lucy sat up and faced him. "What's wrong?"

She was a study, sitting cross-legged between the steering wheel and the back of the car, he thought. In the light from the movie screen, her denin shorts and red-checked halter were blackly purple. Running, biking, working in the garden had tanned her and slimmed her. Her hair, neatly pinned up when they left her father at her home, had fallen in loops and tendrils to her shoulders. He was prepared to look at her all night.

She answered her own question. "I've been thinking, off and on at the oddest moments, about Leyna Shaw."

Leyna was a potential finger-burner. Nick decided to adopt a neutral posture.

"Really?"

"What ever could have happened to her?"

"You know the possibilities as well as I do," he chided gently. "All laid out in *VIP* and all the newspapers, on all the network news programs. Kidnapping, murder, suicide, runaway," he enumerated, "or some combination thereof."

"Yes," Lucy agreed. "But you knew her. What do you think?"

"I wasn't her best friend," Nick protested. "I've known her for a long time; I know things about her. I don't know and can't imagine what happened to her."

"Well, what things do you know?" she prodded.

"Her husband, Jeff Fairbourne, is one of an old moneyed family. The Fairbournes are characterized by magnificent Roman noses, complete insensitivity to the rest of the human

226

race, and the usual bug-eyed acquisitiveness of the truly rich. Also, the family throws up, from the general level of beady-eyed Philistine, at least one idiot savant per generation. Jeff is the last generation's aberration. He told me he intends to be the last generation, period."

"Idiot savant?"

"There have been some genuine classic Fairbourne idiot savants. Jeff is marginal. He has the characteristic extraordinary grasp of the properties of numbers and dates, but he can't make change. He functions, he has a college education or two, et cetera. He's an architect, and his stuff is wonderful on paper, but has a tendency to be disastrous once built. Either somebody notices, just when the ribbons are being cut, that the thing looks like dog puke piled fifty stories high, or all the glass falls out in the first high wind, or else he leaves the plumbing out. He's done that twice. Claims high-mindedness."

Lucy giggled. "That's amazing. And people hire him?"

"Sure. He's a Fairbourne. Fairbournes attract money like rotten meat draws flies."

"So that's her husband. But they were separated."

"Almost as soon as they married. I think it was sort of a spite marriage. Jeff's family had to eat all those crude suspicions that he was homosexual and Leyna could throw all that Fairbourne money in her mother's face. She hates her mother."

"Why didn't they get divorced?"

"Liked things the way there were, I expect. Simple as that. There's no animosity. You saw the pictures of Jeff right after she disappeared. He was genuinely distressed. It was a pretty bloodless marriage, but they both got what they wanted out of it."

She nodded.

He continued: "I can't feature suicide, unless there was something wrong with her, an illness of some kind. She's exactly the sort of person who would cut out rather than go through a terminal illness. Not for lack of courage or for fear of pain, but because she'd hate the indignities, the degeneration, the dependency."

"That was my reaction to the idea," Lucy said. "She seemed . . . tough."

"She was. Apparently she wasn't kidnapped, as there's been

no notes that could be trusted. That was the most likely possibility to me. All that Fairbourne money, plus her notoriety as a journalist."

"Maybe she was, and something went wrong, and the kidnappers killed her."

Nick nodded. "A possibility. One that may never be provable."

"What about out-and-out murder?"

"She had some big-time enemies and a lot of just-plain-people hated her. But I don't know of anybody who would have put out a contract on her, let alone done it themselves."

"But somebody might have. You don't know, right?"

"Maybe. She wasn't the most dangerous journalist in town, for sure."

"So what about the runaway theory?"

"No motivation I know. She was handling her life just fine, it seemed. She wanted to be the famous television journalist, and she was. She liked it. Got off on it."

"I think something terrible happened to her," Lucy said mournfully. Her face, in the light from the movie screen, was troubled.

After a brief silence, Nick agreed, "So do I."

Lucy swiveled around the wheel. "Let's go home."

"To go back to my original question," Nick poked, trying to lighten the mood, "is this what marriage is like? Take the kids to the drive-in, neck a little, and go home before the second feature finishes, without even getting to second base?"

She keyed the ignition. "We'll take the kids in and put them in their beds . . ."

"And turn off the tube and put your father in his bed?" Nick interjected.

"Yes," she laughed. "And then we'll put the driver and her passenger to bed. But you have to leave by five-thirty."

Nick groaned. "What I have to do to get laid."

"I'll drop you off on the way home," Lucy offered.

"I'll take the first offer," he told her hastily.

"Okay," she said amiably, "just so you understand. I'm not having my kids wake up to find Mummy in the sack with good old Nick, or anybody else."

He shook his head. "You're a hard woman."

"It's a hard world."

"But it's hypocritical, Lucy. It's not like you. You're too honest for this kind of charade."

"No, it isn't hypocrisy at all," she insisted, letting the car slide down the slope to the rough-packed lanes between the ranks. "My kids are too young. If they were fifteen, I'd sit them down and say, listen, you know about sex. Mom likes it, too. She has a boyfriend; she sleeps with him. She's not a whore, she's not sleeping with anybody who asks or stands still long enough. She likes this guy. Sex is just part of her relationship with him. You can't explain that to a seven-year-old. All they see is somebody between them and Mum who is either a potential Daddy, or an out-and-out intruder."

"I don't know. I never was in your position. I don't have a seven-year-old. And when I was seven, I thought it the most normal thing in the world to have a father as old as my friends' grandfathers, and another younger father who blew in sporadically from exotic places like the coast of Maine. It didn't change how I felt about my mother. She was still the most beautiful, wonderful woman in the world. Nothing she did could be bad."

"I was seventeen when my folks split, but the marriage had been bad for years, as far back as I could remember," Lucy reminisced. "I was glad. But there wasn't anyone else involved. Just my father and his bottle of rye and his bad back, and his failures; my mother and her precious restored Colonial house. They both took out of the marriage pretty much what they brought into it."

"Everyone's world is a little different, I guess." Nick cleared his throat. "Now that we've talked about divorce, can we talk about marriage?"

Lucy took her eyes off the road long enough to flash him a smile. "Talk to me in six weeks. When school goes back into session."

He folded his arms across his chest as if to hug himself. "Amazing woman."

She laughed.

There was no place to bury her. Roger built up a barrow on the west side of the grounds, near a group of willow-oaks. The silver coffin that had once been an amusing cigarette box and now held Leyna's remains was fitted into the stone-lined cave and the barrow sealed, heaped with soil to cover the rocks, and planted over with turf. In the absence of a marker, Dolly allowed Roger to install a fountain nearby. With that, he lost all interest in the Doll's White House, claiming he didn't have the skills to repair it.

Dolly was furious with him but there was nothing she could do. If she forced him to, he might deliberately bungle it and damage the dollhouse beyond fixing. She had to content herself with cleaning up the water damage in the Gingerbread Dollhouse, which fortunately had not been directly under any sprinkler and had only taken a mild soaking. The Glass Dollhouse was the easiest to clean up; a little window cleaner and some paper towels plus the patience to do it right, and it was back to its old tricks with the light.

Roger immersed himself in the physical fitness program offered by Dolly's Health Club. He gave up sneaking beer, pizza, and Twinkies, and picked at Ruta's crepes and seafood medaillons as if they were so much liver and spinach. His books and apparatus arrived from California and, after rearranging the small, second bedroom in the apartment as a workship, he spent many hours at work on mysterious adjustments to the minimizer. There was no admittance for anyone else, including Dolly, after he installed a lock on the door and pocketed the key.

Dolly plotted to seduce him away from grief. The theatrical instinct that made sex with Roger piquant broke through the bonds of costumes and B-movie roles. At first, he showed himself to be a brilliant improvisor, and then, abruptly, led her into a round of sudden, silent, occasionally violent intimacies, in the course of which Roger was established as the dominator. Increasingly, they were engaged in a ritual looting of each other's bodies and spirits.

The Doll's White House and its mates stood forlornly behind the locked door of the dollhouse room. The big dollhouse began to stink of mildew as well as fire and Dolly could hardly bear to enter the place. She had only to think of the ruin of her pride and joy to spin into a restless depression. It was then she needed Roger. The question she asked of him was always answered the same way, in her bed.

The city summer kept her imprisoned in the apartment or in air-conditioned automobiles or chic shops. Searching for some relief, she hit upon the idea of going away, as if somewhere else in the world would be sweet and green. Her home closed in on her, an artificially cooled capsule floating above the city. So far above the ordinary world did she live that the city was shrunk to the scale of toys. Coming down from her tower to re-enter it, she felt the process reversed, as she shrank and it grew too large to deal with.

She determined to leave for a little while, at least. Perhaps when she awoke from some pleasanter dream, her dollhouse would be restored by magic. In the meantime, she instructed Ruta to have the contract cleaners do the apartment, except for the dollhouse room, and to have the decorator do over the bedroom.

"In purple," she told her dreamily.

It was only on the way to the airport, with the minimizer in its carrycase in his lap, that Roger asked where they were off to.

"England," she said absently, inventorying her handbag to see if she had her cigarettes. "I asked you to bring your passport, didn't I?"

She missed the shadow of delight that slipped across Roger's face and away.

It was a conventional flight because the supersonic planes were booked solid. Roger couldn't sleep, so he patiently ate what the flight attendants offered, and watched the movie. It was a comedy, but he couldn't summon up more than a half-hearted chuckle or two. The familiar melancholy settled on him, thick and heavy as the cloud cover visible through the small windows of the plane.

He peeked at Dolly, in the seat next to him. Sleep was unkind to her. The fine lines were suddenly coarser, the poignant little smudges under her eyes no longer a romantic suggestion of experience. No, she looked like a forty-five-year-old spoiled brat, fucked up and out. The promise of ten, fifteen years, down the line, was in her face. The old woman she was becoming, Roger thought, very like a very old, bad-tempered monkey. She was beginning, in fact, to look like her old man.

He stared unseeing at the movie screen. If they crashed right now, if the plane fell apart in midair, he'd have spent the last precious seconds of his life thinking about Mike Hardesty, summoning up the old bastard's face. It was an appalling consideration. The more he tried to shake the image, the more persistently it presented itself.

He closed his eyes and pushed his chair back to the reclining position. He had to make it to England, where he'd never been before. Never been out of the country at all, except for a couple of teenaged forays into Mexico. Hated it, got the shits both times. His mother had nodded wisely, and told him to take the lesson, for once. He had.

But England was different. His mother would approve of his sucking up a little culture in the mother country. Thoughts of his mother banished those of Mike Hardesty. Roger made a silent promise to call her from London. She'd be thrilled. He would make an effort to be thoughtful. In time, she would grow accustomed to his new life.

The jet lag hit them both very hard. The first three days were an agony of sleeplessness, cross words, and fumbling sex that came to no good end. London was prototypically gray and chilly, a drastic enough change from New York's humid torpidity to bring on a late summer cold in Roger. Dolly smoked incessantly, and Roger's eyes watered along with his nose, until he moved to the second bedroom of the suite, on the pretense of sparing her his germs. He had developed an irritating cough as well. Dolly was not unhappy to have her bed to herself.

She felt better after a while and went out, bored with sexless Roger and his cold. If the day was long, cold, and lonely for Roger, it was not for her. When she returned, she was followed by a bellman burdened with her purchases. Like all the others Roger had seen, he was Indian; the entire staff of the hotel appeared to be one brand of Asian or another. In four days in England, Roger had seen next to no Anglo-Saxons. It was a shock.

The shopping expedition cheered Dolly right up. She ordered a room-service meal for them. She sat on Roger's bed and they ate Dover sole and rice pilaf together, washed down with pots of tea and honey and lemon. Roger admired the clothes she'd bought, and privately thought the stuff looked like something his mother would wear, though she'd need a drastically larger size.

"Let's get out of London," Dolly proposed. "You ought to see more of the real England."

"Ummm," replied Roger noncommittally, though he had not seen any more of London than the view from the inside of a cab from the airport to their hotel on the Victoria Embankment, and from the suite, of the Thames. It looked real enough and if she said it was England, he was prepared to take her word for it.

The next day, they took a train from Waterloo Station to Salisbury. It wasn't the treat Dolly implied it would be, but it was comfortable enough. Naturally, the comfort part couldn't last. It was just Roger's luck. She tucked them onto a bus to Stonehenge, announcing she wanted to see the prehistoric ruins. The bus kept out the rain but was overcrowded with tourists filling out a rainy day with an educational stare, and the atmosphere inside quickly became an unbreathable mix of damp cigarette smoke and bad air. Roger felt like he was in a leaking submarine after the crew had dined on beans for weeks.

After standing in the rain at Stonehenge, shivering and dripping at the nose, and trying to see whatever it was he was supposed to see in a Japanese Giants' stone garden, Roger revised his opinion of the whole jaunt downward. He was ready to quit and go back to un-English, boring London, or any place that offered shelter from the rain, and something to warm his interior. Dolly was thriving like so much fungi in the wet, and hustled him back onto the bus, which was to go on to someplace called Longleat. At least the air in the bus had been renewed while the tourists tramped in the mud and took the pictures that weren't going to come out for lack of adequate light.

Longleat turned out to be a great big drafty old palace that the guide called "a stately home." Roger had to snigger when he heard that; it sounded like stately Wayne Manor to him. That made Dolly give him one of those I-can't-take-you-anywhere looks and he glummed up. He allowed himself to be flogged through the place with the clots of tourists from the bus, again taking pictures that would come out appropriately blotchy, fogged, and unfocussed. Roger did what he thought was the sensible thing: He bought some post cards and a book about the joint to mail to his mother. She would probably be as impressed with the stamps as she would with the stuff about Longleat, which anyone, even his mother, could see was hopelessly unliveable, but at least she would know he had been thinking of her while he was having such a giddy, gay old time, blowing gallons of snot into carloads of Kleenex in merry olde England.

When it was time to board the bus again to return to the Salisbury train Station, Dolly pulled him aside. Roger just wanted to park his duff in a well-cushioned seat and maybe doze a little. Standing in the drizzle, whispering to Dolly, was almost painful. It seemed to begin in his teeth, aching in the cold, but that stopped hurting when she wrapped her nails in his wrist deeply enough to draw blood.

"Let's zap it," she hissed, gesturing to the massive stone pile of Longleat. Roger's hands moved instinctively to clutch the minimizer suspended on his chest, inside his clumsily buttoned trenchcoat. He giggled feebly.

She dug her nails in a little deeper. He wondered if she were searching for a vein. The joke had gone far enough, he decided.

"Are you out of your fucking mind?" he hissed back at her. He freed his wrist by prying up her fingers like staples from a cardboard box, pushed by her, and boarded the bus. He flopped into a window seat, the hell with this ladies-first-gentlemen-last bullshit. In short order, she sat down stiffly next to him, after letting a pair of old ladies in identical green pantsuits board before her. Miserably, Roger realized that the window next to him was cold and wet with condensation. He was going to be dripped on all the way to the Salisbury station. And she wasn't going to speak him. Maybe that was a blessing.

"You need to see some people," Dolly diagnosed. Roger grunted, remembering her last prescription for his health, and rolled the blankets tightly around himself. For two days he hadn't been out of bed except to pee. The sudden prospect of a social life didn't excite him at all.

During his relapse, Dolly decided to nurse him back to health. Smoking and chattering, she stayed in and Ping-Ponged from one end of the suite to the other. No sooner had Roger settled into a comfortable doze than she would descend to plump the pillow, refresh his water glass, ply him with hot tea or chilly orange juice, slap magazines cheerfully onto the nightstand, or inquire did he want the telly on? If he did watch television, she wanted to change the channel for him, or to draw the blinds and have him take a nap. He

234

found himself wondering if she intended to irritate him back to health.

At last, he fled to the bathroom for a moment's peace. There was no reading matter there. It had all migrated to his bedside. He had no cigarettes and no desire for one, not with his sense of taste and smell deadened with the headcold. With all the liquids sloshing around in him, he was still unable to coax forth more than a trickle of pee. There was nothing, finally, to do but look at himself in the mirror. His beard was at the do-or-die point. He either shaved today or let it grow. He stroked the stubble thoughtfully, thinking he looked like a cut-throat pirate. Grinning at the mirror, he strived for a debonair, deadly look. Too bad his teeth were so good. A gap, or a flash of gold would be a nice touch.

Once up, he was unable to really relax again. The bed had a plowed-over look to it and didn't exactly smell sweet anymore. He decided to shower and dress. Dolly fussed and then brightened. Probably she was bored too. She headed for the phone.

She was still on the phone, having an animated conversation with someone in an outrageously affected accent when he whispered he was going out to the barber's.

When he returned to the suite with his infant beard shaped and trimmed, she was waiting for him, a fur coat thrown over the chair she was perched in, making it seem thronelike.

"We're going out for tea," she announced, and tickled his chin under his beard. "Cute." And picking up her handbag. "You'll like her. She's an old, old friend, and a darling, when she isn't a perfect bitch."

The old friend turned out to be really old. Roger felt as if he had slipped into a time warp. Tea was served in a high-ceilinged parlor where a fire burned merry hell in the fireplace even though the temperature outside was a pleasant, if gray, seventy-two. The stone walls of the crumbling old pile they were visiting were probably feet thick, Roger speculated. That would account for the clammy cold of the room.

Them maybe the cold kept the old bird from rotting. She was eighty-five if she was a day, and a horse-faced nurse in a white-winged cap waited on her hand and foot. Nursie poured the tea, as the old lady was apparently too weak to

235

lift the enormous silver teapot by herself, and Dolly was too busy running her mouth.

"Lady Maggie," Dolly introduced her. "Weiler." Significant pause. "Nick's mother."

That made Roger jump. She must have had baby Nickie at the last possible biological moment. She was all shrunk up, like really old ladies often are, and wasn't even any bigger than Dolly, just a wee thing. But her eyes were bright and fiery, and she didn't wear glasses. She was dressed in a long rusty black gown of the same era as the decoration of the room. Roger was unsure about such things, but he guessed the room had last been redone in the mid-twenties. She wore her hair like a flapper, short and tight to her ancient skull, with spit curls underlining her rouged cheeks. The rouge was too bright. His mother's often was; Roger thought perhaps ladies' skintones changed as they aged, and they didn't notice. Or perhaps they just didn't see well enough to do their make-up properly.

Her dress was cut very low, not that the old lady had anything to look at or ever had, to judge from her birdy build, but it wasn't grotesque. Her skin formed a parchment background for the necklace she wore, a massive arrangement of pearls, stones that were surely a small fortune in diamonds, glass beads of a curious silver blue color, and enamel on gold. An abbreviated version of the swirling design hung from her ears. Roger thought they must be uncomfortably heavy, yet Lady Maggie sat perfectly upright. Her head was steady. Only her hands trembled a little and when they did, the chunky gem-encrusted rings that circled every finger twinkled and flashed. Her wrists were surprisingly slim and young-looking, and were completely unadorned.

Lady Maggie and Dolly talked of people, places, and things that Roger didn't know. The old woman tried to draw him into the conversation and Dolly occasionally threw him an arch bone of a witticism, but inevitably his attention wandered to the sweets on the tea table. There was nothing he could add to the conversation but polite noises and he could do that quite adequately with his mouth full.

Nursie came and went with increasing frequency. She was fairly hopping from one foot to another. Roger couldn't figure it out. Then he hauled out his hankie to blow his nose, which was very well behaved, really, when she glared at him and he caught the worried glance she cast at her employer. The ladies were too absorbed to have noticed Roger's snotrag. It answered Roger's mental question; evidently the old woman was as fragile as she appeared. A cold might be disastrous. Dolly had informed him that Lady Maggie rarely received guests anymore. Just the exictement of having tea with them might be a serious strain.

Lady Maggie noticed the fidgeting nurse and sent her away, reminding her that it was time for church. A few minutes later, the nurse, who apparently squatted when Lady Maggie said "Shit," could be glimpsed stumping down the lane in a black hat and coat. Roger refined his sense of this old noblewoman: She might be physically frail, but she had an iron fist.

A little later, Dolly pinched his thigh playfully. It hurt. Roger jumped and almost fell out of his chair when she said, "Roger, darling, would you take a picture of Lady Maggie?"

The old woman laughed. "Might be the last one, eh, Dorothy? Well, I'm not vain. I don't mind the world seeing what a ruin I've become. You sit next to me, and we'll be in it together."

Roger clutched the minimizer in its carrycase. Suddenly, he was sweating copiously. The sweets he'd consumed rolled around his stomach ominously. He wanted to wrap the straps of the case around Dolly's fragile neck. What the hell was she thinking of? Fumbling with the case, he giggled self-consciously.

"Guess what?" he squeaked. "I don't have any film." He blushed.

Dolly's eyes sparked at him. The old lady's face fell, if it were possible for it to fall any more than it already had under the influence of gravity. Despite disclaimers, she *was* vain.

Roger was miserable. He thought her a handsome old lady, and she had been nice to him. But Dolly was going to take this out of his hide.

Soon after that, they took their leave. Dolly promised to see Lady Maggie again before they left London. The old woman's obvious loneliness was rather touching.

In the hotel, Dolly slammed her bedroom door on him decisively, after refusing to speak to him on the ride back. It was exasperating and he became, un-Rogerlike, thoroughly pissed off. He ordered an enormous meal from room service and ate every bite, though it was overcooked and tasteless. Then he ordered up some beer, which wasn't so great either.

Roger took the old woman's call the next day, because Dolly had left early to spend the day at a fancy women's club called the Sanctuary. She still wasn't talking to him. Lady Maggie didn't have the same compunctions. He was invited to come and call on her, even if Dolly was unavailable.

"Bring some film this time," she told him in her honeyed English voice, and laughed. It was a wonderful laugh. Roger thought she must have been a wowzer of a broad, once upon a time.

To his own astonishment, he heard himself saying, "Yes. Yes, I will."

"But let's go out," she proposed.

He was relieved. He would buy a real camera and really take her picture. Nothing could happen in a public place. She was, after all, just another lonely old woman, pulling the same strings his mother pulled in him. She wanted to go out and visit the world again. He was his mother's son still, and could see no harm in it. He was happy to oblige.

She arrived by cab at the hotel, and they found, nearby, a pleasant, mildly expensive place to lunch, where the maitre d' fussed over her. She became, with every attention, more grand and gracious. The maitre d' drew Roger aside to ask who the grande dame was, and Roger told him, but it was obvious the man had never heard of her. He had been doing his job when he met them at the door, cued by her apparent wealth, the extraordinary necklace hanging still on her bony old chest, though she had changed her dress to one of a dark blue color.

Announcing she was allowed a glass of port a day, she settled down to savor it, while Roger had a gin and tonic, a departure for him, but he had developed a dislike for the taste of English beer. Dolly had recommended the cocktail some time ago in her ceaseless re-education of his tastes. It turned out to be inoffensive, if no great thrill, and he ordered another.

He was happy to listen to Lady Maggie's reminiscences, which were mostly amusing and not too obscure. He had nothing much to tell her; she didn't seem to expect that. The grub was several cuts superior to the stuff at the hotel, so he ignored the faint guilt that weighted every spoon and fork full. Five pounds heavier than when he left New York, he was beginning to feel himself again.

Roger took her picture on the Embankment. It was going to be a great picture, really memorable. She was perfect. People loitered to watch them, as he posed her on a bench with brilliant flowers in planters to one side. The passersby smiled. The old woman smiled back regally, happy as a pig in poop.

After seeing her into a taxi, he went walking, finally, touring London. The day had turned off lovely, and he savored the unaccustomed sunshine the way Dame Maggie had savored the port. It warmed his bones.

Dolly was smiling like the cat that caught the mouse when he came in. Too excited to tease him, or bare her claws at him, she pounced with her news.

"You darling! Lady Maggie is having a dinner party for us tomorrow night. Because of you. She said you were a dear boy."

Roger grinned weakly, watching Dolly dance a little jig in the middle of the room. His hopes of a quick and painless end to the affair of the old lady vanished. His day clouded over. Goddamn the old witch. And his witch, Dorothy, too. Two spoiled women, who never could be satisfied with some of him. Had to have more.

"That necklace," Dolly was musing. "That gorgeous necklace. It's Lalique, Roger. Absolutely priceless. I'd love to have it, darling."

Roger had heard all about it at lunch, from Lady Maggie. He'd never heard of this Lalique stuff before today and now it had turned into a stone around his neck. Shit.

"How many other people will be at this shindig? You know it's not safe to use the device when a connection could be made between us and whatever we zap," he protested.

"Twenty people. Some I know, but they're all old pals of hers."

Roger frowned. "That's too many. Forget it. It won't work."

He sat down and untied his shoes. His feet hurt from all the walking. But that was that. He wouldn't do it.

Dolly glared at him. "I want it!"

He shrugged and addressed his right shoe. "Lady Maggie never takes it off between breakfast and beddy-bye, she told me that. We try for it, it means doing the old woman in, too. You want it that bad?"

Maybe he could shock her out of it. That old lady. She made him think of his mother. But he could see Nick Weiler in her features, her bearing. Strange to admire the very things in the mother that he had hated immediately in the son.

Dolly had turned her back on him to stare out the windows at the Victoria Embankment below.

"Yes," she said. "I want it. If she lives, there'll be someone to live in my dollhouse. If she doesn't . . . I don't care. You think about it. You figure it out, Roger."

Roger dropped the shoe in his hand. The carpet muffled the thud of its impact. He scratched his young beard thoughtfully.

"Shit," he muttered.

The party was bizarre, at least by Roger's standards. He was the youngest person present. He figured Dolly was next youngest, and then Nursie, whose gray hair and varicose veins placed her in her middle fifties. Everybody else in attendance would have been drawing social security, if they'd been Americans instead of foreigners. A good number weren't steady on their pins; a couple were in wheelchairs. He was relieved to see no one carted in on a stretcher. Uneasily, he fretted that someone might be carted out on one before the party was over.

Many of the names were vaguely familiar. Dolly certainly seemed to know a lot of them. But looking around at the two dozen ruined faces that, from what Dolly whispered to him, had been movers and shakers in the arts half a century ago, Roger found it easy to imagine that he was surrounded by some antique coven. It might explain the remarkable accumulation of sheer years, close to a millennium, all totted up. He had a vision of them with their fervid eyes, dancing naked on obscene patterns, kissing each other's, if not the Devil's, brownies.

Having nothing to say to anyone, Roger took photographs, in between devouring all that was offered to eat. Noticing Dolly casting covetous glances at the old woman's necklace, he pinched her, delighted to get his own back. The old

240

woman saw it too or sensed it; her skinny, speckled hands sought the necklace instinctively, as if she were modest Venus covering her private parts. The ancient obsidian eyes glittered with anger. When Roger smiled cheerfully at her, she turned away, her lips tight and knowing. Her back was as straight as Dolly's. She was something, Roger thought; the years had not bent her.

Dolly and Roger were among the first to go, leaving their elders and betters to carry on. Lady Maggie's farewell was icy but Dolly managed to kiss one withered cheek and squeeze the old woman's paw. Roger made a stiff little bow and dragged Dolly away. Once out of their hostess's hearing, Dolly hissed. Roger hushed her. Sometimes he had to wonder if she knew there was such a thing as discretion.

Re-entering the hotel, Dolly dropped her handbag all over the lobby. She appeared to be drunk. The staff, and guests going in and out, were amused and whispering. Just outside the elevators, she dropped it again, managing to hold on this time to about half of it. Once in their rooms, however, she sobered instantly, and threw herself on her bed.

"I cannot wait," she announced.

"For what?"

In answer, she threw pillows at him. He ducked and dove and finally shut himself in the bathroom with the minimizer, to check it out.

Somewhat later, he crept out again, wearing a colorless coat and face-shading hat. Leaving by a side door, he walked some blocks to hire a cab. It put him down at a public house half a mile from the old lady's house.

As he walked through the deserted narrow streets, he considered seriously not doing this thing. He did not think the old woman could live through it; at least, if he did it, his vow to give Dolly no more tenants for her dollhouse would be kept. But he knew that once she had the necklace, she would want someone to wear it. It was in his power to walk out of her life. There was money enough in his pockets to take him home. Back to his mother's house. Except he didn't want to go back there.

On the street corner opposite Lady Maggie's house, he stood, apparently lost, looking for street signs. In the dark, the small, discreet signs set into building walls by which the British marked the streets, were virtually unreadable. It was a place and moment calculated to make him feel homeless. The straps of the minimizer's carrycase bound his chest under his trenchcoat. Looking up one unknown street, and then down the one he had come by, he turned, at last, and went where he had been sent and did not wish to go, to Lady Maggie's house.

It was blind and still. The party was long over. He rang the bell and waited.

Nurse answered, as he expected, and when he explained that he thought he had left his watch in the lavatory, she opened the gate and told him she would meet him at the door. As he walked up the drive, lights came on in the house, and he saw her, a monstrous silhouette in her robe and hairnet, passing the Palladian windows. She was more sleepy than irritated, and closed the door behind him with a heavy sigh.

He started down the hall, where he knew the guest lavatory was located. She followed him with heavy, graceless footsteps, clutching herself as if she were cold, or worried that the belt on her robe would untie.

"Herself's all worn out," she told him. "She's been pleased by all the attention, but I hope you'll remember, Miss Dorothy and you, her age. She tires quick."

He smiled conspiratorially at her. "Oh, she's tougher than she looks, though. She's lasted this long, hasn't she?"

Nurse recognized genuine admiration when she heard it. She smiled hesitantly back, revealing tremulous dimples.

"Let me take your picture," he said suddenly, and drew the camera case that hung around his neck from the folds of his open coat.

Her hands flew to her netted hair, her bare and flaccid cheeks, back to her old robe.

"Oh, no," she whispered. "I'm a horrid wreck."

"There's some men," Roger whispered back, "that like fresh-wakened ladies."

"Oooh," her breath escaped her. She wasn't sure but she thought this fancy photographer-fellow of Miss Dorothy Hardesty's was talking sexy to her. She blushed from her hairline to the gathered high neckline of her nightdress.

"Mother Mary," she said at last. Her hands clasped over her mountainous bosom, she backed against the nearest wall and waited her fate, like St. Maria Goretti, to whom she of-

242

fered a quick prayer, even if that young martyr was an Eye-tie.

Her fate came quickly and not without pain. She knew it and opened her eyes very wide so as to see St. Maria Goretti and the Beatific Vision and the BVM, as she fell into the valley of the shadows.

She was uglier than sin, Roger thought, looking down at her, and nudged her with his foot. He felt curiously lightheaded, relieved. The decision was made. He consigned her to one of the kitchen matchboxes he carried in his pockets, and set off to find the old woman's bedroom.

He was forced to open a lot of doors in the big old mansion, and flick a lot of light switches. He hoped the neighbors wouldn't notice. But it was a dull neighborhood, he knew from the old woman herself, full of the rich and elderly who all went to bed when it was dark under the table. She must have heard him fumbling about and known intuitively or on the basis of the most subtle noises that he was not Connie, her nurse of so many years.

She was sitting bolt upright in her bed and staring fiercely at him when he opened the right door at last. She had switched on a small dim lamp by her bedside, and had the telephone in her hand. When she saw him, she dropped it. He heard the angry buzzing of the dialtone with relief. She slipped from the bed and seized a big leather-covered box from her nighttable. It was he who was startled by her quickness into a moment's inaction.

"You can't have it," she cried in a high quaver, clutching the case, not as big as a breadbox but close to it, to her flat bosom. "I saw that wicked girl Dorothy staring at it. She sent you, didn't she? Sent you to murder me and steal my necklace."

"Please," Roger said gently, "please."

She backed away. Her thin bony hands worked at the clasp of the box. It fell open, the jewels falling out, cascading down the fold of her pink silk nightdress to the carpet. She caught at them, and dropped the case. Roger saw she had the necklace. She flung back her head and lifted it to her throat.

"Please," he said, fumbling the minimizer sight to his eye. He saw her through it, saw the slow triumphant smile on her thin lips. Her hands dropped from her neck, and the necklace held.

"You'll have to kill me for it!" she shouted at him. "Kill me for it! It's mine! It's all I have! It's mine!"

He pressed the trigger mechanism.

There wasn't much to the old woman. She weighed eighty pounds, down from her adult weight of ninety-five. She was mostly skull and the brains in it. Everything else was desiccated, dried as if by some predeath mummification. The shock blew her into death like a dandelion seed on the wind. The necklace, with a total weight of three pounds, was driven into her scanty flesh like a fossil fern into newborn stone.

She was very still. Roger knew before he picked her up that she was dead. He was queasy in his stomach, and wanted very badly to get out of this place, this antiquated bedroom in an obsolete palace. He wished he were home in L.A., breathing a good gray smog, and feeling warm again. But conscientiously, he zapped the jewels that were scattered on the floor and plucked them up. He dropped them into the same pocket with the boxes that held the remains of the old lady and her nurse, where they fell like clots of sod with faint thumps.

He walked out, careful to touch nothing, leaving the front door wide open. It was at least dry outside, though a little chilly for a summer night, and the air was fresher than the museum dusty air of the house. He felt better by the time he reached another pub, even though it was closed, and no particular refuge to him. There was a phone outside, and he called a cab. It carried him into Piccadilly Circus where he got out and found another. He changed cabs four times before exiting one a block from the hotel.

The most unsettling part of it was not over. It was necessary to spend a silent half hour in the bathroom of the suite, picking the necklace from its bed in the flesh of the old woman. Dolly, lending him a pair of her tweezers, watched the whole operation, now and again telling him how to go about it. He had a hard time concentrating.

In the predawn he left the hotel once again to walk a few blocks down the Embankment. The Thames was the right place, he was sure, to dispose of the pair of tiny corpses. Like in that Alfred Hitchcock movie, *Frenzy*. And all the other murder stories, all the other thrillers. His cold promised a renascence, making his chest full and heavy. His nose dripped and he felt feverish. Not enough food, he told himself, too much goddamn dieting, and as if to underline the thought, he leaned over the side of the bridge and sent his party supper after the little deaders, falling end over end into the river Thames.

They were not the first corpses to be washed onto the littoral of the river, only the tiniest. One tiny woman, stripped of her nightgown by the current but with her hairnet holding her hair firmly in place, washed relentlessly in the eddy of the shallow water. A slighter one, whose thin hands were moved by the water as if she were waving, or searching. A family of river rats carried them off.

13

THE LADY VANISHES

In a mystery worthy of the invention of an Agatha
Christie or Sir Alfred Hitchcock, octagenarian Lady
Maggie Weiler, widow of Lord Blaise Weiler, and once-
mistress of painter Leighton Sartoris, and her nurse of
twelve years, Constance Mullins, disappeared from Lady
Weiler's home in Hampstead following a party the aged
socialite gave in honor of Dorothy Hardesty Douglas,
the former president's daughter, and an old friend.

The puzzle began when a neighbor noticed the front
door of the Weiler mansion, The Mazes, was standing
open, and summoned police, who found an emptied
jewel box on her ladyship's bedroom floor, and the receiver of her bedside telephone dangling off the hook,
the only signs of a struggle. Police could only theorize
that the two women, awakened after retiring, had been
abducted or killed during a robbery or kidnapping at-
tempt. The investigation, stalled by the dearth of clues,
came to a hopeless halt when no ransom demands could
be authenticated within the week.

The dinner guests at the party, the first Lady Maggie
had given in many months, couldn't report anything unusual about the gathering or their hostess. She wore, as
always, the fabulous Lalique necklace and earrings that
were a wedding gift from her late husband, and which
were missing after the apparent robbery.

Leighton Sartoris, himself advanced in years and something of a hermit, was restrained from leaving his island sanctuary in Maine only by the telephoned advice of natural son, Nicholas Weiler, director of the Dalton Institute in Washington, D.C., who assured his father that there was nothing to be done. Weiler, now heir to the other half of his stepfather's estate (he received half of it after Lord Weiler's death) that had supported his mother, himself flew to London immediately only to find the police stymied. He reported that when he visited his mother only a few weeks before her disappearance that she appeared in good health, considering her age, and seemed unworried.

The former president's daughter and her companion, who talked willingly to investigators but apparently had little to report as well, secluded themselves in their suite at the Handsome Hotel before returning abruptly to the States three days after the crime was committed. "Dolly" Douglas talked to reporters at Kennedy International Airport in New York briefly, stating the whole experience had been "a terrible shock."

7.11.80　　　　　*—VIPerpetrations, VIP*

"Pity there's no one to wear it," Dolly said, gloating over the heap of glittering gems in her hand. "Not yet."

Roger's mouth tightened. Dolly didn't see. She was admiring her new necklace, wrapped like a weighty ring around her finger. Roger went on with his unpacking. He had at last beaten his cold, though it lingered long enough to impress the British police with his invalid state. If he had become glum and dull, Dolly failed to notice. She was busy, and when not in public, wearing her distraught face, smugly happy over her new possessions.

Before returning to Manhattan, Roger purchased a pair of salt and pepper shakers with the likeness of the Queen on their sides, for his mother. He declared them, and the German camera he had purchased. Dolly had a shitload of stuff to declare: sweaters, clothes, china, snob food in little jars from Fortnum and Mason's. She paid a stiff duty on them. What she did not declare was the acquisition of either miniatures or jewelry. As she predicted, her bags received the most casual once-over, and her person went unsearched.

247

She ignored the redecoration of the apartment that she had ordered and went directly to the dollhouse room. The first sight of the Doll's White House made her catch her breath and moan. She turned in despair to Roger, who stood blankly watching her. No sympathy there. She sulked past him to her bedroom, threw herself on the bed and kicked off her shoes.

Roger followed her like a small lap dog. If she were going to cry, he thought he might flee to his own bedroom. But she didn't, so he tried to be social.

"Nice to be home, isn't it?"

She threw her hat at him. "Shit! Look at my dollhouse!"

He did so, looking through the door.

"So? It looks the same as when we left."

"It's a fucking mess, Roger!" she cried.

"I know."

What was he supposed to do? Did she think the bloody stinking ark was going to heal itself magically in their absence?

"Stop staring at me. Do something," she sulked.

The pattern for the next few days was set. She was alternately rude, or at best, indifferent, or else so sexually demanding that he felt like a chocolate box at the mercy of a compulsive fattie. While she haunted the dollhouse room, sporadically cleaning up water and fire damage, or more often, just wandering around it, building up a head of steam, Roger avoided it and her. The health club became his refuge. There, he was beyond her reach. Its sweaty hollow spaces were doors and doors from the dollhouse room with its grisly centerpiece. In the gym he could think and punish himself.

It was not much of a surprise when Dolly announced that Lucy Douglas was the only one who could fix her dollhouse. When Roger expressed doubts that Lucy would be so gracious and that, moreover, Dolly had no cover story to explain the damage, Dolly only mocked his caution, warning him solemnly that nothing ventured, nothing gained.

Lucy was startled to look up from her workbench to see not her father or one of her children casting their shadow over her work, but her former mother-in-law. Dolly simply barged in and embraced her.

Lucy submitted stiffly and silently, though how she could have protested over Dolly's relentless babble, she couldn't think. All she could do was look over Dolly's shoulder and meet the uneasy gaze of Roger Tinker, who was standing in the doorway with his hands in his pockets, like a small boy dragged into an adult reunion. Suddenly, Lucy was certain he had taken the missing blade from her workshop, the one she had ransacked the place looking for, worried that one of the kids had kited it. It was irrational; she shook her head at herself.

The children, alerted by the sight of Dolly's Mercedes in the drive, arrived on her heels, and the chaos increased geometrically. Grandmother, it seemed, had a few little things in the car for her darlings. Promiscuous gift-giving had been forbidden by Lucy when the children were infants and had been the occasion of several minor wars between the two women. And here was Dolly, doing it again, knowing that Lucy would never blow up in front of the kids, and was thus neatly trapped between two of her own principles.

Adjourning the noise and confusion to the back porch, Lucy served iced tea, admired Zach's new airplane and Laurie's new doll, the matching T-shirts that announced each child was "Grandma's little angel," and a new record player accompanied by an assortment of children's music. Dolly seeing the set on Lucy's jaw as she told the kids to thank their grandmother, had the nerve to wink. Lucy's hands itched briefly on her iced tea glass as she contemplated dumping the contents on Dolly's perfectly coiffed crown of platinum hair, but willpower won out in the end.

It was Roger, when Dolly allowed herself to be led off to admire Zach's zinnia patch and Laurie's sunflowers, who made the actual rapprochement. Accepting a second glass of iced tea, he munched a Ritz cracker with a slice of banana on it, a delicacy whipped up by Lucy's father for the occasion, and smiled genially around his cracker crumbs.

Clearing his mouth with a swig of tea, he said, "She's embarrassed to death and doesn't know how to go about apologizing."

Lucy sipped her iced tea and cast a glance at her father, who winked at her from his old wicker rocking chair. She said nothing.

"This trip to England was supposed to be recuperative, to get her act together. She's been drinking a lot. Having a hard time. She's messed up about a lot of things. Getting older,

scared about it. I think that's why she picked up with me."
Roger smiled modestly. "And the fascination with dollhouses.
Some kind of need to fill her life. I don't think she means to
hurt people. She doesn't deal with her feelings, gets herself
into trouble."

"Horseshit," Lucy said. "Dolly knows just what she wants.
I'm sure she's having a hard time. But if she hasn't learned to
make her own apologies by now, it's time she did."

Roger suddenly found his iced tea very interesting. His
armpits began to stain his shirt. Dolly had instructed him to
play on Lucy's feelings for the underdog, her need to be fair.
She was being fair all right, and he wasn't enjoying the lying
one bit.

"Whatever," he muttered. "The thing is, she wants you to
work on the Doll's White House again. There was an accident, a fire, and the damage is such that only you can repair
it."

That made Lucy sit up straight. After a brief internal
struggle, curiosity got the better of her. Her father was going
to ask it anyway.

"What happened?"

"She was drunk and smoking, something I watch, especially around the doll-house room. I was away, visiting my
mother." Roger looked hopefully for signs that Lucy was
crediting him, at least, with mother love. There were none.
She sat listening impassively. He plunged on. "She dropped a
butt into the dollhouse without realizing it. I found the filter
later. The smoke alarms went off but she'd passed out, so the
sprinklers went off too, and put the fire out. But the fire damage was already extensive, and the water made it worse." Roger caught a deep breath. It had been a long lie.

"It doesn't sound like her," Lucy observed carefully, "to be
careless around something that means so much to her."

"That's what I mean, she's been self-destructive."

Lucy listened to the voices of her children, to Dolly's rasp.
She was faking her interest in their flowers, talking down to
them.

"Laurie, Laurie, quite contrawrie," her voice distorted the
rhyme, "how does your garden grow?"

Laurie giggled but she would giggle at anything. Lucy
thought her mother-in-law might very well mean to hurt
people, might even like hurting. This odd man, more like an

overgrown kid in his puppy-clumsiness, wanted her to feel sorry for Dolly, to put herself out for a woman who had made a practice of treating her like an indentured servant. She would like to ask Nick; perhaps he would understand. But he wasn't due back from London until the evening.

She made her decision. "I don't think so." Her own voice sounded faint and faraway to her. She met Roger's kicked-puppy eyes.

"I'm very sorry," he said. "That's too bad." Then he smiled again, and she wondered if he really was.

Dolly came up the garden path with the children. Lucy met her glance directly. The eagerness in Dolly's eyes changed to anger, like a sudden massing of storm clouds.

Roger had gone back to noisily crunching up crackers. He seemed oblivious to the awkward silence between the two women.

Lucy's father broke it, clearing his throat, and saying to Dolly, "This business about Nick Weiler's mother was certainly shocking, wasn't it?"

The mention of it dissipated some of Dolly's steam. She smiled at Mr. Novick sadly. "Yes, it was very painful. Poor dear."

The plate of crackers and banana slices was empty, the pitcher of iced tea down to shards of ice, slices of lemon, and a puddle of the tiniest tea leaves. Roger stared at the remains of the snack with the same solemn sadness Dolly gave to the recent tragedy of Lady Maggie Weiler.

He stood abruptly. "We'd better go."

Dolly, relieved, made a show of kissing the kids, and allowed herself to be led away, bearing their bouquets. She had Roger drive, having decided to be queenly, grasping her smelly, bug-ridden bunches of flowers, waving at the kids.

Lucy felt mildly nauseated. Her father patted her shoulder.

"You did the right thing," he reassured her.

"I hope so."

Expecting to hear from Nick, Lucy was startled to hear Dolly's voice when she answered the phone that evening.

"Lucy?"

Lucy tensed. "Yes?"

"Listen, I have been a jackass, haven't I?"

Lucy held her tongue.

"I'm apologizing, Lucy."

"Accepted." It was a genuine acceptance on Lucy's part, if not fulsome. It was a relief to tie up the loose ends of anger and resentment and prepare to put them out of her life.

There was a decent hesitation from Dolly. "Will you work for me again? You're absolutely the only person who can do it."

Lucy laughed in spite of herself. "I doubt that, Dorothy."

She paused. How to gracefully say no without antagonizing Dolly, breaking the brand-new truce?

"I'm already committed to a lot of work," she said doubtfully.

Dolly pressed her. "You'll think about it, at least?"

It would do as an exit, Lucy decided. She could say no later.

"Yes, I'll think about it. Perhaps I can locate someone else to help you."

"Good." Dolly sounded gratified, as if the possibility were all she had really thought she might gain. "Are you terribly busy right now?"

"Well, yes." *No I can't start right away.*

"Then I'll send some pictures, to give you the idea."

"Okay." Looking at pictures didn't constitute a contract. And she was curious to see what Dolly had done.

"When will you let me know for sure?"

"Soon. Two weeks, no more than three."

"Oh, thank you, dear." Dolly hesitated again. "Have you heard from Nick?"

"As a matter of fact, when the phone rang, I thought it was him."

Dolly giggled. "Sorry, dear. I must have been a disappointment." She sobered. "Really, though, tell him for me how upset I am over his mother. He must be devastated."

"I will," Lucy assured her, repressing the sudden urge to sing a song into her ear: *Liar, Liar, pants on fire . . .*

"Well, I won't tie up your line any longer, then. Thank you again, sweetie. Stay in touch." And Dolly was gone again.

Lucy hung up the phone thoughtfully. There was always such a sense of relief when her former mother-in-law left her, or ended a phone conversation. Dolly was like quicksand, or a tar pit, Lucy thought, always trying to draw her in.

"She said *thank you?* And *I'm apologizing?*" Nick was incredulous.

"She did."

"And you told her to stuff it?"

"Not exactly."

Nick groaned. "Don't do it. Break a leg, get pregnant. But don't do it. Please."

Lucy rolled over and slipped out of Nick's bed. Her navy blue nightshirt, rucked up over her breasts, slid down as she swayed gently. Nick reached for her; she danced away.

"I am not going to," she said airily.

Piling pillows behind him, he sat up, and said, "What *are* you going to do?"

"Get some iced water. Want some?"

"Whatever happened to the romance of champagne?" he mocked. "Iced water sounds wonderful."

Lucy flitted away. He heard her humming, and the chink-clunk of the ice-maker in his refrigerator. Both his cats must have heard, too; they stalked in, jumped onto the bed, and curled up next to him, claiming him back from this woman of his. It was pleasant to recline there, stroking his old animals, and thinking about that dark band of navy blue caught above the curves of Lucy's breasts. Thinking about it was all he was going to do at this point; she would want to leave soon, to be home when her children stirred to wakefulness.

She sat down next to him. He took the glass of water with one hand and slipped the other round her waist.

"Fly with me," he whispered, "Let us abandon all our duties and be foolish."

She laughed. "I should shock you into impotence. I should say yes. Then you'd have to leave your real true love, the Dalton."

"Bloody cruel tease," he protested, and nuzzled her. "I do love you more. A little bit."

At that instant, with his nose buried in her hair, his spine was flooded with iced water, as she tipped the glass gently down his back.

"Aargh," he screamed, and jerked away from her, spilling his own glass over the sheets and knocking her hand so that the residue in her glass spilled over his shoulders and into his lap. She leapt back from him and rolled across the bottom of the bed, giggling.

253

"Jesus, Lucy," he gasped, "my bed is soaking wet, and I think I *am* going to be impotent for the rest of my life."

She covered her mouth and lowered her eyelids but her shoulders still shook with laughter.

"Bitch," he complained.

He tore a blanket from the bed and wrapped it around his shoulders as a cloak. "If I catch my death of pneumonia, it's on you. *Will* you tear yourself away from your bloody workshop and take a trip with me?"

"What?"

"Pay attention. Stop your lascivious giggling. I have to go see my father. It's only to Maine, not the end of the world."

"Your father?" Lucy, suddenly sobered, sat up.

"Yes."

Lucy hiccuped.

"On second thought, I'll go alone. I'm not sure you're fit for civilized company."

"Oh, no, you don't. I'm not passing up a chance to meet the greatest living painter in the world. Even if he is your father."

"Is that what you see in me?"

"Christ, no. I never knew you were related until Dolly told me, and by then, we'd, ah, become intimate."

Nick, reassured, stood over her, one eyebrow cocked. "What will you do for the honor?"

"Pig," Lucy answered. "When do we go?"

"Are you sure we're not going to the end of the earth?" Lucy asked, standing by their heaped luggage. Laurie tugged her hand urgently. "Yes, just a minute, sweetheart," she was promised.

Nick, carrying Zach on one hip, winked at her. "Have courage. Look on it as an adventure."

Zach clapped his hands at the very thought.

"I have to pee," Laurie insisted, ignoring, as women will, the call to adventure.

Lucy looked frantically around the Washington National terminal. Travelers crowded its unassuming spaces in all directions. She had never used it before.

"Do you know where it is?" she demanded of Nick.

He shrugged gallicly. "I know where the men's is. Maybe the women's is near it."

The baggage checked, they set off for the restrooms and found the women's quickly by the line outside the door.

"Oh, no," Lucy wailed, while Laurie danced from one foot to another.

"I'm taking Zach to the men's. I'll meet you at the gate," Nick told Lucy, and leaned close to her to whisper, "This is a romantic flight?"

Lucy couldn't help laughing. At least while he was walking away from her, with Zach trotting along next to him, she had his broad back to contemplate. After that, there was nothing but her own wits to distract Laurie from wet pants and hysteria as the line moved slowly into the sickly sweet-smelling facility.

The Delta flight stopped in Portland, a city where Lucy's father had once lived but that Lucy had never seen. It seemed small after Washington, though Lucy knew Washington was only marginally a metropolis, and, viewed from the air, rather old-fashioned with much red brick and masses of green trees. Sea smell entered the airplane as passengers debarked and then others boarded; Nick told her it was Casco Bay, the body of water their plane had crossed to land at the tiny airport with its terrifyingly short runways.

That good smell was left behind in Portland as they flew north and inland to a larger airport at Bangor. The runways there were long and smooth and rather new-looking. There was building, as there had been at the Portland Jetport, but this airport looked expensive and prosperous. In contrast, the city of Bangor, seen from the sky, was much smaller, built on the banks of a river, rather than on a peninsula into the sea, as Portland was. Where Portland was all red brick and trees, Bangor, though green with summer, ran to gray-white masses of concrete, and the center of the city was curiously empty, an interesting but rather inhuman sculpture composed of multistory buildings gleaming in the sun and irregular collages of parking lots.

This was not their day to tour, though; Bangor too was only a waystation. At this airport, they shifted to a small charter plane flown by a young woman with a cheerful Downeast accent and rather startling turquoise eye shadow complementing her young-businesswoman uniform of purple blazer, neat white skirt, and turquoise-and-purple striped blouse. The plane passed low over increasingly unpopulated country; the

255

woods did not stop but seemed sparser, stunted. The land flattened, and was patched with marshland, blueberry bog, and blue water, as the sea's long fingers reached inland. The salt perfume was once again in the air.

Again, they landed, at a tiny one-horse airport in the bush. The children were tired and fractious; only the promise of a helicopter ride staved off the tears. The chopper came in behind them, only a few minutes after their small plane landed. Watching its descent occupied the children until they could be whisked on board.

It was impossible to talk over the thunder of the blades so they all watched the land disappear. In a matter of minutes, they flew over endless blue sea dotted with occasional boats, from sailing craft to fishing and lobstering boats, to tankers and freighters. Here and there an island poked a battered bit of rock and fauna through the cold blue waters. Lucy thought she would remember always the new perspectives of her planet that this perfect day for flying had presented. At first the works of man on the surface of the world had been something to admire, and then had shrunk, with every passing hour, every change of plane, until it seemed as if the human race did no more than infest, by sufferance or indifference, the bits of land it had claimed. And then came the sea, where man's mark simply did not exist, and she shivered, feeling small and vulnerable in this noisy mechanical bubble beating its way through the cloudless sky. Nick, next to her, felt her shiver, reached out to draw her close, and warm her with his body. Behind them, the children had dozed off, oblivious to all that passed, above and below.

The island was one of a chain, most of which, their pilot screamed at them, were too small to support life more demanding than turtles and a wide variety of sea birds. It was a fish-hook-shaped bit of mountaintop peeking out of the sea, perhaps a hundred and ten square miles of stunted trees, sand, and rock. In the folds of the rocky summit, a few rich wrinkles of laboriously created topsoil supported a patch of forest, Sartoris's gardens, and the meadows where his goats and cows grazed. Sartoris's house and studio, the only buildings other than rude shelters for his animals, were nestled in one such wrinkle, in the hook of the island, where the sea came close to its heart.

The chopper took them low over the house, so that its

shape, a hollow-hearted square, was clearly visible. The studio was a curious pie-wedge of a building, two-stories high and ablaze with glass to the north, and roofed in solar panels that collected the sun from the south. Lucy found herself suddenly twitching with curiosity. Nick, reading her wonder-livened face, was pleased, and laughed.

The chopper landed on a smoothed area half a mile from the house, which shone white as old bones in the strong sunlight. A muscular woman of indeterminate age met them with a pony and a small tray. She had smiles for Lucy and the children but her pale blue eyes set in a long bony face sparked with curiosity. She waited patiently for Nick to finish helping the pilot with their bags, and then enfolded him in her long arms like a long-lost son.

"Nicholas," she greeted him, pounding his back with her big raw fists.

He hugged her back, swinging her off her feet.

"Ma," he sang happily. He set her on her feet carefully. "There. Ma, this is Lucy Douglas. Laurie. Zach. Meet Ma Blood."

The woman's olive skin was flushed with pleasure and excitement. She took Lucy's hand, and then the children's, one by one, with great solemnity.

"Pleased, I'm sure," she said, and giggled.

She turned and seized a suitcase in either hand, and swung them up into the trap, even as Nick, protesting, dived for them.

"Himself," she said over her shoulder, "is out milking the goats. He'll be back for tea. Pretty quick. He told me where to set you down."

She hoisted the children into the trap, where they settled, giggling among the heaped luggage.

"Come on now," Ma Blood prodded them.

There was time, Nick assured Lucy, for a brief ocean swim after settling into their rooms. It was a short run from the glass doors that opened from their bedrooms onto the beach, over coarse dunes, to the sea. The ocean was cold, but the children seemed not to feel the chill. Lucy plunged in, thrilled by the unexpected buoyancy of salt water, and the force of the waves that lifted her and pushed her back to the sand.

After splashing with the children awhile, Lucy crouched under a thick towel on the beach, digging her hands idly into the sand for the feel of it, and watched them play. Nick stayed with them, playing at sharks and sea monsters, teaching them to open their eyes under water. The old man spoke from behind her.

"Mrs. Douglas," he identified her.

She jumped, and turned to look up at him. The sun was behind him, his face obscured by a large floppy Panama. But the large, caftan-draped body radiated an unexpected force, his voice, strong and resonant, and the more startling because of its resemblance to Nick's.

She had begun to rise, even as he reached down to assist her to her feet. The hand she grasped was extraordinary, an enormous hand, large even for the heavy-bodied man who extended it. The fingers were as fat as cigars, flattening at their points into calloused, broken-nailed wedges. Liver spots made archipelagoes over their high-boned backs but the wrists and lower arms, where the sleeves of the caftan were pushed back, were knotted with muscle under the aged skin.

"I'm so pleased to meet you," Lucy stammered.

He did not shake her hand, only squeezed it gently. His skin was papery to the touch, dry but not cold, and scratchy where ragged calluses were built up along the fingers.

His face, obscured in shadow, was like one of the two-decades-old newspaper prints which were most commonly reprinted, the most recent of his public faces. Black and white masks, revealing less than they disguised, she thought. The light behind him outlined his bull neck, the heavy musculature that bespoke a massive chest, and the slight stoop forward, a small signature of age. Lucy turned over in her memory the half-forgotten photographs, the trio of self-portraits, from her art school textbooks. The young Sartoris, and how long ago had he been young, had been an athlete, a wrestler, and a horseman, but was rumored to be incredibly ugly of face. She had no clear impression of what he was supposed to look like, and for the first time wondered if the photographs had been deliberately obscure, the portraits consciously distorted. Peering at him, she looked for Nick in him, and saw only shadows.

He looked beyond her, to Nick and the children, cavorting in the surf.

"There have been no children here in decades," Sartoris said slowly. "I had forgotten how queer and wonderful they are. I didn't think there was anyone left on this earth with the courage to make new people."

Lucy laughed. "Not courage, but thank you anyway. I was younger then. I think the right word is foolhardiness."

She couldn't see him smile, but a throaty chuckle emerged from the shadows of the Panama. He gestured to Nick, just then noticing that Lucy was no longer alone on the beach.

"And my son. Is it foolhardiness that led you to him?"

Startled by the faint contempt in Sartoris's voice, she replied, tightly, "I'm sorry, that's none of your business."

Sartoris laughed out loud then and there was pleased surprise in it. "I wish you luck, Mrs. Douglas."

Nick was splashing toward them, with Zach riding his shoulders. Dancing around them, Laurie tried to wet Zach with handfuls of water, and only doused Nick. Zach, from his invulnerable perch, kicked and chortled triumphantly.

After introductions were made, the old man gestured toward the sun, now low in the sky. All at once, the bathers felt chilled and faintly silly, playing manners in scanty swimsuits. Lucy hustled the children up the path toward the house. Behind her, the conversation between father and son came to her in distant rumbles and splashes. When she turned to look at them, just before entering the house, she saw they still loitered in the dunes, face to face, well beyond earshot. Nick was hunched against the gently rising night breezes, his hands shoved into the pockets of his terrycloth beach jacket, thrown on over his sea-wet skin. There was the solemnity of bearers at a funeral in their stance. Lucy could only guess at what passed between them, perhaps something concerning Lady Maggie.

Bringing the children to the terrace for tea a few minutes later, Lucy found Sartoris ensconced in a peacock-backed wicker chair, his back again to the sun. Nick was still showering off the sand and salt.

"Come and sit with me," Sartoris directed the children, patted cushioned wicker chairs to either side of him.

So quickly did they obey him, that he cast a quick, sardonic glance at Lucy, and said, "Well-raised little people, I see."

Without response, Lucy took a chair opposite him. Raising her children this far nearly on her own, she wasn't about to make apologies to anyone for her methods.

"Is your mother very strict?" Sartoris proceeded to ask her children.

Zach nodded *of course*. His attention was on the table, already set with plates of cookies and other delicious-looking tidbits, as well as an awesome stoneware teapot.

"Yes, sir," Laurie agreed. "All the other kids say so."

Lucy laughed a little uncomfortably at this evidence of her neighborhood reputation.

"Would you pour, Mrs. Douglas," Sartoris asked, and when Lucy nodded and moved to heft the heavy teapot, he settled back in his chair. "My mother was *very* strict," he informed Laurie and Zach. "Oh, yes."

Pausing to pass teacups to the children, he went on, "Why, she never would allow me to have all the sweets I wanted at tea. 'Just two, Leighton,' she always said, 'so as not to insult cook,' and if I took more, she'd put me in bed without my supper."

Laurie's eyes were round with sympathy. Zach eyed the goodies nervously. Perhaps he was going to be forbidden more than two as well.

"And now that I have no mother to forbid me such things, I have a doctor who says much the same thing. He leads me to believe that a decent wedge of that gateau, the lovely chocolate one with the walnuts and cherries on the top, would put me right in my grave."

Zach gasped in horror.

"But perhaps a small sliver will only make me deathly ill. Possibly it will even immunize me, as minute doses of poisons are supposed to immunize one against supposedly fatal administrations. Would you slice me just the thinnest piece, Mrs. Douglas? And much bigger ones for Miss Laurie and Master Zach."

"I'd be pleased to," Lucy said cheerfully. Leighton Sartoris's mother, no doubt Pouring at the Great Tea Table in the Sky, must be feeling checkmated.

"And allow me to select something for you. The madeleines all but *parlez vous*. Mrs. Blood is sadly wasted on me. I think she must be ecstatic to have guests to appreciate her talents."

The children, their faces shining with anticipation and a measure of relief that somehow the vaguely threatened limitation had magically dissipated, chorused thank yous and fell to.

"And you," the painter asked Lucy, "what will you have?"

"Oh, just a madeleine."

He cocked his head mockingly. "Don't tell me your mother only permitted *one*? No? You're dieting? The richest country in the world," he disapproved, "and all the women practicing for a famine. All those bones. I should think lovemaking would be positively painful. Possibly noisy, clattering, clicking, like so many castanets."

Lucy studied her teacup and lied cheerfully, "Actually I'm not; I'm trying to set a good example."

The old man barked an incredulous laugh.

"I heard that," said Nick, coming onto the terrace from the house. "I hope you're not trying to set too good an example. If it's food, I'll feel like a pig, and if it's love, well, I'll be very lonely." He bent to kiss the top of her head lightly. "I'll take three of everything."

Lucy's cheekbones grew warm; she bit quickly into her madeleine. Now her plate was rather priggishly empty. Defiantly, she plucked a chocolate-laced croissant from among its brethren.

"Ha, *mon père*," Nick told his father, "she's seen through your crafty ways." To Lucy: "He likes to corner his guests so they feel they can't eat, or they'll be giving into his bullying. That way, he gets all the goodies. And never mind the stuff about skinny women either. My mother never weighed more than a hundred and ten pounds, except when she was pregnant with me, when she got up to, what was it, eight stone. I never heard any complaints then about noisy bones."

Sartoris snorted. "There's no explaining love, is there?"

Nick turned the conversation skillfully to other matters. First, he provoked Sartoris into telling the children about the island, how he came to live there, and how he lived there, nearly self-sufficiently, he and Mrs. Blood, who appeared magically to refresh the teapot and the plates. When the old painter tired, Nick contributed funny stories about goings on at the Dalton. The children, sated with food, fell to giggling and playing at tea party together. The old man, studying

261

them in silence, while Nick talked, noticed their boredom first.

"I'm rather tired," Sartoris announced.

At that moment, Lucy noticed the bluish smudges beneath Zach's eyes, and Laurie's tired giggle. Suddenly, she too was bone-weary.

"Mrs. Blood and I are accustomed to a rather late dinner. Perhaps you will forgive me if I rest for a while before joining you. Ethelyn would be happy, Mrs. Douglas, to prepare a light meal for your little people, and sit with them while you and Nicholas dine with me later."

"Thank you," Lucy said, and in spite of her tense tiredness, smiled.

The old man rose with some effort and touched her hand lightly before leaving.

"Good show," Nick whispered to the children, and the two adults carried the little ones off for a quiet time. Behind them, the last pool of sunset color darkened and disappeared with the light.

Lucy was conscious of Nick's approving glance as she sat down to dinner. She had her hair up, and her shoulders were bared by her simple sundress. Stealing frequent glances at Nick, she couldn't help feeling good. He seemed inordinately, unreasonably happy. The tension she had sensed in him over his mother was gone, exorcised by his father's presence, some private ritual of grief that had occurred on the beach between the two men, by her presence and her children's, she could only guess.

She was proud of him. She had never heard him as intelligent and witty, sparked by the male peacock in him, strutting for her, and pricked by the unspoken criticism of his father. He brought the Dalton to life, exposing his own love of it. In the wake of Sartoris's widening silences, it struck her that Nick was trying to convince his father of the worth of his life's work, of his own worth.

Sartoris had seated himself at the far end of the table, where the diffuse lights from paired candelabra that lit the room barely reached. Wearing a hooded caftan in rough linen gave him a monkish look and effectively veiled even his profile from Nick and Lucy.

"I'm sorry," he said at last, "to be such a poor dinner companion. Like Scrooge, I'm plagued with ghosts. When one arrives at my age, one discovers the most lasting of emotions is regret. Or, in the case of the grievously sinful, like myself, guilt."

Nick was silent, communing with the tablecloth, or his own guilts. Lucy reached out impulsively and took the old man's left hand.

"I thought I could bury her with all the years I've lived apart from her. I thought I could live here and paint my daubs like a dandelion in a bit of Lucite. When I knew she was gone, I . . . knew I was just a quitter, a nasty old hermit with a heart like a raisin."

Nick too moved closer to his father but could find nothing to say that was of any comfort. So he listened.

"She was all alone in that rotten old house, all alone for years. Perhaps it's because some thug or other has carried her off and murdered her . . ." He toyed painfully with his teacup ". . . I'm sure she's dead, I can feel it, but I hope I should have felt the same if she'd died in her bed all alone.

"She was beautiful when she was thirty." He laughed. "We played some awful pranks, the two of us. And when she came to me and told me she was going to marry a rich man who would be kind and generous and faithful, I thought that was the end of it. But it wasn't. I came here and stayed, months, and months, and then found myself drawn back to her again, as if by some invisible thread that connected us heart to heart. *She* ended it, you know," and he seemed to be speaking only to Nick, "after you were born. So much for noisy bones. Still, we were friends. We never quarreled, or hated each other. We just got old and everything, even love, became more of an effort than it was worth. We've been merely rumors in each other's diaries for years. I must be getting senile, to go all damp-eyed and drippy-nosed over a woman I haven't seen since, God, your stepfather's funeral." He blew his nose loudly into his dinner napkin and muttered. "Ethelyn won't like that."

"There's nothing senile about finding out you can still feel for an old love," Lucy said softly, looking at Nick.

He played assiduously with his coffee spoon, his mouth slipping back and forth between a shaky smile and a tightdrawn line.

"One hopes so," Sartoris said, a little too loudly and

clearly. "Enough of this maudlin sogginess." He raised his untouched brandy glass. "To Maggie."

Solemnly, Nick and Lucy joined him.

"And you know," the old man continued, putting down the glass with a thump, "damned if that miserable girl Dolly Hardesty wasn't there. I never knew that bitch to bring anything but trouble with her, like a big black cloak."

"These days," Nick commented, "she has a little elf with her."

Lucy smiled; Sartoris, not understanding, frowned.

"Poor girl, she's your mother-in-law, isn't she? Must have earned a halo by now on that alone. And you worked for her. That silly toy house of hers. Not that it's really silly, I suppose. I daresay your work is as valuable as mine."

"Ho, ho," Lucy laughed it off.

"I'm not getting into this," Nick said, reaching for the brandy.

"Can't, can you? That's the trouble with being . . ." the old man wrinkled his nose in distaste ". . . a curator. You can't afford to offend anyone. Brown-nose the potential donor, lick-spittle for the silly public and the bloody damned critics with their foppish fads. No job for an honest man. Or woman."

Nick shrugged. It was apparently an old argument between the two men.

"Miniatures used to be little bitty portraits and whatnot, when the earth and I were green," Sartoris observed. "Now it's another world. Anything and everything, on a scale of one to one-tenth, or less. Next thing it'll be real people."

"I'm afraid the state of the art's not quite up to it yet," Lucy laughed, thinking the brandy must be getting to Sartoris. "But it's a living, and as you say, an honest one."

"Oh, yes," the old man agreed. "I'll tell you, my dear. I'd almost rather that my own little pictures and pots were classified as toys, playthings, instead of textbook illustrations or interior decoration. Learned dissections of brushstrokes and impasto and optic nerves, for God's sake. Gives me headaches." He sighed. His large hands came to rest on the tabletop. In their complete stillness, Lucy discerned the old man's weariness.

Nick seemed to pick it up, too. "I don't know about you, *mon père*, but my lady and I have had a long day and face our indefatigable companions tomorrow, probably at first light."

"The best time." Sartoris gestured his dismissal. "I must see Ethelyn before I retire. Have a pleasant night's rest."

He sat like a statue in a garden, a shadowed bulk in a ladder-backed chair looking down the white plain of the dining table. It was some hours later, when Lucy approached consciousness at the conclusion of some dream cycle that she thought she heard the measured footsteps of the old man in the corridor, like a mourner at a funeral procession.

14

She thought, when she woke again, that he was still there, only now he was a giant and he was running. Opening her eyes, she found the room was full of daylight, and the pounding of giant steps resolved into the beat of helicopter blades. Turning to Nick, she found his side of the bed empty. He came out of the bathroom, pants on, but still shirtless and sockless.

"Oh, shit," she said, sitting up and grabbing the travel alarm from the nightstand.

"Is that any way to greet true love?" he complained.

Throwing back the covers, she slid from the bed, barefoot and clad only in a thin summer nightdress, and made for the next-door bedroom she was officially sharing with her children. Their cots were empty and unmade, their flimsy pajamas crumpled on the pillows.

Nick, buttoning his shirt with sleep-slowed fingers, had followed her. Driven by the panicky conviction that the children were in danger from giants, she pushed past him and ran toward the kitchen, ignoring his puzzled exclamation.

Zach and Laurie looked up at her when she pushed open the swinging door to the kitchen. They were sitting at an old-fashioned wooden kitchen table, with their mouths full of freshly baked beignets. Ethelyn Blood looked up from the croissant dough she was shaping into half-moons on a baking sheet and smiled. Lucy, realizing that Laurie and Zach, fully dressed and with their hair still shining from the application of a wet comb, were not only perfectly safe but apparently unfazed by her absence from her bed, and she, still in her nightdress, felt more than a little foolish. Summoning an uncertain smile, she shouted "Good morning!" over the steady thunder of the helicopter blades.

Ethelyn grinned, and holding her cupped palms an inch from her ears, rolled her eyes in exasperation with the din. From just behind Lucy, Nick shouted, "Who is it?"

The housekeeper shrugged and raised her eyebrows.

"Where's Sartoris?" Nick roared.

Lucy flinched away from him as his shout hurt her ears, and Laurie and Zach grinned at the adults' capering, half-mimed conversation.

"He's up," Ethelyn Blood shouted back cheerfully.

Nick glanced quickly at Lucy. The same thought formed full-blown in their minds at nearly the same instant. If Lady Maggie had been the victim of a botched kidnapping, then Sartoris was an even more likely target, living as he did in total isolation with only a middle-aged, if tough, woman as his companion and protection.

Nick plunged through the kitchen, hurtling out the garden door. Lucy followed him. The sound of the helicopter covered Ethelyn's cry of surprise.

She dropped the curl of pastry in her hand. Putting her hands on her hips, she asked in puzzlement, "What are they up to? Himself's on the beach, painting like always." She turned to the children. "Well, you eat up the whole plate of them benyays, somebody'd better. And I was just feeling good to have somebody in for breakfast. Himself, he don't ever eat any. Only time anybody ever comes is when your mama's museum man visits. He takes after his daddy in more than one way, but he does like to eat. Most times. This time," she looked sadly down at her buttery pastries, "he got his mind on something besides Ma Blood's good cooking."

Zach and Laurie shared a hasty glance and giggled. Not only was the food in this place heavenly, there were more goings-on than a circus.

The chopper landed closer to the house than it had for them. Nick and Lucy had only to race through the garden and over the ridge to the orchard where the apple trees bent and struggled as if against a hurricane. At a safe distance from the orchard, the helicopter was even then beginning to struggle upward. Standing just outside the whirlwind of its blades, two people bent over their overnight bags.

The chopper lifted off and drifted away, like a powerful swimmer in calm waters. As the turbulence of its departure diminished, its former passengers were able to show their faces. Lucy, suddenly cold and angry to see her former mother-in-law even in this isolated paradise, turned to Nick, who put his arms around her protectively, perhaps possessively.

Dolly shouted at them, waving her hands, "Darlings, isn't this wonderful?"

Beside her, Roger Tinker, with his chest armored in an assortment of cameras in cases, in the approved Japanese tourist manner, stared slack-mouthed at Lucy in her diaphanous nightgown.

Lucy shot back a defiant glare, and then said, "Excuse me," to Nick, turned her back on the unexpected visitors, and walked calmly back through the orchard. Nick grinned after her, thinking *rah, rah, kid*. Dolly touched his arm, talking into his ear.

"Nick, you'll be chasing Lucy through the fountain in the altogether next. You *are* your father's son."

Nick ignored her sniggering. "What are you doing here?"

She waved a hand airily at the house. "Visiting my dear friend, your darling *père*." Patting his arm, she whispered, "I'm devastated about your mother. London just went sour and ugly. I had to leave. I'm sorry I missed you."

Nick stuck his hands in his pockets and shuffled bare feet in the grass.

"This isn't a particularly opportune moment for you to be here. Sartoris had been hit hard by Mother's disappearance."

"But you brought Lucy and my bon-bons here," Dolly pouted.

"They're family," he said bluntly.

Dolly paused, then, "Oh, I see." She withdrew her arm from his delicately, as if she had just noticed a wet paint notice dangling from his elbow. "Well, darling, it's your bed. And I wouldn't dream of intruding on your . . . grief. But I must see Lucy. It's a business matter."

"She won't do it," Nick said shortly. He nodded cryptically and stalked off toward the house without another word.

Dolly raised her eyebrows at Roger.

"He might have offered to help with the bags. Well, you can manage, just the two of them . . . if you can walk with the lump in your pocket."

Roger grinned. With the weather holding hot and fine, he was looking forward to multiple opportunities to leer at Lucy Douglas. At least there would be some profit to this jaunt. His private opinion was that Dolly was pushing Lucy and that Lucy was not the woman to push. Perhaps he could manage to head off a direct confrontation, act as a buffer. Buffering Juicy Lucy would be okay.

Nick went first to the terrace and then to the beach, looking for his father. He found the old man a little way from doors of Sartoris's own bedroom, that opened onto his own patch of beach. He was sitting on a camp stool, one hand holding the brush, the other supporting it. Nick did not look at the canvas on the easel; from past experience, he knew Sartoris loathed people peeking at his work in progress. The son watched the father dab at the canvas in silence. After a quarter of an hour, the old man stopped, raised his head under the Panama, and stared at Nick.

"It's Dorothy Hardesty and her buddy."

The old man growled, "What the hell does that bitch want here?"

Nick shrugged. "She says to talk to Lucy. Lucy told me Dolly wants her to fix up the dollhouse again. Evidently there was a fire in it when Dolly, while soused, dropped a cigarette in it. Do you want me to hold her off while you work?"

Sartoris was silent. Abruptly, he pulled a paint rag from the waistband of his baggy trousers and wiped his brush. "Bah! I can't concentrate now, with that hurdy-gurdy pounding in my ears, and the thought of Dolly and this villain you say she's kipping with, hissing around my house and island."

Nick nodded. He was afraid of this reaction. The old man seemed dangerously tired.

"Let me help you pack your gear," he offered. It was disquieting that Sartoris, normally so fussy about people handling his equipment, assented with a weary shrug.

When they crossed the sand to the terrace, Dolly was ensconced on the terrace, with a pot of coffee and a plate of freshly baked beignets. Mrs. Blood stood guard over her, watching anxiously as Sartoris shuffled his way toward them. Roger sat in another corner, with the bags at his feet.

The housekeeper nodded to Nick, a *we have this invasion in hand* look, as he mounted the steps to the terrace.

"Where's Lucy?" Nick asked.

"Dressing. The little ones want to go on the beach," Ethelyn Blood told him. With her arms crossed over her chest, she looked as if she were ready and eager for an eviction.

Dolly came to her feet to greet Sartoris, holding out her hands and crying, "Sartoris, what can I say?" Her voice was mournful, her eyelashes fluttering as if to hold back tears.

Roger suddenly found the beach very interesting. There was no one on it to see the shade of disgust that passed, against his will, across his features.

"Dorothy." Sartoris shook his hands free of hers immediately and flinched back from her drawing near as if to embrace him. "What brings you here?" he asked, and passed slowly by her to stare down at the table laid for an outdoor breakfast.

Dorothy was silent for a second and then rushed him again. "Maggie," she whispered, and a tear slipped down her cheek. She straightened quickly, as if regaining control. "Ever since I saw her, after what happened, I haven't been able to stop thinking about you, how you must feel."

Sartoris sat down heavily and reached for a beignet. "That's astonishing. You thought of *me?*"

"Of course. Maggie spoke of you the very night . . ." her voice trailed away delicately.

The old man snorted. "Touching." He broke the beignet gently and nibbled at one piece.

Dolly's face set as if she smelled something bad but was too polite to say so. She sat down, looked at Nick, and winked. He was shocked. Did she think Sartoris was so senile she could mock the old man practically to his face?

"If you don't want to speak of it, we won't," she said soothingly. She reached out to pat Sartoris's hand, at rest on the table.

He withdrew his hand from her reach, and gestured at Roger. "Who's that?"

Roger jumped, his hand held out.

"This is my friend, Roger Tinker," Dolly introduced him hastily.

The old man looked Roger up and down and then employed his free hand to reach for a cup. Ethelyn Blood jumped to fill it.

Dolly gave Roger a chilling look; he dropped his hands into his pockets and slunk back into the corner, a blush heating his cheeks.

"You can't stay here," Sartoris said abruptly. He pushed the remains of the beignet away. "Very nice," he told the housekeeper. She beamed.

"The helicopter won't be back until tomorrow," Dolly protested. "Why not? This house has eighteen rooms if it's got one."

"No room for you. I didn't invite you. Don't want your crocodile tears, either. Call the helicopter and tell it to come back right away. It's probably not as far as halfway back to Bar Harbor by now."

"This is impossibly rude of you, Sartoris," Dolly scolded. She cast an appealing glance at Nick. "Nick, can't you talk to him? You handle him better when he's like this."

The old man hissed. He struggled to his feet. Mrs. Blood moved quickly to his side, her face set and angry.

"My father knows his own mind," Nick said mildly.

Dolly gave way all at once. "Very well. Would you allow me the courtesy of having a word with my daughter-in-law and seeing my grandchildren?"

"Mrs. Douglas's business is, of course, her own," Sartoris growled.

"Well?" Dolly challenged Nick.

Nick crossed his arms over his chest and whistled tonelessly. He wasn't about to interfere even marginally in Lucy's business, and she knew it.

"Better ask Lucy," he said. "But I warn you. She knows her own mind, too."

Dolly sat down, victorious on at least one front. "I'll just wait here for her."

"I'll bring you a phone," Nick offered, "while you're waiting. You might catch that helicopter yet."

He detoured to Lucy's room. The cots were made up; she was tucking neatly folded pajamas under the pillows. She looked up when he entered; he mock-leered at her. She laughed.

"Urgent call?" she asked, indicating the phone in his hand.

271

"If it removes Dolly from our midst, I'd guess so. Sartoris has shown her the door. But she has to call the air taxi. Fair warning: She wants to talk to you."

Lucy, scooping sun-screening lotion and sunglasses from an open vanity case into the commodious pockets of her one-piece sunsuit, grimaced.

"Yuk," she said.

She put on a big straw hat.

"There's something else."

She cocked her head, listening.

"Sartoris. He seems tired. I'm a little worried."

She nodded. "If you think we should go home, it's all right. As a matter of fact, I'm capable of getting myself and my kids home on my own stick, if you think you should stay."

"No, no. Let's all stay a little longer. I think he'll be fine, if Dolly will get on her stick and fly away. He seems happy enough to see you and the kids."

They walked down the corridor, holding hands.

"Where are my old buddies?" Nick asked.

"In Mrs. Blood's pantry. She set them to looking for buckets and spoons appropriate to the beach."

When they arrived on the terrace, they found Sartoris and the housekeeper had retired. Nick guessed Mrs. Blood was fussing a little over the old man, and perhaps, for once it was necessary.

A long conversation with the airport at Bar Harbor ensued, broken by static into an archipelago of discreet shouting. The helicopter was on its way to another job. It would come, barring any change in the weather, at eight-thirty or nine that evening.

Dolly hung up, satisfied. The delay meant that Sartoris would be compelled to serve them lunch, and she would have most of the day her way. Roger was half-asleep in his corner chair, stirring only to burp and fish another antacid tablet from his pocket. He had wolfed the beignets as soon as they had been left to him, and washed them down with most of the coffee, while she glared at him.

Lucy had dawdled after saying hello, through half the phone call, and then left for the beach with the children. She had shrugged apologetically at Dolly; the kids were restless, and with lard cans and old soup spoons, apt to be noisy.

With satisfactory arrangements made, Nick excused himself and disappeared into the house. Reporting to daddy, Dolly thought.

She kicked off her shoes and began to wiggle out of her pantyhose.

Roger applauded. "Take it off," he hooted.

She ignored him. He was being thoroughly awkward, just like a spoiled child, because she had insisted they follow Lucy here and that wasn't what *he* wanted. The last thing she was going to do was let him spoil her fun.

"I'm going after Lucy. Down the beach. If you're coming, you'd better take off your shoes and socks and roll up your pants. And keep your distance. This is private. Between Miss Lucy and myself."

"Oh." There wasn't much Roger could say to that.

He bent to unlace his shoes, wondering if there were things in the sand that might bite his feet. It was a beautiful place; no doubt it had its nasty secrets. He was sorry he had hooted at Dolly. If he'd shut his stupid mouth, she might have played to him a bit. More than that, if he was going to get her off this island without her messing up, it was necessary to stay in her good graces. He stuffed his socks in his shoes and paired them neatly on the wall of the terrace. Dolly was already picking her way across the dunes. He jumped up and trotted after her.

"Lucy!" she called. The sand tugged at her feet. It was still wet from the high tide. "Zachary John! Laurie!"

Lucy, walking a few yards down the beach, turned and waved. Laurie and Zach, a few yards beyond her, dropped their tin pails and spoons and raced back to their grandmother, shouting.

Lucy and Roger, from different vantage points on the beach, watched Dolly scooping up the children in turn, hugging them, babbling at them. Their eyes met briefly, long enough for each to be astonished at the second of open disbelief they saw in each other's faces at Dolly's exhibition of grandmotherly love. Roger colored immediately, and stared quickly out to sea. Lucy, stunned, could only stare at him.

Dolly led the children back to Lucy and released them; they flew back to their pails and spoons and clanked off down the beach, stooping to pluck small, indistinguishable objects from the beach, announcing each find ectastically.

273

Lucy and Dolly fell in behind them, walking much more slowly.

Panting, Dolly made fun of her own exertions, saying, "I don't know how you keep up with them."

The salt air was invigorating but she wasn't dressed for a romp along the beach. She couldn't very well sit on the sand in her white linen tunic, belted over a pleated navy blue skirt. It was a rare misstep for her to arrive anywhere in the wrong clothing. Roger's fault, really, for being a pain in the ass and distracting her. Mocking herself, she twitched the pleats of her skirt.

"Can you imagine? Wearing this on a beach?" She admired Lucy's yellow sunsuit. "You've got the right idea. That's perfect."

"Thank you," Lucy said. "I hope you don't mind just walking along. I want to keep close to the kids while they shell hunt."

"No, not at all. I can't sit down, for sure."

They glanced back at Roger, dawdling down the beach. He too was poking at the sand in search of some kind of treasure, with a long crooked stick he'd picked up crossing the dunes.

"Should we wait?" Lucy asked politely.

Dolly dismissed Roger with a laugh. "Heavens no. Roger can amuse himself."

The two women moved on. Laurie bolted back to show her gleanings. Zach, stolidly advancing as his pail banged against his short legs, gave his attentions to the matter at hand, as usual.

When Laurie had moved out of hearing again, Lucy said, "I have to admit I was surprised to see you this morning."

"Yes, I noticed." Dolly paused. "Your father told me where you were. Well, I had to pay a condolence call on Sartoris anyway."

"You saw Nick's mother that night, didn't you?" Lucy was mildly curious but had taken the police reports at face value. If they said Dolly knew nothing about the disappearance of Lady Maggie and her nurse, then they had solid reasons for ruling out any involvement.

Dolly put on her funeral face again. "It was traumatic. She was an old friend, you know. The summer after my father's presidency was stolen from him, she took my mother and I in. Something of a silly old woman, but very kind. I go back a long way with the whole family, dear. That's why I'm really so pleased that you and Nick are getting along so well. And now he's got all his mother's money, not that he needs it. Pity about that necklace. It was everything it was said to be.

"And then, Sartoris painted my portrait. I was barely fifteen, just a child." There was a trace of pride in Dolly's voice. "I was so flattered." She smiled at Lucy, as if she were confessing a small, amusing weakness. "But it was a nasty crude leering thing. A joke. Typical of the old bastard. You won't like me telling you this, but Nick has some of the old man in him, too."

Lucy, seething under the tight lid of her children's presence, kicked viciously at the sand.

"Sartoris was always perfectly awful. Living proof that age does not mellow, not if you're a right bastard to begin with. Anyway, he's failed shockingly since the last time I saw him. Gotten senile."

"He seems fine to me. A little put-upon," Lucy objected.

"Touché. You should have seen him on the terrace while you were dressing. Proper tantrum he put on. It's not unusual, you know, for childish old people to have ups and downs. He was probably up when you arrived."

"Well, you've known him longer than I have. I'm marrying Nick, not his father."

Dolly smiled. "How nice for you, dear. I must say I was surprised when I called your house, expecting to have to fight to drag you away from your workshop, and your father says you've gone off with Nick. But love wins out, doesn't it? I was surprised you brought the children along. It must cramp your style, a little."

Lucy reddened. She fumbled her sunglasses from her pocket and put them on.

"Excuse me," she said softly, "my private life does have some priority. I told you I'd look at the damage and I will. I will find somebody to do the repairs, if I can't do them myself. I should think you know me well enough by now to know I keep my word. And that I don't like to be pressured."

The threat was explicit enough for Dolly. She had encountered the stone wall before in her dealings with Lucy.

"Oh, dear," she moaned, addressing the sky, "have I said the wrong thing? Again?"

Lucy came to an abrupt stop and stooped to pick up a sea-and-sand-polished piece of glass. She held it up to catch the light, seemingly oblivious of Dolly and their conversation.

"I know you think I'm jealous of you and Nick. Really, I'm not, Lucy. A little concerned, perhaps. I hate to see you hurt. Nick's charming, I'll testify to that, but frankly, out of your league. But you have to do what you have to do, I know. To prove I'm really not out to interfere, why don't you let me take the kids back to New York with me, and you and Nick could have a real vacation? Then, when you're ready to pick them up, you could take a look at the dollhouse."

Lucy looked at Dolly as if she too were a found object thrown up on the beach.

"They're no trouble here. Sartoris likes to have them around. He told me so. But thanks for the offer, anyway."

Dolly shaded her eyes with the edge of her hand and stared down the beach at Roger.

"The offer's open, whenever you want, dear." She paused, and then wailed softly. "Oh, if you could see it, Lucy. It would make you sick. It makes me sick, just thinking about it."

Lucy shifted from one foot to another. If every other word Dolly had spoken was a lie, or self-serving, this, at least, was true. Her mother-in-law was genuinely in agony over the state of the Doll's White House. Lucy herself was more than just curious; it was her own work, in large part, that had been destroyed. It was distressing to her to think of the hours and the effort that went into the work, the beauty of its completion, now lost. She was afraid she might really be sick if she had to look at it.

She told herself that it was to Dolly's credit that she cared about something so much. Even the kids had never seemed of more than sporadic interest to her. The little voices that peeped out showed her that Dolly cared because the thing was Dolly's, and it made her feel small. She had misjudged Nick, trying to make him fit her own high standards, even retrospectively. Their separation had taught her not that she could not get along without him; she knew she could. What she had learned was what he added to her life, the bed of friendship and mutual joys upon which passion could play lightheartedly. Surely, she answered the little voice, Lucy Novick Douglas was at last old enough, experienced enough, to allow that each person might be their own universe, with their own peculiar natural laws. The end of her internal debate was that she agreed again to do something she really was afraid of doing, that she didn't want to do.

"Yes," she told Dolly, "I will come and look at the dollhouse. Soon."

"Good." Dolly took both her hands and squeezed them. "You don't know what this means to me. Please keep on thinking about letting me take Zach and Laurie home with me."

Lucy took back her hands and stuck them in her pocket. She could feel the little piece of glass in one corner, where she'd dropped it. It was smooth, cool, hard, a helpless, hopeless feeling thing, used by the sa.

The two women had fallen behind the children. She walked a little faster to catch up with them.

"It wouldn't take very long to assess the damage," Dolly told her, hurrying to keep up with her.

Lucy nodded.

"Listen, dear, I'm going to get out of the sun. We'll talk again later," Dolly said.

Lucy watched her mother-in-law turn back and set off toward the house, now invisible behind a spit of beach. Dolly shook Roger loose from his beach combing in passing; he paused long enough to wave his walking stick at Lucy in a friendly gesture.

It was hot now on the beach. Lucy's upper lip, hairline, and armpits were dewy. The children were in shorts and T-shirts as a defense against too much sun, but the time had come to switch to swimsuits and cool off in the water.

"Bumbies," she called out, summoning them. As they promptly loped back to her, she reflected ironically that they *were* well raised.

An acid little knot of worry burned under Nick Weiler's breastbone. He didn't like Dorothy being around at all, especially around Lucy. And it upset his father. Unable to do anything more about ridding the island of Dolly, or to keep the two women from meeting, he decided to look in on Sartoris. He made his way to the studio. Like the house, it was littered with Sartoris's work. A museum's security nightmare, strewn about like so many homemade needlepoint cushions, he thought, and he had to grin.

The old man was sitting in his studio at a low, crude table spattered with his favorite yellows and reds. He was slumped in a high-backed chair, his head resting upon his massive chest, his face covered by the disreputable old Panama. The even whistle of the old man's breath told Nick he was sleeping the sleep of old age, sudden, light, and fragile. Nick flopped on a sprung and drop-cloth-covered sofa and waited.

A half hour passed in near silence, the pleasant muffled rhythm of the ocean outside punctuated by an occasional snore or wheeze. Nick closed his own eyes, the better to breathe in the studio smells, the perfume of paint and turpentine, fixative, charcoal, a dozen mundane substances that were the elements of the magic his father worked on canvas, paper, wood, or plaster. The salt scent of the sea was another sacrament, one of release, forgiveness, last rites, he thought. It all brought to mind another day, not long ago, heavy with another perfume, that of roses.

"Phumph." The old man started to wakefulness. His head came up; there was a glint of steely eye from under the hat. "What do you want?"

"Nothing from you," Nick replied easily.

"Don't even want my daubs, eh?"

"Well, I wouldn't turn them down. But I can wait."

Sartoris cackled. "You'll have 'em anyway? Shit. It's true. There's no one else to leave 'em."

"You could find a deserving museum. There's always your beloved motherland."

"Hummph." The painter indicated an old school-marm's desk that was a depository for rags, lard cans, and other debris. "In the bottom drawer, Nicholas."

Among dusty bundles of letters that made Nick's antiquarian pulse beat slightly faster, a new bottle of Wild Turkey. A biographer's treasure trove, turning into a mouse nest, he thought, and then, of course, there might be something of his mother in them. He pulled out the bottle and slowly shut the drawer.

"Since I seem doomed not to work today, I believe I'll have a shot of consolation." Sartoris opened the bottle. "Nothing fit to drink out of here. We'll have to swap each other's germs." He hesitated with the bottle at his lips. "I should hope, considering the company you keep, you haven't got the drip."

Nick held up his hands to show they were clean.

Sartoris chortled. "Anyway, this is a virgin bottle. It needs dedicating. Here's to Mrs. Lucy Douglas, me first."

After a healthy slug, he passed the bottle to Nick, who raised it solemnly and said, "To Mrs. Lucy Douglas, me second."

"Indeed," the painter snorted. "Hard to believe a sensible woman like that would be fool enough to marry Dolly Hardesty's get. Good thing for you both the young idiot took himself out of it."

"Well, she's foolish enough to marry your get." Nick handed the bottle back to his father.

"Ho, ho, is that right? Well, here's to you both, then. Age before beauty," and the bottle glugged again.

Nick took his shot.

The old man offered prenuptial advice. "Don't let her have anything more to do with Dolly. No good."

"There's a little matter of her kids being Dolly's grandchildren," Nick pointed out drily.

"Piss on that. Maybe you should reconsider this business."

"If she can handle it, I can."

Sartoris laughed doubtfully. "Give me that bottle if you're just going to grub it up with your fingerprints. Just get her away from that witch. She's a good girl, she'll make an honest man out of you, if she can't give you back your shot at history."

Nick watched the old man upend the bottle. "You never needed a woman to keep you honest."

"Oh, no. I was never honest, not about women."

"Not even Mother?" Then Nick sobered. "I'm sorry. That was cruel."

The old man shrugged and passed him the bottle.

"If there's anyone sorry about that, it's me. Goddamn but sorry is a waste of energy."

Nick sucked on it briefly and admitted, "I was braced for her dying. I hate to think of whatever happened to her—pain, terror."

"Yes, I know. In my bones, the way old men are supposed to, I feel her death. Shitty world isn't it, my boy. Old fossils like Maggie so much game for predators."

Nick shook his head. "It makes me think of Leyna Shaw. She just disappeared suddenly, too."

"Leyna Shaw?"

"Journalist."

"Ah. I've lost touch. Don't know anyone but you anymore." The Wild Turkey bottle, back in Sartoris's hands, trembled slightly. "Now your woman. The little ones. That's something."

"It's easy to do. Lose touch with one another, I mean."

"When I do read the newspapers, I wonder if I really live on the same planet with all those doodahs and fools and crazies. But I'll tell you, Nick, the one sure benefit of a long life."

Nick had to finish his pull at the bottle before asking, "What's that?" It was becoming an excessively warm day, he thought, and he was going to have to stop this drinking shit before it went much farther.

"It all starts to look the same after a while," Sartoris said.

It might indeed. The old man's eyes were beginning to look a little glazed. Nick looked around idly, admiring the cavernous studio, filled with light.

"Lucy would like this," he remarked, waving away the bottle.

"You bring her here." Sartoris fumbled in his pockets, flipped a small gold key to Nick. "The key of life," he said and laughed.

Nick pocketed it. "You haven't forgotten the aphrodisiac of a painter's studio, have you?"

"Well," Sartoris mocked himself, "a little."

They laughed together.

"I want you to sort out my pictures. It has occurred to me that I am going to die, one of these fine summer days."

Nick nodded. "All right. I'll arrange some time away from the Dalton. Okay if I bring a helper?"

The old man grinned. "And keep that key? So long as the work gets done, eh? I should like to see what Lucy does, these microcosms, someday, too. The idea of art as a toy entrances me. If art has to have an idea behind it, that may be the best one yet."

"This is the man who tore my ass up both cheeks because I didn't think art was going to end if I quit?"

"You disguised cowardice as modesty. I will never forgive

you the waste of your talent. I've changed my mind. I will leave my paintings to Lucy and her children under the proviso that your goddamn museum will never ever have them." The Wild Turkey bottle danced in the light as the painter's voice rose. He pointed a gnarled, multicolored finger at his son. "And me, you can't fuck."

"That's right," Nick twitted him mildly. "You're always the fucker, aren't you?"

"Watch your mouth. I can take the key back, too. No nice-widow-woman in the middle of all this . . ." he took in the studio in one expansive gesture ". . . art."

"Bullshit. You just want someone to sprinkle a little sacred sperm, a dab of sexual perfume, in your fucking temple. Which you can't do for yourself anymore, right?"

"I think," said the old man carefully, looking into the deeps of the bottle, "I will forbid in my will your writing my biography."

It made them laugh again.

When Nick left Sartoris, the bottle capped at the one-third mark, and the old man slipping out for lunch and very likely the rest of the day, the painter managed to lift his head from the old sofa long enough to remind Nick about cataloging the paintings. There wasn't any chance he wouldn't. He would clear his head with lunch and try to survey it, however roughly, that afternoon.

The house was full of Sartoris's work. If he had slowed as he aged, still he had had so many years, and had not for a very long time sold anything of importance. So it was scattered, the bits and pieces of his life's work, throughout the house and the studio. The long corridor walls were filled, every bedroom, sitting room, and wherever else a bit of wall would accommodate a piece of canvas. In some rooms, paintings were racked on storage frames Nick had supplied through the Dalton.

When Sartoris did not appear for the lunch served on the terrace, Dolly took charge as if she were the hostess. She wanted to know what everyone was doing with their afternoon, as if she were day counselor at a summer camp. For lack of any other, safer subjects to talk about, the answers were rendered.

The Douglas children were headed indoors for afternoon

naps. It was apparent they needed them; they were unusually noisy and fractious during the meal. Lucy said she planned on taking a walk, exploring the island. She looked hopefully at Nick, who only picked at lunch, but he shook his head.

"I'm working this afternoon," was all he offered.

Dolly was intrigued. She could think of only one thing he could be working on and that was making sure of his inheritance from the old man. After Lucy took the children off to their room, Dolly moved closer to Nick.

"How much is he giving you?" she asked chummily.

Nick rolled his eyes. "I haven't any idea," he lied cheerfully.

"Shit. Who else has he got? And now you're going to be a family man. Your father's only human. Why should he be immune from the normal desire to see his son married, and a few grandchildren to carry on his name?"

"Really, Dorothy, I don't know. My father, as I tried to tell you earlier, knows his own mind."

"Fine. Be mysterious," she pouted.

Roger, applying himself to cucumber sandwiches, chose that moment to belch. He mumbled an apology and moved on to the brownies. He had nothing much to say to Nick Weiler, and the nothingness was reciprocated.

"Well, what are you going to do?" Dolly asked Roger, just noticing he was still there.

"Go for a walk," he said, around a brownie.

"You'll need it," she twitted, looking at his plate. "I'm taking a nap."

"You need it," Roger said bluntly, and got up, leaving an astonished Dolly gaping after him.

It was a small, and very transitory moment of victory for Roger. Setting off for a jaunt under the hot sun, with a belly full of cucumbers, lemonade, and brownies, proved very soon to be unwise. Queasy and with a mild cramp in his side, Roger loped to a halt in the cool of the orchard behind the house. From there, he could see every possible entry and exit.

Waiting patiently, he became aware of the extra weight of the camera and the minimizer he was carting around on his chest. The leather cases against his cotton shirt seemed to condense sweat like iron shavings around a magnet. His nylon socks were uncomfortably damp and hot also; he took the opportunity to remove them, stuff them in his pockets, and enjoy a few minutes of comparative coolness through his toes. He was just retying his sneakers on his bare feet when he spotted Lucy; she had chosen to leave from her bedroom door, and was headed toward the hills behind the house at an oblique angle from him.

He jumped up and trotted into the camouflage of the trees, ahead of her and parallel to her path. By staying higher than she was, he hoped to keep her in sight. She moved at a very steady, ground-eating pace; he was soon soaked with sweat, and his feet threatened blisters with every step. When she showed no sign of slacking, he grew a little desperate and decided to intersect as rapidly as possible.

Their paths crossed about an hour from the house, on a hillside that overlooked the island nicely. Roger, thrashing through aggressively thorny bushes and undergrowth, had no time to appreciate the view. But when he reached Lucy she was entranced enough with it to be really startled by his sudden eruption from the bush.

Forzen for the moment by the fright, she simply stared at him, her eyes huge, and held her breath.

Roger, sore of foot, uneasy in his stomach, headachy from the sun on his bare head, sweat trickling through his young beard, was distressed to frighten her. He stepped forward, reaching out instinctively to comfort her, and was horrified when she jumped away from him.

"Hey," he protested.

She must have had a sudden vision of how she looked, cringing from him, a strapping girl who stood a head taller than he, and outweighed him, newly slimmed by Dolly's regimen by twenty pounds. The bridge of her nose wrinkled as if she had to sneeze, and then she laughed.

"I'm sorry," she said, "you startled me."

Roger grinned. "You must have really been taken with the view. I sounded like a troop of elephants coming through the woods."

"It *is* beautiful," she admitted, and turned to look at it again.

Roger, who had not peeked back on the path once because he was too busy following Lucy, stared down over the island that lay below them. He could see the curve of the fishhook, and the buildings that were Sartoris's house and studio, only now they were simply sculptural shapes against the green of the earth. The blue sea pounded sand and rock seemingly only inches away. Roger began to feel really queasy again, and it wasn't just lunch anymore. It bothered him to see just how small the island was and how great the sea around it. He wanted, he thought, to see the curve of the earth from a big jet, one more time, and the high towers of Manhattan. And then he remembered Manhattan too was an island, at the edge of this very same great ocean. It was something he wanted to think about but Lucy backed from the view a little just then, sat down on a rocky outcropping, and smiled at him.

"Why did you steal my X-acto blade?" she asked conversationally.

"Huh?"

"My X-acto blade. You kited one from my workshop. Why?" She was sweet and patient, just as if she were asking Zach why he had blacked little Billy Cassidy's eye.

Roger stuck his hands in his pockets. Staring down at his sneakers, a guilty blush heating his cheeks, he knew what he had to tell her. It was only necessary to find the right words.

"Oh," he said, "*that* X-acto blade."

Lucy nodded encouragingly.

Roger stepped painfully forward, plumped down on the stone next to her, and began to untie his sneakers.

"This is a really long story," he said, trying to be as casual as he could, so as not to frighten her off too soon, "and I'm afraid you're not going to believe me."

Lucy, wincing with him as he drew off his sneakers and exposed his blisters to the air, pulled back a little, blinked, and said, "Try me."

Roger took a deep breath, spread his toes in the air, and plunged.

"It's funny. That's why I followed you."

The bridge of Lucy's nose wrinkled again. Roger liked that. It was cute. He hoped she would do it again.

"You followed me?" Her eyes were wide again, too, in mild astonishment.

He nodded. "I have to warn you."

She moved fractionally away from him, across the rock. "What?" Her voice shook as lightly as one of the aspen leaves above them, breathing the sea wind.

Roger patted one of the camera cases on his chest.

"See, this is a camera. An ordinary instant photo camera, useful for taking pictures of kids' birthday parties, and the Washington Monument."

Lucy nodded in agreement.

"But this," he patted the other, very lightly, "is not."

"Oh," she said.

"See, this is my invention. I call it the minimizer."

She stared at it. It looked like a camera case, just like the other one.

"It minimizes things."

"Oh," she said again. Her brow furrowed delicately. "I'm almost sure that's the name of a girdle."

"What?" Roger was stunned.

"Minimizer? You did say minimizer?"

He nodded anxiously.

"Ummm. I've seen it. It's a girdle."

"Oh." Roger was seriously deflated.

Lucy felt sorry for him, with his sweaty, softly fuzzed beagle face, and his ragged feet.

"But that's not?" she asked, trying to get him back on the subject. Whatever it was. She settled back, prepared to be patient. It was pleasant, sitting at the top of this hill after a little exertion, feeling and smelling a sea breeze, and if the company was strange, well, she would have a story to tell Nick that evening, among the sweetly tangled sheets.

"No," he said, shaking off the disappointment he felt over the debasement of his private name. It was more important to tell Lucy what he had to tell her.

"For most of my life, I've worked for the government. On this project. I was fired better than a year ago now. Project shut down, saving money, you know? But I happened to be right on top of the very thing the project was looking for. So I took what I'd found out and applied it, and invented this device. The minimizer."

His prideful touch faltered on the carrying case. The glamor of its name was destroyed. He would have to find another one.

"So?" Lucy said hopefully.

"Well, you see," he looked at her shyly, "this is the hard part to believe." He took another gulp of air. "It makes things small."

Lucy nodded politely, and without comprehension. "Oh."

"Really," he insisted. "Remember Leyna Shaw? And Lady Maggie Weiler and her nurse? Haven't you ever thought it was strange that Dolly and I were around when they disappeared?"

Lucy was frozen on the rock, staring beyond Roger, at the distance-shrunken island below them.

"And the Central Park Carousel? And the stuff from the Borough Museum? I did those." He listed the works. And amended the statement. "I mean, we did."

Lucy stared at him now, unseeing.

"The people died. Leyna killed herself. She didn't like being small, I guess. She did all the damage to the Doll's White House. And I didn't want Dolly to hurt the old lady, so I killed her and the nurse. Set the device too high."

Roger babbled on. It was like listening to Zach confess to torturing the cat or raping his sister.

"Stop," she said weakly, holding up her hand.

He did, staring at her with bird-bright eyes, waiting for her to catch up to him.

"You're crazy," she said flatly.

He sighed, and studied the carrying cases on his chest. There was a painful silence.

"How can you make people small?" she blurted angrily. "How?"

Dolly had asked him that, not in anger, but in curiosity, and he had told her she could not understand. Somehow, he would have to try to make this already hostile woman understand. *Understand.*

He closed his eyes. "With mirrors," he said, "into other dimensions, and back again. I can't explain it any better than that." He pounded his fist into his thigh in frustration. There was so much more, all the modifications that kept a living thing alive, that reduced it to exactly the size he wanted it to be.

She looked away from him, passing her hands over her eyes as if they were tired, or she had a headache.

"Shit," she said.

"I knew you wouldn't believe me," Roger sulked.

"It's crazy," she muttered.

"You'd better believe me," he said softly.

Her head snapped up. "What?"

"Just keep your kids away from Dolly. She wants someone living in her dollhouse. And *she is* crazy."

Abruptly, the woman was on her feet, crashing through the brush, headed back to the house. At least, Roger thought with some satisfaction, he had managed to hit her panic button. Maybe she believed enough to save her kids.

He slid across the rocky seat and picked up his sneakers. Slowly, painfully, he started after her again. He had a lot to think about on the way down. Whether she would tell Weiler, or any of the others. He grimaced to think what Dolly might do or say if she knew he spilled the whole mess to Lucy Douglas, just like that. He had to find a new name for his device. Zapper? Too commercial. Reductor? That had possibilities. The first thing he would do at the house was to flop and take a nap. Perhaps sleep would throw up a new name, some answer.

Late in the afternoon, Dolly woke him with a resounding slap on his bare buttocks. He opened one eye and grunted. There was the sound of her zipper unzipping, the fall of cloth to the floor, the rustle of her kicking it out of the way, promising sounds that stirred him from sleep.

"Your feet look like the rats have been at them," she observed.

"Huh?" Roger rolled over. "Oh. Yuh. Went walking in the wrong socks."

"Poor thing." She didn't sound very sympathetic.

He roused himself. "What did you do?"

Dolly was down to her bra and panties. Two pieces of a bathing suit dangled from her hands. She tossed them on the bed at his feet and reached behind her to unhook the bra.

"Followed Nick Weiler around. Made a nuisance of myself." She giggled. "He wanted to count his inheritance."

Roger watched her breasts falling out of her bra cups like money out of a slot machine. A few weeks ago he would have been drooling. Now the best he could manage was a vague tumescence, about what the *Playboy* centerfold might evoke.

She picked up the top of the bathing suit. "Let's go swimming. Before they throw us out of their little paradise."

Roger lay back and closed his eyes. He felt logy. His mother always claimed afternoon naps were the worst thing for a person. Not really resting and you always felt like you were in slow motion when you came to. His feet itched.

"No," he said, "I guess I won't."

Dolly stopped rummaging for her sun-screening lotion and stared at him. "Don't be a party-poop."

"Ah, my feet are all blistered. That's salt out there in that water. It'll hurt like fire."

"Don't be such a big baby. Salt water's just the thing to soak your feet in."

She finished stuffing necessities into a beach bag, jammed on a wide-brimmed white linen hat, and picked up her beach jacket.

"Are you coming?" she demanded.

Roger, beached on the white-sheeted bed, opened his eyes long enough to look at her. "No," he said calmly, "count me out."

Her gray eyes grew icy. She slammed the door on the way out.

Roger smiled to himself. It was time she recognized whose finger controlled the button on the minimizer.

The long summer afternoon passed. The children played in the sand and in the water, watched over by a quiet, withdrawn Lucy. Dolly joined them, glossy with sun-screen. After trying to engage Lucy in conversation and being rebuffed, she settled down to watch avidly her grandchildren's caperings. At last the wind began to rise, promising the evening chill, and the sunbathers and castle-builders and sea-swimmers retired to the house, with hot, soapy showers and food in mind.

Nick Weiler emerged from his father's studio alone. The old man had shuffled off to his bedroom at midafternoon, wakened by Dolly's poking and prying, as Nick tried to work. She had seemed satisfied once she had disturbed Sartoris, and went away, so that at least Nick could do what he needed to do before the afternoon ended.

Head-tired, and aching in his back and shoulders, he walked to the beach. The day was fading, the beach abandoned. Or given back to itself. The tide had not come far enough up to destroy the children's sand castles, but they were melting, losing their identity. The footprints remained, the prints of Lucy's sandals, still readable to the informed eye. He found a place where she had sat for some time; her bottom had made a small abstract print of its own, rather like the wings of a snow angel. No, he thought, a snow moth, was there such a thing? His head was too befogged to sort it out. All he knew was that he was jolted by this evidence of her presence.

He sat down and rested his head on his knees. Once he had been anxious to bed her, convinced that once he had slept with her, she would be as all the other women in his life, and the terrible need would die.

"More fool you," he muttered to himself.

He could look at her and see the imperfections of her face and body. He knew her personal shortcomings, her temper, her perfectionism. And she knew him; that was the real test. He still loved her, knowing that she knew all his weaknesses. Loved her, was crazy about her.

They would leave the island and go back to Washington. The days would be as they had been seemingly forever; he would work at the Dalton, the summer would end, another year would close. If Lucy married him, none of that would change. There would still be politics as usual, the petty squabbling among the staff, the continuing search for funds, for acquisitions, for publicity, concern over security. He would get older. With a little luck and perseverance, he might become a very powerful person. His father, someday, would still die.

But he would go home to Lucy; they would raise her children together, and someday be reduced again to an apartment in the city and a pair of cats, and each other. It was a comforting vision and a daunting one; he was afraid of wanting it too much, afraid of losing it. For the first time in his life, he thought about his eventual extinction. He was afraid of dying. That's what Lucy had given him. Something to lose.

The others, except his father, were already at the table when he arrived for dinner. Ethelyn Blood patted him on the shoulder as she served, forgiving him his tardiness as easily as she forgave his father the lapse of his drunkenness.

"He only does this once or twice a year now. It does him good to have a blow out. It's hard to be strong all the time, all alone, and getting old. And this time," she glared at Dolly, "he was provoked, Lord knows."

The children, appetites whetted by the long hard afternoon of play, dug into Mrs. Blood's lobster stew, shrimp puffs, and Caesar salad with total concentration. Dolly too enjoyed her meal, and her own conversation, which she must have found fascinating, for she didn't seem to notice that no one else at the table had anything to say.

Roger, looking a little green at the edges, could only pick at his meal and steal anxious glances at Lucy. Lucy, busy avoiding them, studied the tablecloth and the food, but ate mechanically and played with a small, sea-polished piece of glass. Put out with Dolly, whom he was certain was deeply pleased at having disrupted his father's private grieving, and disturbed by his own disconcerting emotionalism, Nick Weiler could only listen to Dolly's bright babble from within a shell of icy irritation.

Dolly had one more triumph. As Mrs. Blood served dessert, the phone rang, informing them that the promised helicopter would not arrive, because of mechanical problems, until first light in the morning. Whether he wanted her or not, Sartoris would be compelled to house Dolly and Roger overnight.

When the children had consumed their chocolate mousse, Lucy stood, excusing herself to put them to bed.

"I'll see you later," she told Nick softly.

And then she skirted Roger's chair by a hugely unnecessary margin, as if he had something catching. She shot a frightened look at him and hurried out, leaving Nick mystified, Roger suddenly and for the first time, deeply involved in his mousse, and Dolly studying him with the interest of a cat at a mousehole.

"I don't believe it," Nick said. He couldn't see her face very well. The terrace was lit only by a few torches; it was romantic, but in a literal sense, unilluminating.

She said nothing for a little while. The only sound was the clink of ice in her glass as she fidgeted with her drink.

"I don't believe it either. He's fucking out of his mind. But I'm not going to do the job. I told you that way back. I told *her* that. I'm going to look at it, and tell her who to hire. What needs to be done. I'm not letting her have the kids for any kind of visit. Not with a nut like that around. He was right to warn me, only he didn't know who or what he was warning me against."

"Why even look at the job either? Tell her to stuff it. What's she ever done for you that you owe her any favors. Stay clear away from her and her creepy boyfriend."

"I gave my word." Her tone was flat and stubborn. She was warning him not to push her.

He sighed. "I wish you wouldn't go anywhere near her. That's all."

And it was. She'd made her decision. The resistance she had wanted to show to Dolly she turned on Nick. She felt stupid and clumsy, and inexplicably frightened, sitting in the near-dark. Tears started in her eyes. He must have sensed her misery. He moved closer and kissed her hair.

"I love you," he told her.

She clung to him.

They necked peacefully for a few minutes, until it became obvious that the chairs would be too uncomfortable to continue in and the moment of going on or stopping had arrived. Ethelyn Blood, hearing soft laughter as she passed through the darkened dining room that looked onto the terrace, smiled. She turned to the bedrooms to look in on the little ones. After that, she thought, she would make herself scarce.

"Let's go to the studio," Nick whispered, making the housekeeper's discretion quite unnecessary.

15

"Lucy positively scuttled around you," Dolly said.

"I didn't notice."

"Don't play innocent. What did you do, pinch her bottom, grab a little tit?"

Roger blushed obligingly.

"You're immpossible," she scolded. "I'll just have to punish you, that's all."

Roger didn't want to be punished. His head hurt, his stomach regretted skipping supper, and his feet stung and itched unmercifully. Enough punishment, and all self-inflicted, he thought.

"Just let me tie you up," she pleaded.

"Ohh," he groaned, "I don't know."

She pouted, beat on his back with her fists. "Goddamn it, you haven't been any fun at all today."

"Ow," he protested.

"You don't want me anymore," she moaned, and tears leaked from under her silvery lashes. "You want Lucy."

Roger felt awful. He had never seen her cry. "No, no," he told her, even if it was a little lie. Sometimes little lies make good Kleenex. Of course he wanted Lucy, he'd have to be out of his mind not to, but she didn't want him.

"Just like Nick," Dolly went on, sniffling, "chasing after young girls."

It was not the moment to remind her that he wasn't just like Nick Weiler, he was only thirty-six himself, and that Lucy wasn't jailbait anymore. Would it soothe her wounded pride to think she was in a losing war with a woman just turned thirty?

He held her, because there was nothing else to do, and she moved subtly against him, arousing him almost before he knew what she was doing. Lay back and enjoy it seemed to apply here.

They must not make any noise, she told him, and gagged him with a pair of panties, after she had tied him to the conveniently old-fashioned brass bed with an assortment of scarves and pantyhose.

It went on a long time. The bonds seemed unnecessarily tight and struggling against them in the throes of the encounter only tightened them more. At the end, he fainted.

He swam through thick hot air to consciousness, into a lightless web of panic. Struggling, he tightened the ligatures around his wrists and ankles until the shooting pain shattered his rage. There was nothing he could do but lie as still as possible. Slick with sweat, and naked, he quickly chilled, and involuntary shivering brought the pain of his bonds again.

After a little while, his vision adjusted to the dark; he could make out Dolly, bundled in the blankets from the bed, sleeping peacefully on a window seat. The gag in his mouth, absorbing saliva, constantly threatening to choke him, kept him silent.

Through the night he dozed off and on, always brought back to semiconsciousness by the sudden tightening of the bonds as his body relaxed against them. The daylight was very long in coming.

He came to again to the sounds of her shower in the bathroom that adjoined their bedroom. It was easier to enumerate the parts of his body that didn't hurt, ache, sting, or itch than to list his damages. His penis, so abused the night before that he thought it might never function again, attested his powers of recovery by standing up proudly. And that was the worst discomfort of all because it wanted not pleasuring but a ten-minute pee.

Dolly came out of her shower humming, laughed to see his tumescent organ peeking at her with its one blind eye, and flicked it casually in passing with a wet towel. Ignoring Roger's writhing, she powdered and creamed her body elaborately. She slipped into bra and panties, then a white silk blouse, gray linen pants, and a mauve ascot.

Sitting down at the vanity, she did her eyes in shades of mauve and wine, her lips in a wine-red lipstick. Her cap of platinum curls was quickly brushed into place, *Cristalle* perfume sprayed on generously, and the jacket matching the pants shrugged on.

Throwing her things into her overnight bag, she smiled sweetly at Roger.

"Feeling a little yukky, darling?" she asked. "Foot and mouth disease, I think. Listen, tell me the truth and I'll untie you. Did you tell Lucy?"

Roger's head bobbed frantically. *Yes.*

Dolly frowned. "Bad boy. You did deserve punishing. That was very, very stupid. I'm afraid I'll have to take your toy away from you. You're not very responsible, are you?"

Roger's whole body rose up at once against the restraints, lifting the brass bed a fraction of an inch off the floor. It settled immediately with a heavy thump.

Dolly, dangling the minimizer in its case before his eyes, laughed again. "Tsk, tsk. What a temper."

She stepped into her shoes. "Since you're not feeling well, I think you'd better stay here a little longer, until you get your feet under you again. Don't worry, the old bastard's not so heartless that he'd throw a poor bed-ridden soul like yourself onto the beach."

The distant thrumming of the helicopter blades punctuated her farewell. Blowing Roger a kiss, she slipped out the door, carrying her overnight bag and the carrycase that held the minimizer. Roger struggled, once again, against his bonds, lifting the bed from the floor once more. But the sound of its thumping descent was blotted out by the helicopter's approach.

Dolly knocked on the bedroom door where Lucy and the children were supposed to be sleeping. Opening it, she found the children stirring, wakened by the noise of the helicopter, and Lucy's bed unslept in.

"Naughty girl, Lucy," she whispered to herself, and bent to gather the children in a hug.

"Grandmother has to go now. That's her helicopter coming," she told them.

Half asleep, they rubbed their eyes, yawned, and leaned against her.

"I want to take your pictures, okay?"

That was easy. Curled together on Laurie's bed like lost children sleeping in the forest, Lucy's little boy and girl waited patiently for Grandmother to take her photographs, just as they had dozens of times before. She had some trouble with the funny-looking camera, but perhaps it was new.

"Goddamn," she said once, and that made Laurie and Zach giggle, to hear Grandmother use a swear.

"There," she said at last, and the flashbulb went off in a blinding red glare.

The pounding steps of the giant broke in on Lucy's dreamless sleep. She knew what it was this time, and sat straight up. Slipping from the bed, where Nick was stirring, clinging to sleep in the face of the noise, she picked up a robe and went out.

Dolly was in the hall, just picking up her overnight case outside the door of the room the children had been sleeping in.

A smile broke over the intense concentration of her expression.

"Lucy, dear," she said, reaching to grasp Lucy's hand and squeeze it. "I just kissed the little ones. They're still asleep. I hope the noise of that machine doesn't wake them."

Lucy looked up and down the hall for Roger.

Dolly answered her unspoken question. "He's gone out to meet the helicopter already. Listen, I'd better run. Take care, dear. My love to Nick."

Lucy stood for a minute, watching her mother-in-law disappear through the door into the kitchen. It was a little chilly, even with the robe she was wearing, and she found herself shivering. Hugging herself, she went back to Nick's room, wondering at the mercurial creature her late husband's mother was. She had discovered almost as soon as she had married that she had wed more than a gangly young flier; she had also, by some evil magic, acquired his mother as part of the bargain. Here she was in Nick's father's house, getting ready to do it again. At least, the old man was on record as being a hands-off sort of parent; she could hope this marriage would not be a triangle from the beginning. Except for Nick, who was getting her kids along with her.

Nick was awake enough to curl up against and to have all those interesting thoughts whispered into his ear. She could almost hear herself giggle as the helicopter beat its way into the air, leaving the island. But it was some minutes before the last ghostly pounding died and the curious thumping began to make itself heard.

On the third thump, Nick stopped kissing her and sat up straight.

"For Christ's sake, what's that?"

Another exhausted thump. Down the hall. From Dolly's room.

Flinging open the door, Nick saw Roger Tinker, trussed to the bed like a chicken spread for boning. Standing there open-mouthed, he was too astonished to say anything. Lucy hurried down the hall after him, peeked around him and backed hastily out, her face flooding red.

The mysterious thumping had drawn Ethelyn Blood, dressed but still wearing fluffy bedroom slippers and pincurls.

"It's Mr. Tinker," Lucy blurted, "all tied up."

The housekeeper patted Lucy's arm, stepped by her, and stuck her head in the bedroom, where Nick Weiler was fumbling at the knots in Roger's bonds.

She gasped, turned on her heel, and swept past Lucy to the kitchen, muttering, "Merry Jesus God." Swooping through the kitchen door and back again in seconds, she rushed by with a wicked looking carving knife, as Sartoris, in his nightshirt, opened his bedroom door and stared blinking bloodshot eyes after his apparently berserk housekeeper.

The knife tore into the silken scarves and nylon stockings with a great hollow ripping sound like great wings, and then Lucy heard Roger cry out in pain. She winced against the wall and hid her eyes, so that she heard but did not see the old man shuffling to her. His huge hands fell hard on her shoulders and she looked up at him, realizing for the first time that he met her eyes bare-faced. And he was not spectacularly ugly, but angelically beautiful, undeniably Nick's father, wearing Nick's face as it would become.

Wonder-struck, she reached to touch him, to feel the reality of the velvety aged skin. The sound of sobbing brought her back to the misery in the bedroom. Ethelyn Blood, her trusty knife in hand, came out and shut the door behind her.

"Keep the children away," she told Lucy. And then, addressing the old painter, "Wicked games, but at least the witch is off the island. I saw her climbing into the helicopter myself, out my bedroom window."

Lucy, reminded of her children, ducked her head into their room, thinking if they'd slept through the helicopter, with luck they might have missed this nastiness down the hall. The shades were drawn, the room merely masses of shadows, but too quiet, she knew, even as she stepped inside. The little cots were empty, still rumpled from sleep, but no longer warm, when she put her hand on the sheets. There were no hastily discarded pajamas; the new day's clothing, laid out the night before, remained in neatly folded piles on the bureau. Just inside the door, their sandals were still paired.

Where were they? Mechanically, she stepped back into the hall. The housekeeper, her arm in Sartoris's, guiding him back to his room, looked back at her, the question on her face: *Are they still asleep?* And her face darkened instantly with this new worry, as she read the helplessness in Lucy's eyes.

"They're not here," Lucy said, but her voice was so low and choked, that Ethelyn Blood let go the old man's arm and hurried back to her.

He turned to stare at them.

"What?" the housekeeper asked, and didn't wait for an answer, pushing past Lucy to look into the children's room.

"They must be in the kitchen, or playing," she said, plainly puzzled, as she stood in the doorway. "You didn't hear them?"

Lucy shook her head.

The two women went into motion together, so fast Sartoris flinched against the wall, getting out of their way. Sighing, he made his own way back to his room, and began dressing.

Dividing the house between them, Lucy and the housekeeper canvassed every room, closet, and hidy-hole in ten minutes flat. Then, together, they hurried to the studio, now calling the children anxiously. And walked, a little out of breath, along the beach nearest the house, and found, to their relief, no small naked footprints into the water.

Returning to the house, they were met by Nick Weiler, who had managed in all the ruckus to pull on a pair of pants.

"Did you find the children?" he asked anxiously.

The women did not have to answer, but only looked at him.

He seized Ethelyn Blood by the shoulder. "My father says you saw Dolly leave. Was she alone?"

Mrs. Blood nodded. "Yes."

Nick met Lucy's frightened eyes reluctantly. "Tinker says she took his device."

Lucy moaned. The housekeeper wrapped one long arm around the other woman's shoulder and squeezed her comfortingly.

"What's this?" she asked.

"Tinker," Nick said, "told Lucy yesterday he has a device that he and Dolly have used to shrink things, and people. He warned her to keep the children away from Dolly."

Mrs. Blood's eyes widened. "I never heard of such a thing," she gasped.

"He warned me," Lucy said faintly.

"What's this?" Sartoris said, behind them. "More devilment? Where are the little ones? Why haven't you found them?"

Nick told him.

The old man, now wearing his old Panama, sitting on the stone wall of the terrace, listened patiently and then asked, "Sounds crazy. I want to talk to this Tinker. Meantime, you call the Coast Guard, or the airport, or somebody that can find out if that woman has the children with her."

"I'll do it," Lucy said, and hurried to a phone.

"She okay?" Sartoris asked Nick.

"Let her do something," Ethelyn Blood said, "do her good. She'll be fine. I'll get some breakfast together. Looks like we'll need it."

Sartoris and Nick found Roger Tinker sitting in a chair in the bedroom he had shared with Dolly. He had gotten into pants, and a shirt, but the shirt was inside out and buttoned wrong to boot. Wincing at every move, he was drawing socks on over swollen and blistered feet. He looked up at them, his eyes dull with disinterest, and returned his attention to his socks.

"Prove it," the old man said calmly.

Roger looked up at him again. "Did ya find the kids?" he asked shakily.

Sartoris looked at Nick.

"No. Not yet."

"She's got' em. And if you check on it, she'll be traveling alone."

Nick's frustration erupted. "You son of a bitch."

"Yeah," Roger agreed. "You got cute tits, Weiler, but you better get dressed, too. We have to catch up with that crazy bitch before she zaps New York, or something."

Sartoris hissed in angry protest but too late; his sweetly rational son had Roger Tinker by the throat and was attempting to strangle him. It was Lucy that saved Roger, and cost Nick his nose, by opening the bedroom door to announce, "I called—" Nick looked her way long enough for Roger to draw back his fist and let fly. The sound of Roger's fist popping Nick Weiler's nose brought Lucy's message to a halt. Nick let go of Roger, who plopped back into his chair, panting. Speechless, Nick backed away, too, bringing his hands slowly to his nose.

Lucy caught her breath; Nick turned to her, opened his mouth, and blood gushed from his nose through his hands. She wailed; behind her, she heard Sartoris smothering a chuckle.

"Ethelyn!" the old man shouted.

The housekeeper appeared on the run, took in the situation with a glance, and was gone. She returned this time not with a knife but an ice pack.

Lucy had shoved Nick onto the bed, and had his head pushed back over the pillows. He winced away when she applied the ice and then gave in to the contemplation of his pain.

"Well, enough of that foolishness," Sartoris said. "What did you find out, Lucy?"

"I called the airport in Bar Harbor," Lucy said. She looked at the old man. "The helicopter was still in the air, but close to them. They radioed it. There was one adult passenger on board."

"So," said the old man.

"So I told you the truth," Roger blurted. He was working

on stuffing his feet into his shoes. "You better get another helicopter out here."

"I'll do that," Ethelyn Blood said.

"Shouldn't we search the island?" Lucy asked Sartoris.

Roger snorted.

Lucy, possessed of a sudden desire to strangle Dolly's former friend herself, tightened her grasp on the ice pack and leaned into Nick.

"Ow," he said.

"Waste of time," Sartoris said. "We'll leave Mrs. Blood here and go after Dolly. If the children should happen to be playing hide-and-go-seek in the bushes, she'll be here when they tire of it. But I think you must face it, Lucy, this fellow's not lying. He may be crazy, but he's not lying."

Roger endeavored to look virtuous but it went to waste. Lucy couldn't bear to look at him. Suddenly she was weeping, and it was Nick trying to hold her, his nose, and the ice pack.

They became fouled in nets of logistics.

"There isn't any way to land a small plane here?" Roger asked.

Sartoris shook his head. "First we came by boat, then after the war, by helicopter."

"The fastest available boat'll take an hour to the mainland on the chop there is today," Mrs. Blood told them, "and then there's a quarter of an hour to the airport, and half an hour on to the big airport at Bangor."

"She could still be there," Lucy pointed out. "I just don't see how she could have made that seven-fifteen flight."

"She didn't have to," Roger said. "Could have booked a private plane, or a car, either in Bar Harbor or Bangor."

"Or Portland, she could have flown from Bar Harbor to Portland by charter plane or helicopter. The seven-fifteen flight out of Bangor stops in Portland, doesn't it? She could pick that up."

"Or a private plane, commuter plane, bus, or car, and once out of Maine, even a train," Sartoris objected. "Why try to catch her en route?"

Roger agreed. "Better to go right to her. We know where she's headed, right?"

"So all we have to do," Lucy finished the thought, "is get ourselves to New York."

"Mrs. Blood," Sartoris said, "see if you can put us on the twelve-fifty-three flight out of Bangor. We'll get there, by boat if we have to, by helicopter if we can. See if there's a helicopter at Bangor that can pick us up here."

There was, and as it fought its way upward, Lucy watched the island shrink away and disappear into the sea with two minds. One of them, much the smaller, insisted none of this was true or sane or possible, but it shrank and disappeared like Sartoris's island into the larger mind, the one that was a sea of grief and confusion, through which she could only struggle endlessly against her drowning.

The four of them—Sartoris, Nick Weiler, Roger Tinker, Lucy Douglas—sat in the helicopter, the molded seats of the waiting areas at the Bangor airport, the Delta jet on the ground, and in the air, speaking to each other only when necessary, carrying their secret like a piece of polished glass or a stone in their pockets, looking just like all their fellow travelers. The jet, climbing high, showed them the world beyond the island again, and brought them to earth at La-Guardia in the early afternoon.

It was all the same, so far as Lucy could see, as it had ever been. Except she didn't know where her children were, or how they were, and she was chasing after the where and how on the word of a crazy man. And if he wasn't crazy, she might be chasing answers she didn't want to hear.

The old man and his son, both of them hiding their faces under broad-brimmed hats, seemed to sense the same thing; they took up instinctively protective positions, flanking her, and each held one of her hands in theirs on the cab ride into the city. Roger, taking the jump seat in their Checker, had only them to look at, unless he wanted to crane his neck to watch the traffic, but he seemed to notice them only occasionally.

He broke the silence, talking to himself. "I shouldn't have made it so easy."

"No," Sartoris said, "you shouldn't have. Why did you?"

Roger's face darkened. "It had to be easy. So it was fast. Foolproof. There was never any time to be careful."

"Like an instant photo camera, anyone could use it?" the painter probed.

Roger wrung his hands nervously. "Yes. Anyone could use it."

"Ah," the old man sighed.

Roger, known to the security guards, gained entrance for them into Dolly's high-rise building and then, with the key she had not remembered to take back from him, into her apartment.

The maid, Ruta, appeared at the sound of the entering, gasped, and clapped a hand over her mouth.

"It's all right, Ruta," Roger told her, guessing that Dolly had told her Mr. Tinker wasn't coming back, and that his sudden reappearance evoked visions of crimes passional in the maid's head, "I've come to pick up some things of mine. It's a friendly visit; I've brought along some old friends of Dolly's. You know Mrs. Douglas, Mr. Weiler, and this is Leighton Sartoris, the painter."

Ruta nodded. Miss Dorothy's daughter-in-law, one of her old boyfriends, and a famous painter who had even been in *VIP*. Perhaps nothing terrible was going to happen. It must be all the old friends were trying to cool out this breakup, not that she minded much if Miss Dorothy ditched this particular fancy man.

"She's in the dollhouse room?" Roger asked.

"Uh huh," the maid confirmed his guess.

"Don't bother with us. We'll just go in and see her for a few minutes."

Silently, they approached the door of the dollhouse room. The sound of Dolly's humming reached them in sporadic bursts from beyond the door. Roger tried the knob; it moved only fractionally. He shot a quick grin at the others. For the first time, Lucy saw what Dolly might have seen in him. There was no time to think about it for Roger was fitting a key into the lock and turning it stealthily. There was a universal holding of breath.

He opened the door.

Dolly, bending into the Gingerbread Dollhouse, looked up, and smiled.

"Hello," she sang gaily, "I've been expecting you."

She hurried forward, holding out her arms as if to embrace Lucy. Lucy jumped backward, was caught by Nick, who wrapped his arms around her protectively. Dolly gave it up in midmotion, resignedly bringing her hands together in a little clap. She cocked her head at her visitors.

'It's sweet of you all to come. But since Lucy is finally here, I do want her to look at the Doll's White House."

She stepped aside, reached calmly to pinch Roger's cheek, and giggled.

"Played a trick on you, didn't I, pumpkin?"

Roger had already surveyed the room, knew what she knew, and where the minimizer was. But first he had to get to it, and hoped to distract her. Perhaps showing Lucy her damaged dollhouse would do it.

Lucy, dry-mouthed and sweating, wanted to scream. *Where are my children?* But Nick's arms restrained her, even his even breathing seemed to tell her to stay calm, if she hoped to extract the answer from Dolly. She couldn't care less about Dolly's dollhouse at this point but it seemed she would have to play the game out. Dolly held the markers.

Nick let her go. She moved woodenly toward the dollhouse, suddenly afraid that *where* might be the enormous, ruined dollhouse. Walking slowly around it, she saw it had been given a new base, big enough to hold a scale model of the grounds. Curious, she touched the grass and an electric shock went through as she realized it was real. A merry-go-round had been placed in the garden; her fingers trailed over its elaborate decoration and stopped. Now she could see, as well as smell, the fire and water damage.

It was obvious but also not serious, mostly a matter of scorching and smoke stain. She rubbed her fingers across one stain. The fire had begun in one room and sucked oxygen, like any other housefire, from the windows. Like any other fire. Removing the wall, she looked into the bedroom where the fire originated. Here the smell was really nasty. She fingered the draperies and noticed immediately the tiny slits in the cloth, the rips at the level of the fixtures, which were themselves bent, as if a strong downward force had been exerted on them.

She removed another wall and stared into the Blue Room. A stain like a rusty puddle marred the carpet like the shadow of a cloud on a sunny day. With one finger, she traced it across the floor in a line like a vein near the surface of the skin. When she lifted her hand, it trembled.

The others stood watching her, Dolly with bright, curious

eyes, Nick and Sartoris anxiously, Roger in admiration, impressed with her easy passage into professionalism. And then he watched it shatter.

She looked up at them, pale, beginning to shake. Nick Weiler moved to support her.

"I think she's going to faint," Roger observed.

The scramble was not as satisfactory as he had hoped, for only the old man and Weiler seemed particularly concerned. Dolly, cool and distantly amused, looked on avidly, but did nothing to help. But Roger was committed; this was his moment, his chance to put his finger on the Button again.

He jumped for the Glass Dollhouse, where the minimizer, looking itself like some curious abstract sculpture of glass and colored foils, was camouflaged among the angles of Dolly's third dollhouse.

And she anticipated him, sticking out one elegantly shoed foot to trip him up. He fell forward with all his weight, shouting "No!" and crashed into the dollhouse. As all but Dolly watched in horror, the glass structure seemed to explode into him. The room suddenly rained bits of glass, pieces as big as hailstones, slivers, shards, and glass dust. Roger's hands, streaked with red, clawed after the device, which had popped upward, away from him. But Dolly caught it, braving the storm of glass, and his flailing.

She stepped back, aimed the device, and the thing went off immediately. They all felt it, like a sudden breath of death pushing them gently aside, in a wash of red light. Lucy and Nick instinctively shielded their eyes. Only Sartoris really watched as Roger, painted in his own blood from dozens of superficial glass cuts, threw up his hands in a futile gesture of warding off. He appeared to twist away from them like a piece of paper suddenly caught on fire. The shrinking was so incredibly fast as to be almost imperceptible to the eye. One moment, Roger writhed among the glass shards; the next he was curled like a giant shrimp on top of a six-inch-square rhomboid that had once been part of the dollhouse roof.

Sartoris felt his heart stutter, as it was apt to do, and he fought a silent, titanic struggle within himself, willing the muscle to heave once more and then again and again. He sucked in lungsful of suddenly cold air, and was chilled in his bones.

Dolly, her eyes glittering impossibly bright, as a bit of glass in the daylight, turned like a ballerina on a music box, one hand as straight as a hand on a clock, aiming the device at Sartoris, Nick, Lucy in turn. She came to rest.

"Two dollhouses down," she announced. "But you can fix the Doll's White House for me, can't you?"

Lucy, trembling, stared at her.

"At least," Dolly crooned, "this one is still perfect." She danced, delicately, on her toes, a few steps to the Gingerbread House.

For the first time, they all looked at it. Next to it, on the table that supported it, the plaster figures of Hansel and Gretel had been discarded. Within, a small boy crouched in the cage, a little girl, a gossamer chain around her ankle, slept on the hearth rug, abandoned, so it seemed, by heartless parents to the captivity of the cruel witch. And the light caught tears glassing the boy's cheeks.

Grief welled in the old man. His heart felt swollen and abused.

Dolly, entranced with her witchcraft, crooning over the children, let down her guard.

With a feral snarl, Lucy launched herself from the periphery of Dolly's vision, catching her like a tackle around the knees. Losing her balance, Dolly tightened her grip on the minimizer but could not stop her arm instinctively seeking to regain balance, reaching upward. Her hand landed hard against the woodwork, smashing the sensitive nerves of the thinly fleshed back of the hand. Crying out in pain, she let go of the device. It tumbled away, to be snatched up by Nick Weiler.

Dolly, tangled with Lucy on the floor, grabbed a handful of the younger woman's hair, reaching for support. Realizing what she had, she yanked for all she was worth. Lucy screamed; her nails found Dolly's face.

Sartoris backed carefully away from them. He could not interfere; his newly stumbled heart sought rest. It hurt to even look at the two women, fighting each other with such complete and deadly passion. Closing his eyes made it worse; he could hear it still. Slowly, he maneuvered toward the Gingerbread Dollhouse, thinking he would, if he could, protect the children.

His swollen nose aching, Nick stared at the device in his hand numbly. Whatever it was, he didn't know how to use it.

He held it distastefully between thumb and forefinger, feeling that it was profoundly evil. He was afraid to put himself between the thrashing women, who were using their teeth, nails, and elbows on each other with savage abandon. Some male part of him quailed before such unleased female violence.

They were nearly equal in their struggle. Beginning to tire, they had to think their moves. The savagery, slowed, became more intense. The more powerful Lucy shoved Dolly against the window wall of the room. She was determined to beat her mother-in-law's skull against the glass and sought leverage under Dolly's chin. Dolly, maddened with desperation, sought Lucy's throat with her small, silver-tipped fingers. The balance shifted abruptly; Lucy began to fade as her oxygen was cut off. Dolly's eyes bulged with effort.

Shaking off his trance, Nick Weiler dropped the minimizer onto the grounds of the model White House and moved toward the women.

Lucy made one last, violent effort. In a spasm of strength that seemed to ripple from her head to her feet, she seized Dolly and slammed her against the window. It cracked. A head-sized chunk of glass fell silently away. Dolly's nose spurted blood and she fell limply against Lucy.

The dead weight of the older woman pushed Lucy, on the edge of exhaustion, backward. She began to keen. Leighton Sartoris flinched. Without volition, Nick shouted, "Stop!"

Lucy thrust again with all her strength, pushing Dolly away. The limp body seemed to fly backward at the window, where it encountered the glass. The glass bulged and gave way. She was gone.

Lucy turned away and collapsed into Nick Weiler's arms. It was Sartoris who watched and witnessed from the gaping window, Dolly's falling body, like a rag doll's, turning limply in slow motion, over and over. It became smaller and smaller, until it was faceless, a black stick figure hurtling downward. There was no sound, no cry. It met the earth and disintegrated. Sartoris closed his eyes briefly. Then he turned back to the living.

Despite the presence of Leighton Sartoris and at least three other witnesses, including her maid, Ruta Lansky, former daughter-in-law, Lucy Douglas, and Nicholas Weiler, director of the Dalton Institute, the facts of

Dorothy Hardesty Douglas's death were curiously murky. A sketchy official account released by the police suggested that the former president's daughter became suicidally depressed as a consequence of the apparent drowning deaths of her two grandchildren. Lucy Douglas, the mother of the missing children, sustained numerous cuts and bruises, and Weiler, a broken nose, while attempting unsuccessfully to restrain Douglas.

The day of Dolly's death began on the island off the Maine coast where Sartoris has lived a hermitlike existence for several decades. Dorothy Hardesty Douglas, her son's widow, Lucy Douglas, Lucy's children, Laurie, age 7, and Zachary, age 4, Roger Tinker, a family friend, and Nicholas Weiler, Sartoris's natural son, were visiting the island in the wake of the apparent kidnapping and possible murder of Lady Maggie Weiler, Weiler's mother and Sartoris's long-time mistress. Early that morning, Dolly Douglas left the island, alone. A call to the airport at Bar Harbor from Lucy Douglas asking if Dolly Dougles were the only passenger on the helicopter ferry suggests that when the children were discovered missing, Lucy Douglas suspected her mother-in-law of taking them. The fact that Sartoris, Lucy Douglas, and Weiler, the younger Douglas's fiancee, followed Dolly to Manhattan supports the idea that they believed she had taken her grandchildren.

Loose ends: Why was a sea and air search for the missing children not begun until after Dolly's death? And what are the whereabouts of Dolly's recent live-in lover, Tinker, who might or might not also be among the missing? An unconfirmed report of a dinghy missing from Sartoris's boathouse forms the basis of one theory: that Tinker, with Dolly's knowledge, possibly at her behest, may have attempted to abduct the children with the intention of meeting Dolly at some prearranged, secret place and that the abduction ended tragically in the notoriously rough waters off the island. If the theory has any basis in fact, the loss of the grandchildren and lover might be grounds enough for Mike Hardesty's daughter's suicide, let alone possibly felony charges ranging from kidnapping to murder (manslaughter occuring during the commission of a felony is automatically first degree murder).

But it seems unlikely that the whole truth will ever be known.

8.22.80   *—VIPerpetrations, VIP*

They came back to the island. It was, as always, impossible to speak over the noise of the helicopter as they flew over the sea, but they held hands as the dark speck in the blue grew rapidly, magically, until it was a real place again. And then they could see the old man and Ethelyn Blood, waiting for them with the pony and cart.

Lucy was much thinner, Sartoris noted, as she ducked out of the chopper. He gathered her up and kissed her cheek. It was wet. She had veiled her eyes behind dark glasses, an act of courtesy, to spare him her pain. Over her shoulder, the old man peered anxiously at his son, who shrugged, and muscled the bags onto the cart.

In a few minutes they sat on the terrace in companionable silence. The day was pleasantly warm, but with the fading heat of an autumn sun. Ethelyn Blood served, with some ceremony, hot tea spiced with oranges. Its delicate scent mingled with the salt smell of the sea, brewing in them a rich sense of the day.

"Have you told Lucy the whole business?" Sartoris said at last, putting down his tea cup.

"No," Nick answered, reaching out to take Lucy's hand.

She was, except for the convulsive reaching out to Nick, stone still in her chair.

"I am sorry," the old man began. She turned her shaded eyes toward him, but he could not be sure she really saw him. "The trash in the papers, I mean, and keeping you shut up so long."

She looked away from him, out to sea.

"Would you believe the truth if you had not seen it?"

"No," she murmured, in a voice so low he had to strain to hear it.

"Of course not. And Nicholas and I thought there would be a great deal of room for abuse of the device."

She laughed harshly.

"You were in shock. It was my decision to keep the business as secret as I could. I removed the children and Tinker from the apartment, as Nicholas told you, by means of a small jewelbox of Dolly's. It was quite small enough to fit into my jacket pockets and no one, apparently, had any idea of searching an old relic like myself. I held out no hope to you; I really thought it unlikely they would survive. From what Tinker told you, the thing killed Maggie and her old nurse; we could not be sure, either, that Dolly had operated it correctly.

"We were able to convince the police that Dolly's death was accidental, that she attacked you and you had to fight back. They called it suicide, saving themselves the cost of legal action against you, and further investigation. The fact of the children having been lost weighed in your favor, I suspect. There was one great hole in the whole yarn, of course."

"The maid," Lucy said.

"Yes. Silly woman. She'd seen Tinker. Fortunately, she went all hysterical and the police discounted her evidence. *I* said we'd come without Tinker, just the three of us. There are benefits to notoriety. It did turn out that Tinker has a mother, who has written a number of letters to the police. Rather a pathetic thing, I gather, but the police find her amusing."

Lucy smiled wanly.

"How is your father taking it?"

"He thinks I've finally turned my brains into oatmeal, sniffing glue. He entrusts me gratefully to Nick, believing a good steady man will at least look after me."

"Little does he suspect," Nick murmured, "who looks after whom."

"Do we have to talk about this anymore?" Lucy said in a tiny, finished voice.

Sartoris sighed, patted her hand. "Not much more. Let's go to my studio."

She stood up, whipping the sunglasses from her face. It was still bruised, and purple shadows were pooled under her eyes.

"I want to see them," she whispered.

Carousel music, high and faint and so distant it might be coming from another world, reached their ears before they entered the studio.

The dollhouse, with much of the fire damage already repaired, sat in a former sandbox that was now a garden more wonderful than the house had ever been. The Carousel, in the middle of a maze of roses, raspberries, and sunflowers, turned round and round, pumping out its tinny music. The children rode the horse, her children, who did not see her, but went on playing at knights and queens.

Lucy cried out once, but Sartoris hushed her, and drew her a little away. "There's more to settle. The sounds of our voices are harsh on their ears. You have not asked, so I did not tell you. Tinker lived, too, despite a nasty loss of blood. He has a workshop in the dollhouse, and works there nearly all the time. He is trying to find a way to reverse the process. We have had conversations. He has instructed me in the use and repair of this gadget and told me such of the whole truth as he knew. He takes good care of the children, with the help that Ethelyn and I give him."

Lucy's hands flew to her mouth. "That monster!"

Sartoris considered her for a moment, as if he were memorizing her. Then he shuffled to his old desk and drew out the minimizer from the drawer in which he kept his Wild Turkey.

"The process is irreversible at this moment. If anyone can ever do it, it is that little man. Yes, he is a sort of monster. He confesses he knows very little about the long-term effects. It's possible, he says, that he will have the natural life span of a mouse, or some other small rodent."

Lucy looked at him calmly. "Please," she said softly.

Nick reached for her again, as if to restrain her. She let him hold her, kissed his cheek, and stepped out of his arms. He covered his eyes.

After she was minimized and placed on a bed inside the dollhouse, under the ministrations of Roger Tinker, the two men stood and watched the Carousel's gyrations for a while.

At last the son turned to his father. "My turn," he said, trying to joke.

The old man hesitated. "Nicholas, I'm very old. I'm not the man I was at seventy-five. I doubt I have as much as five years left. Every day I feel how much I've slipped, how much I've lost. Who will take care of you? And them?"

"There's Ethelyn. And Lucy's father. He'll believe when he sees."

Sartoris gave in. It would be done. They embraced.

"Good-bye," Nick whispered, "I love you. Remember I'm not going very far. We'll be closer than we've been in years. And don't worry about us. We'll survive."

And they did.